Also by Anthony Sciarratta

Finding Forever: A 1970s Love Story

Faith in the Unknown

THE LETTER

a novel

Anthony Sciarratta

Post Hill
PRESS

A POST HILL PRESS BOOK
ISBN: 978-1-64293-422-9
ISBN (eBook): 978-1-64293-423-6

Cover art by Cody Corcoran

Post Hill Press
New York • Nashville
posthillpress.com

Published in the United States of America

For my Eva Abrams...

CHAPTER 1

Victor Esposito hadn't slept soundly in years. He always had one thing on his mind, the idea so pleasant in memory yet still painful. He bore a scar on his heart that was a permanent reminder of what once was, taking in the memory of enjoyment even though it was followed by pain. The story behind Victor's sadness wasn't a complicated one. He had fallen in love with a woman who he couldn't ever have. She completely captured the essence of his being, inspiring him to be the best version of himself. These feelings were pent up deep inside Victor's heart, only surfacing periodically throughout his life's work. Not a single person knew who this woman was or if she was even real. To the rest of the world, she was only a fable that Victor created and the star protagonist in the books he wrote.

There had been many women in Victor's life, but none of them could compare to *her*. He constantly looked for the tiniest piece of her personality in the women around him. It could have been the simplest thing, something so minute that it could keep his attention for a few seconds longer to keep interest in a conversation over dinner. Some would say that was cruel, but a woman could certainly tell if a man's mind was in another place.

He counted the raindrops as they dribbled onto his window. Victor glanced at his clock, noticing hours had gone by, still not being able to properly count the raindrops. It was nearly one o'clock in the morning when Victor abandoned the tedious task he bestowed upon himself. Dragging himself out of his bed to look outside his apartment window, he was taunted by the New York City skyline. Every time he looked out into the night, he was reminded of the woman he loved. He knew she was out there somewhere.

In this late hour of the night, his phone rang. He glanced at it with anger, tempted not to even bother answering. In a spur-of-the-moment decision, he picked up the phone abruptly.

"Yes?" he said with a twinge of anger.

Victor heard nothing. There was not a single sound coming from the other line. It was almost as if someone was holding their breath.

"Hello?" Victor repeated.

Eva Abrams listened attentively on the other line. She had had one too many glasses of wine. From her bedroom, she would call Victor on the first Friday of the month. Eva always felt lonely on that day of the week. She chose to call on nights it rained because she knew Victor would be up counting the raindrops that fall from the sky. It was his way of trying not to think about her. Eva was desperate to hear his voice yet never able to work up the courage to speak. She never said anything and only held her breath, fighting the burning temptation to be heard. Eva glanced at her husband sleeping beside her, making sure he wasn't awake.

Victor moved the phone down towards the receiver when he heard a heavy breath. He placed the phone back next to his ear and attentively waited for someone to speak. Victor wouldn't dare to think it was Eva who called him, never able to give himself that kind of credit. A nagging voice in the back of his mind told Victor to wait on the line a little longer.

Eva finally gathered the courage to say something. As she began to put the words together, her husband rolled over to her side of the bed and grabbed her hand. Eva's husband was a good man. He supported, cared for, and loved her. He was generally known to be an all-around nice guy. He was especially known for being proper, which even showed through his name, Stanley Abrams. Eva frantically slammed the phone down on the receiver. The crash of the phone made his dreamy daze disappear. Stanley turned on the lamp next to his bed and faced Eva.

"Who was that?" Stanley asked.

"I don't know," Eva replied. "I didn't hear anything on the other line. There was only silence."

Stanley kissed his wife. He shut off the lamp.

"Go back to sleep, sweetheart," he said.

Stanley turned over to his side of the bed, taking more than half of the covers with him. Eva turned to her side. With tears in her eyes, she held her breath as she always did. Eva had a lingering feeling that wouldn't go away. The energy surrounding the feeling was dark and loomed over her like the clouds of a gathering storm. Eva always believed in the presence of demons on this earth. Not the kind you'd see in horror movies, but the kind that keep a person feeling down. The kind of demons that taunt your mind, nagging you. This nagging wasn't so much of a voice or temptation, but more of a premonition.

Victor only managed to sleep for a few hours. At four o'clock, the sun still hadn't risen. He threw on clothes that were sprawled out across the floor of his room, not even looking to see if they were clean. He walked outside his apartment door and into the hallway of a pristine apartment building in Manhattan. The hallways were lined with a bright red carpet, and the ceilings were painted with gold. Any person would envy Victor's living arrangements, but he didn't care. Material things never mattered to him because he knew the money he made wasn't going to come with him when he died.

The elevator door shone. Victor saw the reflection of himself in the door. With a scruffy beard, messy hair, and a broken smile, he waited for the elevator to reach his floor. Victor realized how unhappy he looked as he desperately wished his life had turned out differently. The sad part is that his life had been an amazing journey thus far. At the age of forty, he had already accomplished so much. Victor was an accomplished author, his first book being a massive hit. A string of successes followed with later novels, leaving the world only begging for more. People envy this kind of success, but for Victor, only one thing mattered.

Being notoriously impatient, Victor repeatedly pressed the button to call the elevator. The elevator doors opened and a cool breeze suddenly passed by. A man stood inside who was dressed sharply—almost too sharply for this time in the morning. His hair was greasy, shining off the gold-plated ceiling in the correct lighting. He wore gold jewelry on his fingers that matched his olive tan. The man held the elevator door open for Victor, who walked inside. The cool breeze became more glacial as the door closed. The man smiled sadistically.

"I know you," the man said. "You're Vic Esposito. The writer."

"Yeah," he smiled. "That's me."

The man shook his hand. "I'm Louis."

Louis continued to speak.

"I love your work. Would you mind if I asked you a question about one of your books?"

Victor was always respectful to his readers. There was never a question he didn't answer, an autograph he didn't sign, or a picture he didn't take. He always believed it was important to treat his fans with mutual respect. He was no different from them.

"Sure thing," Victor said.

Louis placed his hand on Victor's shoulder. Victor felt Louis' icy fingertips through his shirt. There was something about this man that made Victor feel uneasy. The dark aura around him felt threatening to his existence. It was almost as if this man could snap his fingers and take away everything that was good in Victor's life.

"You seem to have so much faith in a higher power. I could tell you really have a strong connection with God."

Victor looked at this man, cross-eyed. This was a question he had never been asked before.

"I have faith in God," Victor replied confidently.

Louis laughed. Victor could sense his doubt. Louis was dangerous, but Victor was not afraid. Louis was the kind of man who was able to smell fear, preying on people who lacked faith and those who didn't believe in God watching over them. No matter the circumstance, Victor had faith God would guide him through it.

"You sound really confident," Louis said. "Are you sure there's nothing God has denied you? Something you really want but could never have? You seem like a guy who always takes the moral high ground. How much fun could the moral high ground be?"

Victor looked at this man with disgust, as he finally realized who this man was. He was face to face with the definition of evil. Louis was the reason why humans were flawed. From the beginning of time, he had been tempting mankind. He was the snake in the Garden of Eden, the angel cast down from heaven above, and the temptation of Christ in the desert.

"What's wrong with you?" Victor said. "You think you know me? You have no clue who I am or what I've been through."

The elevator stopped at the sixth floor. The doors opened, and Louis walked outside of the elevator bank. He turned back to Victor.

"Have a nice day now," the man said, smiling. "I've been around a while. I think I know my way around anyone I come across."

He walked out of Victor's sight, and the warmth returned to Victor's blood. The elevator doors closed as Victor aggressively pressed the button that would take him to the ground floor. Victor fell into a hypersensitive state he experienced when anticipating the worst possible scenario. He was in tune with the universe and his feelings, having a connection with the world others couldn't understand. As an empath, he experienced life with a heightened sense of awareness. Being naturally anxious, he dismissed the feeling as worrisome paranoia.

CHAPTER 2

Manhattan was particularly quiet this early morning. The only sign of life was a newspaper truck driving down an abandoned street. Victor continued his usual morning stroll to a small bodega. The bodega was empty aside from a young mother walking around with her child. The pair didn't look like they had much, but they seemed content with what they had. Victor watched as the child picked out his favorite snacks for his mother to buy. As the young girl placed the snacks in a small basket, her mother discreetly took them out and replaced them with healthier options. The owner of the bodega lifelessly stood behind the counter.

"Poor kid just wants a greasy and salty snack," Victor thought to himself. "C'mon ma, you can do better than that."

Victor walked over to a small coffee machine and poured himself a cup of day-old New York coffee in a traditional blue and white paper cup. He took a carton of his favorite whole milk, Farmland Dairies, from inside the refrigerator and splashed some into his coffee. Out of the corner of his eye, his attention was drawn to a man entering the store. The man was clearly homeless. His eyes were bloodshot, his arms filled with needle-sized red marks, and his soul weighed down by his bleeding heart. Victor could tell the man was high on something. This was common to see in New York City, or any city for that matter. Victor wondered about this man and what he was trying to forget. He felt for those who suffered from addiction.

Victor dismissed the man from his thoughts, but still remained cautious. The milk curdled at the top of his steaming hot cup of coffee. He threw the coffee into a nearby trash can and quickly made himself another cup. He buried his head into the back of the refrigerator, searching for a carton of whole milk that wasn't expired.

The woman, with her child, and the raggedy man waited patiently in line. The woman had finally given in and gotten her child a greasy snack. The woman took money from her purse and handed it to the owner of the deli. Victor watched as the man behind her desperately stared at the money. As the money hit the palm of the cashier, the man pulled a gun from his belt. He violently grabbed the woman, holding the barrel of the gun against her temple. The barrel of the gun felt cold against the side of her skull. With an icy stare, the bandit threatened to shoot the woman if his demands weren't met. The child cried at the sight of her mother in such a helpless state.

"Empty all the money into a bag!" the bandit screamed. "Now!"

Victor heard the commotion from across the deli, quickly hiding behind a stack of boxes and slowly making his way towards the front of the store. The owner of the deli nervously emptied the money from the register. Watching the barrel of the gun pointed at the woman's skull, Victor imagined the owner felt that the power of life and death was in his hands. His movements would determine whether or not a child would lose her mother. He filled a plastic bag with money as his hands trembled. The fear overwhelmed him, and the owner accidentally dropped money onto the floor.

"Don't move," the bandit said coolly. "Don't fucking move, I said."

The bandit pressed the gun against the woman's head, leaving a thick red mark where the barrel met her temple. With her head between his bicep, the man dragged the woman to the corner of the store. The owner slowly put his hands above his head, showing the bandit that he wasn't ready to be a hero.

"I'm going to pick the money up off the floor," the owner said calmly.

The woman tried to calm her crying child with a soothing voice.

"It's okay, baby," she said. "Mommy is going to be okay. Just close your eyes."

"Shut up!" the bandit screamed.

He tightened his grip on the woman's neck. Victor attentively listened to the conversation as he walked out of hiding with his hands in the air.

"You don't want to do this," Victor said.

The bandit nervously pointed his gun at Victor.

"No one believes me," the bandit said. "I'm going to shoot someone tonight. Nobody move!"

Victor calmly put his hands to his sides, gently speaking to the bandit.

"I'll walk behind the counter, pick the money off the floor, and hand it to you," Victor said. "Does that sound okay?"

The bandit smiled. "Yeah, that'd be fine. Try anything funny, and it's not only going to be the girl that dies. No one is going to make it out of here. You'll have three deaths on your head. Including the kid's."

As Victor made his way behind the counter, the bandit watched his every movement. Victor picked up the money, wrapped tightly in a plastic bag, and walked half the distance to where the bandit was standing.

"I'll throw the money over to you," he said. "Let the girl go first."

The bandit laughed. "Are you really in a position to negotiate?"

"I'm not negotiating," Victor said. "I'm asking you nicely. Could you please leave the girl out of this? She has a child."

The bandit tightened his grip on the woman.

"You got balls, man," the bandit said. "I respect that, but I'm not dumb enough to fall for this shit. It's either you hand me the money, or someone's going to die."

Victor didn't trust the bandit. He knew the owner of the deli had called the police with a button he pressed below the cash register. Once the bandit heard the sirens, he would use the woman or child as a hostage to get away from the police. Victor couldn't risk that happening. He would never put either of them in harm's way. No child should ever witness something so horrific. Without a clear plan of action in hand, Victor threw the bag of money to the center of the room.

"Go get the money then," Victor said.

The bandit anxiously looked at the money that lay between them. He slowly moved closer to the money, holding his hostage close to his body. As he inched towards the money, the cop sirens rang loudly outside the deli. The bandit could hear the sound of heavy boots marching on the cement as the cops surrounded the store. He improvised and pushed the woman away from him, allowing her to return to her child. The woman shielded her child from the horror that was unfolding by covering her eyes. The bandit grabbed the money off the floor, then aimed the gun at the women's head.

"You called the cops?" the bandit screamed. "Now I have no way out. If I can't make it out alive, why should she?"

Victor still remained calm. "No one has to die," he said. "We can get you help. There's always room for a second chance."

"Not for me," the bandit said with a smirk. His eyes raced back and forth between the woman and his gun. He cocked his gun and pointed it at the innocent woman desperately trying to shield her child. Victor could see in the bandit's eyes that he already made his decision. Victor had lived a better life than many and would never be able to live with himself if he let a mother and daughter die. God had blessed him in so many ways, and it was his turn to give back.

An instinctual feeling in the pit of Victor's stomach guided him to make a decision; it didn't take much thinking. One of his best qualities was also his worst. Victor was self-sacrificial. He was always known to be a protector, especially when it came to people who he felt were innocent. In this moment, Victor would finally make the ultimate sacrifice, one most people would never make.

The bandit fired his gun, and Victor jumped in front of the woman, shielding her from the bullet. The bullet pierced Victor's skin and struck him in his chest. His body crashed onto the floor as the blow rendered him lifeless. The last thing Victor heard were the screams of a mother and child as the world around him fell black. It was almost a pleasant feeling because, for once, his anxious mind finally stopped running. His body lay on the floor motionless, his eyes wide open. The blood poured down the side of his shirt, dripping onto the floor.

The bandit dropped the gun at the scene and burst through the front door of the store, ignoring the warnings of the police to surrender. Almost instantly, he was shot and killed. The police wasted no time and quickly stormed the store, armed to the teeth. A group of policemen tended to the woman and child, who were still clinging to one another. The woman screamed, begging the police to shift their attention to the man that saved her. She insisted Victor was still breathing.

"That man saved my life," the woman said crying. "He saved both our lives."

An ambulance was readily waiting outside, having arrived soon after the police reported sounds of a gunshot.

Eva, who had finally managed to fall asleep, suddenly jolted to life. A wave of anxiety crashed over her mind, causing sweat to drip down the side of her face. She felt a sharp pain in her chest. Eva had nothing physically wrong with her, but this horrific pain wouldn't go away. She rolled off her bed and onto the floor in silent agony. A few more moments, and the pain dissipated. Eva knew that this pain wasn't her own. She carried herself to the bathroom. Eva was surprised the noise she made didn't wake her husband up, as she glanced at Stanley who was still sound asleep.

Whenever Eva was upset, she spent time in the bathroom. The running water masked the sound of her tears. The steam from the shower filled the room as Eva cried hysterically. She sat on the cold tile floor, wrapped in a ball, wanting to scream but not able to make a sound. Eva didn't know exactly what was wrong, but she did figure that it was Victor in pain. The negative feeling that had been nagging her throughout the night finally surfaced. Eva now knew what she felt was a premonition as the questions poured into her mind, but she didn't know who to call or what to do. The sadness was so overpowering, Eva felt it in her bones.

Victor was rushed to the hospital for emergency surgery. Miraculously, he was still breathing, hanging onto his life by a thread. Victor's mind was black and his consciousness was empty. His body showed no signs of life. Victor was pushed through the various wings of the hospital and put through to emergency surgery. The massive loss of blood had already caused trauma to his body. At this point, the doctors knew they needed to control the damage. His chance to live through this was slim. Even if he did manage to survive, his life would change forever.

The police contacted Victor's mother, who rushed to the hospital in a matter of minutes. His remaining family members were either dead or not on speaking terms with him. Barbara was the sole person to contact in case of an emergency. The trauma of the event forced Barbara into a massive hysteria. The hospital almost admitted her until she agreed to take medication. This situation would be traumatic to any person, let alone a parent.

Barbara Esposito sat emotionlessly in the waiting room, paralyzed by the medication that numbed her mind. Her tears dried as the tranquilizers set in, draining the emotion. She quietly waited, wondering if she'd ever be able to see her son again.

It wasn't long before the media got wind of what had happened. Victor's work was read by millions of people in the United States and around the world. His fans, or readers, were in mourning for a person they felt they knew so well. He put himself and his life experiences into everything he wrote, making almost any story relatable to the average person. It was like his readers had lost a close friend who they knew everything about, having lived through precious life moments together.

The media mercilessly hounded Barbara for statements and potential updates. Victor had always felt the news was for people who enjoyed hearing what's wrong with the world. The five o'clock news was always filled with depressing stories, which strangely draw people in. Misery does love company, so it would make sense the media would eat up such a juicy story. The news spread, leaving the world holding on to their breath as Victor held on to his life.

Eva paced around her kitchen table, repeatedly calling Victor's phone number. Her intuition haunted her—she was desperate to discover the source of this pain. After the fifth phone call, Eva felt faint, plopping down on a couch in the living room of her home. Well known as a minimalist, she was content with a comfortable couch, a bookshelf, and a small television. Although she lived in a beautiful Long Island home, she didn't need much more than what little she had.

Eva closed her eyes, taking a deep breath as she tried to rid her mind of this feeling. Victor and Eva had agreed to live separate lives long ago. She knew she shouldn't intrude in Victor's life, but she couldn't help herself from wanting to. Her thoughts swarmed, followed by deep breaths and a sudden cease in her onslaught of phone calls. The painful feeling Eva had in her chest was shackled to her. The feeling was heavy, as if she was trying to drag a large boulder.

Eva tossed and turned on the couch, accidentally turning on the television by lying on the remote. The first thing she saw was a breaking news announcement about a shooting in Manhattan. Eva changed the channel because she hated the news, but it seemed to be that every other news station was mentioning the story. While she flipped through the channels, she heard a news anchor say, "Victor Esposito."

When she heard Victor's name being mentioned, Eva instantly knew. She placed both her hands over her chest, in the same place Victor got shot. For the first time in her life, Eva watched the news like she was playing *Clue*, trying to find out who killed the writer with a gun in Manhattan. She stared at the television, totally emotionless, with eyes that were drained of their usual bright green glow.

Her whole world collapsed in a matter of moments. The man she loved was fighting for his life, and she couldn't do anything but wait. Eva had never expected something like this to happen, and the initial shock hadn't left her mind. She lay on the couch in total denial, barely able to breathe.

Eva always thought Victor would be the one losing her first. She had never had an easy life, and because of it, Eva suffered from chronic depression. When she thought back on it, there were parts of her life that could have been considered living nightmares. Because of this sadness that followed her, Eva tended to be a little reckless. Whether it was driving too fast, smoking, or not taking care of herself, Eva exhibited self-destructive patterns. It wasn't extreme, however, and it manifested itself in a subtle way. Victor was one of the few to see through Eva's actions, knowing she didn't want to die and that her reckless attitude was her way of crying out for help.

On the outside, Eva was a strong, independent, and intelligent woman. She truly embodied each of those great qualities, but not many saw her dark side. No one would ever guess she had endured so much suffering. Deep in her heart, she was truly afraid of the world around her. The world was a dangerous place, and she wanted someone to care about her living in it. Eva wanted someone to notice when she did something wrong, but she didn't want that attention from just anyone; rather, she wished it came from a man who truly would die for her.

Eva had a few boyfriends in her life, and none of them took the time to care about her in this way. They never got jealous if another man directed their attention at her. They never thought to ask why she'd suddenly start smoking cigarettes or driving recklessly, when neither was a consistent character trait of hers. These cries for attention were ignored.

What Eva wanted was a small reaction. It could have simply been a phone call to check in on her. Eva forced herself to be independent, but there was a part of her that desperately needed to be nurtured. Eva was needy and clingy, but she never wanted to let that part of her show. She feared being pushed away for having needs.

Her husband, Stanley, was the definition of stability, and that's what Eva had needed at the time they met. Coming from a life that was so unstable, Stanley was a breath of fresh air. He was truly a levelheaded, good-hearted man. He didn't have a vicious bone in his body. Stanley only had one major downfall: he wasn't the most romantic man. He never noticed the little things about his wife. When she'd cut her hair differently, he wouldn't notice. If she seemed a little sad one day, he wouldn't think to ask what was wrong. He never took the time to appreciate how beautiful Eva was or hold her in his arms and say how thankful he was to be with her. It wasn't that Stanley didn't appreciate her; he just wasn't the kind of man to ask those things. It wasn't in him to be that way.

Stanley entered the living room holding a steaming hot cup of coffee, dressed and ready to start his day. Stanley dressed appropriately for his character, even when he wasn't going to work. He donned a button-down, open-collared shirt with slacks. That was his daily go-to outfit.

He watched as Eva motionlessly lay on the couch. Stanley noticed she seemed to be in some form of a trance, her eyes glazed over. He glanced at the television, then back at his wife. He could clearly see she was upset about Victor. Still, he didn't think it was actually a big deal. Stanley knew Eva was an avid reader of his books.

"Damn," he said. "I liked that guy too."

Eva was constantly forced to hide her emotions. Her husband could never know that her mind was in two places. Spiritually, it was with Victor, but mentally, it was with Stanley. It had become more difficult for Eva to hide it as the years passed. Some days it was worse than others. There would be random nights where Eva would drink to numb the pain. For her, that would only mean two glasses of wine. It was enough to get her through the night.

"You're acting like he's already dead," Eva said defensively. "They said he's hanging on."

Stanley shrugged his shoulders.

"He got shot right in the chest. What are the odds of coming back from that? He's probably not going to make it."

Eva put her feelings aside once again. She hoped Victor would pull through this. She had always liked the idea that there was a small chance they'd run into each other. Now that small hope was gone. It was only a matter of time before her husband would get wind of this. Eva didn't know how much longer she'd be able to contain her sadness.

Stanley's words repeated in her mind over and over again, finally registering in her brain. The sadness bottled up; her cheeks were turning red, and her eyes were welling up with tears. The tears dripped down her cheeks as she tried to hide her face in a pillow, unable to look at her husband any longer. Eva became increasingly more callous, forced to live in denial of her feelings.

Stanley thought it was a little odd Eva was reacting this way to the news. The story itself was horrible, but Stanley couldn't see why Eva was taking it personally.

"Why are you crying?" Stanley asked. "You're acting like you knew the guy."

Eva wiped away her tears, trying to keep her emotions at bay. Her husband could never know what had been going through her mind all this time. Eva and Victor had never had any physical contact. She had never broken her marital vows. She couldn't even bring herself to give Victor a friendly hug goodbye. The temptation would have been too great, even with a gesture that small.

Eva's self-control was unparalleled. How could you see someone you know is perfect for you and never act on your feelings? Eva was only human, and it was normal to respond to the love she had for him. Having these strong feelings without fulfilling them left Eva in a great deal of pain. She had always held out hope that one day she could have Victor and they'd finally be able to have their chance. Her head sunk as she figured destiny had other plans instead.

Dr. Silverstein walked out of the emergency room, his clothes stained with Victor's blood. He looked around for Victor's family members and spotted Barbara, who he figured was his mother. This was the part of his job he hated the most: telling families the bad news. It was something he had to live with on a daily basis. His words became more scripted and his feelings more numb as the years of being a doctor passed.

"Ms. Esposito," Dr. Silverstein called out.

Barbara rushed over to the doctor, grabbing his shirt as she begged him to give her some sort of good news. He gently pushed her away from his body and held her hands between his own.

"Victor is out of surgery," Dr. Silverstein said. "He's in critical condition. We did all that we could, but it doesn't look good. The trauma forced him into a coma. Beyond that, we don't know the extent of the damage to his brain. In these types of cases, we wait a little over a month, but in between that, anything could happen."

Barbara stared at Dr. Silverstein with horror.

"My son," she screamed aloud.

In between her tears, there were violent bursts of anger.

"You bring him back!" Barbara yelled. "You bring my son back to me."

Barbara threw herself violently onto the floor. A team of nurses carried her away from the doctor and back to a seat. Her son was everything to her. He had spent many years of his life working to make his mother happy, and now she was unable to contain her anger that something she held so dearly to her heart was being taken away from her. Father Time teaches children that they will one day have to bury their parents, not that parents will have to bury their child. Barbara was the youngest of four, and had already had to say goodbye to her parents and siblings. Her husband passed away when Victor was only a teenager.

"I want to be with my family," she cried to herself. "I can't live alone. I can't live without my son. Not my son."

Louis sat in the hospital waiting room, calmly reading a magazine, quietly listening to the doctor's conversation with Barbara. He watched the commotion unfold with pleasure. Louis walked past the doctors and Victor's family, remaining in the shadows, totally unseen to others around him. The shadows danced on the walls around Victor's hospital bed, and swiftly, Louis was at Victor's side.

The man-made machines pumped life into Victor's body as he lay in his hospital bed. A feeding tube accompanied the breathing tube in this unnatural state of being Victor was forced to endure. At the mercy of man's creation, Victor needed these machines in order to survive. It was now up to his mother to decide Victor's destiny. Should she allow her son to peacefully die a hero, pulling the plug and allowing her son to slowly dwindle away? These are the kinds of decisions that could break any person. You would constantly ask yourself what the comatose patient would want. Then, there's always the question of "what if?"

Louis stood next to Victor's bed, placing his hand on Victor's shoulder.

"Men," he mumbled to himself. "So naive to think that they have the power to control life and death."

He allowed the breathing tube to run through his fingers in total curiosity of the human attempt to preserve a life.

"I bet you have a lot of regrets now. You had everything: Money, health, and a great career. Being a good guy isn't all it's cracked up to be, huh, buddy?"

Louis tapped Victor on the shoulder twice and walked out of the room filled with satisfaction and delight. He disappeared into the shadows in the hallway as Victor's mother rushed back inside.

Barbara was used to seeing her son filled with energy and interest in the world around him. He'd spent his days as a child asking his mother how the world works and why things were the way they were. These questions were almost impossible to answer, but Victor would demand an answer anyway. Her answer on why the bus stopped at the bus stop was met with content.

There weren't any questions Victor could ask her now. He was stripped of his personality—his inquisitive, creative mind that captured readers. Seeing him drained of this contagious energy would be hard for anyone who was close to him. Victor was the kind of man who could brighten the mood in any room with a funny joke or story. The stories always involved his travels, as he had narrowly escaped troubles in countries around the world.

Victor's life was in his mother's hands. He was once again a helpless baby in dire need of a mother's wise intuition. It was up to her to decide if the doctors should allow him to die peacefully on his own. Barbara pulled a chair next to his bed, and her chin sunk into her chest as she cried.

"My poor baby," she whimpered.

Barbara held his hand tightly, lightly trailing her fingers through his hair.

"It was only yesterday that you were my little boy," she said. "Now you're all grown up. You made a life for yourself. You did everything you said you were going to do."

Barbara wiped the tears away from her face.

"The doctor said you could move on from us at any moment. Hold on a little longer. She's coming. I know it."

CHAPTER 3

Eva's eyes were glued to her television. She hadn't moved from the couch for hours. The newscasters were giving updates to the public by the moment, surrounded by cameras that bombarded the entrance to the hospital. The live television broadcast was being shot from St. Peregrine's Hospital in Manhattan. Eva recognized the location and jumped into action, grabbing her car keys as she ran towards the door of her home. Stanley screamed her name, watching her scurry.

"Have you gone crazy?" Stanley asked. "What the hell are you doing?"

Eva stopped. She turned around and faced her husband.

"I have to go," she said calmly.

"Where?" he asked again.

Eva walked towards Stanley and hugged him.

"We've been married for almost twenty years," she said. "I've been nothing but good to you. I'm asking you, this one time, please don't ask me where I'm going."

Stanley looked into his wife's eyes. He didn't know what she was going through, but he could see she was in pain. He could see the news about Victor had triggered her in some way. He knew his stories meant the world to her. Stanley would have never guessed that they were all about Eva. To write a book about someone, to capture every groove of their face, curve of their body, and thought in their head, takes a great deal of studying. The way Victor captured Eva was so different from the way other people perceived her. It was a special bond they shared that no person would ever come to understand.

Stanley kissed his wife goodbye, allowing her to leave his arms. It felt like the weight of the world was crashing down on Eva as she danced around the raindrops, running towards her car. Thunder crashed and boomed across the sky, reminding her of the enormous hangover of misery she felt from this day. The rain felt like hail pounding down onto her body, sinking her shoulders down. As she got soaked, she learned it was impossible to dance around the rain. Stanley watched as Eva frantically skidded out of the driveway and onto the street, scratching his head in mystery of what his wife was up to next. He always knew that she was quite strange, but this was strange even for her.

Stanley awkwardly stared at Eva's bookshelf, noticing for the first time that it was filled with every one of Victor's books. He pulled one of Victor's books from the shelf, sat down on the couch that still had Eva's imprint, and began to read. Stanley was curious to see why his wife had been unusually impacted by the news. He couldn't quite put his finger on it, but he knew the way his wife was acting was too out of character, or so he thought.

<hr />

Eva aggressively drove into the hospital parking lot, making herself a space near the entrance. Still soaking wet from the rain, Eva left a trail of water along the hospital floor as she approached the receptionist's desk. Gasping for air, Eva asked for Victor's room number. The receptionist refused to give Eva any information because she wasn't an immediate family member. Eva didn't normally lose control of her temper, but this time she did, slamming her hands down on the receptionist's desk. Her face turned red with furious anger.

"Listen to me, God dammit," Eva screamed. "You're going to give me that fucking room number. You hear me? I made that man who he is today. I'm the reason he's a writer. I'm his muse—that's more than family! No one is going to stop me from seeing him. Either you give me the room number, or I'm searching every room in this hospital."

The receptionist's desk was covered with spit from Eva's screaming. The veins in her skull were popping out of her temple, showing the red-hot blood that was pumping through her body. The crowd of people around her gawked at Eva after listening to her plea, noticing she was truly a force to be reckoned with. The receptionist fearfully wrote Victor's room number down on a piece of paper, and slid it over the top of the desk and into Eva's trembling hands.

At the speed of sound, Eva was outside of Victor's room. She could have outran a gunshot, or the Road Runner himself. She quietly crept through the halfway-closed door, like a little mouse finding their way into the crawl space of a house. Eva braced herself to see Victor for the first time in what seemed to be forever. The memories of his warm and protective energy rushed back as she realized she was going to see a shell of the man she once knew. Eva wasn't going to be able to see the look on Victor's face when he saw her, which instantly filled her with regret. She now wished she could have told him how dearly she wished their lives turned out differently. The regret hounded her. She wished she had had the courage to speak to Victor the night before. In what seemed to be an endless journey through purgatory, Eva slowly entered Victor's room.

Barbara made sure the room remained empty, still sitting attentively at Victor's right side. She knew how Victor hated making a big fuss about anything, and he wouldn't have wanted anyone seeing him like this.

Eva stood in the doorway of the hospital room, completely frozen in time. Her knees buckled, not able to hold the weight of her body any longer. Eva collapsed onto the floor, gasping for air between her screams of pain.

The man who loved Eva unconditionally was dying, and she couldn't do anything to save him. Victor had picked Eva up when she was at her lowest point, loving her for the woman she was, flaws and all. The two shared the type of love that could heal the most painful emotional scars.

A day didn't go by without Victor saying a prayer for Eva. She was the type of person that was painfully unaware of the world around her, and the idea that she was out in the world alone drove Victor crazy. He couldn't always physically be around her, but he felt that praying was the only other way he could reach her. To her amazement, there were days when she truly felt his prayers and the shroud of protection he tried putting over her.

Even with a bond this strong, Victor never pushed Eva to leave her husband. He knew Eva would never do anything to hurt her family. Coming from a broken home, she knew the effect it could have on children. Eva also never wanted to hurt her husband, who was good to her. She did love him, but the kind of love she felt was different. She viewed him more as the father of her children than a soulmate.

Eva was easily the greatest thing that had ever happened to Victor, inspiring him to slowly become a better man. Being the first person to realize Victor had talent, she had encouraged him to tell his wonderful stories and find his inner voice. Victor wasn't a writer at heart, but it was Eva's love that made him one. Every great writer has an inspiration, and Eva was his. She was his one wish, his one regret, and his lifeline. Her happiness always came first, even if it meant his own pain.

Barbara turned around when she heard Eva crying and walked over to help her off the floor. Barbara took a good look at Eva, who she could tell was slightly older than Victor. Barbara couldn't believe this was the woman who captivated her son, the woman who made him into the man he was. Eva was beautiful, standing tall with bright green eyes. Her body frame was slim, yet she still had curves in the right places. Even as an older woman, her looks had never faded. Eva's skin was still radiant, making her girlfriends begin to believe that she was immune to wrinkles. Some of those close to her would say she never aged. Many often said she resembled a country version of Olivia Newton-John.

"You're her," Barbara said.

Eva nodded.

Barbara held Eva's face between her hands.

"You look different than I expected."

Eva still wasn't able to speak, or take her eyes off Victor. She walked over to his bed and gently sat at his left side.

Barbara continued to speak.

"He really loved you. I think he may have even loved you more than me, and I gave birth to him."

Eva smiled, remembering how Victor would joke about how much she'd love his mother. Eva could already tell they would have gotten along. Barbara walked out of the room to give Eva her privacy. Eva held his hand between both of hers.

"It's me," Eva said. "I'm here. I'm finally here."

Eva tried holding back her tears as she continued to speak. She felt guilty that they hadn't spoken in almost ten years. Victor may die never knowing the way Eva felt about him. Because of the nature of their situation, she never felt right telling him.

"This is what it took for me to come and see you," she wept. "Why didn't I do this before? Why did you have to get shot? Who asked you to do that?"

Eva slammed her hands down. She screamed at Victor and deeply resented his need to please people in this moment.

"For once in your life, you could have been a little selfish. You could have worried about yourself. Now you're sitting here, fighting for your life."

Her anger quickly dissipated as the sadness took over her mind. Eva crawled into Victor's hospital bed, laying her head on his body, then gently placing her hand on his chest. Eva whispered.

"You can't leave me. I need you. You promised you'd never leave. Who's going to be here to protect me? You always took the time to care for me. To lift me up when I was down. I can't live without you here."

Victor didn't respond. Eva could only hear the sound of the machines breathing for Victor.

"You have to come back," Eva said. "This is some sort of a joke, right? You used to tease me all the time. You'd always make jokes about moving far away. Tell me this is a big joke.

You're going to wake up soon, and we're going to laugh. Then I could give you that big hug you always wanted. I still have to make you those lemon cupcakes. I never forgot about them."

Eva ran her hands through Victor's hair. She was trying to stay strong, but the pain proved to be too much. Tears dripped off her nose onto Victor's chest as she sobbed between every other word. Eva hardly understood what was coming out of her own mouth.

"If you don't like lemon, I could always make something else instead. I know how you always wished I could have made it for you. I promise I'll do it. No more boundaries, no more waiting. We could make it work. All you have to do is wake up."

Eva gently nudged Victor, desperately wanting him to show some sign of life.

"Wake up," she said. "You'd be waking up next to me. You don't have to sleep alone anymore. I'll be here now."

Eva continued to push Victor. The reality of the situation finally hit her when she realized Victor wasn't going to respond. There was no way of making him come back—his life was in God's hands now. There wasn't a need to hide her emotions any longer, so Eva decided to be true to herself and fulfill an inner promise to her aching heart. She refused to accept that this was the end of their story.

"Don't make this goodbye," she said crying. "We still have so much to do. I promise things will change. We could sing all the songs from *Grease*. We could go out to the movies…. We could do it all…just like we always wanted. That sounds great, right?"

The more Eva pushed Victor, the more she was met the same heartbreaking answer. Victor wasn't going to wake up.

"Right?" she asked him again.

When a person witnesses death, it pushes them to tuck their fears away. Death forces them to realize that sometimes in life there are going to be regrets. It suddenly becomes important to leave no question unanswered. Eva knew that, in some way, Victor saw what was going on, and he could hear what she was saying. Even though his body was failing him, his soul was still alive.

Eva stared into Victor's closed eyes, holding his face in her hands and rubbing her thumbs on his cheeks. Eva kissed Victor on the cheek and stayed nose to nose with him.

"I love—"

Dr. Silverstein entered the room, interrupting Eva. He jumped at the sight of her lying next to Victor, wasting no time scolding her.

"Who the hell are you?" he screamed. "Are you crazy? You're going to make his condition worse lying on him like that."

He shooed Eva off the bed, quickly checking the scars on Victor's chest. Eva gasped at the massive scar she'd been accidentally lying on. The doctor was relieved to see that Eva hadn't reopened the wound.

Dr. Silverstein continued yelling at Eva, noticing he was standing in her shadow, as Eva was almost five inches taller than him. She pointed her finger down at him.

"Do you know who I am?" Eva said angrily.

Dr. Silverstein slowly backed away from Victor.

"No," he said. "But there are rules here. This is a hospital!"

Eva laughed at the idea of rules. She was never good at following them anyway.

"Rules?" she said. "Screw you and your rules. I'm not going anywhere. I'm staying here with Victor. He needs me here to take care of him."

Barbara witnessed the fighting from the doorway of the room. She crossed her arms and carefully watched Eva. Barbara had never seen a woman have such raw emotion for her son before. She had a hard time believing this love he claimed to have found even existed, and that it really wasn't a figment of his mind's creation. Barbara had never been crazy about the idea that her son apparently had this mystery woman hidden from her, but now the skepticism was slowly disappearing.

Barbara could see the argument was going to escalate and quickly rushed to Eva's defense, explaining to Dr. Silverstein who Eva was. He didn't like the idea of potentially exciting Victor, if he could hear anything, because his condition was so critical. The slightest amount of stress could trigger a bad reaction.

"She's family," Barbara said warmly. "Leave her be. We're the only two people who should be allowed in this room."

Dr. Silverstein nodded and returned to Victor's bedside, continuing to monitor his condition. He sighed when he noticed there hadn't been any improvement.

"I stand by my first diagnosis. You're going to have to make a decision in the next few weeks," Dr. Silverstein said. "His condition hasn't changed. If you decide to leave Victor like this, you'd be preserving his body. There's a good chance he may never come back."

Barbara sighed. She was totally numb to the situation between her medication and the initial shock. The doctor's news infuriated Eva, who was still adjusting to the situation. She broke down and begged the doctor as she cried.

"Please," Eva said. "There has to be something we could do. I know he's in there somewhere."

Eva's screaming and crying scared the doctor away, and he ran out of the room without any hesitation. Barbara and Eva sat down next to each other. The two most important women in Victor's life finally met. If he had been coherent, the very sight of this moment would have made him filled with joy mixed with a slight tremor of fear. The damage these two could do if they decided to join forces would be intimidating to any man.

The hopeless look on Barbara's face was unparalleled. She didn't have much faith in anything after her own life experiences. Now in her seventies, the stress and chaos of life shook the core of her being. There were few years in her life that weren't unstable. Because of this, Barbara, like many in the world, lacked faith in God. After enduring this suffering, how could she have faith?

Barbara wouldn't take it upon herself to decide whether or not Victor should die, even though the decision lay with her. Without a wife or child in the picture, the choice was left solely to Barbara. Victor would never put the burden on Eva, who he never thought he'd see again. By default, it was Barbara who had to decide. Knowing her son so well, she was sure that if Victor knew Eva was here, he would have wanted Eva to make this decision. With little hesitation, Barbara blurted out her thoughts.

"I'm leaving this up to you."

"What?" Eva replied frantically.

"It should be you," Barbara repeated. "He would have wanted you to decide. You're the one who will know if he's going to come back or not. Victor has no children, no wife. You're the only mark he left on this world. His life's work is because of you."

Barbara held Eva's hand.

"I can't do it," Eva cried. "I can't let him die."

Barbara tried to compose herself as she started to cry again. There was no amount of medicine that could keep these feelings at bay. It only caused her emotions to barricade in the back of her mind, eventually overflowing when more bad news surfaced. The agony that showed in Eva's eyes was equal to Barbara's. Victor always thought women were smarter than men, not being as easily hindered by life's circumstances. That was likely because he had been raised by a strong mother and had fallen in love with a woman who was equally strong. Although Victor worried about Eva often, a part of him knew that she was strong-willed, and could survive on her own.

"I'm going to get a coffee," Barbara said. "Spend time with him. He's been waiting for you."

Barbara left the room. Eva crawled back into Victor's hospital bed, pulling down his gown and staring at his scar. She gently kissed the skin next to it.

"I've always wondered what it would be like to be this close to you. To feel your body between my hands. It feels like I'm finally home."

The doctors didn't dare bother Eva as she fell asleep in Victor's arms, fearful of the way she'd react. She was forced to sleep in the tiny corner of the bed, yet Eva had never felt more comfortable before. It was the first time Eva had slept soundly in years, feeling the safety and comfort of a man who loved her.

CHAPTER 4

Awoken by the sounds of the machines pumping life into Victor's body, Eva was in a daze, refusing to believe that this had actually happened. She rubbed her eyes open, hoping this was a nightmare. It didn't take long for reality to set in once again as Barbara slipped into the room. Barbara closely watched Eva cling to her son's lifeless body.

"He wasn't kidding," Barbara said just loud enough so Eva could hear her. "You really would do anything for him."

Eva jumped when she heard Barbara's voice, quickly rolling out of Victor's hospital bed in embarrassment.

"I didn't mean for you to see that," Eva said. "That was something he always wanted.... Victor always wished he could hold me in his arms."

"I wish I had what you and Victor have," Barbara said. "At least you could say a man loved you that much."

"I can," Eva mumbled to herself.

Barbara hugged Eva, holding her close like she was a daughter of her own.

Since becoming famous, Victor traveled often. He always enjoyed experiencing other cultures and visiting cities around the world, even if those places were considered dangerous.

Naturally, Victor was a superstitious man and always feared the unknown circumstances life could bring. He had left something for Eva in the event that anything happened during his travels. Barbara knew very little about who Eva was, but Victor had insisted when he left the box with Barbara that Eva would come asking around if anything ever happened to him. Victor was adamant Barbara give Eva what he'd left her no matter what.

Barbara had forgotten about the box years ago. She'd left it in the closet of Victor's childhood room. But with Eva showing up at the hospital, the memory of the box slowly entered Barbara's mind once again. Even though she was a nosy woman, Barbara had never thought to look inside. She knew it was too personal a matter, and the box was sealed shut.

"I have something for you," Barbara said. "I don't know much about your relationship with my son, but he left something for you in the event that anything bad ever happened to him."

Without any hesitation, Eva followed Barbara to her car. Barbara drove her through the Midtown Tunnel, getting off at Exit 19 on the Long Island Expressway. Eva was skeptical of the towns around her as she passed through the industrial side of Maspeth. She found it hard to believe that Queens wasn't made up of only bridges and tunnels. Middle Village was one of the last Italian neighborhoods in Queens, remaining a stronghold for not only Italians but also for many European immigrants over the years. The people were of working middle-class families, living in homes around Juniper Valley Park, where residents took their children to play. This town was well known for its reputation of safety, avoiding the violent crimes New York City faced over the years.

Barbara's home was a castle of brick, towering almost four floors above the crowded street. Eva opened the car window, allowing her hand to flow through the waves of wind that brushed against the car. She observed the areas around her in total curiosity, eager to see the area where Victor had lived for most of his life. She noticed many of the homes in the area looked the same. None of them were really wide, but instead built high. Flowers, bushes, and small pine trees around patches of grass lined the driveway leading up to the door. It was typical of a Queens resident to surround their home with perennials, wishing for a feel of the suburbs like their overtaxed counterparts in Long Island. Eva stared at a peeling statue of the Virgin Mary that sat atop a rock on a patch of grass. Eva liked that Victor came from a humble home. She never grew up with much money and always appreciated everything she had.

Barbara pulled into the driveway, quickly unbuckling her seatbelt. Even though she tried to pay attention during the ride, Eva didn't have the slightest clue where she was. Eva was never keen when it came to getting around any area she wasn't overly familiar with.

"Is this your home?" Eva asked.

Barbara nodded.

"The home Victor grew up in?"

Barbara nodded again.

"Victor left something for you a long time ago. Now would probably be the perfect time to give it to you."

Barbara got out of the car. She walked up the brick-paved path to the front door. Barbara placed the key in the door, jiggling the lock a few times. The door swung open with a creaky sound that Eva could hear from inside the car. She closed her eyes, inhaling through her nose then slowly exhaling. She often referred to this process as centering herself.

"Please, God," Eva said to herself, "give me the strength to get through this."

It was easy to see that Barbara's house was well kept. The couches were covered in a hard plastic that looked sticky and uncomfortable. There was a strong smell of citrus Pledge in the air, as the wood furniture shined in the light. After seeing the kitchen, which looked as though it hadn't been used in years, Eva had a fleeting thought she may have entered a doll house. Everything Barbara owned had a place, including the commercial deli slicer and espresso maker on the marble countertop.

Feeling the essence that swept through her body when she first walked inside, Eva tried to take in the energy of their home. She was very in tune with the universe in this way. The Esposito house felt like an actual home, which was something Eva never had growing up. She knew Victor had faced many hardships in his life, but he always had some sort of a supporting cast and a pleasant place to come home to. His mother was the matriarch of this empire, and it was clear everything would come crashing down if she wasn't around.

Eva wanted to have that kind of a special family connection, often wishing for exactly the kind of home Victor had, a loving place where she was safe. Eva pictured being a part of Victor's large family, knowing they would warmly welcome her with open arms. Victor had bragged about how well she'd have fit in if things had been different. Many of the family members Victor had talked about passed away long ago.

Barbara watched Eva aimlessly walk around the house as if it was her own. Eva inspected every knickknack, studied the pictures on the walls, felt the fabric of the couches, and even took the time to look through the refrigerator. There was something odd about this place—maybe because it was where Victor had lived, but she couldn't help but feel welcomed.

At heart, Eva was innocent and childlike. Barbara enjoyed the pleasant and harmless aura Eva radiated. Eva looked as if she couldn't hurt a fly, at least not purposely. This quirkiness about Eva was endearing, and Barbara could tell that's what likely drew in her son.

"Come upstairs," Barbara said.

Eva followed Barbara up the steps of her home and to a small room on the second floor.

"Is this Victor's room?" Eva asked.

Barbara nodded.

Victor hadn't lived at home since his mid-twenties. Everything was exactly the way it had been the day he left. Barbara hadn't wanted to disturb anything, comparing Victor's room to the shrine of a Greek god. His room wasn't considered average for a twenty-year-old in the mid-nineties. There was a seventies-style bed that was slightly elevated from the floor. The light pouring in from the window bounced off the colors of the wall, which was painted two different shades of blue, one light and one dark, like the colors of the ocean.

Iconic movies like *The Godfather*, *Raiders of the Lost Ark*, *Grease*, and *Rocky* were paid tribute with large printouts of the original movie posters covering the walls. They were cramped together with barely an inch of wall space to be shown. Victor would spend hours watching movies with his father, keeping his mind off the busy world around him. He was known to be a film buff, looking back on moments like this as a positive time in his childhood. Film was Victor's coping mechanism and his only way to hide from reality. He could easily get lost in films, finally able to escape his own mind. He was often a prisoner of his own thoughts, endlessly worrying and always nervous.

Eva sat on Victor's bed, once again slowly taking her time to soak in the energy in his room. The smell of Victor's scent on the sheets passed her nose, even though it had been over ten years since seeing him. She examined the posters, making a different facial expression at each one as the memories passed through her mind. Eva concentrated on one in particular, staring at the print of a hand with puppet strings.

Eva had never seen *The Godfather*, which was a big "no-no" in Victor's book. Hearing this, knowing Eva loved movies herself, Victor had begged Eva to watch what many considered to be the greatest film in history. It wasn't that she didn't have an interest in watching it, but for some reason, she could never bring herself to watch it alone. Eva also didn't like watching violent movies unless they had meaning behind them. The idea of contract killings turned her off to the film. She often opted to watch a good Quentin Tarantino violence-filled revenge scene. Victor knew she'd enjoy the film if she was aware of the vengeance behind the violence. She preferred things to be personal, not strictly business.

Weeks went by, and Eva still refused to watch *The Godfather*. It crossed his mind that she may not have wanted to watch it without him. He felt that Eva wanted to save that moment, always having something to look forward to. His assumption was correct, because Eva would have enjoyed Victor dissecting the film into pieces for her to understand. She was probably the only woman willing to sit through a near three-hour movie while Victor rambled on about the significance of sending someone a dead fish. Some would argue that's the definition of true love, while others would call it insanity.

Barbara opened a large white door in the corner of Victor's room. Eva saw the first speck of dust in the house fly past her as the door flew open. The closet was messy, filled with coat hangers, clothes, and shoes. At the bottom of the closet was a large cardboard box. Barbara grabbed it off the floor, gently placing it down on Victor's bed next to Eva.

"Here," Barbara said while catching her breath. "Victor told me if anything ever happened to him, he would want you to have this. He was always very superstitious during his travels."

Eva smiled, not thinking to even question the meaning behind this. She could only focus on the idea that Victor had never forgotten about her. During the years of silence that went by, he had odd contingency plans put in place. Eva's mind quickly drifted off, now only focusing on what was inside this mystery box. She decided not to patiently wait for an approving nod, and ripped open the box with little care.

A bottle of wine from the fields of Tuscany had been carefully placed inside, surrounded by white wrapping paper. The label didn't look like any wine she had ever seen before. It must have not been mass-produced, and strictly available at one of Tuscany's many family-owned vineyards.

Victor wasn't able to physically spend time with Eva, so she could never take part in any of his adventures. In his own peculiar way, Victor took Eva with him everywhere by constantly reminding himself of her. Everywhere he went, he found a way to share his life with Eva, searching for her in the smallest details of his adventures. While touring Italy, a unique bottle of red wine reminded him of her.

"He never shut up about this box," Barbara said. "He always told me that if anything ever happened to him, you had to see it. I guess he never thought you'd accept it while he was here."

Eva giggled.

"I would never take gifts from him," she said. "I never felt right about it."

"Why?" Barbara asked.

"Well, the thing is, I'm married. I also have three children. I always thought it would have been a betrayal of my marriage if I took anything from him."

Barbara's eyes opened up wide as she finally realized why Victor could have never been with Eva. Barbara knew there had to be about a ten-year age difference between the two, but she could never figure out why Victor never attempted to make it work. She fully understood that Eva would likely never want to leave her family or want Victor to stop living his life waiting for her.

"I see," Barbara said. "Does your husband know?"

"No," she replied. "He really keeps to himself. We talk about the house, the bills, the kids, but we never have much time for anything else. He works a lot of the time then sleeps the rest. I truly do love him. He is good to me, though I can't help but feel there's something missing. We don't have a romantic love but rather a different kind of love for each other."

Barbara shook her head.

"At least he's nice to you," Barbara said. "My husband wasn't nice to me."

"Yeah," Eva sighed. "That doesn't make me feel any less lonely. Sometimes I just really need to lie there with him. We don't even have to be talking. I've always liked the idea of being in a man's arms. Feeling his hands on me, not even in a sexual way, but a nice tight squeeze on my shoulders."

Barbara shrugged her shoulders. "What woman doesn't want that?" she said sadly.

After Eva had closely examined the wine, she noticed another box sitting below a few layers of tissue paper. Eva placed the wine aside and slowly opened the second box, wondering what Victor could have possibly done next. What more could he have left behind for her? Inside the second cardboard box were oddly colored cowboy boots. They had a red and turquoise pattern on them, spattered with pictures of birds.

Eva gasped.

"What?" Barbara asked with concern.

Eva's eyes filled with tears. There wasn't a gift that could have possibly meant more to her. It wasn't the gift itself that mattered, but the meaning behind it. Eva had briefly mentioned the boots to Victor on one occasion. She'd never brought it up again, but Victor remembered she'd said it. He remembered everything Eva ever said.

"I can't believe he remembered," Eva whispered.

Eva pulled the cowboy boots out of the box. She placed them on her lap, letting her hands run over the leather.

Barbara thought out loud, "They're just boots. What's so special about them?"

Eva's head sunk. Barbara could see the tears dripping off her face as she held the boots tightly in her arms. Along with the initial shock that Victor would remember such a small thing about her, Eva felt massive guilt. She'd never done anything this special for Victor because she wouldn't allow herself to. How would her husband feel if she were to give another man a gift? It wasn't fair to him. There had been many times Eva had special gifts in mind for Victor. Eva had even gone as far as buying one, but she never gave it to him. Eva couldn't handle the guilt she'd feel. Now that really didn't matter, because she was feeling guilty no matter what she did.

"When I was young, I was a practicing musician for many years," Eva said with a flicker of happiness. "I was obsessed with becoming a country star. It meant so much to me. I flew down to Tennessee and started singing country songs in any bar that I could find." Eva paused to wipe the tears away from her face. She continued, "To fit my look, I wanted a pair of cowboy boots, specifically red and turquoise cowboy boots. For some reason, I don't like any other kind. I searched for years and couldn't find a single pair of boots with the colors I wanted. Somehow, Victor did."

Eva carefully put the cowboy boots back into the box and placed the cover back on. She looked at Barbara hopelessly full of love with nowhere to put it. Eva was trapped, not knowing what move to make next. Barbara saw the internal struggle inside Eva, but was unable to find any comforting words. Eva got up off Victor's bed and hugged Barbara tightly, looking for any form of emotional connection she could get. Who better than the woman who created Victor, the only person who understood the pain that would come if she lost him?

CHAPTER 5

There isn't a doctor in the world that knows what's going on in the head of a comatose patient. Some doctors say that a person in a coma can hear all that you say, while some think that theory is simply not true. The case was the same with Victor. Dr. Silverstein encouraged Victor's family to speak to him, but he made no guarantee what was being said could be heard.

The idea of an afterlife has been a heated debate for centuries. People of different ethnicities, religions, and creeds have weighed in on the issue. With little proof, there are only a handful of people who can say they know there's life after death. Most of those stories aren't considered believable, and humanity always comes up with scientific explanations for these visions.

Victor woke up lying in the middle of a vast desert. Every star in the sky was bright, lighting up the night. A full moon shone in the middle of a dark blue sky. The moon seemed so close, Victor could almost touch it with his hands. Before he sat up, he felt the ground around him, his fingers digging into the desert sand. The last thing he remembered was hearing a gunshot.

A man sat next to Victor's lifeless body. He wasn't too tall, standing at what is average height. He had a thick black beard and dark eyes. His hair was frizzy, and his clothes were torn. He looked as if he'd been in the desert for weeks.

Thick smoke passed over his eyes, waking him up to the smell of burning wood. With a deep gasp for air, he jumped to life. Fear struck his heart, as he found himself in what looked like the middle of nowhere. He remembered being in a bodega not too long before. Victor rose to his feet, finding himself wearing no shoes. The cool wind of the desert blew through his hair as his feet sunk into the desert sand.

Victor was extremely skeptical of the strange man sitting behind him near the campfire.

"Who are you?" Victor asked cautiously.

"I'm Benedict," the man responded calmly.

Victor looked around him, noticing there wasn't a single sign of civilization. The only sources of light were the stars in the sky and the fire at his side. Outside of the fire's reach, there was only darkness. The dark ring outside the light emitted an energy that made Victor feel anxious. He sat down across from Benedict, making sure he stayed close to the light.

"Where am I?" Victor asked.

Benedict didn't respond and quietly pushed the logs around the fire with a thick wooden stick. Victor stared at the man, analyzing Benedict's body language, trying to get some sort of a read off him. There wasn't a trace of fear inside of Benedict; he was too calm. He seemed at peace with the world.

"What's the last thing you remember before you woke up here?" Benedict said.

"I remember hearing a gunshot. Then everything went black."

Tears came to Victor's eyes as he thought of the little girl and her mother who'd nearly been killed. Victor hoped he had done all that he could to save them.

"You saved two innocent lives. Why did you decide to save the life of a little girl and her mother instead of your own?"

Victor gasped. He backed away from Benedict.

"How did you know that?" Victor screamed.

"Answer the question, and I will be happy to explain everything," Benedict said calmly.

"The mother and child were innocent," Victor replied angrily. "How could I ever let that bandit hurt a child in front of her mother, or vice versa?"

"Am I dead?" Victor asked quickly.

Looking at Victor, Benedict smiled.

"You're not dead yet."

Cindy Rossini sat by Victor's bedside. She had short brown hair that was shoulder length. She was much shorter than Victor, standing only at five foot two. She carried herself in a way that was prideful. She came across as sweet and innocent, but on the inside, she was a woman who had disdain for men. Maybe she had a good reason for it, as most men don't have the best character. Cindy had been one of Victor's girlfriends; they had dated for years.

She stared at Victor, not with anger or disdain, but with sorrow. Despite treating him so poorly, Cindy didn't wish death upon Victor. She didn't think he deserved to die. Victor was a huge part of her life, in more than one way. Victor would never forgive her for the hurt she'd brought into his life, but Cindy only felt it was right to pay her respects.

Cindy felt guilty for the pain she'd put him through over the years. The guilt consumed her when she'd heard the news of the shooting. She knew that, because of her, Victor hadn't been able to hold an emotionally intimate relationship for most of his life.

"How long has it been? Maybe almost ten years?" she asked Victor. "I know I'm probably the last person you'd ever want to see."

Cindy didn't dare touch him, as she knew Victor would have never wanted that. She chose her words carefully because if he knew she were here, he'd ask her to leave. Victor could never handle the way Cindy had broken his heart. Cindy had been someone Victor deeply trusted, confided in, and spent many years of his life trying to please. Yet he had been met with a betrayal unlike any other. For almost a whole year during their relationship, Cindy had been sleeping with another man.

Victor had grown suspicious when Cindy began to act strange at one point in their relationship. There'd be some days where she'd be distant and some where she was loveable. She'd fiercely protect her phone, being sure to run and pick it up whenever it rang. There would be nights where Cindy would go missing for hours at a time. The lying consumed her life, as she wasn't able to keep up with her cover stories. Her naturally-filled body shape became frail as she stopped eating from the guilt that haunted her. Victor hung on to the thought that Cindy would never hurt him, refusing to see how she could be so cruel as to lie and sneak around.

Cindy never had the chance to make things right with Victor. The broken trust between the two of them was something that could never be healed. The deceitfulness

Victor discovered within Cindy forever altered how he felt about her.

Victor had not only been betrayed by Cindy, but by those who he considered to be friends. Friends, acquaintances, and those closest to the couple had lied, electing to watch him slowly suffer. They refused to get involved in the situation, wishing to remain neutral instead of taking sides. This one tiny woman had forever altered Victor's reality. She'd created an alternate reality that forced him to suppress his instincts in the name of love. As he constantly questioned his faith in their relationship, Victor started to believe he was the problem. A year's worth of blaming himself for what happened changed the inner workings of his mind. The loving and forgiving man had become a bitter cynic who couldn't trust a single soul, including God.

The massive guilt Cindy once felt years ago came back, manifested in the pit of her stomach and causing physical pain. She looked at him—a once strong, powerful, and loving man, now reduced to nothing. Still, a part of her was not sorry for what she had done. She justified her actions by finding faults in Victor, using them as excuses for her actions. Hearing these faults named in a detailed conversation before their relationship ended had Victor convinced he'd done nothing right. Victor started to believe he would never mean anything to a woman he loved, causing his self-worth to reach rock bottom.

Cindy gathered the courage to hold Victor's hand, battling past the remorse as her eyes welled up with tears. Some, those who knew the two of them, would say that Cindy's tears were fake. The crying was a response to her guilt. Had nothing happened to Victor, she wouldn't have gone to these lengths to make things right. Deep in her mind, a part of her was happy Victor was dying. She was extremely envious of his life and the success he had achieved since they'd split. Cindy had always wanted Victor to stay with her despite what she'd done to him. The chance to revel in Victor's fame and fortune could have been hers, but the opportunity passed her by. She chose lust over love, deceit over trust, and doubt over faith.

Eva walked into the room as the stroke of Cindy's hand touched Victor's body. She stopped abruptly when she saw Cindy sitting at his bedside. Eva stared at Cindy, first in a state of shock, asking herself a barrage of questions: "Who is this woman? What is she doing here? How did she find him? Why is she touching him like that?"

The way Cindy held Victor's arm made Eva's eyes bulge, teeth clench, and stomach turn. Eva had never seen another woman in Victor's life, refusing to picture him with anyone else besides her. This was a selfish thought because she was the married one. Yet, as much as she wanted Victor to move on and find someone, the selfish part of her was too overbearing. Victor was Eva's, and he wasn't to be shared with anyone. Eva never wanted another woman to please him, hold him, make him laugh, or touch him. The thought of him making love to another woman broke her heart. Eva had never been more possessive of a man in her entire life. The worst feeling of all would be Victor telling another woman that he loved her. Now, seeing what she thought was another woman care for him first-hand, these fears became reality.

Her thoughts continued to swirl, and Barbara approached the door of the hospital room to find Eva totally stoic.

"Why are you standing at the door?" Barbara asked.

Eva didn't reply. Barbara gently brushed Eva out of her line of sight to find Cindy sitting at Victor's bedside. Cindy turned around to see Eva and Barbara standing behind her. She mumbled under her breath, "Shit."

Barbara lunged at Cindy in a fierce rage. As much as Eva would have liked to watch Barbara tear Cindy to shreds, Eva stopped the attack. Cindy jumped from her seat like a gazelle that had narrowly escaped the attack of a hungry lion.

"You destroyed my son!" Barbara screamed. "For years, you destroyed my son. He treated you like a princess, and you spit in his face. Why would you betray a person who was so good to you? You could have just let him go instead of dragging him through the mud. You don't know the pain you caused him."

Barbara broke down in tears thinking about the suffering Cindy had put Victor through. Eva held Barbara in her arms, comforting her, then guided Barbara over to a seat in the corner of the room. Eva calmed Barbara down and marched over to Cindy, staring down at what she thought was a midget. She had trouble picturing Victor with a woman so tiny. Then she realized that it might have been her jealousy talking.

"Who are you?" Eva said angrily. "Visiting is for family only. By the way Barbara just acted, I don't think you're family."

Cindy grinned. "I'm Cindy," she said. "Victor's ex-girlfriend from many moons ago. We spent years of our life together. I only thought it was right that I pay my respects. Victor did treat me very well."

Even though she was so short, Cindy was not afraid to push Eva out of her personal space.

"By the way, I was like family at one point. I was with the Espositos all the time. Holidays, birthdays, vacations, you name it. I don't remember seeing you around. Who the hell are you?"

Eva clenched her fists together, beginning to put the pieces together in her mind. She was the only woman to break Cindy's spell on Victor, showing him that she wasn't anything like Cindy.

"You hurt him," Eva mumbled under her breath.

"What?" Cindy asked.

Eva screamed, "After whatever you did to him, do you know how long it took me to get him to trust me? I had to show Victor that I loved him for the man he was. I didn't force him to be someone else the way that you did. His soul was shattered when I found him. It took months of rebuilding, work, and fixing. There was one point where he couldn't even feel. Where he shut me out because he was so afraid of being hurt."

Cindy barked back at Eva.

"That's right, I did try to change him. It was for his own good. He can't go about his life being an old man at such a young age. He should have tried to be open to living in the world he was living in. You can't live in the past the way he did. The way he dressed was so unattractive. That man could listen to eighties rock for hours on end. I couldn't take it anymore. He needed to get with the times. The only person I know who loved Bon Jovi more than Victor is my mother."

Cindy pushed Eva with one finger, not having the slightest clue who Eva was or why she was attacking her in this way.

She asked herself, "Was she his lover?"

Cindy thought that it couldn't be. Eva definitely looked older than Victor—that wouldn't make any sense to her. She couldn't picture a man preferring a woman that was older than him as opposed to a younger woman. The last Cindy had heard from the tabloids, Victor was single and never had a steady girlfriend since her.

Cindy continued to rant. "Who are you anyway, his long-lost aunt? I don't remember seeing you around anywhere."

Eva's face turned red in disbelief that Cindy had the audacity to call her old.

"Who am I?" Eva said sarcastically. "Who am I?"

Eva paused for a moment, viciously smiling. With saying only a few words, she knew she could ruin Cindy's day. Eva was the sweetest person in the world, but when a person double-crossed her, she could be wicked.

Cindy patiently waited for Eva to respond, thinking Eva wouldn't be able to come up with a witty response. She assumed Eva was a woman starved for love, trying to find the man Victor painted in his novels. Cindy didn't have the slightest clue who Eva really was, and figured she was just another groupie.

"I'm the novel girl," Eva said calmly.

Cindy didn't understand what she meant.

"Novel girl? What, you're his editor or something?"

"I'm the woman he writes his novels about. I'm the woman he dedicates his books to. I'm the woman who made him who he is today. I'm the woman who encouraged him to read and write. I'm his first love and the only woman to ever truly love him the way he deserved to be loved."

Cindy froze in total disbelief as she analyzed Eva's appearance. Out of curiosity, Cindy had read Victor's books. Eva looked exactly like the woman he had described in not one, but all of his novels. The blonde hair, the green eyes, her height, and even the frame of her body fit the description. Cindy had always wondered who Victor's dedications were to, and it finally started to make sense now. His books were dedicated to a mystery woman, always under the same name, a person that no one could ever find. Now Cindy was standing toe to toe with the so-called novel girl, a woman she could never compare to.

———

Victor continued to interrogate Benedict, convincing himself that he was dreaming. Maybe this—the gunshot, the deli, and now being lost in the desert—was one bad dream. There was no other explanation for randomly waking up in a desert. Was traveling at the speed of light suddenly possible? Victor smacked himself in the face, only to feel the sting. If this were a dream, he would have woken up. There wouldn't have been a feeling of pain.

"This is all a bad dream," he mumbled. "This is all a bad dream."

Benedict smiled again. He thought Victor was amusing, always thinking he could control the world, that he could bend fate with his very hands and protect those he loved from harm despite the circumstances. Some would say Victor was delusional; others might have believed in his willpower.

"You're not dreaming, Victor. This is real. There's nothing you can do about it. Right now, you're in a coma. You got shot in that bodega, you were taken to the hospital, and now you're on life support. You're fighting for your life. The only thing that's alive is your conscience and your soul. That's what makes it possible for you to be here right now, sitting here next to me."

"Excuse me?"

"You heard me. I know it's a hard pill to swallow, but let it sink in."

Victor sat back down in the sand, placing his hand over the fire to see if he could feel the heat. He burned his hand and quickly retreated.

"If I'm in a coma, why can I feel pain? Why can I feel the heat from the fire?"

Benedict laughed. "I already told you. You may be in a coma, but where you are right now is very real. You're in limbo, lingering between the afterlife and life on earth. You're at the crossroads between life and death. You're still able to feel, to hear, and to touch. This could go one of two ways, depending on your health. Once you start to lose the feelings of a human, that means you're moving towards life after death, or you could wake up out of your coma and all could be well."

"Well, how does it look so far?" Victor asked. "Am I going to pull through?"

Before Benedict could answer his question, he was interrupted by booming voices coming from the sky. The voices were faint, but he could still hear them. It sounded like two women arguing with each other. Victor noticed the voices sounded familiar.

"What are those voices?" he asked. "Why do they sound so familiar?"

Even though you're in a coma, you could hear what's going on around you. You could hear what people are telling you. In a way, you are conscious of what's going on.

"Who's speaking to me?"

Benedict stood up and dusted the sand off his clothes.

"Do you think you're ready to handle that?"

"What else do I have to lose? I'm half dead apparently."

Benedict snapped his fingers. Suddenly, he was in the hospital room watching Cindy and Eva argue over his dead body. His mother was still crying the corner. Cindy was steaming that Victor had written novels about Eva, hating the idea that Victor had found happiness and was not wallowing in his own misery. Cindy knew a man would never love her that way, and she hated knowing that Eva had found that love.

Cindy crossed her arms. "So you were my replacement?"

"Replacement?" Eva laughed. "If that's what you want to call it, sure."

Cindy shrugged her shoulders. "Well, I came before you, didn't I?"

Eva pointed down at Cindy's face. "He never loved you," she said calmly. "He may have thought he loved you, but he never did. I know that for a fact. I've experienced the way Victor loves firsthand. He respected me both as a person and a woman. That man would have died for me if I asked him to. No matter if I got fat, old, or into a horrible accident, he would still love me the same. His feelings for me never changed, even after years of not seeing each other. I don't think you can say he'd do the same for you. He only wanted to do those things for me. There's not another woman on the planet who made him feel the way I did. When you destroyed him, I put him back together, piece by piece."

Eva paused to catch her breath. She continued, "I'll tell you one thing. Even after all that you've done to him, he still never wished a bad thing happened to you. I know for a fact he would never want to see you, but he still wished you the best. We all know you're here to satisfy your own guilty conscience. Now do us all a favor and leave."

Cindy quietly walked out of the room, knowing she had lost the war of words with Eva. Eva ran back over to Barbara, trying to calm her down for what seemed like the fifteenth time. Victor, looking on the whole time, was in awe. Seeing Eva and Cindy in the same room was enough of a reason to make him uneasy.

"You ever hear of that saying: over my dead body?" Victor joked.

Benedict chuckled.

"That's Eva," Victor said calmly.

Benedict nodded. "Eva's been with since you've been in a coma. She's been here the entire time. She hasn't left your side. Cindy came in only when Eva stepped out with your mother. They went back to your house so your mother could give Eva the box you've been keeping for her."

Victor didn't care that Cindy was there, and didn't waste his energy figuring out why she'd show up to his deathbed. He didn't care if Cindy was sorry, whether her feelings were fake or real. Victor kept staring at Eva. He analyzed her from head to toe, admiring her facial features and her beauty.

Victor was quickly reminded of how humans felt love, feeling the strike of a thunderbolt causing his heart to pump from his chest. This is why humanity fights to stay alive, to find the true meaning of what it means to be alive.

"She came to see me?" Victor said in disbelief.

"She loves you," Benedict said. "Of course, she did."

Victor quickly dismissed Benedict's comment. "She never told me she loved me. She never told me. She wasn't allowed to. She couldn't."

Victor put his head down.

"Eva broke her rules and boundaries," Benedict said reassuringly. "She admitted to everything earlier today. She slept next to you in your hospital bed."

Victor shook his head in disbelief. "Then why didn't I hear it?"

Benedict patted Victor on the back, reminiscent of how a father would comfort his son. "Because you weren't ready to hear it yet."

Benedict guided Victor out of the hospital room. Victor blinked, ending up back in the desert next to the campfire. He gazed into the fire emotionlessly, watching the wood crack from the unbearable heat of the fire. For once, no thoughts ran through his head; his mind was blank. Benedict stood beside him, quietly waiting for Victor to process what he had said. Benedict could see that Victor was deep in thought.

Eva was Victor's North Star, guiding him through a depression by showing him what unconditional love feels like. She had looked past his sadness, despair, and anger to find a man with a beautiful soul, someone with so much love to give and no woman to give it to. Almost instantly, Eva had been drawn to him.

Victor had never thought about writing until he realized he could control the world through his stories. He created a life for himself and Eva, one that would be perfect. He could live multiple lifetimes, in any place he wanted. He could even create a place that wasn't of this earth, traveling on a rocket ship to Mars where he'd have an extra thirty-nine minutes a day to spend with Eva.

Every time Victor released a new novel, Eva religiously ran to the bookstore to buy it, reading it in no later than a day's time. She was always anxious to see what new world he created for them next. For Eva, it was also an escape from her own chaotic life.

After five minutes of silence, Victor turned to Benedict with a hopeless look on his face.

"Why did you show me that?" Victor asked.

"Because you needed to see it. You've always doubted her love for you. It's time you accept the truth."

"I never doubted it. I never allowed myself to feel it. I refused to see that she cared for me. She could never say the words to me. Nothing was ever confirmed. I could see it in her face, in her smile, and even in the way she acted towards me. Of course, I knew, but it still killed me that she could never say it."

Victor pulled his hands up to his face, wiping the tears dripping off his nose away. He missed the little things about her. The sentimental moments counted the most. He'd think back on the way she'd call his name, the distinct smell that she had, or the feel of her soft skin accidentally grazing his. There's no telling what he would give to relive one of these timeless moments.

"Maybe it's time you allow yourself to be happy," Benedict said. "Give yourself the credit. You don't know what she's going through on her end."

Victor's frustration was overwhelming, and his sadness quickly turned into rage. Now, he'd never been farther away from Eva. He was dying, and there was nothing he could do to change that. Instead of trying to figure out how much Eva loved him, Victor should have accepted that she *did* love him. This topped the list of his regrets. Yet, he would ask himself, how could he truly allow himself to accept her love if it could never be truly fulfilled? Why would he put himself through that pain?

"I can't allow myself to be happy," Victor screamed aloud. "Tell me something, since you seem to know everything. Why can't I be there to take care of her when she's sick? Why can't I see the look on her face when I read her vows at our wedding? She can never look at me and say, 'Victor, you're going to be a father.' I can't hold her in my arms in the middle of the night. If another woman were to lie on my chest, it wouldn't feel right. That's Eva's spot. The worst part of it all is that I can't even touch her. I can't bring her in for a dance. I can't hold her hand. I can't make love to her."

Benedict could see the life draining from Victor's body as the reality of his words set in. He hadn't told a single soul about Eva, finally deciding to confide in a desert nomad. Benedict was surprised by the raw emotion coming from Victor, and was left speechless. He assumed Victor's love for Eva was strong, but their bond was indescribable. This was the strongest desire for a person Benedict had ever seen. It was poetic and inspiring but filled with tragedy. Benedict started to think that maybe Victor really could bend fate with his very hands.

CHAPTER 6

With her emotions still flaring, Eva drove herself home, passing red lights, stop signs, and making sure to hit the pedal a little extra hard at crosswalks. Her hands trembled as she gripped the steering wheel. Her mind was still cloudy, a part of her lost trying to navigate the new world that had been placed at her feet. As Eva pulled into her driveway, she noticed her husband's car already parked there and let out a large sigh. Eva knew she had to explain this to her husband eventually. She just didn't know how. What possible reason could she give for running out of the house so abruptly? What could she do or say? The questions were endless. Her husband was a smart man. It was only a matter of time before he figured out what was going on.

Eva watched the bright orange and yellow sky through the car window, waiting for the sun to set on the day. Today, nature seemed a little more beautiful to her. Maybe it was the high of love that had whistled back into her life.

"Where did the time go?" she thought to herself.

Eva walked around to the trunk of her car, placing the key inside and opening it to find Victor's box. She decided to leave it there, only taking the bottle of wine. She dragged her feet to the front door with the wine in hand, feeling like shackles were tied to her ankles. Bracing herself for what would come next, she reached to put the key in the front door, wallowing in the guilt of leaving Victor alone for the night.

Stanley quietly sat on the couch with his feet up on the coffee table, something he knew Eva couldn't stand. Lucky for him, it was a Sunday. He had the luxury of taking this time to try and figure out what was going on. Stanley hadn't moved the entire day. He sat in one spot, reading one of Victor's novels from start to finish.

There was something odd about Victor. Why was his wife so attached to Victor's stories? Stanley reread parts of the book over and over again. He knew there was missing something. The character descriptions seemed odd to him. The female protagonist resembled Eva. Her attitude, her backstory, and even the way she was described were offshoots of reality. Was this why she enjoyed his stories? Maybe she saw herself, or tried to find herself, in his story?

Eva found Stanley reading Victor's novel. A stack of Victor's entire works stood next to him, aligned in a specific order. This didn't alarm her too much; she knew he wouldn't be able to connect the dots. Stanley closed the book, looking at his wife with great concern. He wasn't angry at her but confused. Stanley trusted Eva, which he had every right to. For her to hold a man like Victor off for so long spoke volumes about her character.

Stanley rushed up to Eva, questioning her with suspicion.

"What happened today?" Stanley asked. "Why were you acting so crazy?"

Eva's head sunk to her chest. "I can't explain it. I just needed to go."

Stanley lifted Eva's chin up with one finger, then placed his hands on her shoulders.

"Look at me," he said. "Tell me what's wrong. You can tell me anything."

Eva's mind was racing.

"Should I tell him?" she thought. "Is it finally time to let my husband know that I fell in love with another man?"

The worst part of the situation was that her feelings weren't cut and dry. It wasn't that she fell out of love with Stanley. She loved him very much. It was just a different kind of love.

Eva took Stanley's hands off her and gently placed them at his sides.

"When I'm ready, I'll tell you," she said quietly. Eva reassuringly kissed him. Stanley watched as she made her way into the kitchen. He saw the bottle of wine in her hand, not thinking to question her about it. Stanley knew she enjoyed her wine.

Eva's words repeated in his mind as she walked away. He stared at Victor's novel, deciding he would continue to search for an answer. There was something he was missing, and Stanley knew that Eva wouldn't tell him until she was ready.

Eva rummaged through her kitchen drawer, pulling a bottle opener out with glee. The smell of the wine already made her blood feel warm. Victor had chosen this particular bottle from a small wine shop in Florence. This brand of wine wasn't available in America, and was exclusive to Tuscany. The Italians believed mass-producing this type of wine would lead to a decline in quality.

The wine looked perfectly colored as it filled her glass. Eva knew to let the wine sit before she drank it, allowing the wine to breathe. The wine touched her tongue, instantly relieving

Eva of her pain. Her lips were now colored the same shade as the wine.

Eva sat in her bed, trying to find comfort in this situation. The more Eva drank, the angrier she became, which was strange for her. Eva wasn't an angry drunk, but something was bothering her. She couldn't quite pinpoint the feeling, until it swiftly hit her, like a wave crashing over her mind.

It was Cindy that bothered her. The anger was coursing through her veins at the thought of Cindy holding Victor's arm. She couldn't believe that Victor had dated such a woman. Cindy was the total opposite of Eva. In a strange way, Eva was angry and jealous that Victor had cared for another woman before her. She didn't like the idea that Cindy sought out his attention enough to read his books and that she came to see him while he was sick. Eva was territorial over Victor. She didn't want anyone else to have what was hers.

The long and exhausting day took a toll on Eva's mind. Only a measly two glasses put Eva to sleep. Until the moment her eyes shut, her thoughts ran. Even while she was asleep, the thoughts continued to hound her. The comforting feeling from the red wine helped Eva fall deeper into her sleep. Then, the anger took over her mind, revealing her true feelings while she dreamed.

Eva dreamed she was sitting next to Victor on a couch in a room that resembled an office or study. It was a small yet colorfully painted room. The walls were a burgundy red color, and the floor was lined with a grey carpet. The lighting was dim; only a small lamp lit the corner of the room. Strangely, this room didn't have any doors. There was nowhere either of them could go.

Eva hadn't realized she was dreaming yet. As far as she knew, this was real. She attentively analyzed the details of Victor's body. He didn't look sickly anymore. His cheeks were rosy, and his body shape, full. His broad shoulders and thick arms gave him a powerful essence. His chest was large and defined. His face sported a few days' worth of stubble. He looked exactly like he did the last time Eva saw him.

Victor discreetly looked at Eva, who was wearing a dress that perfectly molded to the natural curves of her body. The dark green color of the fabric matched her light green eyes. The two colors complemented her blonde hair, making her eyes glow. The dress only came down to her knees, showing off her legs. Victor stared at her legs and moved his eyes to her thighs. Eva noticed Victor staring at her. She loved the way he admired her body.

"We can't," Victor said.

"But why not?" Eva replied hastily.

Her scent grew stronger as Eva slowly inched towards Victor. He couldn't help the feeling in his loins that got more powerful by the moment. When she wanted, Eva could be a dangerously seductive woman. Her eyes screamed want, her whisper was sensual, and her touch was soft. It was evident Eva had a burning desire for him in her soul.

As Eva grew closer, Victor backed away to the far corner of the couch. "Stop," he said quietly. "We can't do this. We can't."

Although Victor told her to stop, he didn't want her to. He was enjoying every moment of Eva wanting to seduce him. This moment was years in the making, filled with sexual tension that was desperately seeking to be expressed. After a decade of frustration, these feelings were dangerously present.

"Why?" Eva whispered softly. "Isn't this what you want?"

Eva crawled closer to Victor and backed him into a corner. The guilt fled his mind as soon as he decided that he needed to have her. Any sense of morality he had left evaporated. When Eva reached Victor, she crawled on top of him and felt how badly he wanted her. Eva got pleasure out of watching him try to resist, knowing she was going to win. It was only a matter of time before Victor begged her for more.

Eva's silky lips looked perfectly shaped as she leaned in to kiss Victor, feeling his heart beat faster against her chest. She kissed Victor once on the lips, leaving him paralyzed. Victor was in awe of what was happening. Something he had wanted so badly, for so many years, was finally a reality. He could smell her womanly scent becoming stronger. The feeling of her soft lips parting his was silky, just as he'd always imagined.

She whispered in his ear, "I don't want to share you with anyone."

She placed her hands under his shirt as she kissed him, feeling his chest beneath her hands. Victor's warm breath caressed Eva's neck while she anxiously pulled his shirt off. He tried to resist her, failing at every attempt. Eva kissed Victor's shoulder, moving down to his chest. Her hands moved across his body, inspecting every crevice. Slowly, Victor gave in. He placed his hands on her waist, gripping her tightly.

"Isn't this what you've always wanted?" she whispered again.

"Yes," Victor said calmly.

The sensation of Victor's hands on her waist swept through her body. A gesture so small had monumental meaning for the two of them. They'd been apart for too long, with too many boundaries. Eva could feel the warmth between her legs. Her body was aching for his. She felt a sensation coming on, yet he had barely touched her. She anticipated the moment he would be inside of her—waiting, yearning, and needing.

Eva continued kissing her way back up to Victor's lips. He could feel the warmth of Eva's lips on his skin and the passion between each passing moment that went by. There was nothing he could do any longer. He needed Eva to be his. The feelings in his heart were too powerful.

Eva unbuttoned his pants, slipping her hand inside. She whispered in Victor's ear again.

"You see this?" Eva grabbed Victor as she spoke. "This is mine. It's all mine to have fun with…to play with…to…."

Before Eva could continue speaking another word, Victor's dominance awoke. He ripped her dress in half with his hands, revealing her breasts as he pulled her into his body with fiery lust. Eva completely molded to Victor's body, allowing him to cup her breasts and warm her cold body with his hands. Their tongues swirled around in each other's mouths. Eva loved the feeling of Victor's hands on her, safe yet still erotic.

Her breaths were heavy sighs of relief. Eva had finally won her prize, experiencing what she had been craving for so long. Victor's dominance was one of the sexiest things about his personality. He looked at Eva like she was only his, and that's exactly what she was. She loved knowing Victor's strength was profound. He was a good man with a bad boy attitude lurking in the shadows of his mind.

They kissed intensely, not thinking about anything else but each other. They were releasing years of frustration, pent-up sexual energy, and imagination. Everything was new to them. They took such joy in exploring their bodies, getting to know one another like never before.

Victor got off the couch with Eva's legs still wrapped around his waist. He carried Eva. She refused to let him go. Victor threw her down on the desk, knocking the lamp onto the floor. His pants casually slipped down to his ankles. Victor pulled the rest of Eva's torn dress over her head. For a moment, he stopped to admire her naked body, taking his time to run his eyes over every curve. He loved everything about her, even the imperfections. To him, she was completely perfect. Eva watched him as his eyes glanced over her with heavy breaths as she anticipated Victor's next move. The longer Victor stared, the more she noticed the desire in his eyes.

Victor broke his silence, spread her legs, and pulled her closer to him. Victor kissed her lips, then whispered, "I love you."

"I love you too," Eva said with a deep breath.

In a flash, her dream suddenly ended. Eva awoke from her deep sleep with heavy breaths and sweat dripping off her forehead. She was thirsty, not for water, but for Victor. Her feelings from the dream were real. The warmth between her legs was still there. Parts of her body were quivering and trembling. Such a powerful dream had her on the verge of an orgasm but still left her feeling unfulfilled. She needed him, and a dream wasn't going to cut it.

The morning light shone on her face. She looked beside her to find Stanley sleeping quietly, curled to his side of their bed. Eva quickly shook off the drowsiness as she walked downstairs to the living room. Eva combed through her bookshelf, trying to find something to read to Victor. She was confident Victor could hear her words. Even while he was in a coma, she felt their love was strong enough that, wherever he was, Victor would know she was with him.

Eva had one book in mind and was looking to see if she'd kept it after all these years. Her fingertips grazed the spine of each book until she found her novel of choice. *Lady Chatterley's Lover* by D.H. Lawrence stood in the far corner. She wiped the dust off the classic novel. Her aunt had given her this book when she was barely twenty. It had a bad reputation because it had been banned at one point in the United States for sexual profanity. The beauty of this novel was that it was a true love story. It wasn't the story of some hot affair that was meaningless. It was the story of two people who were meant for each other. The story was too realistic for people to handle. It dove into a woman's mind, which was a tall task for a male author to accomplish.

This novel specifically had significant meaning in Eva's life. Why? The answer was simple. The message this novel was sending was concise. The best type of a relationship is with someone you truly love. The best sex is with someone you love. Anyone could have a meaningless fling, but one hundred pages pass before the main characters kiss in this novel. Sex is the final pillar in any relationship, roping together mental and emotional intimacy. *Lady Chatterley's Lover* was the story of a woman who was in a meaningless, emotionless, relationship and found love that awakened her in a way she thought she never could be.

Eva took the book off the shelf and went back upstairs to change. She was making the best of this, trying to hold out hope that Victor would pull through by some miracle. This was the only other way Eva could be close to him. By reading him such a powerful love story, she felt it was the only way she could share her love with him.

Victor and Benedict walked through the desert with nothing in front of them but endless miles of sand. There was still no sign of civilization, only the endless barren desert. Victor had been following Benedict for miles in silence. They hadn't spoken since the previous night at the campfire.

"Where are we going?" Victor asked with an annoyed tone.

"I'm not sure," Benedict replied. "We're lost in your mind. You created me. I'm nothing more than a guide in the world you created."

"I should have created a map," Victor fired back.

Benedict remained calm. He knew Victor was frustrated. It was understandable.

"This endless road will continue until you face the feelings you've been hiding for so long."

Victor's anger was slowly growing as he continued to walk alongside Benedict. He felt like there was no escaping the mental prison he was trapped in. Victor decided to play along for now, but he had a feeling there was something Benedict wasn't telling him.

"What do you want to know?" Victor asked. "I was under the assumption you knew everything."

"I only know what you allow me to know." Benedict continued to walk, with Victor closely following him. "Tell me about Eva. How did you meet? What's your story? Why can't you be with the woman you love so dearly?"

Victor sighed, "We'd better have another few miles of desert because that's how long it's going to take me to explain how everything started."

Benedict nodded.

Victor continued, "I met Eva at a Tony Bennett concert. I went to the concert by myself because I didn't know anyone who would go with me. Not too many people would jump at the chance to see him. I mean, he's not Jon Bon Jovi or anything."

Benedict rolled his eyes as Victor continued rambling.

"I had an aisle seat, and sure enough, Eva sat down right next to me. Like me, she had also come to the concert alone. Neither of us spoke the entire show. We just looked into each other's eyes, noticing the raw emotion as Tony sang away. At the end of the concert, I introduced myself to her. We sat and talked until everyone left the theater. There was something about her that made me feel so comfortable. I was drawn to her."

Benedict looked at Victor's face, noticing his cheeks were rosy thinking about the memory. He finally smiled for the first time since being in the desert, coming to life a little more.

"Continue," Benedict said.

Victor had no problem rambling on. He loved to talk.

"We met for coffee the very next day. Something small and casual. Nothing too over the top at first. As we talked more, our feelings grew. There was something in my mind that told me to take our relationship really slow. I always felt like a part of her wasn't with me whenever we saw each other. After the third time we met, I asked her out to dinner, and she declined. I was confused and even a little hurt. She insisted there was a good reason why and that she'd like to continue meeting because our talks meant a lot to her. I agreed because I genuinely enjoyed her company. I wouldn't have called us friends because the sexual tension was strong from the beginning. We were both dancing around an unseen issue. I was afraid to continue asking what it was, and she was afraid to tell me. First, we met once a week, then twice, and eventually three times. We were totally content with coffee and talking."

Benedict knew Victor was stalling, thinking it might have been too painful for Victor to talk about.

"It sounds like you're leaving something out," Benedict said. "I know it's hard, but you have to let it out."

Victor quickly wiped away a few tears that dripped from his cheek. He didn't want Benedict to think any less of him for crying.

"We became attached to each other. I always thought she was a tiny bit odd, which made her really interesting. It was the little things about her. She was a very unique woman. I'd never met anyone like her."

Benedict stopped Victor from speaking.

"You haven't mentioned her response to any of this," he stated.

Victor sighed once again. "The only thing that stuck out to me about her was that her words were limited. She could only be so emotional with me, and I never knew why. Her eyes screamed love and compassion, yet nothing came out of her mouth. She would slip every so often. I caught her, more than once, accidentally saying how much she cared about me or how she treasured a moment between us."

Benedict was getting impatient. He wanted Victor to get to the point already.

"And then?" Benedict asked.

"A few months before we met, I got out of a horrible relationship. She picked up the pieces of my heart and put them back together. She made me feel like I was worth something, like I was a catch. I wouldn't be an author if it wasn't for her. She was the inspiration for my stories."

Benedict noticed a bright smile on Victor's face as he thought back to the story of Eva's life and how it impacted her.

"Eva was an artist herself. She was a struggling musician through her twenties. Eva never had the right encouragement, and she wanted to make sure I had it. One day, we went to a guitar store, and I watched her play. She was so breathtaking. I fell in love with her right there and then. We were meant to be, and we both knew it. Nothing was ever the same after that day. I looked right into her eyes and told her I wanted her to be mine and that I couldn't stand the idea of her being with anyone else but me. I wanted her to bear my name, to be Eva Esposito. I couldn't control this dominant urge I had. No woman had ever made me want more than Eva did. As I spoke these words to her, she looked deeply into my eyes. I saw what she was feeling and that she wanted those things too. We inched closer to one another until our lips were only centimeters apart and she started crying, prying herself from my arms. Then she told me why she was so distant."

Benedict heard the sadness in Victor's voice and could tell that he hadn't talked about this often. It was something he had never had the chance to think about. It seemed like Victor hadn't even had the chance to process it in his own mind, even after all these years.

"What did she say?" Benedict asked anxiously.

Victor sighed, "She was married. I fell in love with a woman who was married. Married with three beautiful children. We never did so much as touch each other. She never would dare betray her vows, and I respected her for that. I never pushed her either, doing the best I could to behave myself."

Benedict was waiting to see if Victor and Eva eventually had an affair. He frowned upon the idea of adultery, knowing that this wasn't an ordinary romance. Before he offered council, he carefully asked another question.

"Are you sure nothing ever happened between the two of you?"

Victor laughed. His reaction wasn't a nervous one, though. The laughter came from a place of security.

"No," Victor said stoutly. "Who am I to break up a family? Besides, I've never seen a woman love her children more than Eva. She's a loyal wife and mother. How could I ever push her to leave her family?"

Even though Victor loved Eva, he wanted what was best for her, and that was to be with her children. Eva never wanted to destroy her family and hurt the people she loved the most. He put her happiness before his own. Victor had power and sway over Eva, yet he hardly used it. Victor was trying to be selfless. In an odd way, this made Eva want him even more. She knew that behind that moral high ground talk were powerful feelings and deep desires waiting to be unleashed.

"So then how did you get to this point? By the way you looked at Eva when she came to see you at the hospital, it seemed like you hadn't seen her in years."

Victor couldn't hold back the sadness any longer. He stopped walking, standing completely still as he covered his eyes with one hand. He sobbed, like a man grieving his dead wife. Benedict had quietly watched the emotions Victor had through this entire talk. Happiness, sadness, anger, and now devastation.

"We agreed not to see each other ever again," he said through his tears.

Benedict put his hand on Victor's shoulder, offering him a sign of comfort.

"It sounds like you really loved each other," Benedict said sadly.

"She's such a good person. Better than I'll ever be. She always wanted the best for me. Even though she never said it, I knew she loved me. She never wanted me to leave her like everyone else in her life did. If she would have asked me, I would have kept meeting her every week, but the guilt consumed her. Our feelings got too strong and she never wanted me to wait for her because she was ten years older than me. Eva wanted me to live a full life, like she had. She always wanted me to have a family and children. She always said I'd be the perfect dad for a little baby girl. She was afraid of holding me back from my own life."

Benedict didn't understand why they couldn't be together in some way. Why couldn't Eva just leave her husband if it was what she wanted to do? Then he realized that Eva was afraid because she couldn't give Victor the life *he wanted*. She didn't want Victor to wait for her to leave when she might never be able to do it. Her biggest concern was hurting the people around her. She never wanted her children to come from a broken home the way she did. She didn't want to hurt her husband, who was very good to her through the years, and she didn't want Victor to waste his own life waiting for her. She didn't want him to miss out on the chance of meeting another great girl and having children of his own.

"She was the one, wasn't she? She was the one to leave you?" Benedict asked.

Victor shook his head, validating Benedict's words.

"Why did she leave me?" Victor cried.

Benedict knew the answer to this question, but he knew it wasn't going to be well received.

"Because she loves you," Benedict said.

Victor screamed, "But she never said it! Why did she never say it?"

"Come with me," Benedict said. "I want to show you something."

CHAPTER 7

The early morning sun shone in Stanley's eyes. He was happy it wasn't raining anymore, thinking that indicated Eva's feelings would finally change today. He rolled over to grab her hand, hoping she had moved on from her inner conflict. He found himself gripping empty blankets. Stanley heard Eva downstairs. It smelled like she was preparing breakfast. Excited by the smell of fresh eggs in the morning, he quickly got ready for work. Stanley dressed in the same clothes he wore every day. He donned a button-down shirt, a blue tie, slacks, and shined shoes.

Stanley was a Wall Street broker, making his bones at the ripe age of twenty-three. He'd been working in a brokerage for years now and had worked his way up to the top of the food chain. His success came with a price: Stanley spent his time mostly away from home. Early mornings in and late hours home. He wasn't a workaholic, but Stanley spent more time at work than he should have. Still, there were no complaints, because he did provide for a family of five.

As he combed his hair, Stanley looked into a mirror hanging above his dresser. Yesterday's thoughts lingered in his mind.

"What was it about his book?" Stanley kept asking himself.

What was it about the words he so carefully took the time to put together? Stanley noticed Victor's writing style—extreme detail, down to the curve of someone's face. Why was this affecting his wife?

The one thing that Stanley did notice was the description of the female protagonists through the first and second books. They were very similar, and it seemed like he constantly wrote about this one ideal woman. Stanley was stuck on the notion that Eva somehow put herself into his story.

"Maybe because the description was a little similar to hers?" he thought to himself as he buttoned up his shirt.

Stanley could see why Eva enjoyed the female protagonist in his stories. They were always endearing oddballs. Eva was an oddball herself and had always encouraged her children to be themselves, no matter what that entailed.

Stanley spent so much time working he never had much of a chance to spend time with his family. It was always Eva taking the kids to and from school, guitar lessons, and sports tryouts. He considered himself a lucky man to have a wife who was such a good mother. Stanley thought their relationship was healthy because he treated Eva with respect. When they fought, there wasn't much yelling, only tension that would eventually blow over. But things had changed between them over the years.

He first noticed a change in Eva when the last of their children left the coop. She went through a few months of depression and began drinking every night. The drinking wasn't excessive, but a glass of wine or two every night started to seem suspect to Stanley.

Eva went through these bouts often. She was troubled in this one way. Stanley dismissed it as harmless and let Eva go through these bouts with little commentary. Eva appreciated that she never had to hide her vices from Stanley. Still, she wished he cared a little more. Eva was clearly trying to garner some sort of attention. She wanted someone to worry about her. Deep inside her heart, she was needy but forced herself to be completely independent. She never could rely on anyone outside of a few people.

Stanley never talked much and when he did, it was about the kids or work. When he saw Eva going through what he dubbed her routine, he would just shrug his shoulders. It wasn't that he didn't care that she was drinking; it just wasn't in him to be overly protective and concerned. He was very passive in everything that he did. Stanley didn't feel the need to sit her down and talk her through things, thinking Eva was self-sufficient enough to go through these journeys on her own. For a man who was smart, he was severely mistaken in this one instance.

Eva only wanted a simple, "Are you okay?" She wanted the feeling of her husband's strong hands on her shoulders or a warm hug. Eva needed to be *wanted*.

Despite these shortcomings, Eva loved her husband. He gave her life new meaning and stability with a wonderful home in suburbia and beautiful children. She wasn't the type to give up so easily, having no problem putting her energy into a relationship when a man showed her the proper love and respect she deserved. Stanley gave her that and more. He allowed her to finally take a breath in the whirlwind that was her life.

Even though he was Eva's husband, Stanley didn't know Eva the way Victor did. It wasn't fair to compare Stanley and Victor, because when Victor was with Eva, they only talked about each other. The only thing Victor and Eva had to worry about was talking. They couldn't physically interact in any way, making their relationship purely emotional. It gave them a chance to focus on their feelings, a type of relationship most people never get to experience. While emotions slowly blossomed, they could only put off their yearning for physical contact for so long.

Stanley and Eva were forced to tackle the issues that come with marriage, such as children, bills, sicknesses, and other hardships. Victor served as an escape from this, making Eva's relationship with him a little unfair. Eva could never deny that, fair or not, Victor and Eva were stuck in the middle of a love affair. Feelings that were so addictive, they'd do anything to spend five extra minutes together.

Stanley wasn't the most passionate man and that made their situation slightly worse. He didn't see Eva the way Victor did. It was naturally a part of Victor's anxious personality to analyze Eva, noticing everything about her. If he felt she had the slightest hiccup coming, he'd ask what was wrong.

Victor hated when Eva hurt herself by smoking and refused to let it go unnoticed. He begged her to quit, often threatening to never see her again if she didn't. He was vocal about his feelings, and it was a refreshing experience to know that a man could act this way. Victor's words were always strong and powerful. He wasn't afraid to say how he felt and quickly took charge when he felt Eva was doing harm to herself. He was a man among men, a literal tough guy who was sensitive to a woman's needs.

Eva prepared her husband his daily breakfast: black coffee, with two eggs over easy and two pieces of whole-wheat bread with melted butter on top. Eva never gave herself the proper credit for being such a good cook. She was constantly comparing herself to the fond memories of her grandmother's cooking. Eva would spend most of her nights as a child eating at her grandmother's house. She never shied away from cooking anything, from fish to steak, or even baking. The food, still steaming, was waiting on the kitchen table for Stanley. Sitting across from where Stanley would usually be, she prepared herself a bowl of freshly-cut persimmons. She got her fill while they were in season because they only grew five months out of the year.

The three empty seats around the kitchen table only added to her depression. She missed having breakfast with her children, sending them off to school and preparing their lunch. She missed the endless hugs and kisses when they got home from school and the fighting to tell her about their day. The greatest gift life gave her was the opportunity to be a mother.

The last of Eva's three children had left only a few months ago, and she hadn't been normal since. She'd never felt so lonely, even though she'd been married for almost thirty years. Since she was twenty-five years old, she'd been with Stanley. He had promised her a life at home, and she had graciously taken that offer. Eva made sure she was the best wife and mother that she could be, never depriving her family of anything.

As her children got older, they needed less of her care. During her long-overdue downtime, she often reminisced of her career as a musician and began to write music again. When she wasn't taking care of her children or playing her guitar, she spent her time praying. Eva protected those she loved with a shroud of prayer, hoping that God would bless the lives that meant so much to her. Now she enjoyed playing Christian music, which she felt made her worship time more playful.

Stanley walked out of his bedroom and down the steps. He looked at the pictures of his children on the wall and smiled as he made his way into the kitchen. He kissed Eva good morning, then sat across from her. Before he spoke, he took a sip of his coffee.

"Thanks for the breakfast, sweetheart," Stanley said. "You should have made yourself some eggs too. You're always eating that oddly-colored fruit. What was it called again? Something with a P? Peach? Pomegranate? Prickly Pear?"

Eva interjected, "Persimmon." She ate another piece before she spoke again. "They only grow a few months out of the year, so I want to get my fill while I can."

"I'm just saying some protein would be good for you, that's all."

Stanley folded his toast and dipped it into the egg yolk. He noticed a book sitting next to her and pointed to it.

"A new read?" he asked.

"No, I read this book many years ago. I just haven't read it in so long. Something reminded me of it."

Stanley didn't even think to ask which book it was. He couldn't keep track with the amount of reading Eva did. Stanley could tell that Eva's answers were empty. She wasn't giving her normal quirky responses. Stanley knew this was more than a mood swing, and he wasn't going to let another day go by without knowing what was wrong.

He took in a deep breath and exhaled. The words that had been stewing in his head finally came out.

"I think we need to talk."

"I think so too," Eva said. She responded too quickly. Eva braced herself for the conversation she never thought she'd be having.

"What is it about Victor Esposito?" Stanley asked. "You've been acting strange since we heard he'd been shot. I read some of his books. I don't understand what it is."

Hearing his name come from her husband's mouth was devastating. She twirled her fingers around nervously. If she said nothing or came up with an excuse, it would put an even larger strain on their marriage.

Eva's head sunk. She mumbled her words. "His books are about me."

Stanley let out a really deep laugh that didn't stop for a minute straight, making it clear he wasn't taking her seriously. He wiped the tears of laughter away from his eyes.

"That was a good one," he said letting out small giggles. "Now really, what is it?"

Eva glared at Stanley with a cold face.

"You said you read some of his books?"

Stanley nodded.

"How could you not even realize they're about your own wife?"

Stanley's face turned pale as he saw the serious look in her eyes. The truth slowly dawned on him. The comparisons he made weren't so crazy—the little tiny details about her life story, personality, and even the description of her body. How could he read novels inspired by his wife and not even realize it?

"But I don't understand," he stuttered. "How are they about you? They're love stories. They're all romance. Did you—"

Eva cut him off.

"I never had a relationship outside of our marriage. I never broke our vows. I never took a gift from him. I never fed into any of his compliments. And he never made an advance on me."

Stanley noticed the cold look on Eva's face. He saw her distaste.

"I don't understand," Stanley said.

Eva nervously laughed.

"That's the thing. You never understand. What's so funny about a man writing a book about me? Am I not worthy or special enough? Am I that much work to be around?"

Eva's eyes were watery. One tear slowly traveled across her cheek and onto the table. Stanley watched her in silence.

Eva repeated herself, "Why is it so shocking that a man loves me enough to write an entire collection of books about me?"

Looking into his wife's eyes, Stanley could see that he had lost her. He didn't do enough to make her feel wanted and he took her for granted. The working, overtime, and selfishness finally came to a head. Stanley could see the strain in their relationship. She needed him to be her rock, and that was something he never lived up to.

"When?" Stanley asked.

"Ten years ago, when I went to the Tony Bennett concert that you couldn't make. I met him there. We met for coffee for about a year straight. Victor respected that I was married with a family. He never pressured me. He just enjoyed my company and loved being around me."

Stanley's voice got deeper as her story progressed. He slowly became more aggressive as Eva told her story.

"You expect me to believe that this man had no bad intentions? You think he met week in and out just because he enjoyed being around you? You really think he wasn't sitting there, waiting for you to make a mistake? Like he wasn't imagining screwing you every second he had coffee with you?

Eva's face twisted with anger and disgust. A person who meets you for a year straight knowing they can't touch you clearly just doesn't have sex on their mind. A whole year? Especially a man?

"No, I don't think he had any bad intentions. I told him that I'd never leave and that I'd never betray my marriage. He understood completely."

Stanley laughed as the anger coursed through his veins. He didn't think about why Eva did this but instead blamed her for doing it. Even though she didn't cheat, which he believed, Stanley was still hurt that this had been going on for so long. He balked at the idea of their so-called puppy love.

"Keep believing that. There's no such thing. That kind of love doesn't exist. You're creating this in your mind. You'll be over it in a few weeks when he's not around anymore. He's a man, like anyone else. No one waits around that long for a woman. No one. You were probably one of many women he wrote books about. I bet you he uses that line all the time."

The more Stanley spoke, the more depressed Eva became. She, too, found it hard to believe that someone could love her this much. She spent months going back and forth, constantly contemplating whether or not her feelings were real.

"Why don't you believe someone could love me this much?"

"That's not the point here," Stanley screamed. "So that's where you went yesterday? You ran to go see him? You spent the whole day sitting next to him? It's nice to know what I'm worth compared to that guy."

Eva's cheeks turned red. Stanley didn't understand what she was going through. She had tried everything to not let this affect her life and to balance these feelings in such a way that no one would get hurt.

"He's dying!" Eva screamed. "How could you compare your-self to someone who's dying? You don't even know what went on. I left him! I cut him off and said I couldn't do it anymore. I felt like I was betraying you! My feelings were getting too strong, and it was pulling me too far away from you, so I never saw him again. Before yesterday, I hadn't seen him in almost ten years."

Eva's feelings were laid out on the table for her husband to finally see, the guilt finally leaving her mind. There were no more secrets and pretending. Everything was out in the open. She cried into her hands as Stanley heard her admit for the first time the way she felt about Victor Esposito.

"I love him," Eva said. "I love both of you, but I love him too. I don't want him to die. He saved me. He saved my life. You don't understand."

Stanley spent no time consoling his wife, feeling no desire to. He simply took his briefcase and left for work. He truly thought this was harmless and that when Victor passed, this would be over with. His passive attitude continued to lead him down the wrong path.

Eva heard her front door slam shut, not even caring that her husband left. She knew this fight was years in the making. It took meeting Victor for her to realize how sad she really was. Eva realized she had run away from the one person that made her happy. She had pushed away the one man who loved her in the most selfless way possible. Eva, unable to indulge in her feelings for someone she couldn't have, had been afraid of getting too close.

As her tears left a trail behind her, Eva opened a screen door leading to her backyard. She walked across a wooden porch onto grass and knelt before a beautiful garden with bushels of flowers and vegetables growing. The colors of the garden were endless. Vibrant yellows, greens, and reds stretched across the grass, lighting up the yard.

Eva had spent her time carefully planting this garden from the day she had moved into her home. It held a special place in Eva's heart because it reminded her of her grandmother, Juliette. Eva had been very close with her grandmother throughout her childhood. Juliette was the only parental figure Eva had ever had. She had also had a beautiful garden, filled with colorful flowers and fruits. The only difference was that birds would always visit her grandmother's garden, specifically cardinals. Eva had put a birdbath next to the garden, but it had been years since any birds had visited.

"Hi, Nana," Eva said quietly.

She ran her hands through the flowers in the garden. Eva always came to the garden to talk to her grandmother. She felt her presence here.

"I miss our long talks on the couch while we watched those cheesy soap operas together. I miss how you comforted me with your cooking. I still don't know how you did it. You were there for me through everything."

The wind slightly blew and gently pushed against her arms. It felt like her grandmother was listening, gently placing her soft hand on Eva's arm. Juliette had seen Eva through the darkest times of her life. Eva always looked to her for comfort, even long after she had passed on from this world.

"I'm in love. I'm in love with a wonderful man. His name is Victor."

Eva smiled as his name passed her lips.

"I know you would have approved of him. He really loves me. His love for me makes me feel like I'm in a fairytale. He even loves the things I hate about myself, like the little red mark on my cheek. You know, the one you always used to point out? I remember you saying it was a mark God left when he created me to remind me how beautiful I am."

Eva touched the red mark on her cheek. She remembered the nights she spent playing pinochle with her grandmother and grandfather. She had always enjoyed spending time with them no matter how old she got. If it hadn't been for her grandmother, she wouldn't have had any positive memories from her childhood.

"I love him, Grandma," Eva wept. "I love him, and he's going to die. He's going to leave me here by myself. He promised me he'd never leave. Please, Grandma, don't let him go. What can I do? Tell me, and I'll do it. I only want one more day with him. I want to make everything right."

The dirt soaked up Eva's sadness as her tears dripped down into the garden. She had nowhere left to turn—she needed help from beyond this earth. The only person left who could help her was God.

Two cardinals, both colored a beautiful shade of red and black, flew into the birdbath next to the garden and showered themselves in the water. With her eyes swollen, Eva looked up at the birds that had finally returned. She approached them, expecting the cardinals to fly away.

The tears in her eyes vanished, followed by the doubt and worry that fled her body. She looked on quietly as the birds mingled with one another. Eva knew her grandmother had heard her prayers and was telling her to have faith. It was comforting to know that she was still watching over her until this very day.

Eva was no stranger to signs from the beyond, often dreaming about those she loved that had passed away. For the first time since she'd last seen her, she felt her grandmother's warm love again.

"Thanks, Grandma," Eva mumbled.

Eva walked back inside and prepared to spend another day at the hospital. She packed a gigantic purse of things to bring with her. Even if she wasn't out for the whole day, Eva was known to be a bag lady and carried just about everything someone could need. Her bag was filled with snacks, Diet Coke, Advil, and cigarettes. This time, Eva decided to leave the cigarettes behind, remembering Victor would have been angry at her for smoking.

As Eva walked towards the door of her home with her purse wrapped around her shoulders, she suddenly stopped, realizing there was one more thing she was missing.

Eva dropped her bag to the floor, ran up the stairs to her bedroom, and heroically lifted her mattress above her head. Between the mattress and the boxboard was a sealed letter. The cream-colored envelope was blank, with no name addressed on the front. With one hand holding up the mattress, Eva delicately grabbed the letter.

CHAPTER 8

Benedict snapped his fingers and a bright light flashed that caused Victor to shield his eyes. The desert around them disappeared, and they were suddenly in the middle of a massive garden. Trees towered around them, blocking the rays of a beautiful and bright sun. A slight breeze blew through the air every few minutes, cooling Victor's skin from the hot desert. Bushels of flowers filled the ground beneath him, cushioning his feet like brightly-colored pillows. Victor found himself at the center of this garden. He looked around him for Benedict, who had vanished.

"Great," Victor said. "Thanks for nothing, Benedict."

There was no path or any clear walkway. Everything looked the same. The only difference he spotted in the terrain was that there were flowers. There were rows of tulips, roses, and daisies, aligned in a specific way. Victor decided to walk along the rows of rose bushes, following the trail to a small opening between the branches of two trees. Light was pouring through the other side.

"This is where someone is supposed to tell me not to go towards the light," Victor laughed to himself. "Where else do I go? I don't have much to go back to anyway. There's only my mother left, and Eva, of course. But what good is being alive if I can't be with her?"

Victor asked himself these morbid questions, and a part of him didn't mean to ask them. There was truth in everything he said, though. Victor didn't have a wife or children. He didn't have Eva in the way he wanted her. What was there to go back to? His life wasn't going to magically change, and he accepted that.

On the other side of the passageway of trees was a patch of grass that was closed off from the rest of the area. The sun shone down on only one spot. In the middle of the grass was a birdbath that stood about five feet high, carved from white marble. The marble glistened in the sunlight, appearing like a shrine would.

A flock of cardinals suddenly swooped into the birdbath, making a splash and startling Victor. He smiled when he saw the first sign of life since he'd been trapped in this world. Victor slowly approached the birdbath, trying his best not to scare the birds into flying away. The birds weren't startled by Victor. Instead, they welcomed his presence.

One of the birds lay quietly in the birdbath, struggling to play with the rest of the flock. Victor picked up the bird and noticed it was injured from the harsh landing. It appeared to have hurt its wing. The bird nestled comfortably in Victor's hands, rubbing its feathers between his fingers as if they were a warm nest.

An old woman wearing a white gown watched from a distance as Victor tended to the injured cardinal. She had long, flowing grey hair and beautiful skin that shone in the sunlight. Her nose was neither too big nor too small, but rather, it was just right for the size of her face. It complimented the rest of her facial features, making her stand out. The sun radiated off her impeccable skin, showing no blemishes.

Victor gently held the bird between his hands. He spoke to it softly, "You'll be alright, little buddy. Hang in there."

The woman walked up behind Victor and carefully listened as he talked to the bird.

"I know exactly how you feel. You could say that I had a little accident myself."

The other cardinals freely roamed the birdbath chirping away. Victor was upset the injured bird couldn't join in on the fun.

"You'll get to fly with your buddies again real soon. There are some things we can't explain in this world, but I have a feeling you're going to be okay."

The old woman smiled at Victor's words of encouragement to the little bird. She broke her silence.

"There are many things we can't explain," she said.

Victor jumped when he heard another voice and quickly turned around to see the woman only a few feet away from him. Victor didn't feel threatened by her. She didn't look harmful. Nothing surprised him anymore. He almost expected these things to happen. Victor anxiously asked her a boatload of questions.

"Who are you? Where am I? What are you doing here? Where's Benedict?"

The woman giggled. She answered every one of Victor's questions. "My name is Juliette. You're still trapped in the world you created. I'm a friend. And Benedict put me in charge now."

"In charge of what?" Victor fired back.

Juliette snickered. "Babysitting you, of course."

Victor noticed Juliette's personality was warm and light-hearted. She was playful and bubbly, almost reminding him of Eva.

"Great," Victor sighed. "Another spirit guide, or whatever you wanna call it."

Victor made imaginary quotes with his fingers when he used the word *spirit guide*. His doubt was still strong. It was difficult for anyone to get into his stubborn mind.

Juliette inched towards Victor. As she got closer, Victor could feel a motherly warmth radiating from her. The type of love someone feels when they visit their grandparents' house for dinner and get smothered with warm kisses.

The flock of cardinals began to slowly fly away. Each bird took its time, soaking in the last few moments of the water running through their feathers. Juliette and Victor watched the cardinals fly away into the trees. The only bird left was the injured one in Victor's hands.

"What do you have there in your hand?" Juliette asked.

Victor opened his hands to reveal the injured bird.

"This cardinal swooped down into the birdbath and hurt its wing."

"Can I see it?" she asked.

Victor gently handed over the bird. Juliette closed her hands, concealing the cardinal. She said a prayer aloud.

"God, everything you created in this world is wonderful, including this little bird. You have cared for animals, and the Bible tells us to care for them the way you would. I ask for the healing of this bird in the name of our Lord Jesus. Amen."

Juliette opened her hands, and the cardinal spread its wings. It flew in the direction of the other birds, following them into the beautifully full green trees.

Victor was awestruck by the power of that small prayer. He was even more impressed that Juliette was able to harness that power and so quickly call upon God for help. As Victor watched the bird fly away, Juliette noticed there were tears in his eyes.

"Why are you crying?" she asked.

Victor wiped the tears away from his face.

"I'm like that little bird," he said sadly. "To a bird, a broken wing means death. You saved that little creature's life with such a small and beautiful prayer. I'm sure Benedict told you that I'm in a coma. My mind is here, in this world with you, but my body is failing me. Part of me wants to leave the world I came from. I don't have much to go back to. Another part of me knows I'd be leaving the world too early. What could I even do to get back there? These questions and doubts are running through my head. I feel like my life is slipping away from me slowly, and I keep trying to catch up, but I can't. Just like that little bird."

Juliette attentively listened to every word that Victor said. A small stone bench was adjacent to the birdbath. Juliette walked over to the bench, sat down, and patted a space beside her. Instead of being witty with his questions, Victor quietly complied to her invitation to sit. With his head sunk low, he sat next to Juliette.

"You have everything to go back to," Juliette said hopefully. "I know this firsthand."

"But you don't know me," Victor said. "Both you and Benedict just met me. Even if I created you both in my mind, there's a chance you still might not know the person I am."

Juliette placed her hand on Victor's shoulder, gently rubbing it like a mother would.

"My dear boy," she said, "I am not a creation of your mind. I am very real. You may not know who I am, but trust me when I say that you've heard of me before. This is the first time I've met you, but I feel like I've known you my whole life. Someone has been speaking very highly of you to me. I was anxious to meet you when Benedict let me know you had arrived."

Juliette's words frustrated Victor. How could both she and Benedict know who Victor was? How could they know anything about his life? How could they know all of the things that had happened to him, yet, in the same breath, ask him to tell them what had happened to him? None of this was making any sense. Victor knew something wasn't adding up.

"I don't understand," Victor said. "Can you please let me know what's going on? What is this place I'm in? This world can't be created by me. I've never seen any of this before."

"Like Benedict said, you're stuck in between worlds, dancing back and forth between life and death. The afterlife and life on earth. I came into your world from heaven above."

Victor tried not to laugh. He was a believer in God, but for some reason, he found it hard to believe that Juliette was sent from heaven. He didn't know who this woman even was. Why would she take the time to help a stranger?

"So you're telling me you're from heaven? The heaven? The heaven where God is from? Where people go when they die?"

Juliette nodded. "I was called upon to help you along in your journey. To bring you back to the world where you belong."

"Who called upon you?" Victor asked.

Juliette replied quickly. It was like she couldn't wait until she got her next word out.

"Eva," she said.

"Eva?" Victor said with confusion. "But. But. How? My Eva? Eva Abrams?"

"She was my Eva before she was your Eva," Juliette said jokingly. "I'm her grandmother. She liked to call me Nana when she was a little girl."

Victor's eyes lit up with joy. He wasn't sure whether to be happy or sad. He wished Eva could be here to see this. Victor's instant reaction was to cry, but he was excited to meet the woman Eva had spoken so highly of.

"You're Nana! I can't believe it! Eva spoke about you all the time. She raved about your cooking. Can you cook something here?"

Juliette and Victor laughed together. She had heard every one of Eva's prayers. From the day she left this earth, Juliette had been watching over Eva. Juliette was there even when Eva didn't feel her presence. Juliette had been there when Eva's children were born, when she got married, when she suffered from depression, when she fell in love with Victor, and now, Juliette was here to see her through this.

"I would love to, my dear, but there are more important matters. I'm here to tell you that you can't give in. You need to fight to stay alive. I see that you're tired. I see the pain you've been through. Trust me when I say that you don't know everything. Eva needs you. You can't even begin to understand the impact you've had on her life. You don't—"

Before Juliette could say another word, Victor cut her off. He couldn't take hearing that anymore. Benedict and Juliette kept trying to tell him Eva cared without any proof. Were they mind readers? Victor judged the way Eva felt by the look on her face. That was it. Maybe she said a few kind words here and there, but other than that, Eva was speechless when it came to her feelings about him. Hearing Juliette repeat this infuriated him.

"Eva asked to never see me again!" Victor screamed. "How could she need me that much? I spent days telling her how much I loved her. I did whatever I could to make her happy. I saw in her eyes that she loved me, but she never said anything back. Nothing at all! She always stayed emotionally distant from me. Still, I kept barreling past it just to spend time with her, hoping and praying one day something would change. If I had had such an impact on her, why did she never say anything? Why did she never cry in my arms or give me a warm hug? Why did she let me walk away?"

Juliette shook her head in shock that Victor didn't have a clue about the extent of the struggles Eva had been through. Victor had an idea, but Eva never divulged too much information. She always kept things hidden away because they were too painful to talk about. Without even realizing it, Victor had helped her through it all. He had helped her heal deep wounds that may have never healed if he hadn't been there.

"Eva had a very horrible childhood, Victor. There were parts of her life that could have been considered living nightmares. All she had growing up was her sister and me. Both of her parents had abandoned her by the time she was seven years old. Her father left to start another family. Her mother was around half the time and wasn't the most hands-on parent. When her parents were around, she faced severe mental abuse, something she still finds hard to even think back on. Eva never had any direction and was basically a child left to fend for herself. There was no parent to sit her down and hold her when she cried. She didn't have anyone to tell her right from wrong. If it hadn't been for me stepping in, I feel like she wouldn't have any good memories from her childhood. As a teenager, she never had any money. Some days it was hard just to find food to eat if I wasn't around for whatever reason. Eva had no clue what it was like to be unconditionally loved. She didn't know what a healthy relationship looked like. There were no role models. Because of this, she spent most of her life suffering from depression."

Victor sat in silence, filled with horror. He could have never imagined that Eva had gone through this. She had turned out so well in many other ways. Despite having a hard life, she never had any malicious intentions towards anyone. She never went out of her way to be mean. She always wanted to help and please those around her, so long as they had her trust. The only person she treated poorly was herself. She constantly battered herself with feelings of worthlessness that came from her childhood.

Victor never would have guessed that her problems were worse than average. She had never mentioned a thing. Now he began to see why Eva may have needed him in her life. His love for her was unlike anything she'd ever felt before. He truly made her feel special. No one had ever gone out of their way for her the way Victor had.

Juliette saw the confusion on Victor's face as his mind processed her words. Victor was still trying to put the pieces of her story together. He tried to remember anything Eva said about being depressed or childhood trauma. Juliette was preparing Victor for one of the most important events in his entire life. She kept hinting at something he needed to know.

She wanted Eva to tell Victor herself, but Juliette needed Victor to know the backstory first.

"Victor, she never told you, did she?"

"What do you mean?" he asked.

"When you met her, Eva was mentally ill. She——"

Before Juliette could finish her sentence, storm clouds gathered. Thunder boomed across the sky, making it hard to hear anything that Juliette said. The wind ferociously blew, and the ground below them shook. Bright flashing lights filled the sky above.

Juliette tried her best to scream over the sounds of the thunder and the rush of wind. "Take care of her," Juliette screamed.

"I can't hear you," Victor screamed back.

Juliette hugged Victor tightly, squeezing him with every ounce of love she had. Even though she hardly knew Victor, Juliette loved him as if he were a son of her own. She knew he was the one to truly make her granddaughter happy. That, on its own, meant the world to her.

When Juliette let go of Victor, she disappeared into the wind. She completely fell apart, turning into nothing more than a pile of dust. Victor looked up into the sky and saw the bright flashing lights from above get brighter. The booming sound of the thunder almost sounded like words to him. He couldn't quite understand what they were trying to say.

The winds became harsh, violently pushing Victor around. With his feet planted on the ground, he forced his way over to the birdbath. He held on to the marble structure, wrapping his arms around the base. Over the wind, Victor could faintly hear people screaming. There were too many voices talking at once.

He didn't recognize any in particular. No voice reminded him of anyone he knew.

Victor felt guilty for doubting Eva's affection. He'd been through too much in his life to accept her love so graciously and confidently. Part of him didn't even want to believe she loved him, because he could never have her. What was the point?

He felt comfortable creating a story for the two of them in each of his books. In his stories, he could have her to himself. He could carefully choose a life for the two of them. His love for Eva was so strong that his biggest fear in life wasn't death. It wasn't dying in a plane crash or getting hit by a car. His biggest fear was losing the love of his life, Eva Abrams.

The winds grew stronger, and Victor's grip only grew tighter. He never let his hands slip from the birdbath, refusing to give in. Juliette's words kept repeating in his mind, over and over again. He was worried about Eva. What could she possibly be hiding from him? There were still things Eva had never told Victor, parts of her life that she had never divulged because she knew it would only draw her closer to him. Sharing such intimate and personal feelings would only have deepened their attachment.

In the midst of this massive storm, Victor was only concerned about Eva. He needed to find a way home to the woman he loved. Victor knew that he wouldn't be allowed to leave this world until he completed his journey. The first step was to accept that he was worth the love of such a beautiful woman. He promised himself in that moment that he would fight to have her, even if it meant fighting himself.

CHAPTER 9

This was the third day Victor had spent in a coma, with no sign of life, remaining in the exact state that Eva had left him in. Barbara was asleep in a chair next to Victor's hospital bed, still refusing to leave his side despite the doctor's orders. She wrapped herself in a blanket, snoozing the early hours of the morning away.

The heart rate monitor beeped slowly, as it had been for the past seventy-two hours. Victor's heart rate had been steady since his surgery, but the doctors knew this was only the beginning of the troubles they were set to face. The surgery had been tremendously strenuous on Victor's body, and they expected complications down the road.

A nurse came into the room to do a routine checkup on Victor. This nurse, named Laura, was a godsend. Laura had long brunette hair and dark almond-shaped eyes. She was in her late twenties, only a few years into her profession as a nurse. Laura had read many of Victor's books, and they had changed her life. She'd been inspired to find a man who loved her the way Victor painted love to be. She had instantly recognized him when he was brought here and was anxious to take part in anything involving him. She treated his mother with extra kindness, refusing to badger her about hospital rules and boundaries.

Laura checked Victor's vital signs, quickly noticing he was running a fever. It wasn't a slight fever either. It was high enough that Victor was in danger of being harmed. The monitor showed a temperature of one-hundred and three degrees. Laura immediately called another nurse, who then rushed into the room to take Victor and run tests on him. They worked extra carefully not to wake his mother, who would barrage them with never-ending questions.

Victor was tested for over two hours with results that weren't so positive. His white blood cell count had increased significantly, also indicating that he was fighting an infection. The doctors had been expecting this because most comatose patients tend to develop infections, but they were shocked that it was happening to Victor this early on.

The nurses whisked Victor from room to room, running test after test. First, they drew additional blood samples to rule out specific infections that comatose patients are prone to. They shined a bright light in his face from the ceiling above as they examined him. Over his lifeless body, two leading doctors at the hospital argued over whether or not Victor would pull out of this. It was unprofessional, but there wasn't anyone around to hear them. They were numb to these kinds of injuries, seeing the worst and the best of them for most of their careers.

After they finished drawing blood, the doctors took him into another room for a brain scan to monitor his activity. Victor was stable for now, but the most important thing the doctors had to figure out was if it was possible for him to have some quality of life eventually.

The tests pressed on as Eva waited patiently in the chair beside a slumbering Barbara. Not seeing Victor in the room didn't alarm her; she figured the doctors were doing routine evaluations. Eva patiently waited for him to return, looking through *Lady Chatterley's Lover* to find pages she'd like to start reading. Skimming through the book, Eva remembered how sensual it was. She blushed at the idea of the words from this book passing from her mouth to Victor's ears. She glanced over at Barbara beside her.

"She better go home before I read this," Eva thought. "I'd be mortified if she heard me reading this to her son."

Eva giggled to herself, always lighthearted about these things. The situation was pretty funny. Only she would choose to read this kind of book to a comatose patient. Maybe this would spark some sort of life in him, especially if he knew Eva was the one reading it.

"Could the prospect of sleeping with me bring him out of a coma?" she thought to herself. She played around with that idea, suddenly smiling deviously. "It could," she thought confidently.

While wandering the hospital hallway, another patient caught her eye. It was an old woman lying in bed. Eva guessed that she was in her eighties and inching towards the end of her life. She wasn't moving or speaking, only breathing. It was clear she was a shell of her former self, a beautiful soul trapped in the prison that are our bodies.

Eva watched as the woman's husband, who was around the same age, stood by her side. The woman pointed to her feet, which were bare. The husband quickly moved to attend to her, placing extra fuzzy socks on her feet, then covered her with blankets. The woman smiled at her husband, who kissed her before he sat back down.

Seeing this brought a specific memory to the forefront of Eva's mind. She thought back to the last day she saw Victor. She felt like her throat was closing, reliving the vivid memory and revisiting the pain. Her scars were still raw, as if it had happened yesterday.

Eva sat completely alone on a bench at a park near her home. She looked up into the sun that shone down on her skin, warming her. Eva was deep in thought, contemplating the decision she'd made the night before. It was the perfect day for a stroll through the park. The grass was freshly cut, leaving a strong scent of nature in the air. Children played on the jungle gym across from the bench. Eva enjoyed watching the fathers play with their children.

Eva had asked Victor to meet her at the park because she was tired of meeting at the coffee shop. The coffee shop was always where she felt the most comfortable. For some reason, she felt the least tempted to act on her feelings for Victor while she was there. She could never understand why, but a good reason would definitely be the many glaring eyes around.

Victor walked with a cooler over his right shoulder. He scoured the park with his eyes for Eva, following a cement path until he saw her watching the children play. Victor was careful not to break her concentration. He carefully sat down next to her, saying nothing, patiently waiting for Eva to speak first.

"I miss them being that small," Eva said.

"Your kids?" Victor asked.

"I miss those chubby baby thighs and fingers. I miss the feel of my babies' skin on mine when holding them close to my chest. It's the greatest feeling in the world."

"Yeah," Victor sighed. "I wish I knew what that was like. I always wanted to be a father."

Eva smiled, turning to Victor with her bright green eyes and long, flowing blonde hair. She stared at him, noticing the profile of his face as he stared down at the pavement. Eva examined his hair, eyes, and nose. She imagined what a child between the two of them would look like. The very thought of that dream brought her happiness—more babies, with a man like Victor, who would be warm-hearted, understanding, protective, and stern all at the same time. He would be the kind of father that has tea parties with his daughter, then takes his son out to play football. A father with a gentle soul and soft eyes that a little girl or boy could come home to as they cried about their bad day at school.

Eva could see this far ahead into a relationship with Victor, though she'd never admit it. Eva was too afraid to. Why would she go into a relationship thinking everything was going to be perfect? That would set the bar too high and leave room for disappointment. She dreamed about a life with Victor in total secrecy, not daring to tell a soul that this was her deepest fantasy.

"You'd be a great dad to a baby girl," Eva said. "Little girls fall in love with their daddies. They're the first representation of a man in their life and a huge role model for what their relationships should be like in the future."

Victor blushed at such a beautiful compliment.

"I'd be the kind of dad that sits on the porch, cleaning out a shotgun barrel before my daughter goes out on her first date."

Eva gave Victor a full and hearty laugh. She could truly picture that. Victor was a possessive person and didn't like anyone stepping on his toes.

Victor placed the cooler between them on the bench.

"I told you no gifts," Eva said, doing her best to act stern. Victor's puppy dog face broke her down.

"I know," Victor said. "But I never listened to you before, and I won't listen to you now. I enjoy buying these gifts for you even if you won't accept them. Every time I try to give you a gift, I want you to know that I remember what you tell me. I want you to feel special."

Eva didn't know how to respond to that statement. How could she really? Here was a man who wanted to make her feel special, taking the time out of his day to think about her and go out of his way to try and give her a meaningful gift. Victor had already tried many times to give her a gift. He was met with the same answer, over and over again. This time, Victor had a feeling she couldn't resist.

"Just close your eyes," Victor pleaded. "At least do me that favor."

Eva complied, desperately trying to hide the smile on her face. Every time Victor got her a gift, it was thoughtful. It wasn't jewelry or anything expensive because Eva wasn't the kind of woman that could be bought. Victor made sure that his gifts were always closely intertwined with her personality, coming from a place deep in his heart.

Victor quickly unpacked the cooler, placing two paper plates, forks, cups, and napkins on the bench. He saw Eva trying to open her eyes.

"No peeking!" he yelled.

Eva shut her eyes again. Not being able to hide her smile any longer, she forced her true feelings to show. A smile on her face glistened for the first time in years, showing all of her pearly white teeth.

Victor rushed to finish setting up the rest of their dinner. He quickly took a bottle of Diet Coke and seltzer from the bag, followed by what appeared to be balls of food wrapped in foil.

Eva drank an odd combination of Diet Coke and seltzer, filled to the top of a cup with loads of ice. This was her favorite drink aside from red wine. It was a combination she'd come up with because of the reports that diet soda wasn't healthy. She figured diluting it with seltzer would make her want less.

Inside the foil were Sicilian arancini—most people in America refer to them as rice balls. Victor had made them from scratch, following an old family recipe. Victor was careful to keep the ingredients extra fresh, as Eva was particular about the taste of the food she ate. If she didn't like something, she would refuse to eat it. She wasn't the type of person to eat food even if it wasn't good just to avoid hurting someone's feelings. Victor knew he was taking a chance but was confident because he remembered she loved rice.

Victor organized everything neatly on the bench, using it as a picnic table. He carefully unwrapped the rice balls that were still warm. He'd just taken them out of the oven only a half-hour ago. To add the finishing touch, Victor took a candle out from inside a pocket of the cooler. It was small, but he thought it would do the trick. Eva heard the clicking of a lighter as Victor tried to light the candle. She opened her eyes and looked at the dinner set before her. Eva watched in total shock as Victor struggled to light the candle because of the wind blowing.

Victor noticed Eva's eyes were open as she sat there with her jaw dropped. No person had ever gone to this kind of trouble for her before. Yet this man, who knew he had no chance of being with her, still went to the trouble.

"Before you say anything," Victor said nervously, speaking fast because he wanted to get every word in before she got angry with him, "I wanted to bring wine, but I knew I was trying my luck with that. So, I brought the Diet Coke and seltzer instead. I made Sicilian rice balls from scratch. It took me around five hours."

Eva was still in silent shock as Victor continued to ramble from the nerves of anticipating her reaction. He really didn't want to be rejected after going to all this trouble, even though that's what he expected.

"If the candle makes you uncomfortable, I can put it away. I know it's not a date."

"I like the candle," Eva said strongly. "Leave it."

Victor smiled brightly as his cheeks turned a rosy red color. Filled with excitement, Eva grabbed the rice ball and cut it in half with her fork. She took a bite.

"This is amazing!" she cried out. "What's in it?"

"Chop meat, carrots, risotto, peas, and cheese wrapped into a little breadcrumb ball. Then fried with top-notch Italian olive oil."

By the time Victor had finished his sentence, Eva had already eaten the rice ball, bouncing off the walls with excitement. It was hard for Victor to absorb the reaction he was getting. He found it endearing that Eva was this excited over home-cooked food. Then he realized that maybe her reaction wasn't strictly about the food. It might have been that Victor had taken the time to make this for her and remember her favorite drink. The idea of someone going out of their way, to make her smile, excited Eva like never before.

"I feel really special," Eva mumbled. "No one has done anything like this for me before."

She looked at Victor with her innocent green eyes and smiled.

"There's one thing though," she snickered. "I only drink Poland Spring seltzer with lemon flavoring."

Victor laughed. "You nut," he said. "Out of all the good things, that's what you pick out."

Eva giggled. "I'm sorry, but I had to tell you, so you know for next time!"

Victor knew Eva was only teasing him. He'd never seen her happier, though he did wish one thing was different. He knew that if there were no boundaries between them, he would be getting a much different response from her. He craved her kiss, a tight hug, or deep affectionate words that she couldn't offer him. He often wondered how Eva would show her love back to him. His love might not be returned with food or a gift but instead in a way even more special than a material item.

"There's one more thing," Victor said with glee.

Eva paused as she ate another rice ball, giving Victor her full attention.

"What could be next?" she joked. "I hope it's a puppy. I've always wanted a Shih Tzu."

Victor pulled a white plastic bag from the inside of his jacket. Eva noticed that he did look a little extra bulky while sitting down. The gift was neatly placed between two plastic shopping bags.

"A long time ago, you told me that you have poor circulation and that, because of it, your feet are always cold. I wish I could be around to fix it for you. I'd hold your feet with my hands if I had to, but I think this should do the trick."

Victor handed the bag over to Eva. Bits and pieces of the plastic bag flew into the air as she ripped it open. She tore right into the bag the way a little child would, not thinking to open it the regular way.

Eva found herself holding two pairs of purple socks. These weren't any ordinary socks but rather thermal socks. They were specifically designed to improve circulation to the feet, making them warm more often. They also had a gentle grip around her ankles, which was important to Eva. Comfort was her number one priority when picking out clothing.

"You got me socks?" she whimpered. "Thermal socks? So my feet stay warm?"

Victor nodded.

"You care about my feet being cold?"

Victor nodded again.

"I want you to be comfortable, always. Besides, if you wear them, it's like a part of me is with you. I love the idea of you wearing something I got you. It's the only way I can really touch you. It's like we're cuddling in a weird way. I'd much rather be a dress or a T-shirt, maybe even a bra, but I'll take the feet, I guess."

Eva loved Victor's corny and witty sense of humor, which was right up her alley. A man could never get anywhere with her if they never made her laugh.

"Thank you," she mumbled. "Thank you for caring so much about me. No one has ever invested any time in me like this."

"It's because I love you," Victor said.

Eva tried her best not to crack a smile. She didn't make any eye contact with Victor; otherwise he would know she loved him too. Eva worried that if she ever let those words cross her lips, it would be just as bad as sleeping with him. She would never be able to look her husband in the face again.

Eva was going through different kinds of emotions, noticing that Victor couldn't have been sincerer. Without realizing it, Victor was bringing Eva closer to cracking as he indirectly pushed her towards him. Eva's mind was split. She'd always had mixed feelings about the situation. A part of her wanted to receive Victor's love and care, but another part of her was angry he was telling her that he loved her. It only made things worse and made her feel less wanted in her own relationship.

"I told you never to say anything like that," Eva said coldly.

"I've never felt this way for a woman in my entire life," Victor said. "I know I can't do anything about it. I'm not asking you to leave your family, but I wanted to let you know."

The more Victor spoke, the more amplified her feelings became. She was losing her inner battle and falling in love with Victor. She refused to give in. The amount of hurt she'd cause her children would be unbearable. She'd never be able to look at them and say she was divorcing their father or that she cheated on him. Eva wasn't even fully sure if she wanted to leave. She still loved her husband very much.

"Stop it!" she screamed. "Stop it already!"

Victor was taken back at the way Eva yelled.

"Do you know what you're doing to me?" Eva asked. "Can't you see it? Cut the good boy shit already. You're not a good boy. You're trying to seduce me! For God's sake, you even brought a candle to light. What happened to you saying you'd never push me? That flew out the window real quick. And I also said no gifts! So many times. I can't take them."

"You're not so innocent either!" Victor screamed back. "I see the way you look at me, like I'm some piece of eye candy. Half the time you're eye-fucking the crap out of me! What about those dresses you wear?"

Their emotions were finally coming to a head—Victor and Eva were on their way to their first major conflict. This was a side of each other they hadn't seen yet. Eva acted like her choice of clothing was a surprise, even though she'd been purposely wearing dresses and clothes she knew would draw Victor's attention. She did stare at him, more often than not, biting her lip in a way she thought was discreet.

"Yeah, that's right," Victor said. "Don't give me that fake surprised look. You knew exactly what you were doing. You were seducing me just as much as I was seducing you. You're not innocent in all of this."

When Eva was angry, she'd scrunch her nose and lips in a cute way. She was a dangerous sparring partner though. She enjoyed fighting and was always in it to win. Eva was extremely intelligent and wouldn't stop until Victor accepted that she was right.

"Well," she paused. "Well."

"What?" Victor screamed. "What now? I only do this because I love you! I love you so much, and I want to show you what I could offer you if life was different."

The guilt she harbored in her heart grew as her feelings for Victor did. After an entire year of inner conflict, her true feelings poured out of her. What was eating her alive flew out of her mouth and was in the open for both of them to deal with.

Eva cried profusely, making it hard for Victor to understand what she was saying.

"I have to go home and contemplate the fact that you might love me more than my own husband does," she said sobbing. "Every time we do this, that's what goes through my head."

Victor was silent as he tried to absorb what Eva said. For once, he was now feeling the guilt. Eva was right; he may not have been such a great guy. Seeing the pain in her face, Victor realized this wasn't fun and games anymore. The back-and-forth of her feelings was taking a toll on her mind, displacing her from reality. Victor decided to reveal something personal, something he thought he'd never have the gall to tell Eva.

"I pray for your husband," Victor said.

Eva took her head from her hands and looked up at him.

"You pray for him?"

"I pray that he makes you feel special. I pray that he takes the time to make sure your feet aren't cold. I pray that he treats you better than I ever would. I pray that he's a better man than I'll ever be."

Eva understood what Victor was trying to do, but this was another testament to how much he loved her. His selflessness only made her want him more.

In these few moments of thinking, Eva quickly decided she could no longer keep lying to herself. She couldn't keep staying out and disappearing for a few hours a day, even though her husband hardly noticed. The guilt had begun to consume her life. Her feelings for Victor were growing stronger every day and she was too tempted to make her fantasies come true. Eva knew it was time to move on. The words that passed her lips were quick, and she knew she'd never be able to take them back.

"I can't do this anymore, Victor," Eva said, still trying to speak clearly in between her crying.

Victor met Eva with silence, not daring to scream or yell, which he desperately wanted to do. He remained quiet, because he had foreseen this day coming, knowing that their relationship would only be able to survive for so long.

"Why?" Victor asked with tears filling up in his own eyes.

Eva replied quickly and stoutly, "This needs to end, and we should never see each other ever again. No phone calls, no letters, no coffee, nothing. I can't live this lie anymore. It's not fair to the people I love. Take your socks and rice balls back."

Victor tucked away the hurt, the feelings of losing someone he looked forward to seeing daily. He tried not to think too far ahead because it would only destroy his concentration for the moment. Victor knew he couldn't go a full day without seeing her, yet she asked never to see him again.

Victor was known to be notoriously stubborn, so stubborn that he felt that his will was powerful enough to bend the fates around him. He would accept Eva's conditions under one of his own, the one thing that might be able to get him through the pain of not seeing her.

"This hurts me more than you could ever imagine," Victor said softly. "If this is what you want, so be it because I love you. But at least tell me the truth about one thing."

"Okay," Eva said, wiping the tears away from her eyes.

"Tell me how you'd love me," Victor mumbled. "I want to know the way you'd show your love. You've seen the way I show mine. How do you show your love for someone? Would it be a special gift you had in mind or a song you wanted to sing for me? How would you love me, Eva?"

The tears streamed down Victor's face as he finally gave into his own emotions and feelings. He didn't feel comfortable crying in front of Eva, let alone in the middle of a park. None of this mattered anyway. The only thing that mattered to him was her response. Victor desperately needed to hear her answer in order to survive without her. Her answer would be just enough for him to get by.

Eva stoically watched Victor cry. Her heart wanted to scream one thing, but the words from her mouth said another. One sentence that would break Victor's heart and send him in a downward spiral that he'd never recover from.

"I love my husband," Eva said as she looked away from him. "I think it's time that you go."

Without saying goodbye, without a hug or a friendly kiss, Victor packed up his cooler and left. He did not take the socks or the rice balls, never wanting to see either of them again.

Eva kept herself composed as best she could, waiting on the bench until Victor was completely out of sight. She got up to leave, then stared down at the remaining rice balls and her thermal socks.

Eva shook herself awake from the trance she was in. She tried not to get emotional, remembering a moment she wished she had back. Looking down at her feet, she rolled up her pants. She did take the thermal socks home with her and wore them often. Whenever she washed them, she had the second pair ready to go. Victor never knew, but she treasured them because he had gotten them for her. The socks warming her feet were only a bonus.

Laura wheeled Victor down the hallway with Dr. Silverstein following. Eva was upset to see that he was still in his same state. A small part of her had been holding out hope that he'd woken up overnight. She moved out of the way so the nurses could wheel him back into his room.

The commotion woke up Barbara, who asked a barrage of questions, just as Laura and the rest of the nurses had predicted. Laura gently rubbed Barbara's shoulders, trying to make her feel more comfortable for what was coming next.

Eva watched Laura's every move whenever she was around Victor or Barbara. Eva didn't like Laura very much, and that hatred grew every time they saw one another. Eva heard the way Laura talked about Victor's books. She was enamored by him. Eva tried her best to avoid Laura getting a type of Florence Nightingale syndrome.

The strange part was that Eva wasn't this jealous normally, but then again, she'd never seen Victor with another woman. She'd never seen Victor's attention directed anywhere else but to her. When she wasn't with him, she put it to the back of her mind.

Laura spoke softly to Barbara. "Victor had a slight fever this morning," she said calmly. "We gave him the proper medication to try and bring it down. After a few hours of testing, we were worried he might have pneumonia, but it was nothing more than a sign of his body still fighting on. It's very common to have a fever after surgery."

Barbara hugged Laura. "Thank you so much, sweetheart. You've been so good to me and my son. It means a lot."

Eva tried not to reveal her true emotions but inside, she was filled with jealousy. Barbara saw Eva standing there and quickly introduced the two, as they had never formally met.

"Eva, this is Laura," Barbara said as she joined both their hands.

"Eva is a frie—" Before Barbara could finish her sentence, Eva quickly interjected.

"I'm his wife," Eva said confidently. "His old ball and chain. The woman he made a vow with at the altar. His soulmate."

Laura's eyes opened up widely. The tabloids had said Victor was a well-known bachelor. He had hardly ever been seen with a steady woman since he'd become a famous author.

Barbara smirked as she knew what Eva was doing and actually liked the way Eva took charge over her son. It was a sign of good things to come. Barbara also liked Eva's bold and brash attitude, which reminded her of her own.

"Wife?" Laura asked with confusion. "I thought Victor was a bachelor."

Eva shook her head. "We ran off to Vegas and got married right before this. Only a few months ago."

Laura detected the jealousy, but she completely believed Eva's lie. She could see the sincerity in her face. Laura saw the way Eva clung to him and knew of the endless hours she had spent with him since Victor had gotten here.

Laura noticed a book in Eva's hand. She pointed to it.

"Excellent," she said. "You're going to read to him. That's fantastic. There was a study that showed coma patients are more likely to come out if they hear the voices of their loved ones often. If I may ask, what book?"

Eva proudly showed her the book. "*Lady Chatterley's Lover*," she said.

Laura's eyes opened up wide again.

"The book that was banned for the sex talk?"

Barbara snickered as she still knew exactly what Eva was doing to this poor nurse. She was also a little taken back that Eva brought such a book to read to Victor. At the same time, she understood why. She figured that nothing between them had ever happened.

Eva nodded again. "The very same. Gotta keep the spark alive, you know? Even in his coma. I'm sure it will help him along if he knows I'm here waiting for him. If you catch my drift."

Laura shrugged her shoulders.

"I guess so," Laura said. "The good news is that he's showing some brain activity, so that's a huge sign of improvement. I'm not a doctor, but in my own opinion, he might actually hear what you tell him. I can't guarantee it, but you never know."

CHAPTER 10

Victor slowly opened his eyes, as they had been shut tightly during the storm. He could feel the wind becoming gentle. The sounds of the crashing thunder got further away. The dark storm clouds dispersed, revealing a bright sun that broke through, shining on the entire field of grass again.

Victor let go of the birdbath, shaking away the pain from his hands. His grip was so strong that his skin stuck to the marble like glue, and his hands were now glowing a fiery red color.

He dusted himself off and looked around him. The area hadn't changed much. The trees looked untouched from the storm. There wasn't a single leaf or flower out of place. Everything looked exactly as it had before.

Victor did notice one thing: the water in the birdbath was still there. It was glowing a clear blue, like the color of the ocean water in Hawaii. Victor dipped his hands inside to feel the cool water calm the angry burn on his hands. Whisking his hands through the water, Victor watched as the red burns disappeared. His hands no longer ached and felt soft, like the skin of a baby.

Smiling with happiness, he spoke aloud, "Thanks, Juliette. I hope to see you soon. Don't forget that you owe me some homemade cooking!"

Benedict was watching from the passageway between the trees. Victor hadn't noticed him yet. In what seemed to be the norm of how people greet each other around here, Benedict appeared behind Victor, surprising him yet again.

"Did you miss me?" said Benedict.

Victor immediately recognized his voice, not bothering to turn around to see who it was.

"You son of a bitch," he said laughing.

This time, Victor was more lighthearted to Benedict's antics. When Victor turned around, he noticed a few of Benedict's facial features had changed. He didn't look like the same man as before. Instead of his scraggly beard, he only had a thick mustache. Instead of his coarse and curly hair, he had short hair that was balding. Benedict also looked like he had gained weight. His belly was blown up and round.

This sudden change in Benedict's appearance made Victor suspicious of him. Victor remembered Juliette saying that she knew Benedict and had even spoken with him. She also said she wasn't a creation of his mind. If those things were true, then maybe Benedict had lied to him. Maybe he wasn't a creation of his mind but, in fact, someone else entirely.

"Wait a minute," Victor said. "The way you look, it doesn't make any sense. What's going on here?"

Benedict smiled. He'd been waiting for Victor to catch up.

"You could say I put on a few pounds," he laughed.

His laugh reminded Victor of his childhood for some reason. The sound of Benedict's voice was familiar to him.

"No, no," Victor said abruptly. "It's everything. The hair, the belly, the mustache."

Victor scratched his head. It wasn't clicking in his brain yet. Who could this man possibly be?

"Your name isn't Benedict? Is it?" Victor asked.

"No," Benedict replied with laughter.

"And you've been lying to me this entire time about who you are?"

"For the most part," he laughed again. His laugh was hearty and full. Victor could tell he was getting a lot of enjoyment out of this.

Benedict hugged him tightly.

"I missed you," he said. "I'm sorry I missed the most important parts of your life. I was always there, I promise, watching you go through it all."

Victor was scared to hug Benedict back. The hug felt warm to him, as if this man were a part of his family. There was a connection between the two, a deep one. Victor just couldn't put his finger on it.

"I'm sorry," he mumbled. "I'm still not sure who you are."

Emotionally, Victor was blocking Benedict out. This is why Benedict didn't appear as the person he was from the beginning. It would be too much of a shock to Victor and would have impeded his spiritual journey.

"Walk with me," Benedict said. "Come through this passageway, and you'll know who I am."

"I came from that way," Victor said. "There was nothing there."

Benedict shook his head.

"There was always something there. You just chose not to see it."

Victor followed Benedict back through the passageway of trees and the path of flowers. As they crossed through to the other side, Victor instantly knew who Benedict really was. He saw a familiar place from his childhood, a beautiful home, surrounded by trees and fields of grass. The windows sparkled in the sunlight.

Victor turned to Benedict, who now finally looked like the man he was supposed to be. Benedict was really Victor's uncle, Paul Calamera, the brother of his mother, Barbara. Victor had lost his Uncle Paul to a rare cancer at a young age. He had never gotten the chance to know him as a young adult or even as a child. His memories of him were very limited. Even though Victor never knew him that well, he had always felt a connection between them.

Paul shared many of the same characteristics as Victor. They both loved music and instruments, sharing unbelievable talents. They were both known to be the friendliest and most caring when it came to those in need. They were also both the patriarchs of their family.

Victor hugged Paul tightly.

"We're back at your house," he said. "I don't even remember how many years it's been. I hardly even remember what you look like in person, only in pictures."

Paul hugged Victor back, as if he were a son of his own.

"The last time I saw you, you were only a few years old. You know, I waited in the hospital all night for you to be born."

Victor smiled.

"I've spent so much time being strong that I haven't had any time to be scared. I'd never admit it to myself, but I'm really scared, Uncle Paul. I don't want to die."

Uncle Paul placed both hands on Victor's shoulders, counseling him the way a father would.

"It's okay to be afraid," Paul said. "Listen, I have to take care of a few things in the backyard. We're throwing a little party for you because we don't know how long you're going to be here. There's something you have to do first, so listen closely."

"We're?" Victor asked curiously.

"We'll talk about that later," Paul said. He continued, "I know it's hard for you to believe, but Eva loves you. She always has, and she always will. She loves you just as much as you love her."

Victor went to interrupt him, but Paul quickly silenced Victor.

"I don't wanna hear any more nonsense. You won't accept it because it's too hard, I get it. But now, that's going to change. There are things that you don't know, and you're finally ready to hear them."

"Okay," Victor said without any rebuttal.

"Walk upstairs and go to the room down the hallway on the left side. Don't come out of the room until you feel that you're ready. This is the final step in your journey. You'll be able to see and hear everything that Eva says to you. She's at the hospital right now, waiting to read you some book."

Uncle Paul raised both his eyebrows and nudged Victor's shoulders.

"Aside from that, you're not to come out of that room until you reconcile everything with Eva. You're going to work everything out, then if you're lucky, we'll try to send you home."

Victor couldn't have been more confused. How could he reconcile with Eva if she couldn't hear anything he said? Would he have to become a poltergeist? This world was a strange one, even for a man like Victor.

"But how will she hear or see me?" Victor asked.

"Spirits can visit the dreams of the living," Paul said. "Visit her dream later tonight, after you hear what she has to say to you. You'll know when the time is right to come out of that room."

"I trust you," Victor said.

Paul pointed to the front door of his home.

"Now go. The rest of your life is waiting for you."

Six novels and ten years later, Victor still couldn't find the words to tell Eva how much he loved her. Hundreds of questions passed through his mind as he walked towards the door of the house.

The memories rushed back to Victor's mind as he approached the front porch. He remembered the summers he'd spent as a kid in this very house. He truly missed being a child when times had been simple, and his worries, few. His biggest concerns had been which way he should jump into the pool and what he should eat next. Now, he was fighting for his life in a place he wasn't even sure was real.

Victor placed his hand on the doorknob, taking a deep breath. He always liked to know what he was getting into, fearing the unknown. He liked everything to be set in stone and planned ahead of time. In this world, nothing was. He had to deal with the idea that he may never be able to go home. Even worse, he was forced to realize that he may never see Eva again.

With little effort, the door swung open. The house looked exactly as Victor remembered it. The smell of the air in Paul's home was the same. Everything felt real, like Victor had somehow traveled back in time. It was a truly amazing feeling to relive the positive memories. They helped ease Victor's anxiety and made him feel more vulnerable and open as the moments passed.

The steps were only a few feet away from the door. Victor wasted no time looking around the house. He held on to the banister, pulling himself up step by step. Victor could hear the creak of each step. The noise seemed to get louder as his heart beat faster.

Now at the top of the steps, Victor peered down the hallway. There were four rooms: two on the left and two on the right. The doors to the rooms were closed except for the one in the far-left corner, like Paul had described.

The one open room had a bright light pouring out that spilled into the hallway. Victor, still nervous to move towards any form of bright light, trusted his uncle.

Victor took one last deep breath and exhaled, letting out the anxious energy in his body. He bravely marched towards the door, ripping off any anticipation anxiety like an old bandage. Victor found himself standing directly in the light, noticing that it came from a large window in the room. He quickly stepped inside and shut the door behind him.

The room was completely empty, with no furniture, curtains for the windows, or closets. The wooden floor shone like it had been polished that very morning. The walls were plain white, with no scuffs or dents.

Victor looked around him, nervously waiting for something to happen. He was expecting something a little different than this. He thought someone or something would appear, but nothing happened.

He thought to call upon Paul. Did he do something wrong? Did he somehow manage to find the wrong room?

These questions kept passing through his mind. In a quick spur-of-the-moment decision, Victor decided to stop questioning everything. He chose a corner of the room and sat down. He thought about praying, something he hadn't done in a long time. Victor was a believer in God, but his relationship with him was tumultuous. When something tragic would happen, Victor would tend to shy away from God in anger, not purposely, but because he couldn't handle the idea of these bad things happening.

"It's been a while, hasn't it? During one of the darkest points of my life, I turned to you. I wanted you to help bring me out of my relentless depression, to change my life for the better, and to be hopeful again. I don't think praying is like wishing on a genie bottle, but something inside me knew that you heard me. I persisted and was relentless in prayer. Then I met Eva. Without her, I would have never been inspired to write anything. Millions of people around the world have been inspired by our love story, which has been one of the most rewarding experiences of my entire life. It means they saw how real the feelings involved were. So maybe I wasn't as crazy as I thought."

Victor clenched his fists tightly, feeling regret for what he was about to say as he tried to be selfless. If it meant Eva being happy, Victor had no problem taking the road less traveled. True love is wanting happiness for your partner no matter the circumstance.

He continued, "If I don't ever make it out of here or back to where I came from, I want you to do one thing. Watch over Eva, protect her, guide her, and help her live a happy life. I pray that her children go on to live full and healthy lives. I pray they thank their wonderful mother for their success. I even pray for her husband, believe it or not. I pray he sees what a great wife he has and that he smothers her with kisses every morning when she wakes up. I hope that he holds her, loves her, and treats her better than I even would. He's a lucky man, and I hope he knows it. No matter what happens, know that I don't have any regrets for the life that I've lived or the path I've chosen."

Victor whimpered. The words passing his mouth were painful to think about and process. What had he done? He was giving up. He was giving into the circumstances life had brought him. He wanted to scream at the top of his lungs in anger. Why should he be the one to suffer? He wanted Eva for himself, not for her husband. If he could, he would want to put her in his pocket and take her everywhere with him. Victor wanted to spend the rest of his days with Eva, not caring about anything else that was going on in the world. He only wanted her love. Yes, these thoughts were selfish, but it was probably what she wanted too.

These angry thoughts quickly boiled down to sad ones. He gathered the strength to pray for one thing. He hesitated, only because he would feel betrayed if nothing happened, but he was willing to take this risk.

He mumbled, "Please, let me see her one more time. Just once more. I want to see her one more time before I die."

CHAPTER 11

Victor finished his prayer, opened his eyes, and found himself staring at his own lifeless body. The pumping of the breathing machines and the beeping of the pulse monitor rang in the background. The smell of sanitizing agents was strong in the air. He quickly smacked himself in the face two times. When he felt the sting of his hand, he knew that he was physically present in the hospital.

He got up from the corner and slowly walked over to his body, noticing how fragile he looked in the hospital bed. It was a scary feeling to watch himself wither away. He was literally witnessing the life get sucked out of him. He couldn't believe what had happened to his body in only three days.

Victor noticed an extra-large purse on a seat next to his bedside and laughed because he knew it was Eva's. Victor curiously looked through her bag to see if she was still smoking from time to time. It was a habit he hated, only because he never wanted Eva to get sick. He wanted Eva to live a full, long, and wonderful life, feeling that's what she truly deserved.

Eva's purse infamously held her Diet Coke and seltzer bottles. Victor saw them and instantly laughed, thinking back to the first time he noticed it. He continued to rummage through her bag, something he felt guilty for doing, but he knew that Eva could be reckless. He hadn't seen her in ten years and wanted to make sure that she was doing well.

Hearing the rattle of pills at the bottom of the bag made him uneasy. He quickly glanced at the label.

"This is medication for depression," Victor thought to himself.

Juliette's words repeated in his mind. He remembered her saying that Eva went through something she had never told him about.

Victor heard the door to the hospital room slam shut. He jumped, dropping the pills back into the bag. He turned around to see Eva at the door, staring at Victor. His heart sank. He had been caught. How could he allow himself to be caught going through her bag after ten years of not talking? Eva marched towards him. He closed his eyes and braced for the stern lesson he was going to get on why he shouldn't go through her bag.

Eva walked right past Victor and sat down in a chair next to the bed. Eva walked right through him. Victor turned back around and stared at Eva as she sat by the bedside of his real body. She held his hand, aimlessly watching him, waiting for some sort of movement.

"Eva," Victor said aloud.

She didn't hear anything. Victor said, "Hello? Can you hear me? Eva?"

Victor continued to talk only to be met with silence. Eva wasn't hearing anything he said. He waved his hand back and forth in front of her face. Even with the sudden movement, Eva remained completely still. She couldn't see that he was there.

Eva continued to stare at the real Victor, not noticing or hearing a single thing that he said. He sighed. It was just like when he visited the first time with Paul. Eva couldn't see he was there.

"What's the point of this?" he screamed. "I can't talk to her."

Eva opened *Lady Chatterley's Lover*, turned to her page of choice, and began to read aloud. The novel was a classic, and the language, difficult to understand. It took time for the words to process in Victor's mind. Somehow, Eva understood every word. She was always smarter than he was. They were two different kinds of smart, but Victor was never afraid to admit that. Eva was an extremely intelligent woman and it was one of the most attractive things about her.

While she read, Eva ran her hand across Victor's forearm, gently rubbing him. He could almost feel her soft touch. Eva's voice was sensual and soft while she whispered words in his ear. The way she calmly and slowly read to him was erotic. Her voice soothed his every worry. Victor felt the troubles leaving his mind, only focusing on her voice.

The part of the book Eva chose to read was a sexual one. She read to Victor of Lady Chatterley's affair with a man she had fallen in love with. This man, named Mellors, was not her husband but rather a lover who took her body to a place she could never forget. The detail of every movement, feeling, and pleasure running through each character slowly passed Eva's lips. The intensity of their love grew stronger by the moment. The book was so very detailed in description, taking both Victor and Eva to an intimate place in their own minds.

The possibility of Victor hearing what Eva was reading to him made this feel pleasurable. Even while he was in a coma, Eva tried to tease him with what he could have if he woke up.

Eva pictured the part of Victor that would ignore the damage an affair would cause. She knew that part of Victor was always there, waiting to be unleashed like a shackled beast in a cage. Underneath his moral and proper exterior, Eva saw that he wanted her for himself. She saw the dominant, possessive, and aggressive side of him that he was afraid to let out.

Every time they met, Victor anxiously waited to see what Eva was wearing. Without admitting it, this was a game they played week in and week out. Eva would dress in clothes she thought Victor would find attractive, and Victor would do the same, teasing each other to push and see who would break first. There were moments they worked each other up to nearing the point of no return, all without words and instead with what seemed to be harmless implications.

Victor didn't have the slightest clue Eva was fantasizing about him after every meeting. The more they met, the more erotic their situation became. It was taboo. She was a married woman, and the idea of an affair was hot. He was something she couldn't have, adding wood to a burning fire. Eva loved that he was moral and put her happiness before his own, but she knew this was only a small part of him. Eva was anxious to see the side of him that wasn't so moral.

Every night, she'd pick a different part of his personality to fantasize about. One night would be the dominant and aggressive side, the part of him that would book a hotel room and drag her there, only to have his way with her and teach her a lesson for the times she'd teased and provoked him. He'd turn her into his slave for the night, knowing she was enjoying every second of his aggressive behavior. The idea of Victor watching her as she enjoyed being completely dominated by him made her blush.

Then there was the sensual side of him. There was the side of Victor that would slowly make love to her, taking his time to please her and making sure her pleasure was even more important than his own. He'd hold and love her as the moments passed, kissing every corner of her body and exploring what was new. They would grow closer as the night moved on, soaking up the intimate love they shared. There'd be whispers of, "I love you" throughout the night. Cuddling would be impossible until they were both fully satisfied.

Eva also had different sides of her own personality she wanted Victor to see—the side of her that didn't want to be dominated, but to dominate. Even though Eva was married, Victor found comfort in the idea that Eva went home to the same man every night. Eva, on the other hand, didn't have that same luxury with Victor. Eva had to deal with the idea that Victor could date whatever woman he wanted. He wasn't going home to one woman she could compete with. The idea of him being with another woman infuriated her. It wasn't only about sex but also about sharing emotional thoughts or feelings with another woman. The thought passing her mind drove her crazy. Eva wanted Victor to herself and refused to share him with anyone. If she could lock him away with her forever, she would. Eva knew the impact he had on women and why they'd try so desperately to have him. He had a way with words, a handsome face, a great sense of humor, and a big heart. She knew any woman would be putty in his hands if he allowed it to happen.

These feelings awoke the dominant part of Eva, allowing her to have a fantasy about taking the reins. Eva wanted to show Victor what he'd been missing out on, making sure he'd never think of another woman ever again. She wanted to give him such mind-blowing pleasure that he'd become obsessed with her, making him beg and plead for more, forcing him to submit to all of her demands. She wanted to watch Victor, as powerful and dominant as he was, lose his mind over her, to crave her body and plead for one more moment of experiencing her.

Eva wanted Victor to only think about her in every way—sexually, emotionally, and even physically—and with every beat of his heart. These thoughts and fantasies raced through her mind as she continued to read. Victor quietly listened to every word of the story, trying to take in the feelings she was having. He could sense the sexual excitement building in her body and loved watching her get aroused by reading a book to him.

A nurse barged into the room, interrupting her reading to Victor. He jumped at the sound of the door opening. He was terrified his mother would walk in on this. God only knew the weeks of nightmares he'd suffer after that.

"You can't keep the door closed," the nurse said. "The door should always be open so we can monitor him properly."

Eva didn't reply. She only grunted at the nurse interrupting her reading to him. In her mind, Victor was going to be okay. He needed to stay alive for her. Eva never thought Victor would leave her alone. He promised he'd never leave, and Victor never broke a promise he made to Eva.

The nurse quickly checked Victor's condition as Eva anxiously waited for the nurse to leave, tapping her foot on the floor while the moments passed. Victor stood quietly by and watched this odd situation unfold.

Eva could be the bubbliest and kindest person, but sometimes she truly disliked talking to the people around her. She was the kind of woman who hated going to a store and being approached by the sales associates asking if she needed help. Her circle was always small, having had one or two best friends throughout her life. This was a choice she made because she preferred to have a few good friends instead of many bad ones.

The nurse left the room as Barbara abruptly made an entrance. Eva quickly slammed the book shut and threw it into her bag. Eva didn't want his mother seeing she was reading the book to him. Barbara knew Eva was going to read it at some point, but Eva would rather she not see it.

When Eva nervously tossed the book into her bag, she didn't notice that her letter fell onto the floor. She had placed it inside the book for safekeeping.

Eva fidgeted with her bag, not noticing when Barbara picked up the letter from the floor.

"Is this yours?" Barbara asked.

Eva turned around to find her letter in Barbara's hands. Her heart sank as she saw the envelope crumpled between Barbara's fingers. Barbara immediately caught the concerned look on Eva's face.

"Yes, that's mine. I needed to mail it out today."

Eva went to grab the envelope from Barbara's hand, but she pulled it away. Victor moved closer to the altercation, watching closely as the two most important women in his life stood toe to toe.

"It's not addressed to anyone," Barbara said. "And it's already sealed too."

Eva didn't like that Barbara needed to know everything and didn't appreciate the way Barbara was interrogating her over a personal matter.

"Quite honestly, it's none of your business," Eva said powerfully. "Give me the letter back. I was just leaving to mail it."

Barbara's eyebrows raised in shock at the way Eva stood up to her. With her long arms, Eva yanked the letter out of Barbara's hand, almost tearing it in the process.

"I'll be leaving now," she said calmly.

Barbara stood by powerlessly as Eva grabbed her bag and marched out of the hospital room. Victor snickered at the way Eva stood her ground. Barbara had finally met her match. She knew, from that moment on, that Eva wouldn't tolerate her overly dominant personality.

"You could literally ruin a wet dream, Mom," Victor laughed.

Barbara suddenly jumped when she heard whispers of a voice.

"Who's talking?" she screamed aloud.

A light flashed before Victor's eyes as the sound of his mother's voice faded away.

"I'm going to go blind with all these flashes," Victor thought.

He found himself back in the empty room once again. This time, the sunlight in the room dimmed. It was getting dark. Dusk approached, and Victor still couldn't find a way to speak to Eva. Why could his mother hear him and Eva couldn't? Victor thought that maybe Eva wasn't ready yet. It might be possible that she chose not to hear him.

Victor looked out the window as his eyes followed a stream of grey smoke that filled the air. He tried to open the window, but it was locked. Victor could see that there was a group of people in the backyard of Paul's home. A large umbrella was covering their faces, so he couldn't recognize anyone specifically. He was curious to see who else was in Paul's house and marched towards the door to open it.

The handle wouldn't budge, like the door itself was completely stuck. On a second attempt, Victor used two hands to try and nudge the doorknob. The door still didn't move an inch.

Victor placed his foot on the wall next to the door and tried to pull it open without turning the knob. The door didn't even make a creaking sound almost as if it was cemented into the wall.

Victor screamed at the top of his lungs in frustration, feeling the walls closing in around him. He didn't know where else to turn or what to do. He was trapped.

Then a thought came to the forefront of his mind. The whole time he'd been here, he had tried to force some sort of an occurrence. He had tried to force a feeling to come up inside of him or force an answer from Juliette or Paul. He now realized that was the wrong approach. It might be better to allow these occurrences to happen on their own.

He went back to his corner of the room and sat on the floor with his eyes closed and breathed. He let his breath take over his mind, allowing air to flow into his nose and out of his mouth as he quietly reflected on his thoughts.

CHAPTER 12

Eva was sitting in the driveway of her home, waiting to see her husband. Eva found herself waiting in the driveway often, like a part of her never wanted to go home. So much had changed in her life over the years. She'd barreled through life so quickly that she had never had a chance to truly enjoy the more stable part. There was always something keeping her mind occupied.

The hardship she'd been through was tough to match. She wished she could forget most of her childhood all together. Eva even thought about writing a novel about it at one point, but it was too hard to relive the memories.

Eva never blamed anyone for her troubles, refusing to be a martyr. She never held any resentment against her parents for what they'd put her through, not being the type of person to hold grudges. She clearly wasn't an Italian, to whom nothing mattered more than a grudge.

The many memories of her life passed through her mind as she thought about the years of struggling. There was never much money for her to spend. She hardly got by. To be alone from such a young age took a toll on her. The boyfriends she had weren't the most attentive. They'd let her go off and do whatever she pleased. While some would welcome this laid-back attitude, Eva wanted someone to care. She wanted a man to worry if she'd been gone all day or if she had a cold. The really simple things mattered the most.

Eva wanted to be loved unconditionally and needed a man who would stick by her no matter what was happening in their lives. She'd rather a man who cared too much than a man that didn't care. Enter Victor, the ball of anxious energy that she fell in love with.

Victor was the kind of man to call if he hadn't heard from her in an hour. He'd notice if Eva brushed her hair one morning and ask what she'd done differently. Victor could sense sadness and feel happiness. He'd know just when to pick her up when she was down, or to be sad with her instead of cheering her up. Eva fed off his anxious energy, noticing the way he saw every little change in her mood, facial expression, or even her clothing. Every time they met, he analyzed her, sniffing out anything that could have been off. Some would call him a bit much, but Eva called it love.

There was one day in particular that Eva thought back on. It was the day Eva learned that Victor's feelings for her went beyond words. He showed Eva that he could love her through anything and nothing could come between them.

Seven months after they'd met, Victor showed up to the coffee shop for what had become their normal weekly meetings. He agreed to meet Eva at twelve in the afternoon on this day. Victor was early, as usual, making sure he wasn't wasting any of his already limited time with Eva. He arrived promptly at eleven-fifty, counting down the seconds on his watch until the next minute passed. Eva always arrived at the time she said on the dot, give or take a minute or so.

Victor sat in anxious thought, always nervous about the idea of seeing Eva until she walked into the room, taking his troubles away. He'd taken off work today and decided to meet Eva earlier than they normally planned. Victor hoped that he could fenagle spending a few more hours with her because of the change in time. The minutes passed by, and Eva still hadn't shown up yet. Victor became uneasy when it was five minutes past twelve, and Eva was uncharacteristically late.

Victor, at first, began to think the worst possible scenario. He was worried Eva had finally given up on their odd relationship. This decision would have made sense. How much longer could they have lasted? They were already prolonging a painful goodbye. It was possible that Eva couldn't handle telling him this and decided not to show up instead. Even though this fear was real, Victor could never picture Eva doing something like that without saying anything first.

A woman working at the coffee shop suddenly called out to the crowd of people sitting around.

"Is anyone's name here Victor?"

Victor shot up out of his seat, almost knocking the table in front of him onto the floor.

"I'm Victor."

"There's a phone call for you. It sounds urgent."

Victor raced over to the phone, realizing it was only Eva who knew he would be here. The woman handed Victor the store phone.

"Eva?"

"This is Long Island Jewish Hospital in Manhasset," a voice said on the other line. "We're calling because a Ms. Abrams listed you as one of her emergency contacts. She said the best way to reach you was to call this location. She got into a car accident earlier today, but she's perfectly alright. She only has a few scratches."

Victor dropped the phone and ran out of the coffee shop. He frantically got into his car and made his way to LIJ, which was only a ten-minute ride away. Normally he would be riddled with nerves over something like this, but Victor stayed calm as he drove to the hospital. Behind his exterior feeling of being calm, he was dying on the inside. He knew that the minute he saw Eva with even a scrape on her knee, he'd be beside himself.

Eva lay in her hospital bed, still confused from her accident. A man had run a stop sign and hit her passenger side door. Her airbags had gone off on all sides, knocking her head back and forth. The seat belt had gripped into her skin, leaving red cuts on her chest and shoulders. She had passed out for about a minute after the crash as a crowd of people gathered around the two cars. The paramedics had thought they were dealing with a fatality.

The doctors in the hospital ran multiple tests, making sure she didn't have any neck or spine injuries. Eva walked away from a major accident with only a bruised arm and a few scrapes. She didn't remember much after the accident, only that she had pulled herself from the car seat and had lain down on the pavement in silence.

She was lost in her own mind, still trying to piece together how she got to this point. When the nurses asked her for an emergency contact, she told them to call the coffee shop and ask for Victor. She knew he'd be very worried if he didn't know why she didn't make their date.

Eva wondered if Victor would come to the hospital to see her, which was definitely breaking one of their set boundaries. Victor had many reasons not to come, knowing that her husband or children could have already been there. Given the arrangements they made, this would be the right thing to do, but Eva wanted him to break this rule. She needed to be cared for and worried about. If Victor visited her with this risk at hand, Eva knew that he would love her through anything.

It wasn't long before Eva heard someone running down the hallway in the distance. She smiled, knowing by the sound of the anxious footsteps that it was Victor running to her rescue. Eva quickly tried to fix herself, brushing her hair with her hands and making sure her hospital gown was tied. She heard a large thump as Victor barreled through the door to her room.

Without saying a word, their eyes met, conveying two different messages. Victor's eyes told Eva that he was desperate to save her. He looked lost and fearful that he couldn't control the situation. He couldn't do anything to stop her pain, and it killed him that he was forced to stand by and watch her suffer. It didn't take long for him to break down, as the severity of the situation finally hit him. The woman he loved had almost been taken away from him.

Eva's eyes told Victor that she was helpless and desperate to be cared for. She wanted to be in the arms of a man who would promise to care for her until she got better. She pictured in her mind what Victor's care would feel like. She dreamed about him smothering her in kisses and being safely held between his arms throughout the night.

The first thing Victor noticed were the scrapes on her hands and feet. He could see the end of a gash that was showing where her chest met her neck, peeking out from the collar of the gown. Her left arm was swollen and bruised, propped up by two pillows.

He pulled a chair beside her bed, staring at her without saying a word. She turned to face him as best she could, dragging the IV with her. Victor took his hand and gently touched her face. She molded the side of her cheek into his warm palm. Eva was always cold and enjoyed that Victor was always warm. They had never touched each other before, making Victor nervous about what was happening. He had butterflies in his stomach, reminding him of how pure love could be.

Victor loved the feeling of her soft skin on his fingertips. He felt her face with his hands, gently running his thumbs across her eyes. Eva remembered how gentle his touch was. There was something sensual and comforting about the way he touched her. Victor stopped at her perfectly shaped lips, admiring the way her kiss would feel. Feeling the softness of her lips on his fingers, he dreamed about what it would be like to kiss her. Eva let out a small moan of pleasure, knowing this was Victor's way of kissing her.

"I almost lost you," Victor mumbled.

Eva's eyes welled with tears, but she tried to hold them back. She didn't want Victor to see her emotional investment in him.

"I don't know what I would do without you," he cried. "I'd be left alone, forever. I look forward to seeing you. Our time is already so limited."

Victor stared at her bruised arm and the scrapes on her hands. He pulled down the collar of her gown, seeing how far the gash went into her skin. Her breath was suddenly heavy as Victor stared at her wound. He couldn't handle the idea that Eva could have easily died today. She would have died without ever knowing how he felt about her.

"I would die without you," Victor said as he broke down in tears. "I would die without you here. I need you."

Eva tried not to let the tears escape her eyes, but there were too many to hold back. They streamed down her face, taking the place of words.

"Why couldn't it have been me? You're so innocent and fragile. I know you're strong, and I know you've been through a lot, but the first thing I noticed about you was your innocence. I wish I could take your pain away."

Eva smiled through her tears as she realized she had found what she was looking for her entire life. Here was the man who put her before himself. She would proudly do the same for him, because he deserved it.

"I had a dream about you last night," Eva said softly.

Victor smiled and wiped away the tears from his eyes.

"I had a dream about you and your grandfather. I really liked him. I saw you give him a big kiss on the cheek, the way Italian people greet each other."

Eva moved closer to Victor, craving the warmth he was radiating.

"When I woke up, it made me think about what it would be like to be with you. To feel the love that you give others and that big kiss."

They laughed together. Victor loved to see the way Eva smiled. Her face always was filled with color when she laughed. It was the kind of laugh that came from her belly and was hearty.

"I always wonder what it would be like to be with you too," Victor said.

Eva enjoyed that Victor was taking care of her, needing this form of attention from a man. She liked the idea of being waited on when she was too tired to move.

"Would you mind getting me a glass of water?" Eva asked with a sad face.

"Of course." Victor shot up out of his seat and went to fetch Eva a glass of water.

Only a minute after he'd left, Stanley entered the room. He walked over to the chair Victor had been sitting in only moments ago, throwing his suit jacket over the back of it. Fear struck Eva's heart, as she knew Victor could come back any second. She forgot that Stanley was her actual emergency contact and that she specifically told the hospital staff to call Victor to let him know what had happened to her.

"What happened?" Stanley asked with concern. "Is everything okay? I left work as soon as the hospital called."

"Someone ran a stop sign," Eva said nervously. "He hit the passenger side of my car. I got out of the car, and the first thing I did was lie down. I don't remember much else aside from the airbags going off."

Stanley patted her hand.

"Well I'm glad you're okay," he said with a warm smile. "This accident could have been serious. What did the doctors say?"

Eva held up her bruised arm.

"I have a few bruised bones in my arm and a gash on my chest from the seatbelt. That's about it."

"Thank God you're okay," Stanley repeated.

Victor walked down the hallway, back towards Eva's room. He stopped when he heard another man's voice. His heart sank, knowing that Eva's husband was in her room. Victor wasn't scared of him, but he was scared of ruining Eva's life. How could he ever look at himself again knowing he destroyed a family? There wouldn't be a way to explain why Victor was there. The way Eva looked at him would be a dead giveaway.

Victor pressed his back up against the wall next to the door, curious to peek in and see what was going on. He eavesdropped on their conversation. Victor's mind told him to turn around and walk away. He shouldn't witness Eva together with her husband. It could be heartbreaking for him, not to mention an invasion of her privacy. His heart quickly took over, forcing himself to see how invested Eva was in her marriage. It was only a natural curiosity given their situation.

Eva nervously waited for Victor to accidentally walk into the room. Her uneasiness was clear to her husband, who quickly picked up on it.

"Is something wrong?" Stanley asked. "You look really bent out of shape."

"No," Eva said nervously. "Nothing's wrong. I'm shaken up from the accident."

Victor poked his head inside the room, wanting to see what her husband looked like. He could easily sum up the kind of man he was from looking at him. Eva never talked about him much.

Victor saw a man who was taller than him, standing about six feet to his five foot seven. He was of an average build with early greying hair. He looked a lot older than he probably was. Victor could see that Stanley was sophisticated and well put together, which he knew was Eva's type. Victor could tell she sought out stable men.

"What a suit," Victor thought to himself with jealousy. "I bet he's a Wall Street guy."

Victor pulled himself away before he got caught, still leaning on the wall next to the door. He noticed three teenagers running down the hallway, two boys and a girl, all of them different shades of blonde hair. They reminded him of the children from *The Sound of Music*. He instantly knew that these were Eva's children. The daughter looked like a spitting image of Eva if she were younger. It was amazing to see. The other two were twins, having the same facial structure, body frame, and hair color. Each child ran past him, not thinking to wonder why he was leaning against the wall outside their mother's hospital room door.

"Mom!" they all screamed at once.

Each of them crowded around her, bombarding her with kisses and hugs. Victor peeked back in again to witness this sight. He saw how happy Eva was to be with her children. He could tell she was a great mother. Victor had mixed feelings about witnessing this moment—his instant reaction was sadness, because he wished he could have this life with her. He thought to himself that those should be his children and they should be enjoying their family together. He couldn't change any of that now. He only wished to go back in time and find Eva somehow, so he could be the one to spend his life with her.

He also felt genuine happiness for her, knowing that this was what she wanted and that, despite her feelings for him, this was something they couldn't share together. She always told him it was her dream to have a family and a bunch of little babies. Victor would never do anything to take this away from her, but at the same time, he wondered what Eva would do if she had a choice. He realized he would never have the answer to that question, because it was near impossible for a man to read a woman's mind.

As her children smothered her with love, Stanley moved in to kiss Eva, gently holding her chin with his fingertips. Eva knew she couldn't tell Stanley not to kiss her. He would question why because she'd never done that before. Her children also would think the same because they had hardly ever seen their parents not display love. She was forced to take the risk of Victor seeing. She shook beneath her skin, knowing the pain she could cause by this one tiny moment.

Stanley's lips touched Eva's, and he could feel her trembling. There was a part of him that knew something was wrong, but he figured it was the trauma from the accident. As her husband kissed her, she opened her eyes to see Victor, standing in the door. The look of pure sadness and helplessness of his face could never be etched out of her mind. She could do nothing to take what he'd seen back. Eva watched as he disappeared only a moment after she'd seen him. They never spoke about that day, both nervous to unravel the feelings behind it. Eva knew she did nothing wrong, and Victor knew he couldn't complain about what happened, but that didn't mean it didn't hurt them both.

Eva broke free of her vivid memories of Victor and realized she'd been sitting in her car, staring into space for over twenty minutes. She popped open the trunk to finally take her cowboy boots, picking up the box and carrying it inside with her. She decided to not suppress her feelings any longer. With one free hand, she opened the door to her home.

On a normal evening, Eva would see Stanley sitting on the couch watching some television as he slowly drifted off into a deep sleep. He wasn't anywhere in sight, which was strange for him. Eva figured he was avoiding her after their argument today. She didn't know what to do at this point or how to handle their relationship. Surprisingly, she noticed this was still not at the forefront of her mind.

Eva crept up to her bedroom and saw Stanley with his body turned to his side of the bed, facing away from hers. She walked abruptly into the room, so he knew she was there. Still, he didn't turn around to greet her or apologize.

Stanley was dealing with this the way he dealt with everything, by not bringing it up. He expected Eva to forget what was said and for their lives to go back to normal. That's what he was hoping for at least. Stanley felt perfectly fine sitting in relationship limbo with Eva. He provided for her, kept a roof over her head, and treated her respectfully. Stanley thought she should be more than happy with this because most people don't have that kind of stability.

Eva walked into the bathroom, shutting the door behind her. Her muscles had been extra achy from the stress of the past few days. Eva thought a warm bath would help relieve her of the muscle aches in her body. She turned on the water and put bubble bath liquid into the tub.

The water quietly crashed onto the porcelain, and the bubbles slowly filled up the tub. Eva liked to listen to the sound of the water flowing. It relaxed her. She undressed herself, staring into a full-body mirror that hung behind the door of the bathroom. Eva took off her clothes aside from the thermal socks that Victor had gotten her.

She examined her body closely in the mirror, wondering how Victor would react if he saw her naked. Even better, she thought of wearing only the socks he had gotten her, with the rest of her body naked. Eva knew that would really get him going.

"He'd love my body," Eva thought to herself. "He wouldn't be able to keep his hands off me."

She giggled.

"Who am I kidding? I wouldn't be able to keep my hands off him either."

Eva ran her hands across her chest and down to the middle of her stomach. She imagined her hands were Victor's. She imagined his warm touch, his fingers feeling her soft skin and moving across her body. The warm feeling in her groin roared as if she were twenty again. She reached her hand down between her legs, touching herself at the idea of Victor taking her. Eva's knees buckled and her legs quivered as she pleased herself.

She continued to look into the mirror, watching her body go through these sensations. She couldn't stop thinking about Victor seeing her like this, seeing the pleasure that he was giving her. She loved the idea of Victor admiring her body, wishing to please her every need. The little thought of him touching her body was erotic.

"I should have taken him when I had the chance," she thought.

Eva stopped her pleasure-filled fantasy to turn off the water before the tub overflowed. She crawled into the bathtub, soaking up the heat of the water. Surrounded by bubbles, Eva leaned the back of her neck on a small pillow she kept in the bathroom for when she bathed.

Like a child, she played with the bubbles in the bath, always finding the humor and joy in every situation. Her tense muscles finally became relaxed as her body fell into a comfortable groove. Eva closed her eyes and tried to ease her mind as the heat of the water soaked her troubles away. She listened to the sound of water dripping from the faucet into the tub. Eva counted the drops in her mind. After the twentieth drop, she fell into a deep sleep.

CHAPTER 13

Victor felt his breath travel from his lungs, into his nose, and finally out of his mouth. When he breathed like this, it was an easy way for Victor to analyze his feelings. Most of the time, he felt numb, trying to tuck away any painful feelings he could avoid. Eva had taught Victor this breathing technique to help him deal with the stresses of everyday life. She believed it was important to have all of your feelings, both good and bad. Victor never wanted to have a bad feeling, so his mind naturally protected itself by shutting down.

Victor thought of what he'd been through since he'd started this journey of self-discovery. He thought back to the lessons Paul and Juliette had been trying to teach him, both different but equally important.

Paul had mentioned to Victor that he couldn't see Eva yet because he was not ready. He had come too far to let Eva slip through his grasp so easily. Juliette, on the other hand, had wanted him to realize that he didn't know the full story. There was something Eva had never told him. They had both hinted at a feeling or some sort of occurrence he was missing.

Victor knew the answer to this question, but the real question was, could he accept the answer? Could Victor really bring himself to put aside the years of emotional pain and abuse he'd gone through to see that Eva was different? Could he really trust that, even though she'd never vocalized any feelings, she loved him as much as he loved her? It was a monumental emotional hurdle that he had to make in the next few minutes.

"She's different," Victor mumbled in his meditation.

The thoughts swarmed in Victor's mind as tears trailed down his cheeks. His lips quivered as his body shook from the overwhelming sadness that came over him. The tears traveled across his forearms and onto the floor. He was at his absolute most vulnerable point. Victor continued mumbling the words aloud to himself, trying to plow through the emotional pain.

"I'm pretty damn sure she loves me."

The tears came down faster when he realized the sincerity of his words.

"Eva loves me," he repeated. "She really loves me. How could I not see that, all of this time, she really was in love with me?"

Victor took his last deep breath, exhaling the final remnants of the negativity he'd been facing. He opened his eyes, and he noticed a huge change in the empty room he found himself in. Victor was now in a beautifully decorated room.

The room lit up around the now vibrant colors on the wall. Beautiful shades of turquoise and red made the entire energy in the room feel different. A large bed stood in the center of the room, leaning against the wall. It looked like the bed of a queen or king. The covers and pillows were lined with a dark gold color that complimented the mahogany nightstand and wardrobe adjacent to the bed. The smell of the wood was so fresh, like it had been carved that morning.

Victor had passed his final test. In order for him to truly see and feel the awe-inspiring world around him, he needed to have faith. That was something he had been lacking for years. Victor had stopped seeing the world through the eyes of a person who was hopeless. It was truly a magical place, one that was in tune with human emotions. This was why it had taken Victor so long to see that Benedict was really Paul. Victor had passed Paul's house without realizing it for the same reason.

The golden covers of the bed seemed to be ruffled, like there was something in between them. Victor got up from the floor and approached the bed, not knowing what this world had in store for him next. Based on the past experiences he had, he knew there was a surprise for him somewhere. He wondered if this was another test, or even a trick his own mind was playing on him.

Victor pulled the covers down as they passed over Eva's body. She was dressed elegantly in a turquoise dress, matching the color of the wall. Victor watched Eva for a few moments in total silence, trying to soak in what was happening. He was worried Eva wouldn't be able to hear or see him once again.

He watched as she peacefully slept, thinking about how he had missed her so dearly. It gave him a sense of relief when he finally got to see every curve of her face, the shape of her nose, and even the way her hair fell around her shoulders. To Victor, she was the most beautiful woman on the planet and he admired her beauty more than anything. Seeing her once again reminded Victor that no woman could ever compare to her. He sat next to her, gently grabbing her hand.

"Eva," Victor whispered.

"Mmhhm," Eva said.

Victor sighed with relief when Eva finally heard him. There was no more fighting to be done. She was here, completely within his grasp. Victor picked up her hand and kissed it.

"Eva," he said, louder this time. "Wake up."

"Let me stay in my bubble bath," she mumbled.

Victor chuckled. "You're not in a bubble bath."

He kissed her on the cheek this time. Eva finally opened her eyes and fully awoke from her sleep to see Victor staring into her eyes.

"Hi," he said quietly.

Eva wasn't surprised because she'd been dreaming of him often, thinking these dreams were another tease, not reality. She tried to hold back her emotions.

"Hi," she said softly.

Eva sat up from the bed, looked down at herself, and noticed she was wearing a green-colored dress again. Eva smiled, hoping this would be yet another one of her wildly erotic dreams. The turquoise-colored dress seemed to be trendy in her sexual dreams.

"Is this a dream?" Eva asked.

"Yes and no," Victor said. "You're dreaming right now, but I'm really here with you. I visited your dream. This is really me and really you. Right now, we're together in a world that's between life and death. That's where my soul has been the whole time I've been in a coma."

"What?" Eva asked with confusion. "A dream is a dream. Don't tease me like that."

Victor pulled Eva's hand towards his body, guiding her closer to him. She willingly followed his guidance, as her face came closer to his. They stared at each other, nose to nose. Their hearts were beating rapidly as they shook from the nerves of being this close to one another. Victor stopped only a few centimeters from Eva's lips, then their lips lightly grazed each other's. From such a small touch, Eva felt a sensation unlike ever before. Finally, he kissed her, unleashing a new flow of emotions that they'd never experienced with each other.

Such a small kiss was years in the making. After the heartbreak, longing, wanting, and fantasizing, their love for each other showed through their first physical contact. Eva allowed Victor's tongue into her mouth, meeting his with her own. They refused to let go of each other, soaking up every waking moment. She grabbed Victor's face with her hands, pulling him closer to her.

There were no thoughts going on in Eva's mind. She was only focused on kissing Victor, making sure their first meeting was one to remember. After years of emotional starvation, Eva felt truly loved, satisfied emotionally and physically. His kiss was gentle and filled with desire. There were butterflies in her stomach, the nervous feeling of joy that one gets when they first kiss the person they love. It was a feeling that assured Eva she had been right all of this time.

Victor let go of Eva. He watched as she sat in total amazement of what had happened.

"Did that feel like a dream to you?" Victor asked.

Eva shook her head, looking at the way Victor was mesmerized by her. No dream she'd ever had compared to this. This dream felt too real, like her mind and soul were in another place while her body lay sleeping somewhere else.

"This can't be a dream," she laughed.

Eva's smile was one of the few things that brought happiness to Victor's life. He could tell she was a naturally sad person. Watching her laugh and smile made him genuinely happy. He ran his hands up and down her body, feeling her soft skin. How he wished he could lie with her for hours on end, feeling that soft skin on his own. She was so smooth to the touch.

It was overwhelming to feel the different kinds of emotions Eva brought out of Victor. He shielded his eyes away from Eva, moving off the bed and away from her, covering his face. She followed him, not letting one moment pass when they weren't together.

"What's wrong?" she asked nervously.

"Ten years!" he screamed. "It's been ten years since I've seen you. You never told me a thing. Not a single feeling! Not an 'I love you,' or an 'I miss you.' Nothing! You never told me how much you cared or worried about me. I had to figure it all out for myself. It made me think that maybe this was all in my head. For a while, I even thought it was easy for you to let me walk away and that you never thought about me again. To never hear from someone for ten years, you start to think they don't care anymore."

Eva tried to speak, but Victor continued to ramble on.

"But then you stayed with me!" he cried out. "You ran to see me when I was shot. You stayed with me the whole time I was sick. You got jealous of Cindy. You read to me. You hardly ever left my side."

Seeing Victor cry like this caused her heart to grow heavy. She had never intended to cause Victor this much pain, but their situation had been doomed from the start. She could see that he was in disbelief of what was happening.

"Stop!" she yelled with tears in her eyes. "Stop it already!"

Eva marched over to Victor, grabbed him by the face and kissed him, then continued to hold their faces together with force. She pushed him away before she spoke again.

"I love you," Eva said through the tears in her eyes. "I always knew you were the one for me. There was something about us. The idea seemed right to me."

Victor tried to speak again, but Eva screamed at him in retaliation.

"For once, stop talking!" she shouted. "You always do the talking. Now it's my turn!"

Eva pointed at Victor, trying not to smile at the goofy look on his face while she was trying to be serious.

"Do you understand that just because I didn't say anything doesn't mean I didn't love you? I spent three days a week with you, sneaking out of my house whenever I got the chance. I called you in the middle of the night to hear your voice, every other Friday, for almost all of those ten years. I fought with myself not to write to you. I spent hours fantasizing about what it would be like for us to make love. Oh! And let's not forget your socks. I wear your socks every single day. The only days I might not is if I'm going to the beach. Is that good enough for you?"

Eva tried to catch her breath, having taken no time to breathe while she was ranting. That anger had been pent up for some time now. Victor tried to speak yet again, and Eva spoke over him. She didn't want him to have any rebuttals, excuses, or doubts.

"I don't want you to touch another woman besides me. The idea of you being with another woman makes me want to kill someone. I never want you to have a girlfriend. I never want to you get married. I only want you to spend every single day with me! Every day. I only want you to be with me and that's it."

Victor's tears dried, and his smile shone through the sadness. That was what he'd been waiting to hear. He loved seeing Eva a little angry and possessive over him. In the back of Victor's mind, he knew Eva felt this, but it was truly nice to hear it come from her.

Eva broke down and cried profusely. Those feelings had been pent up inside her for over a decade. She had buried them deep inside her heart, never telling anyone what happened between them.

"One more thing," she said through the weeping. "When I said we should never see each other again, I wasn't only thinking of my family. I was thinking of you. I didn't want you to waste your life waiting for me. I harbored guilt every day. Guilt for betraying my husband and guilt for taking advantage of the way you felt about me. I never wanted you to be alone because of me. I wanted you to be happy, and now you're dying."

Eva moved closer to Victor as she molded herself into his chest and wrapped her arms around him one at a time.

"You're dying," she repeated.

She could feel the anxiety inside of him as she wiped her tears on his chest. His muscles were tense, his body was warm, and his heart was beating rapidly. She could sense the nervous thoughts running through his head. This was all happening so fast that Victor couldn't believe it was real.

Victor's thoughts were racing. "I'm afraid of her leaving me. Everyone leaves me. I never want her to leave me. I lost her once, and I never want to lose her again. I don't want her to hurt me. I love her. I love her. I love her."

Eva looked into his eyes and saw the blank stare. He was lost in his own anxious world. She could see the doubt getting to him. In this moment, she was angry—not at Victor, but at whoever had hurt his gentle soul, whoever had damaged him so badly that he had to work hard to see that she would always love him.

Eva wanted to take Victor's pain away with her love, forcing him to accept the way she felt about him. Eva knew Victor too well and figured that he was overly concerned with avoiding the pain that comes with love.

"Look at me," Eva said.

She held his face with both her hands, feeling the trembling fear in his body. Love could be painful sometimes. For Victor, feeling this much love for Eva was scary. It was the unknown possibilities that caught his attention. If she wanted to, Eva could crush him. His heart was in her hands, and that thought petrified Victor. To be this vulnerable was the scariest thing that could ever happen to him.

"What are you so afraid of?" she asked.

"You hurting me," he mumbled.

Victor wiped the tears away from his eyes. Eva couldn't handle seeing him like this. A man who had so much love to give was breaking down. A man who had no clue how dearly he was loved. A man she would never hurt. He had always been her rock, and now it was her turn to be his. Eva's heart broke seeing the pain in his eyes. She tried to compose herself, but the tears refused to stop.

"Ask me not to hurt you," she said.

"I can't."

"You can do it," she said with encouragement.

They continued to break down as the words passed his mouth.

"Eva," he said through his tears, "please don't hurt me. I love you. Don't hurt me."

She rubbed her hands along his cheeks. The feel of her soft skin calmed him.

"I'll never hurt you," she said. "I promise you, I'm different. I'll never hurt you."

"They all said that," Victor said with a twinge of anger.

She wiped the tears away from his face. "I would never lie. I love you. I would never do anything to hurt you. I promise."

Eva held Victor close, looked into his red, teary eyes, and kissed him. She kissed him slowly, not once, but twice. Both times, parting his lips. There was a burning love that was unrivaled behind her soft kisses. Her kisses were warm and sensual, masking the pain he was feeling. In each other's arms, they stood there, embracing the moment. She felt their souls beginning to connect again for the first time in ten years. They weren't two people; they were one.

"I never want to leave this spot," Eva mumbled. "I always dreamed of lying in your arms."

"I always dreamed of you never leaving my arms," Victor replied.

These intense feelings of love triggered a deep emotional response in both Victor and Eva. Their desires for one another grew ten times as strong and they needed to find another way to show their love for each other. These feelings needed a new outlet, and there was only one thing left Victor and Eva hadn't done.

Victor's hands moved up and down Eva's back, causing a shiver to sweep through her body. Her legs started to quiver as she could only think about his hands being on her. He noticed her reaction of acceptance and continued to move his hands down to her backside.

"I always thought you had a cute butt," Victor laughed. "That's the one part of you I never really got to see. You always showed off the curves of your body, and even your chest to me, but never your butt."

Eva blushed at such intimate words. The idea of Victor wanting to take the time to explore her body was exciting. She felt the warmth between her legs firing up. Still, her mind was in another place. The guilt started to consume Eva when she remembered this could be technically considered cheating.

"Do the same rules apply in the spirit world?" she thought to herself before gently pushing Victor away from her.

"I don't know if I can do this," Eva said.

Victor nodded, taking in what she said and thinking about it for a few moments.

"Do you trust yourself?" he asked.

Eva nodded.

"Do you trust your feelings?"

Eva nodded again.

"Would you ever do anything you wouldn't want to do?"

"No," Eva replied.

Victor kissed her before asking his final question.

"Do you trust me?"

"Yes," Eva moaned. "I would trust you with my life."

"You raised a family. You sacrificed all that you could, and now it's your turn to be taken care of."

Eva stared aimlessly into his eyes.

"Let me take care of you," Victor said softly.

Victor moved one finger up and down her right arm. She was completely frozen in time, and would allow Victor to do as he pleased. She was his to enjoy. The Victor Eva had been dying to see was finally here—the side of him that wouldn't take no for an answer. The chivalrous, moral man she knew was going to disappear for a little while.

He kissed her lips once more, this time pulling her waist into his body with aggression, causing a jolt of excitement to shoot through her body. Without even doing much of anything, she was already dripping with anticipation of what Victor's next move was. Victor started leaving a trail of kisses along her body. First, he kissed her eyes and then her lips. He loved hearing the moans coming from her, encouraging him to continue his journey. Softly, he kissed her earlobe and moved to her neck, his trail of kisses still lingering.

Victor pulled down the straps of her dress and watched as it quietly fell to the floor. Before touching her again, Victor stared in amazement. He was dying to explore her, wanting to see what he'd been imagining for so long.

Eva watched his eyes scan her. This time, she wasn't nervous but instead empowered. She noticed the way his eyes melted at the sight of her breasts and curves.

"The way you look at me," she mumbled while looking down at herself.

"What about it?"

"I love seeing the enjoyment on your face when you look at my body."

Eva used her empowering feelings, and quickly took charge of the situation. In only her panties, she undressed Victor, grabbing his waist where his shirt met his pants. She slowly pulled Victor's shirt over his head.

His body was filled with hair, which was a sign of manliness to Eva. He was the opposite of her in this way because she was naturally hairless. Eva took pleasure in undressing Victor, noticing every curve while quietly touching him. She felt his chest, the part of his body she loved the most. Victor wasn't the most defined man, but he was stocky in every sense of the word.

She could feel his chest muscles by a simple touch, and trailed her fingers along the veins in his forearms leading up to his bulky shoulders. His abdomen was hard, but Victor still sported a little belly. Eva really enjoyed his little belly. She didn't want a man that was filled with muscles or a man who was too skinny and flat. Victor was the right proportion for her to enjoy. The one part of him that surprised her was his butt, which was well-shaped for a man.

Victor was every ounce of man Eva could have ever wanted. The way he carried himself was sexy and his presence alone was a turn-on for her. Victor's opinions were strong, he owned up to everything he ever said, and he never cared what other people thought of him. He was truly loyal, not only to her, but to anyone he cared for. He was naturally territorial and jealous. This wasn't in an overbearing way, though; he displayed exactly the amount of jealousy a woman needs to see from a man.

With her hands on his chest, she felt Victor's heart racing. It was comforting to know Victor was just as nervous as she was. Wasting no time, she unbuckled his belt while kissing his chest, then her hands slowly reached down his pants. Eva jokingly slapped him with his belt before she threw it aside.

"Too kinky for you?" she joked.

"Not as kinky as the quirky underwear you're wearing," he laughed back.

Victor and Eva always had fun together no matter what they were doing and truly enjoyed each other's company. Eva wore orange-and-white-striped normal women's underwear that wouldn't appear to be sexy to most people. He couldn't help but notice the brightly-colored stripes that stuck out so vividly.

"I think they're sexy," Victor laughed. "But I know another look would suit you better."

"What's that?" she said as she played with the lining of her underwear.

"No panties!" he laughed.

"I may need your help for that," she asked innocently.

"You have to finish me first."

Eva obeyed him, unbuttoned his pants, and pulled them down to the floor. She came to her knees, looking up at Victor who was above her. He held his breath as she gently grazed her body against his manhood, slithering her way back up to face him. Eva loved making him uneasy.

"You're such a tease," Victor said.

"I'm a bad girl. I can't help it," she pouted.

"Bad girls need to get punished," he laughed.

Victor placed his hand behind Eva's head and motioned for her to get back on her knees. Without any words exchanged, she obeyed his order, knowing exactly what he wanted.

Eva was a powerful and independent woman, but that didn't mean she didn't enjoy being dominated by Victor. On her knees, she gave into what he wanted. He held his hand behind her head, guiding her first with a gentle touch, then with slight aggression. She loved the taste of him, enjoying every moment of giving Victor the pleasure he was seeking. She felt a fire between her legs start to burn, one that filled her with delicious satisfaction.

Eva truly believed his penis was hers, wanting him to be inside of her and never leave. Only she needed to know what his sweet love tasted like. The way she handled him told Victor what she was thinking, and he welcomed her possessiveness.

Eva stopped for a breath, and Victor picked her up, swinging her onto her feet. She clung to him as he carried her over to the bed, throwing her down below him. He kissed her lips, as he slowly moved his hands down her body. It was his way of examining her. He craved the feeling of her soft skin. She trembled as his hand traveled across her breasts, then slowly down the curves of her hips, and finally to her groin. He took off her panties, instantly noticing how wet they were, and threw them across the room.

Victor's hands now traveled up and down her thighs, the part of her body he loved the most. Her thighs were perfect to him, not too big nor too small. He admired them, just as he admired the rest of her. Eva watched as his eyes and hands made their way across her. She relished in the moment of Victor's admiration. She loved the way he touched her. His touch was sensual, and his hands always kept her guessing. She never wanted his warm hands off her. Now between her thighs, Victor spread her legs and admired the true beauty of Eva for the first time.

Victor could feel the moist warmth radiating from her. Eva's enjoyment was dripping out as his hands touched her. Her womanhood was a truly beautiful sight to him—a true work of art. Never had he enjoyed just looking at a woman this way before. Victor's hands passed over one last time before they finally entered her.

Eva watched Victor as he truly enjoyed watching Eva's body go through sensations. She could see him taking in every moan and sigh as he continued to please her. Victor pulled his fingers out of her and she grabbed his hand tightly, pushing him back towards her.

"No," he said stoutly.

"Why not?" she moaned.

Victor's actions spoke for his words. Before she could say anything, he kissed her breasts, and her moans grew louder. He teased her too much, making Eva only want more from him. She needed to feel him now. Eva grabbed his hair and pushed his head down towards her groin. She held his head between her legs, pushing his face further into her. He obeyed and tasted the sweetness that was Eva. She knew he loved the way she tasted by how his tongue traveled around her. There was no hesitation from him; he only wanted more.

Victor only focused on the fact that she was his. All of her was his, and he wanted her forever. They shared an undying, selfless love and a desire to please one another on different levels, with their selflessness evident in their concern for one another's desires and pleasure. It was true romance at its finest. What else could one expect from years of boundaries? Victor and Eva were only human. The one difference between them and other people was that they were two humans who truly were in love with each other.

Eva's screams grew louder as she tightened her grip on his hair, pushing him further down inside of her. She only wanted and needed more of him, only could think about having him inside her. Not another thought passed her brain. His touch overpowered her mind as she felt herself shaking. A wave of pleasure was coming her way. She kept pressing his head down harder, almost to the point where he couldn't breathe. Eva finally let out screams of pleasure, not fearful of showing Victor how much he was pleasing her.

Victor smiled as he continued to please her even after her orgasm.

She thought to herself, "And he's still going? What a man!"

Eva pulled Victor's head up. Even with his face all wet from her, she still kissed him. Eva never had felt such love from a man before. The way he wanted to please her was truly genuine and came from a place of love.

Victor pried himself away from Eva and stood at the corner of the bed. He pulled her towards him by her ankles, her legs wide open beneath him. There was no more anticipation of waiting. The moment was finally here. After ten years of waiting, Victor finally entered her, consummating their love. In this moment, Eva finally felt at home. She felt that she was where she was supposed to be. His body was her home. Eva never wanted Victor to leave her. She wished he could stay inside her forever.

Eva watched as the sweat slowly traveled down Victor's chest, across his body, and eventually onto her. She stared into Victor's eyes, the eyes of a true man, one who was willing to please his woman. He cared only for that. The both of them shared in the pleasure a relationship should bring. They were both rightfully selfish and selfless, seeking their own pleasure yet seeking to please.

Eva and Victor refused to stop making love. They would only rest when they were truly at peace with their sexual escapade. They wouldn't be able to cuddle without being fully satisfied. At the rate they were going, that could have been never, but every good night eventually comes to an end.

Victor and Eva collapsed onto the bed, lying naked in each other's arms. She let out a large sigh of relief. Eva could see that Victor was finding comfort in this vulnerable situation. Eva ran her hands across his body, wanting to feel every inch of his skin on her hand. Her hand ran from his inner thighs up to his chest and then back. She soaked in the moment, just enjoying being able to touch him in this way.

"How much longer do we have?" Eva asked.

Victor kissed her lips softly, wishing she'd never asked that question.

"I'm not sure," Victor sighed. "There is something I should probably tell you though."

"I'm listening."

"We're at my Uncle Paul's house, who's been dead for over thirty years."

"Okay," Eva replied. "And?"

Victor knew he was in love with a woman who was totally nuts. Only she wouldn't have been startled by such a claim.

"That doesn't startle you that we're at a dead person's home?"

Eva laughed. This was quite familiar to her.

"Dead people visit me in my dreams all of the time. This is nothing new for me."

Eva always confused Victor. He tried to center himself and grasp what she'd said.

"This is different, though. You're really experiencing this. We're in another form of reality."

"That's okay!" she laughed again. "I live in another world as it is."

"You really are nuts," Victor laughed.

Eva shrugged her shoulders.

"And you're stuck with me."

"Paul is waiting for us downstairs. I think we should go before this ends."

"I'd be happy to meet your dead family," she giggled.

CHAPTER 14

Victor and Eva found the dresser in the bedroom filled with clothes specifically tailored for the both of them. It was clear someone had been expecting them. Eva wore a beautifully printed white dress that was free-flowing while Victor wore beige slacks with an open, white button-down shirt.

Victor walked over to the door of the room, expecting yet another battle to open it. He took a deep breath and placed his hand on the doorknob. With little effort, the door swung open. Victor's jaw dropped at the sight of that.

"What's the matter?" Eva asked.

"Nothing, just something with this door," he mumbled. "Follow me."

Together, they walked into the hallway and down the steps of Paul's home. The colors of the walls were more vibrant and made the house look brighter than before. Everything about the home was strikingly lively, reminding Eva of the dancing furniture from *Beauty and the Beast*. She hummed along to the music from the iconic movie, picturing the furniture coming to life. Victor was more struck by how polished Paul's home suddenly looked. The house was now furnished with Brazilian cherry wood floors.

Loud music was playing from speakers in the backyard, encouraging Victor and Eva to follow the noise. They could faintly hear the sound of people trying to talk over the music playing. The smell of burning coal filled the air around them as they made their way into the kitchen. Shadows of people moving along to the music playing could be seen through the other side of the screen door leading out to the yard. Victor and Eva looked at one another, each searching for an answer.

"What do you think's on the other side?" Eva asked him.

"I think that's my family," he said. "I'm scared to go."

"Why?" Eva asked him. "You should be excited to see your family."

He never thought positively about much in his life, sporting a continuously worried look on his face. His mind was too dark, and he often needed Eva to brighten his day. She was his shining star in the dark night, guiding him to happiness—that is, whenever she wasn't making him want to pull his hair out.

"What if that's heaven?" Victor blurted out. "What if that's the other side? What if this was my journey to the afterlife? This may have been God's way of letting me say goodbye to you for the last time."

Eva thought about his questions and internalized what he said. She actually thought he might be right. Eva was afraid to lose Victor forever, but something in her heart told her that Victor wasn't going anywhere. Eva turned to him and held his face.

"You can't die," she said with tears in her eyes. "You can't die because I need you. You can't leave me. You just can't."

Victor heard the desperation in her words. Ten years without him had felt like a lifetime. She'd do anything to make sure he'd never leave her again.

Victor had never felt this kind of love from a woman before. This was all new to him, even from Eva. It had taken her years to bring out these feelings even if they had always been there. Victor put his arms around Eva, deciding in this moment that he could not leave her, never wanting to see this scared look on her face again.

"I'll never leave you," he said calmly. "I'll never leave you."

Holding hands, they opened the screen doors and walked outside together. The porch lights blinded their view as they took their first steps outside. The smell of freshly-cooked food hit their noses like a tidal wave, mixed in with the smell of chlorine and freshly-cut grass.

They were met with loud cheers by voices that sounded familiar. It reminded Victor of a time he truly missed: way back when he was a little boy.

When hearing the shouts and screams, Eva picked out a few voices that sounded familiar to her as well. Eva loved the idea of being part of an enmeshed family, and the more caring and involved the family was, the better. The voices she heard sounded much like a loving family.

The Calameras were a quirky bunch. They were known for many things, but the two most notable were dancing and dirty jokes. There was always a joke to be said, a story to be told, or a dance to be learned. Whenever someone would come over to their home, they were always greeted with food and loud music. It wasn't just any old music, however; it was music that had soul and made you want to get up and dance.

Vito and Camille, a clearly tumultuous couple, were sitting down at the patio table, playing gin rummy. Vito had a love affair with gambling and cold cuts, usually spending most of his time down at the social club. If he wasn't there, Vito was home, cooking his famous meatballs or practicing playing cards. Camille was his right hand, partner in crime, and nagger in chief. She was known as the queen of entertaining, having no shortage of dirty jokes. A staple of her personality was her childlike innocence, much like Eva. She had always enjoyed dressing up for Halloween and did so until she was in her late seventies. For Camille and Vito to be quiet was rare. They were usually laughing or fighting, moods that were decided by a mere coin flip.

Juliette and Fred Bolton played cards along with Victor and Camille. Juliette was the perfect homemaker and the quintessential grandmother. She filled Eva's life with joy, love, and food. Whenever Eva was upset, Juliette would make her famous apple pie to take the sorrow away. As cliché as it sounds, her secret ingredient was love. Eva could always taste the amount of love she put into her cooking. Only Nana could make a hard-boiled egg taste like a gourmet meal from France.

Her husband, Fred Bolton, was a fun-loving, yet still an old-school, kind of man. Fred was a hard worker and provided a living for Juliette, so she was able to be a homemaker. His long hours at work were rewarded by a kind and loving wife who supported him. No matter how tired he was, Fred always made time to spend with his family. They spent their weekends playing board games with Eva for hours. The Bolton family weren't as loud or animated as the Calameras, but they definitely had one thing in common; their love was unconditional.

Uncle Paul manned the barbeque, cooking sausage and peppers, a dish he was known for making. While cooking, he danced along to the doo-wop music playing on the radio.

Paul lived to entertain, learning from his mother Camille. He loved having people over his home and never had a shortage of company. Paul went out of his way to help those he loved, and even strangers, on only moment's notice. He was also a man of many talents, able to do anything from balancing a chair on his nose to flying a plane.

The Calameras and the Boltons had spent their time getting to know each other as Eva and Victor's relationship grew stronger. The two families had spent endless amounts of time together. Though their personalities were different, they shared a deep love for their grandchildren.

For the first time in decades, Victor and Eva saw family members who had passed on many years ago. They were healthy, now living without the sicknesses that had taken them from earth. Eva cried at the sight of her grandparents and was instantly met with a warm hug from the only people who she felt had truly cared during her childhood.

"Nana! Grandpa!" Eva cried out.

"Hello, my darling," Juliette said. "I've missed you so dearly."

"There's my little girl," Fred joked as he hugged both Eva and his wife.

Victor's reaction wasn't quite like Eva's. He was hesitant to let his feelings out, still in total shock of what was going on. Vito and Camille got up from the patio table and walked over to him. Paul followed, closing the lid to the barbeque.

"Hello, doll," Camille said as she pinched Victor's cheeks. "Gimme a kiss."

Victor kissed his grandmother, holding her close to him, refusing to let her go. As his relationship grew with Eva, he felt closer to his grandmother. Victor felt Eva and Camille would have been the best of friends. They both embraced their natural need to be quirky and were never embarrassed to be themselves.

"My grandson!" Vito screamed. "My grandson, the famous writer! Who'd ever thought that when I was feeding you in a high chair, you'd be a world-famous writer!"

Victor hardly knew his grandfather because Vito passed away when he was only five years old. From what he did remember, Vito hadn't changed a bit. He was wearing a flannel shirt and his go-to fisherman's cap—a look he was known for. When he walked, Vito never lifted his feet, dragging them across the floor. Though he may have never looked it, Vito had a way with words, especially with women. He was a well-known ladies' man, a true connoisseur of charisma.

Lastly, Uncle Paul, with his big belly and jolly smile, came waddling over to Victor and hugged him. Paul reeked of burnt sausage, and to Victor that smell was too familiar. When the Calameras cooked, they stunk up the whole house with the smell of meat grilling.

The greetings ended, and finally, the two families turned to each other. Eva motioned for Victor to stand next to her, grabbing his forearm and whisking him over to the seat next to her grandparents.

"Nana," she said with excitement. "I want you to meet Victor Esposito, my—"

Before Eva could finish her sentence, Juliette rushed to hug Victor.

"Fancy seeing you again," Juliette joked. "It's only been a few hours."

Victor snickered. He turned to Eva, who was staring at the two of them in amazement.

"We've already met," Victor smiled. He held Eva's hand tightly. Victor was happy, but on the inside, he was nervous. For a dream like his to come true was overwhelming. First, he had made love to the woman he thought he'd never have. Now, he was having dinner with family members he'd missed his entire life.

"I could die in peace," he thought for a quick moment. "That's probably not such a great thing to say now," he repeated in his mind.

Eva tugged Victor's arm like a little girl in a candy store.

"You met my grandmother?" she screamed. "Since when?"

"She came to me in this world," Victor said. "Juliette said she knew about me and that you would talk about me to her for hours—so much, that she feels like she's known me my whole life."

Eva blushed. She turned to her grandmother and screamed in embarrassment, "Nana!"

Juliette giggled and shrugged her shoulders. Fred Bolton worked his way to Victor, slipping in front of Juliette and Eva, holding his hand out for Victor to shake. Victor shook his hand sternly, giving it a tight squeeze. Before their eye contact broke, Fred pulled Victor in for a hug.

"Welcome to the family, son," he said softly. "I know you're a good man. More importantly, you're a good man for your Eva."

"My Eva?" Victor mumbled.

"First she was our Eva, and now she's your Eva. She's yours now, so take good care of her."

Victor felt as if Fred was handing Eva off to him at their wedding. The moment was beautiful, one that will be etched into Victor's memory forever. He took Fred's words seriously, and would work tirelessly to take care of the woman he so dearly loved.

Victor continued shooting the breeze with Fred, spending time getting to know the patriarch of the Bolton family. Camille quickly grabbed Eva's hand, stealing her away from Juliette for a few moments.

"I love your nose," Camille said.

Eva smiled brightly. "Why, thank you. I don't believe we've met. I'm Eva Abrams."

Eva could feel that Camille's energy was similar to hers. She could see the fun-loving, childlike personality in Camille instantly.

"My real name is Costanzia, but everyone calls me Camille."

"What a pretty name!" Eva said enthusiastically. Eva admired the beauty of other women and always made it a point to fawn over them, feeling that women should stick together in this way.

"You know," Camille said, "as a baby, my grandson always promised me I'd stay alive to see him get married."

Camille put her head down in sadness.

"It was a dream of mine to see a grandchild get married. In life, you can't get everything you want, but I happened to get something a little better."

Eva felt the love radiating from Camille, seeing that family meant everything to her. Eva could also sense the sadness in missing out on a part of Victor's life that Camille wanted to be there for.

"What's that?" Eva asked.

Camille gently pinched Eva's cheek.

"Meeting you!" she said happily. "My grandson loves you more than anything else in the world. You're his life, and that means you're mine too. All I've ever wanted was to see him in the arms of a beautiful, strong woman. Now, I finally get to see that."

Eva's cheeks filled with a light red blush, knowing she had approval from the matriarch of the Calamera family. Eva could tell that Camille's words were genuine and felt a sense of responsibility for Victor, one that was stronger than ever before. He was widely loved by his family and many others around him. Eva felt a duty to protect him, the same way he protected her.

Eva didn't have to say anything else to Camille—her facial expressions did the speaking for her. Beginning to choose the words to respond was an overwhelming task. Instead of saying anything else, Eva hugged Camille the way she would have hugged her own grandmother.

"I'll never stop loving him," Eva said.

Such tender words made Camille cry of happiness, filled with joy that her grandson had found something she'd never had. She'd split from Vito years after their children had moved out of the house and had died alone, waiting and longing for the love of a man that would sweep her off her feet. Camille didn't want Victor to face that same fate. Too many people die this way, and she didn't want her grandson to be one of them.

Vito and Paul waited by Camille's side to meet Eva and were anxious to specifically hear one thing in particular. They both wanted to know how exactly Eva had helped Victor become one of the world's most well-known authors.

CHAPTER 15

The Calameras and the Boltons sat down at the patio table in Paul's backyard, finishing the antipasto platter. Vito probably ate more than half the plate on his own, with Camille smacking his hand away a few times. A basket filled with half-loaves of Italian bread sat at the center of the table. Paul brought over a pile of sausage, peppers, and onions, freshly steaming from the barbeque. He separated the hot and sweet sausage on two different sides of the plate.

Juliette had prepared apple pie with freshly-picked apples and homemade pie crust. She was bubbling with excitement for Victor and Eva to have a piece, but she was forced to wait until after dinner. Before she ate, Juliette made sure to see that Eva was eating a hefty amount of food.

Victor and Eva sat next to each other near the head of the table. Eva quickly finished her sandwich and then plopped on Victor's lap, placing her arms around his neck. She sat so comfortably on top of him as the rest of the family reveled in their love affair. They could see how much Victor and Eva loved each other.

With his mouth filled with food, Paul called out to Victor. "There's one thing everyone wants to know here."

"I thought you guys knew everything already," Victor joked. "You all seemed to have the answers the whole time I've been here."

Juliette quickly interjected, "We only know what you tell us. When you pray and think about us or talk aloud to us, we can hear you. Other than that, we only know what you allow us to."

Victor nodded like he knew what they were talking about. He had stopped following the crazy rules of this world long ago. He had decided not to read into things anymore, taking the spirit's words at face value.

"What's the question of the hour?" Victor asked the table of people.

"How did you become a writer?" Paul asked. "None of us know how you became a writer. When you were a little boy, you never mentioned anything about writing. I don't even remember you being interested in reading either."

They looked at Victor, anticipating his answer.

"I wasn't," Victor said candidly. "I was never a writer, and I never thought about becoming a writer."

Eva laid her head on Victor's neck, looking up at him. She felt the light scruff on his face rub against her skin. Eva watched the happiness pour out of him as he told their story. The smile that was imprinted on his face as he gathered his thoughts was one that she would never forget. Eva couldn't help falling in love with such a sensual and compelling man.

"So," Paul asked, "what made you decide to write a book?"

He answered with a bright smile, "Eva."

"Well, that much we could assume," Juliette said. "Stop being shy. Tell the real story! We're family here."

Eva knew Victor was being modest about himself and his writing. In her eyes, Victor was one of the few last real men, if not the last. People often confuse manliness with a specific look, personality trait, or persona. People consider a *real* man to be an all-powerful, dominant being. The world sets silly rules like men should never cry or have any sort of feelings that aren't deemed tough. The epitome of the strong, silent type. Victor was none of these things, and that is why Eva felt he was truly the last real man.

Victor had two simple rules that he followed. The first, only fear God, never men, because men could never match the power of God. The second, was treat your friends and others around you with respect, unless they give you a reason not to. It was rare to see him be outright angry with anyone unless they double-crossed him. He was genuine and had a hard time lying about anything. Victor was very emotional. His feelings always showed through his eyes. He wasn't afraid of his feelings and instead chose to get in touch with them. Victor faced his demons and acknowledged his good qualities.

What Eva thought was the most important was Victor's sensuality. He could get in touch with a woman's feelings and had a knack for understanding their thoughts, easily learning a woman's life story by merely looking at her face. His touch was soft and comforting yet, at the same time, able to send shivers down their spines. Any woman who ever got close to him could clearly see there was something more to him than to the average man. His love and care could be as dangerous as an addictive drug. Eva craved it, and it was a craving unlike any she'd ever felt before. He incorporated these feelings into his writing which is what made his work so powerful.

Victor looked down at Eva, who seemed to always find the perfect way to melt into his body. His hands started to tremble—not with fear, but with the energy of the emotions that were surfacing.

"I was a carpenter, spending my early mornings working in the buildings of Manhattan. I did freelance work on the weekends too. It could be grueling at times, especially in the burning hot summers, but I enjoyed it. I always loved to create things with my hands. I never wrote much of anything before I met Eva."

Victor paused for a moment, reminiscing on the time they had spent together.

"I'd never met a woman like her before. My first impression of her was innocence. I saw a lost soul within her. A woman who was looking for a life partner who would latch onto her and never let her go. She sought an unconditional love, one that even the toughest life couldn't alter. Eva would return that same love if she ever found such a man. I like to think she found that man in me."

Victor spoke, and the table of people quietly listened to his every word. There were no more questions to ask. This powerful story brought out feelings deep within their own hearts. Fred slowly grabbed Juliette's hand. Vito and Camille, although they had been separated when they died, did the same.

"Our love was a forbidden one. I found out Eva was married with children. She professed to me that she'd never do anything to hurt her family and her husband. I accepted this, but that didn't mean that I gave up. I could tell that Eva longed for something more, no matter what she said. I never wanted her to leave, but I did want to show her that I loved her. The most I would get back from Eva was a deep gaze, one that told me her feelings without them needing to be said. Still, never hearing the words took a toll on me. I was desperate to the point where I would have been satisfied with a long hug. I thought that a few moments of holding her in my arms would be enough to get by."

With her arms wrapped around Victor, Eva squeezed him tightly, relishing in the moment. He finally had Eva in his arms. The tightness of the hug felt safe and he knew he had nothing to fear any longer.

"One day, I had pushed the boundaries too far and she asked to never see me again. I had broken her down and unleashed her feelings. At the time, the idea felt right, but I never saw that I was tearing her life apart even further. I was making everything harder. I think Eva finally realized that we kept prolonging a horrible ending."

Even though he had been angry and hurt, Victor had a hard time blaming Eva for her decision. She had done what was in the best interest of her family. Her decision hadn't depended on her own life but instead on the lives of others around her. How could Victor ever blame her for wanting the best for those she loved the most? In a way, Eva had even felt like she was doing right by Victor. She had wanted him to have children of his own, and Eva could never have given that to him. The only person she hadn't done right by was herself.

"Eva found me lost and depressed, and she left me the same way. My life fell apart and I soon realized I couldn't function without her in my life. The only thing I had left were the memories of the time we'd spent together. I wrote down the memories as accurately as I could recall, trying to find a way to preserve the feelings we shared. I read them over again whenever I felt like I was slipping into a depression. I fantasized about what my life would be like if things had worked out. I wrote down these little fantasies about anything I could think of that I'd like to do with her. These fantasies eventually became stories because my thoughts never ended. When I finished, I had a book's worth of material to work with. I brought our relationship to life because I couldn't have her. I wanted Eva to know how I pictured a life together with her and that no matter what happened, she will always be special to me. I wouldn't have any of this if it wasn't for her."

Juliette got out of her seat, leaving Fred still looking for her hand. She walked behind Victor and Eva, wrapping her arms around them. She pulled Victor and Eva in for a hug, squeezing them tightly.

"The two of you are beautiful," Juliette said aloud. "Do you know how amazing it is that your relationship was purely emotional? To be selfless enough not to force or push each other into anything more than talking? That takes a great deal of strength on both parts. You took the time to learn about each other first, without anything physical involved. Your relationship is based off your innermost personal feelings, and the physical part is only a bonus."

Camille looked at Eva and Victor, smiling with happiness. She hadn't seen Victor this happy since he was a little boy. Her heart was bursting with joy for her grandson and Eva.

Vito was proud of the man his grandson had become and of the girl that he had met. Vito prided himself on being a great judge of character, and he could see that Eva was perfect for his grandson. He felt it was a matter to celebrate.

Vito screamed aloud, "Let's hear some music, Paul!"

CHAPTER 16

The sun went down on Victor and Eva's welcoming party and even without sunlight, their families refused to stop the party. The lights around the porch shone brightly, along with a group of fireflies that lit the way. Classic music blasted over the speakers from Paul's Victrola that he had dragged into the backyard. Without waiting a moment, Camille and Victor started dancing on the porch. They were followed by Paul, who danced next to the Victrola, ready to change the record when the song was finished. After Paul, Fred guided Juliette off her seat and onto the middle of the porch for a dance. Eva and Victor watched their families dance before getting up themselves. They took in the moment, knowing it would be the last time they ever saw them like this. Together, they danced the night away, bringing back the memories of Paul's legendary parties. This special meeting, granted by God himself, struck Victor and Eva in different ways.

Eva loved the idea of having a big family. One where everyone cared what you were doing, where you were going, and especially whether you were hungry. She loved that Victor's family appreciated her for the strong woman she was. They loved her as much as Victor did because they knew the positive impact she had on his life. Combining that with the warmth and memories of Eva's own family, mainly her grandparents, made her feel completely at home. If she had a choice, she'd never want to leave again. Paul's house was the retreat she needed from her life.

Victor loved how different Juliette and Fred were from his family. It was a sort of culture shock for him, because he was used to a loud and brash family his whole life. Fred and Juliette were both soft-spoken people who were comfortable with anything. They hardly ever yelled or screamed, which was a form of relief for him. No matter what, Victor still loved his crazy family for what they were. Yelling or not, they had treated him well. He had grown up with support from each of them, and he never forgot that.

The night grew darker, and the music died down. Victor and Eva ignored the idea of ever leaving this place, but they could feel an end was coming soon. Neither of them mentioned it, even though they felt their worries creeping up on them.

Paul checked a clock nearby, knowing too that this special day was coming to an end. He pulled Victor aside, not wanting Eva to hear what he had to say.

"It's time to go," Paul said sadly.

"But we just got here!" Victor replied.

Paul shook his head and pointed to the sky.

"I know, but it's not up to me. There's a higher power that we all have to answer to."

Victor hugged Paul tightly. He whispered to him.

"Don't tell Eva," he said. "Let everything fade away on its own. I don't want her to get upset. Saying goodbye will be too painful."

Paul patted Victor on the back, letting him know he acknowledged his request.

"Can you give me one more dance with Eva?" Victor asked.

Without saying anything Paul played a final song.

Victor walked over to Eva, who was talking to her grandparents. He got down on one knee and grabbed her hand.

"May I have this dance?" he asked her.

"You're not asking me to marry you?" Eva replied sadly.

"One step at a time," Victor joked.

Eva smiled and followed Victor onto the patio. They danced along to "The Way You Look Tonight," cheek to cheek. Halfway through the dance, Eva rested her head on Victor's shoulder. She was completely comfortable, slowly rocking along to the music in his arms. With their eyes closed, they danced as slow as their bodies would allow them.

Victor held Eva tightly in an effort to stop her from leaving, but he knew the magic of this world was too powerful even for his strong-willed heart. This time, he could not bend fate with his very hands. He was a helpless victim to God and the world he created for him.

Anxiously waiting for the moment to pass, Victor blinked, and Eva was gone. The warmth of her body disappeared. The only sign left of her was the imprint of her chin on his shoulder. He looked back and saw only Paul standing on the porch. Juliette, Fred, Vito, and Camille had disappeared too. It was almost as if they had never been there in the first place.

"Will it hurt?" Victor asked Paul.

"Will what hurt?"

"Dying."

Paul smiled at Victor.

"Not a bit."

As Paul finished his words, Victor noticed an instant change. First, he couldn't hear the wind blowing in the night, the rustling of the leaves on trees, and even the buzzing of a nearby fly. Second, his sense of smell left, and he was unable to smell the freshly-cut grass and the charred meats that were cooked on the grill. Lastly, Victor lost his sight as the world around him faded to black.

CHAPTER 17

Eva jolted to life when her head sunk under the water of the bathtub. She splashed around the water in shock, pushing herself up to the surface. Eva gasped for air, trying to catch her breath. Stanley heard the commotion and banged on the door to the bathroom.

"Eva!" Stanley screamed. "Are you okay?"

Eva couldn't answer him as she choked on the bath water.

"I'm knocking down the door!" Stanley said worriedly.

Eva heard a large thump, but the door didn't budge. She finally answered after her coughing fit was over.

"I'm okay," she said with a hoarse voice. "I fell asleep in the bathtub."

Stanley banged on the door again, this time in anger.

"Are you out of your mind?" he yelled. "You're going to kill yourself like that."

Eva climbed out of the bathtub and patted herself dry with a towel. She opened the door to the bathroom and found Stanley's nose at the tip of where the door was supposed to be. He looked worried about Eva for the first time in years.

"I'm worried about you," Stanley said.

Eva didn't answer him. Wrapped in a towel, she charged past him. She picked underwear, socks, and a bra from her dresser, then scurried to the closet. Eva searched through an endless number of hangers. She stopped at one specific emerald green dress and flung it off the hanger and over her shoulder. Eva marched back into the bathroom with her clothes in hand, slamming the door behind her.

Stanley jumped at the large bang the door made. He hadn't spoken to Eva since their fight yesterday. What could he do to take back what he said? He had to make up for years of neglecting her without even realizing it. His wife was in love with another man, and there was nothing he could do. He could only hope that Eva still loved him enough to continue working on their relationship, even if a part of her would always love Victor. In Stanley's mind, Victor was already dead, so he knew that he had the upper hand.

"How can we not talk about yesterday?" Stanley yelled.

The door swung open and Eva slowly walked out of the bathroom towards Stanley. There was a lump in Stanley's throat when he saw the look on his wife's face. He could see the throbbing anger in her right temple.

"Let's talk about it," Eva said calmly. "Let's talk about how I haven't even existed for half of our marriage. Let's talk about how I raised three children by myself while you were at work. There's nothing wrong with that, but I could have used a little appreciation. Just a little! That's the only thing I would ever ask for. You never cared if my feet were cold. You never cared if I smoked or drank. You just shrugged your shoulders and said, 'She'll get it over it.' Yes, I go through those bouts often, and I'm glad you didn't pressure me to stop. But I wanted to at least see that you cared! A little tiny bit of worry would have been nice. It's amazing that, even though I've been living with you for over twenty years, I've never felt lonelier for half that time."

Stanley crossed his arms, not taking in most of what Eva said. In his eyes, he provided for her, gave her a great life, and never disrespected her. What did he have to be sorry for? So he had some shortcomings. No one is perfect. That isn't a reason to end a marriage. Stanley could see it in Eva's eyes that there was no going back from what he'd said. The love between them was gone and the only thing holding them together was their children.

Eva had always appreciated what Stanley had done for her and the way he had changed her. He had plucked her from an unstable life and gave her the world. She looked back positively on their relationship even if the romance wasn't always there. Raising three successful children in this crazy world is an accomplishment for any parent. The only problem was, for Stanley, she was only a wife, not a best friend and lover.

"We have children together," Stanley said coldly. "What are you going to tell them? That you left their father for a famous author who's half dead and in a coma? All because he wrote some books about you?"

The more Stanley called Victor "dead," the more Eva hated him by the second. He'd been saying Victor was going to die constantly. It seemed like Stanley was wishing Victor dead, which would make sense given the present situation. Eva would have no choice but to stay with him then. Where else would she go? She would never risk upsetting her children this much if Victor died, even if they did have lives of their own now.

She grinned through her teeth. "Don't you dare say that again."

Eva took a deep breath, keeping herself from getting too angry. "And they're not some books."

Stanley was amazed at the way Eva defended Victor. He couldn't say anything bad about him. What was it she saw in him? That was the question he kept asking himself. What was it that drew her to him? Why him?

Eva picked up her purse from the floor, threw it over her shoulder, and continued trudging towards the door. Stanley marched after her, finally having enough of what he deemed to be total nonsense.

"Eva!" Stanley screamed. "If you walk out that door, our marriage is over. More than twenty years of a relationship, thrown away. Think about the kids! Think about our lives. Do you want to grow old alone? Stay with me here. Forget about that guy."

She stopped right in her tracks. Stanley knew that if he kept mentioning the children, she would be guilted into staying. He knew that one of Eva's biggest fears was to be alone. If Victor died and she didn't have Stanley, Eva would be by herself. Stanley had no choice but to show her these potential realities, even if it was brutal and manipulative to mention. He would do anything to keep her, and he went about it the way any desperate person would.

Stanley's words took a few moments to sink in. Eva's eyes glazed over as the vivid memories of her life flashed before her eyes. Eva remembered the abuse she had faced, the deep struggle to find inner peace in her childhood home. Those traumatic events were engrained in her memory, along with negative feelings that never left her. They lay dormant in the back of her mind, waiting to be awoken again. She'd never wish this pain on anyone. Her biggest fear was to live totally alone, without someone to love her. Eva would do anything to avoid feeling that emptiness, or causing someone to feel it. Would leaving her husband give her children that same feeling? Would they question the way they had been raised and their childhood the way Eva had? This was important to think about. There was plenty she wanted to say, but only this came out.

"I love you, Stanley," Eva said warmly. "I love you because you were good to me and you're the father of my children."

Eva took a deep breath, swallowing the lump in her throat. She knew what she was about to say next would hurt him, but it needed to be said. They couldn't live a lie any longer.

She continued, "The love I feel for Victor is a different kind, one like I've never felt before in my life. It's the kind of love that makes me feel safe wherever I go. A day doesn't go by that I question if he cares about me. Victor worried about me at every turn. He could tell if there was one hair out of place on my head…. And I quickly grew to have that same love for him. To mend his tortured soul the way he did mine. Even though I never told him, I worried about him constantly. I knew if there was the slightest change in the tone of his voice. I knew him, better than he knew himself."

Stanley was awestruck that not a single thing he said seemed to visibly faze her. Eva was not one to lie, hardly ever hiding the way she felt. For her, it took too much work and effort to fake emotional reactions. Stanley knew this about his wife.

Her eyes were steel blue. The skin on her cheeks tightened as these cold words passed over her lips. Stanley could see that she took no pleasure in saying this.

"I don't think you could ever love me the way he does," Eva said with complete assurance. "It's something you can't describe with words. He could barely describe it in his own novels."

Eva kissed Stanley on the cheek.

"Goodbye, Stanley," she said softly.

She turned her back to her husband of over twenty years and walked down the steps of her home.

Stanley said nothing and turned his own back to her, quietly walking into his bedroom and shutting the door behind him. He was ashamed of himself for not being more careful about losing his wife's love. Stanley couldn't believe the way he'd been acting the past couple days. How could he assert that his wife wasn't special enough to write a book about? Deep in his heart, Stanley knew this was for the best. He himself was afraid of change in his own life. The convenience of Eva was too easy for him, and he enjoyed that. Now, it was his turn to see what it was like without her.

Thoughts of regret didn't swarm Eva's mind any longer, as she was confident in her choice. Even if Victor never pulled though, she'd never truly be alone because Victor lived in her heart. He had promised never to leave her, and she believed him. Victor had lived inside of her for all of those ten years. They may have physically been apart, but Eva had never been truly alone.

The steps below her feet felt light, like she was walking on clouds. Eva felt a heavy burden lift off her shoulders. Her mind wasn't racing with thoughts; instead she felt relief.

Eva checked not once, but twice that the unaddressed letter she carried was still in her copy of *Lady Chatterley's Lover*. It was still perfectly sealed with no bent edges. It looked like it had been written that very same day. The dream, vision, or premonition she had had the night before, she didn't know what to call it, had inspired her to finally open the letter. She'd sworn many years ago to never think about the letter again—that is, until the time was right to give it to its rightful owner. That letter contained things so personal about Eva's life and she knew there was only one person who ever deserved to hear it.

"I'm almost there," Eva thought as she made her way towards the door. "I'm coming, Victor. I'm free to be yours now."

The house phone rang loudly with a ring that seemed to be amplified as the wave of sound hit Eva's ears. She planted her feet into the ground and turned to glance at the phone.

"Could it be one of my children?" she thought. "Hardly anyone called here besides them."

Her heart began to beat rapidly as she anxiously walked back over to the phone. Eva's intuition was telling her to pick up the phone, but she was too late. The loud rings suddenly stopped. She looked up the dark stairs of her home and heard her husband talking on the line.

"Hello?" Stanley answered grumpily.

"This is St. Peregrine's Hospital," said the receptionist. "We're calling for a Ms. Eva Abrams?"

"What is this call regarding?"

"Ms. Abrams requested we notify her about Victor Esposito if it was an absolute emergency."

Stanley forced away a smile. He felt guilty at the idea of finding some pleasure in the death of this man, but he couldn't help it.

"She's not here at the moment, but can I take a message? I'm her husband."

"Tell her to hurry here now because there are some complications with Victor's condition. I'm not at liberty to say anything more."

"That's sad to hear," Stanley said with a sigh of relief. "I'll inform her of the news."

The receptionist from the hospital hung up the phone. Stanley lay down in his bed with his hands cradling the back of his head. He crossed his feet, relaxing with a deep breath.

Eva tried listening to Stanley's phone call but couldn't make out what it meant. She quickly dismissed her nervousness and left the house. There were still lingering thoughts about the call that she pushed away. Eva felt something wasn't right, but she held out hope it had nothing to do with Victor.

CHAPTER 18

The darkness around Victor slowly came to a dim light as he shook off the drowsiness to notice he was sleeping in his own bed. Victor recognized his plush blue sheets and ripped the covers off to find his legs underneath. He wiggled his toes, feeling the life inside him. He leaned over to the left side of the bed, looking at the dark outline of a lamp. The light flickered on, revealing that he was in his apartment.

A clock on the wall said it was four o'clock in the morning. He remembered waking up around the same time the morning he was shot. Victor's apartment looked the way he'd left it. There was a stack of newspapers in the corner near the bed, all of them already read. Victor checked the food in his refrigerator, looking at the dates of milk he'd bought. Everything was normal, but Victor was smart enough to know that this wasn't one big dream. What happened with Eva couldn't have been fake and he refused to believe he had imagined any of it.

Victor noticed a newspaper wrapped in plastic that sat on a glass table in the middle of his apartment. He unwrapped it. The front cover showed a picture of Victor at a book signing event, where he was waving to fans. Victor read the headline aloud, "Writer Victor Esposito Shot While Saving Two Lives."

Little pieces of the newspaper rained around him like snow-flakes as he tore the paper to shreds in furious anger. He looked up at the ceiling, not knowing what test was coming his way.

"I thought I learned my lesson!" Victor screamed aloud. "Can I just go home already?"

A loud demonic laugh boomed from behind him, unlike the laugh of any normal person. It was too heavy, filled with bass and no life. Victor wasn't scared of the voice. It seemed cartoonish to him. There was nothing that could surprise him anymore, so he fearlessly turned around to greet the person.

Louis was pouring himself a drink at the kitchen counter. Victor's attention didn't turn to Louis; he instead focused on the bottle. Louis happened to be drinking Victor's thirty-year-old Macallan, which was worth over five thousand dollars. Victor wasn't fazed by this, knowing Louis was trying to get on his nerves.

"Enjoying that drink?" Victor asked playfully.

Louis took a sip, letting the scotch swim around the crystal glass.

"That sure is a good quality scotch."

"Choke on it," Victor mumbled.

Louis heard his comment but chose to ignore it.

"Drink?" Louis asked pointing to a second glass.

Victor shook his head.

As Louis walked closer to Victor, an unnerving clank his heeled shoe made on the floor rang in Victor's ear. There was something about Louis that Victor didn't like from the second he saw him. He remembered that chilly feeling when Louis touched his shoulder in the elevator.

"Who are you?" Victor asked.

"Me?" Louis chuckled again. "I'm an angel."

"I didn't know angels drank scotch and wore suits."

"A different kind of angel."

Victor pointed to the door. He had had enough of Louis following him around.

"Get out of my house."

Louis agreed without fighting.

"I will. I know there's no convincing you that you've been treated poorly in your life. For what? To end up half dead in a coma. It's such a shame. You could have been great. How great could a man be without the use of his cock?"

Victor ignored Louis's comments, although they stung. He did wonder why somebody like him would have spent his life in sadness, then get shot on top of it. He thought of Eva in this moment, worried he would be denied her love. Victor felt if that were to happen again, he'd be better off dead.

The negative thoughts filled his mind, as Louis started to manipulate Victor. He preyed on people like Victor, the hopeless romantics of the world who thought that the power of their love could best even the worst circumstances life brings. Louis knew that it took a special kind of person to persevere and have faith in God even when life takes one's faith away.

"Please, God," Victor thought, "give me the strength to get through this. I have faith. These thoughts aren't real. They're just in my head."

"God can't help you now," Louis answered like he had heard Victor think.

Victor still refused to respond, which he felt would give life to Louis and his thoughts. Louis quietly walked towards the door of Victor's apartment, knowing Victor was stewing. He stopped at the foot of the door.

"You could have had all the fun in the world. Money, broads, health, and fame. People would kill to have your life, and you chose to give it up because of a woman? What kind of a man are you?"

Victor didn't answer, only looking lost in his own thoughts. "Did I truly waste my life away loving someone who I could never have? Was there ever really a happy ending for me? The only place this got me was dead."

Louis was getting to Victor. He failed to see that, in reality, these thoughts were only a figment of his imagination. Of course, there was some truth to it. The truth was that Victor was afraid of these things happening. He feared it the same way a person fears a car crash or bungie jumping. It could happen, but it's never set in stone. The idea of the fear held Victor back.

Victor often felt that if he had faith in God, he could get through anything. Everything, both good and bad, happened for a reason. There was always a means to an end. He lived by those words, hoping that one day he would overcome his eternal sadness and live in some sort of happiness. He was holding on to his faith by a thread. The fear was taking over his mind, forcing him to act impulsively.

"Faith over works," Victor told himself.

Louis had a knack for tapping into the biggest fears of people, making them see a reality that was skewed. He was the very demon that Eva spoke of. It wasn't the kind that a person sees in horror movies; instead, it was the kind of demon that brings people down, a force denying them of the true happiness life could bring. Louis could see Victor was about to crack, and that strong willpower he'd sustained his entire life was withering down to nothing. Louis wanted to finish off his work, saving Victor's biggest fear for last.

"All those years you spent alone," Louis said softly. "Coming home to an empty bed, with no warm smile or kiss, no hot plate of dinner waiting for you after a long day of work."

Sweat started to drip down the side of Victor's forehead. Eva's words repeated in his mind. He kept seeing the look on her face, with tears in her eyes, as she held his hand and spoke the words that had finally made him see he meant everything to her. Her words repeated in his mind over and over again.

"Ask me not to hurt you." Answering with, "I'll never hurt you, Victor."

Louis pounced on this thought like a jackal, hearing every one of Victor's thoughts.

"She promised to never hurt you, huh? Can't tell you how many times I've heard that one before."

Victor still said nothing, holding on to the promise Eva made him. He trusted her implicitly, but his natural reaction was to run. He was too afraid to find out the answer. It was cowardly in a way, but what man could withstand the pain of being betrayed by someone he'd give his life for? There had been too much hurt in the past, and Louis knew that.

"Faith over works," Victor thought to himself again.

"I donate to charity every year," Louis joked. "I still got cast away. So much for that investment."

Victor finally spoke, gathering the courage to face his attacker.

"A man without a heart is a man without a cock," Victor said stoutly.

"What are you trying to say, boy?"

"I say what I mean, and I mean what I say," Victor joked. "All I hear is you whining because you don't have a heart, which means you don't have a cock either."

Louis put his hand on Victor's shoulder and gripped it tightly.

"Are you really trying to measure your penis with the devil?"

"No, it's not about measuring. It's the perception. The meaning behind the words."

"What's this perception?"

"This money, fame, and the 'broads' that you speak of, are manifestations of anger because you feel emasculated from being cast down from heaven. Translation...you think you have a small penis."

Louis dug the knife in deeper, knowing he had Victor only moments away from cracking. Louis wanted to prove that he could take away Eva's love. He wanted to prove to God that, after all that he'd given Victor, he would still not believe in Eva. After the signs, visions, and even seeing his dead family, Louis knew Victor would still succumb to fear.

"So you spent a life wallowing in your own self-pity over a woman who you could never have and I'm the guy with no dick?" Louis chuckled.

"You know," Victor said calmly, "I don't really care about anything you're saying to be honest."

"Only guys with no dick think that they could buy a woman's love."

The smile was wiped off Louis's face instantly. He'd seen Victor practically biting his nails only a few moments ago. Louis didn't have the slightest clue what could have changed in a matter of seconds.

"Are you so sure?"

Victor nodded.

"You can't buy Eva's love. Anything I'd ever given her was a nice gesture, and I'm sure it made her feel special.... But it never had an impact on how she felt about me. She would never care if I didn't think of buying her anything. Eva didn't fall in love with the gifts I got her. She fell in love with the person I am. She fell in love with the way I think, the way I operate. Both good and bad. She fell in love with my soul."

Louis sensed that the worry was leaving Victor's mind. He could see that he was slowly becoming more confident in the wake of his death. Victor trusted his judgment of the person Eva was, but even if what Louis was saying was true, had Victor lived his life in a way that was so bad?

"I spent my whole life waiting for a woman like Eva," Victor said proudly. "If I die, I can say that I left earth knowing I loved someone. I can die saying that I did my best to show Eva how much I love her. Whether it was wrong or right, I don't know, but I tried. I tried, to the best of my ability, to love someone else. To me, that's the greatest reward life could have ever given me. Nothing else matters."

Louis finally lost his collected attitude. Victor's hopefulness infuriated him, and for good reason too. There are millions of other people that would be content with a life of fame and fortune, but to Victor, it meant nothing. Why was he different? That was why Louis had taken an interest in Victor. He could see that there was only one desire his heart had.

"The money! The fame! All mean nothing to you?" Louis screamed.

"What's a life worth living if you can't enjoy it with someone you love?"

"You could buy love!" Louis screamed again. "You can buy the love of whatever woman you want."

Victor smiled and shook his head.

"Not Eva," he said confidently. "Any other woman, I'd entertain the idea, but not her. If I don't make it out of this, I can die a happy man. I know that Eva loves me, and that's the only thing that matters to me. I'll never truly be alone, whether I leave this world or not. She'll always live on in my heart."

CHAPTER 19

E va drove into the hospital parking lot for the fourth day in a row, amazed by how much more complicated her life had become in only four days. The sound of her car's engine slowly died as she turned the key. She sat helplessly in the car, mentally preparing herself to see Victor hooked up to machines.

"Is this one big bad dream?" Eva asked herself.

She thought about the night before, the "dream" she'd had about making love to Victor. How could it feel so real to make love in a dream? It felt like her body actually experienced what happened. She woke up with the blissful pleasure of a morning after intense sex. Eva smiled at the nasty thoughts running through her mind, but quickly shook off the vivid images before leaving the car.

The doors swung open as Eva entered the hospital. The receptionist sitting at a desk nearby looked at Eva with puppy-like eyes that drooped down to the floor with sadness. Eva had grown to know her well after the first time she visited the hospital. The rest of the hospital staff called her Andrea, but Eva gave her the nickname Andy. Andrea didn't quite roll off her tongue the correct way, and she felt awkward messing up her name constantly.

Eva walked right past Andy without a word. She could see that Eva didn't seem to be upset, and this was shocking to her. She shouted Eva's name, who instantly hurried back to the desk.

"Ms. Abrams!" Andy yelled.

"Yes?"

"Did you receive my message?"

"What message?"

Before saying another word, Eva thought back to the phone call that Stanley had answered. Her cheeks grew red with furious anger when she realized Stanley had decided to have the last laugh, making a last ditch attempt to punish her. The anger quickly fled when she realized why a call from the hospital had probably come. On the verge of tears, Eva pushed Andy to give her an explanation.

"What's wrong? What message? Tell me?"

Tears came to Andy's eyes. She couldn't stop shaking her head with sorrow. Before the receptionist could even answer her question, Eva ran to Victor's room. Her feet thundered against the floor, making a loud clacking sound as she made her way towards the elevator. Eva aggressively pressed the button, anxiously watching the numbers at the top of the elevator light up.

Inside was Louis, picking his teeth with a toothpick. Eva saw there was someone else in the elevator but disregarded him completely. Eva slammed her finger on the button that had a large number three on it as Louis attentively watched her.

Eva suddenly felt chilly, which was surprising after the way she had run to the elevator bank. A cold shiver was sent down her spine when Louis tapped her shoulder to get her attention.

"Are you okay, miss? You seem a little disturbed."

Eva didn't answer him. The elevator seemed like it was taking a little too long to get to the third floor.

"You're here for Victor?" Louis asked with a smile.

Eva turned to him with fire in her eyes. Her teeth were clanking together from the adrenaline pumping through her veins.

"I know who you are. You have no business being here."

Louis laughed snidely.

"Oh, but I do. Didn't you hear? Victor's not doing too well."

"I'm not afraid of you," Eva yelled. "I'm not afraid of you, and I'm sure Victor wasn't either."

"He wasn't afraid of me, and then he got shot. Victor should have listened to me. He should have had his fun while he had the chance. What does it pay to live your life being a good man when it's so short? He didn't enjoy anything. He was too busy being miserable over *love*."

Louis shook his head, laughing at his own remarks. He continued, "Where did love ever get Victor? It practically got him killed, in a life of loneliness, and constant pain. What for? What God would hurt such a beautiful soul? Your God, I guess. But hey, what do I know? I've only been around for a few thousand years."

Eva knew that Louis was a fallen angel, one that walked the earth in search of those who don't have enough faith in a higher power. No matter the religion or creed, these types of demons look to take advantage of those who have lost their faith, those who have experienced tragedies and question why something so horrible could happen to them. Eva had always believed in the presence of demons on this earth, tempting one to believe the wrong things and to stray away from hope and love, the core of what makes us human beings.

These words hurt Eva. She was beginning to blame herself for what happened to Victor. Had she truly condemned him to a life of misery? She thought back to her dream again and how happy their families were together. No one else but God could have made such a thing happen.

The elevator door opened. Eva ran out, once again choosing not to acknowledge what Louis had said. He smiled as the elevator doors closed, enjoying the pain and worry that he felt Eva experiencing. Louis saw that he couldn't get through to Victor or Eva. Both had fended him off with the courage behind their faith in God and their love. Neither had let his hurtful words impact their lives or feelings. He was powerless in the wake of true love.

From the moment the elevator opened its doors, Eva could hear the commotion from down the hall. Doctors were yelling at one another, Barbara was wailing outside of the hospital room, and the machines keeping Victor alive were sounding off like alarm bells. None of this seemed to be leading up to a positive answer, but Eva didn't want to believe anything until she saw it herself.

She barreled past the crowd of hospital staff standing by the door anxiously watching what was happening. Eva passed over Barbara, who was face down on the tile floor, crying, between the hallway and the door.

"My son," Barbara screamed with tears in her eyes. "They're taking my son from me."

Barbara's cheeks and eyes were red from crying, and one side of her face was completely imprinted into the tile floor. The tears streaming down her face showed no sign of stopping.

"Why?" she wailed. "Why does it have to be my son? He's such a good boy. My little baby boy."

Eva caught the attention of the doctors standing over Victor, noticing the heart rate monitor was flat. Victor's breathing tubes had been removed, and a nurse was manually pumping oxygen into his lungs. Another nurse was rubbing an adhesive gel over the defibrillator machine paddles.

"Clear!" one nurse shouted.

The nurse shocked Victor's chest. The shocks went through his body and had no effect. He still remained lifeless.

"Clear!" the nurse shouted again.

Eva watched as they continued to pump Victor's body with shocks of electricity. Every shock had the same result. He wasn't breathing or moving. Victor was lying there helplessly. A man who always went out of his way to help others had no one to save him.

"Clear!" the nurse shouted for the third time.

Like the first day she saw him in the hospital, Eva felt her weight collapse beneath her knees. Everything in the room moved in slow motion as if it were a scene from a movie. The noises were drowned out by Barbara's screaming and the rest of voices sounded like blurry words that didn't make any sense.

"No," Eva mumbled to herself.

The tears were now pouring down her face, causing her cheeks to swell from the sadness. Her eyes were swollen, her heart was pumping out of her chest, and her head was throbbing with pain. Eva had never felt this out of control before in her life, like she didn't want to live anymore. She wanted to go back to Paul's house, knowing she was nothing without Victor here.

Eva crawled over to Barbara on the floor, holding her head in her lap. Eva tried to be strong for her. They were both losing the most important person in their lives. Together, they both cried as the nurses tried everything to revive Victor.

"Clear!" the nurse shouted for the fourth and final time.

The nurse shocked Victor's body one last time. Victor lay motionless, his eyes still closed and the heart monitor still ringing flat.

"Why couldn't it be me instead?" Eva mumbled through her tears. "Let me take his place, God. Please let me take his place. I love him. Don't let him go."

The nurses pronounced Victor dead in a matter of seconds. They turned to Eva and Barbara, offering their condolences.

Laura entered the room and gasped, shocked to see that Victor had passed. Tears filled her eyes as she thought about the wonderful stories Victor had created in his life, stories that inspired her to find true love in her own life. Laura saw Eva and Barbara wailing on the floor, holding each other tightly.

Eva tried to collect her thoughts, pulling herself up from the floor. She guided Barbara to a seat nearby, carrying her with Laura's help. They left Barbara in the seat, curled up in a ball. Eva picked her bag up from the floor and reached inside to pull out the unmarked letter from her copy of *Lady Chatterley's Lover*.

She pulled a chair next to Victor, practically slamming it down on the tile floor. Eva sat down and ripped open the pristine, unmarked letter she'd been keeping for ten years. Laura paid attention to every one of Eva's movements, curious to see what she was going to do next. The doctors in the room lurked near the doorway, wondering what Eva was going to do with the letter as well. The people in the room slowly started to make the connection between Victor and Eva. They thought about the way Eva carried herself, coupled with the emotional and sexual attachment to Victor. Her flowing blonde hair and bright eyes that changed color and country girl looks. She was the living version of Victor's novel girl or girls, the famous trademark to his stories. It made sense, that Eva had been the one that got away, the inspiration that sparked his entire career, the only woman who had captivated his soul, and the only woman he had ever loved.

With her hands shaking, Eva unfolded three pieces of loose-leaf paper with writing in blue ink. Her voice trembled with the passing of every word. She felt like there was a rock in her throat. Her tears smudged the ink, making the letter hard to read. Eva read the letter aloud, hoping that Victor would somehow be able to hear every word. This was her gift to him and the way she showed her love. This was what he had been waiting for.

To my Victor,

If you're reading this, it means I finally had the courage to send you this letter. I decided to write this letter and seal it the same day that I told you never to see me again. I want to let you know what I've been feeling since we met. I want to tell you all the things I should have said, the words I was screaming in my mind and never had the courage to actually say. I was too afraid of the consequences. I didn't want anyone to get hurt, but I never real- ized that I was hurting you all along. I always felt that you deserved to know how I felt about you and what you did for me.

Victor, you have no idea how much you mean to me. Without knowing it, you saved my life. You found a way to stop the internal bleeding that was my depression. You made me see how special I am. I want to tell you about my life, things I've never told anyone before. I'm going to explain how you saved me from myself. Now you'll know the real story of Eva Bolton-Abrams and how she fell in love with you.

From an early age, I spent most of my life in sadness. My father left my family to start another one. My mother married another man and left me to fend for myself. When my parents did come around, I faced daily abuse, both physical and verbal. The vulgar names constantly fill my mind even now, dragging me down to a place I never want to revisit.

When I turned eighteen, I left home, only to find myself struggling once again. My dream was to be a country star. I sang and played guitar in almost any dive bar I could find. I left my demo at record labels every other week, hoping and praying for a break.

That big break never came. I was stuck moving from apartment to apartment and job to job.

There were some days I tried to stay happy that I had a place to sleep peacefully. I fell in love twice in my life. Once, it was with a fellow musician, who I dated for almost seven years. He was more like a best friend than an actual boyfriend. We eventually parted for the better. I met my husband soon after.

As I got older, my depression grew stronger. I still can't put my finger on the reason, but my quality of life slowly diminished. Maybe it's because, from the day I was born, I've always felt alone. Life took a toll on me, one that I thought could never be fixed. I thought I'd spend the rest of my life trying to escape from my inner sadness.

I spent day after day falling deeper into the grips of my depression. Not a single person asked about it. Not my husband, not my family, no one. They had to see it was there, because I physically changed as the sadness made its way through me. I'd go through periods of gaining and losing weight. I'd drink to cope with the pain or randomly take up a new vice like smoking, waiting for someone to notice. And no one ever did. Nobody ever heard my cries for help. I never even realized I was sending them until I think back on it now.

The only thing that made me hold on to my sanity was my children. My three beautiful children. One of the few things I pride myself on is being a good mother.

Eventually, my depression took even that away from me. It followed me, like a tiger hunting its prey, wherever I went or whatever I did. The demons in my mind tightened their grip. I could do nothing but pray. I prayed to God every night that these demons would release their grip on my mind. My thoughts kept pushing, provoking, and forcing me to see that there was no escape. I thought I would suffer forever, until one day it dawned upon me that there was only one way out.

Then I met you, the man who helped me learn to love again, and my life changed forever. Because of you, Victor, I found my self-worth. I found a man to love me for exactly who I am, a man who cherished being with me every moment, good or bad. No one has done what you've done for me. No person went out their way for me the way you did. You took the time to listen to me, to appreciate being around me, and to genuinely love me.

I never dreamt about a man buying me a special pair of thermal socks because of the bad circulation in my feet. When you made me the rice balls, I didn't know what to do. The excitement poured out of me. It must have taken you hours to make, carefully wasting your time away on little old me just to put a smile on my face. When you lit that candle, I had nervous butterflies in my stomach. I felt like I was going out on my first date ever.

You wrote books about me. I still can't believe it when I say it. You created stories for the two of us, lives of our own. You created families, children, life, and even death. You wrote about an undying love between two people, one that has inspired millions.

Before that, you spent a year telling me how much you loved me, how much you cared for me, and what it would be like to be with me. I never could say anything back because I felt too guilty. I felt my morality slipping away. I felt a betrayal of my God, my children, and my husband. One day, my children will have lives of their own. My husband seems to live in a world that includes me in it sometimes. My God? Well, He'll just have to forgive me for this one.

I love you, Victor. Yes, I said it. I finally said it. I've never felt so much love for someone before. Every time I saw you, I couldn't take the smile off my face. I enjoyed spending every moment I could with you. Every time you left me, there was a part of me that wanted to beg you to stay. I wanted to put you in my pocket and take you home with me.

For years, I kept your books under my bed—that is, until my children decided to play hide and seek there one day. I liked the idea of having you close to me while I slept. It was my way of cuddling with you. It made the pain of not being able to hold you a little easier.

I wear your socks every single day. I make sure that when I wash one pair, I have another waiting to be worn. It's like I have a piece of you with me wherever I go. That was one of the most thoughtful gifts I'd ever received.

You might not know it, but I'm a writer myself. I wrote a little book of my own. It's a journal, a collection of stories between the two of us. I documented every one of our meetings, so I could always look back and remember them. I wrote down things about you I'd never want to forget—words we exchanged, things you said to me and me to you. I remember almost everything you've told me, aside from maybe a few things.

I know I've always told you that I never knew what a life between us would be like, and that was cynical of me. The truth is, I know exactly what it would be like. I was just too afraid to imagine it. I know that we'd get married at a beautiful church, through the eyes of God. I know that you wouldn't be able to compose yourself on the altar and would *probably cry more than I would. We'd waste no time on the honeymoon, locking ourselves in the bedroom for days at a time. I know that we'd have a bunch of babies. Maybe four. Three boys and a girl. Our first child would be a girl, and she'd help me be a mommy and take care of the wild boys. I know you'd be the greatest dad in the world. You'd spoil me and the kids rotten. There'd be special presents and little trinkets every week. We'd cook and listen to Tony Bennett together. Maybe we'd even take our children to a concert.*

You spoke about your family to me on many days. I loved hearing your stories, and I wish I could have met them all. I know I would have loved your mother, but it seems like there'd be some days where we'd butt heads. I know your grandmother and I would have been the best of friends, like you always said. I would have loved to spend the summers at your Uncle Paul's house, playing cards on the porch while a fire warmed us on a cool summer night.

As for my family, I know they'd love you. You're one of the most personable people I've ever met. You could talk about anything. My grandmother, Juliette, would have adored the way you treated me. She would have respected and loved you as if you were a son of her own. I'm sure you would have loved her cooking too. I wish you had the chance to meet her.

We'd grow old and grey together, looking back on our lives in total happiness. We would go through it all: love, raising children, fights, bills, mortgages, pregnancy, health issues, and maybe grandchildren. Then, as time slowly took the life out of us, we'd move on from this world—not alone, but together.

The truth is, I've pictured this and more. I've fantasized, dreamed, and hoped for a life that had you in it. I knew that when I met you, I had found a man who would love me forever, who would love me no matter if I got into a brutal accident, no matter if I was sick or healthy, and even if I couldn't have children.

You'd always be there to protect me, and I'd love to stay safely in your arms. That feeling is one I've hardly felt in my life. I would do the same and more for you. I'd pick you up if you couldn't walk. I'd comfort you in times of need. I'd be your rock when you needed me to be. Most of all, I would love you, more than you'd ever been loved before. I would never let you go.

I truly believe that we can find a way to be together one day. I know that day is coming sooner, rather than later. When it does, the first thing I'd do is make love to you, something I've been waiting to do since we met, and we'd feel that closeness, intimacy, and love like never before.

Thank you for saving my life and giving me a reason to live again. I pray that I have the courage to send you this letter one day. I think I will, when the time is right. Until then, remember, you're mine. God made you for me.

With love,
Your Eva

The crowd around Eva and Victor grew larger as she finished reading her letter. They saw the emotion pouring out of every word that rolled off her tongue. It was like one of Victor's many love stories had come to life. The scene reminded each and every person there of a storybook love. When she finished reading, her letter was filled with teardrops. The paper was so thin, it was one movement away from a rip. Eva looked up from the paper and at Victor.

The doctors pronounced Victor dead at twelve o'clock in the afternoon on Saturday, the fifth of August, in front of his mother and the love of his life, Eva Abrams.

CHAPTER 20

The doctors, nurses, and other bystanders from the hospital refused to leave, watching Eva sit next to Victor's lifeless body. They cried along with her and Barbara, mourning the loss of a great man. More than that, they mourned the loss of a love that never got to be fulfilled.

Eva pushed Victor gently, hoping her touch would send its own shockwaves to his heart and wake him up.

"You have to wake up," Eva mumbled. "I promise I'll be here to take care of you, just like how you took care of me. We can take care of each other."

Eva pushed him again.

"You can't leave me alone."

The people around her cried.

"I'll sing for you," Eva cried. "I'll sing the song you always wanted me to sing for you. I won't feel embarrassed anymore. Watch!"

Eva sang a verse from Olivia Newton-John's "Hopelessly Devoted to You," a favorite of Victor's.

Eva looked to Victor when she finished singing, hoping what he dubbed her angelic voice would bring him back, but that failed too. Eva turned to one of the nurses who was still in the room.

"Could you try one more time?" Eva asked as the tears dripped down her cheeks.

The nurse shook her head with sadness, realizing it was pointless.

"I'm sorry," the nurse said. "It's too late." Eva turned to Laura helplessly.

"Please," Eva said, crying. "Try again. I could never leave him alone."

Laura looked to the approval of a doctor standing nearby, who nodded in agreement. The doctor, though he had a hopeless look, agreed to continue working on Victor.

"We'll work on him for five more minutes," the doctor said sadly.

Laura fired up the defibrillator machine, placing the adhesive gel on the paddles one more time. Eva held Victor's hand and made the sign of the cross, mumbling a little prayer under her breath.

"Please give him another chance."

Eva stepped back away from Victor for a moment.

"Clear," Laura said with a crack in her voice.

She placed the paddles on Victor's chest and shocked him. The nurse waited a few moments before shocking him again. Eva desperately stared at the monitor, waiting to hear the sound of a beating heart. The monitor was still flat. The nurse readied her hands, preparing to shock Victor yet again.

Eva clenched her hands together, biting her lip with hope. The nurse shocked Victor. His body was still. The nurse readied herself for a third and final shot at reviving Victor.

The nurse didn't bother saying clear again. There wasn't a point. Everyone knew what she was going to say every time she shocked him. As the nurse's hands moved down to Victor's chest for the last time, Eva saw Victor's hand twitch.

"Stop!" Eva screamed.

Eva threw herself in Victor's direction, gently grabbing his hand, desperately waiting for him to notice her touch. The nurse holstered the defibrillator panels and attentively watched Victor with the rest of the room. Springing to life, Barbara jumped out of her seat and ran over to Eva's side.

Victor squeezed Eva's hand with the little strength he had. The heart rate monitor beeped with life, showing that his pulse had come back. His eyes blinked, slowly opening up to look at the world around him. Victor gasped for air like he was drowning in an ocean of water.

The nurses cheered, Dr. Silverstein ran into the room totally astonished, and Barbara was screaming with happiness. Eva was the only person who was silent in the midst of the chaos. She moved in the direction of his sight. Their eyes met for the first time in ten years. Victor looked up at Eva in total confusion, barely able to speak because the breathing tube had scratched his throat. Still delusional from being in the coma, Eva could see that he was panicking. He didn't know where he was or what was going on.

Victor's lips trembled as he tried to gather the strength to speak. Eva's tears were dripping onto his face as she drew closer to him. She could see him twitch as her tears hit his face.

Victor whispered to Eva, "Am I in heaven?"

"No," Eva said calmly.

"I'm not dead?" he asked softly.

"No," Eva said smiling.

Eva could see the wheels trying to turn in his mind. For a moment, she worried his memory wasn't there anymore—that is, until she heard what he said next.

Victor gave a small side smile. "I made a promise," he mumbled. "I promised you I'd never leave."

Eva held his face between her hands, seeing his lips were badly chapped from the breathing tube. Eva rubbed his cheeks with her hands as she watched the color slowly come back to his face.

"You did," Eva said. "I knew you would come back to me."

Victor continued trying to speak, but Eva shushed him quiet. "Now it's my turn to take care of you," Eva said calmly.

The doctors carefully interrupted Eva, hoping to not get on her bad side again. She was pleasant to the doctors this time, grateful for bringing Victor back to her. The doctors asked Victor a series of questions as they were curious to see if he'd loss any major functioning of his body. After a full day of testing, the doctors were astounded to find that his brain was completely intact. He'd lost no major functioning of his body. Victor still needed major rehabilitation from the shot to his chest, but he would be out of the hospital after that. The doctors were confident he would go on to live a totally normal life.

While Victor went through his tests, Eva brought Barbara a steaming hot coffee from the cafeteria. There were bags under Barbara's eyes. Understandably, she'd hardly slept since Victor had been shot. She hadn't even gotten a chance to speak with him because she had been so overcome with emotion.

Eva sat next to her in silence, while they both waited to see Victor once again. Eva felt the dark storm clouds over her mind disperse, causing the trembling in her hands to stop. Her heart, which hadn't stopped racing in days, slowly calmed. Her conscience was no longer guilty. She was now allowed to be open about her feelings for Victor. She was starting her life over again, but this time, with the love of her life. Eva truly believed that there would be only happiness from here on.

Barbara noticed the drastic change in Eva's attitude. There was a skip in her step, and she walked around with her head in the clouds, like there wasn't a worry in her mind. Barbara's curiosity got the best of her, and she couldn't help but to ask what her plans were. Her son's best interest was still her top priority. Barbara would not have Victor go through another major heartbreak.

"So what's the plan?" Barbara asked suspiciously.

"With Victor?" Eva answered sharply.

"Yes."

Eva was just as cunning as Barbara. She could easily read or see a person's true motives. Eva also felt that Barbara had every right to worry about her intentions, though Eva was surprised Barbara had to question her at this point, after what they'd been through together.

"I'm going to take care of him. He deserves someone to be there for him…to love him for the rest of his life. I dedicated most of my life to my family, and now it's my turn to dedicate the rest my life to Victor. He dedicated his soul to me. His life work was because of me. In a lot of ways, I am his life…. And I want my life to be his now. I will do everything I can to make sure he gets better."

Barbara nodded approvingly, unable to conceal her smile any longer. Barbara hugged Eva tightly.

"I finally have a daughter!" she screamed. "The daughter I've always wanted. We can get our nails done together and we can shop together. Oh! We can yell at Victor together. That's my favorite."

Eva giggled. She loved Barbara's personality, even though she could be brash. They were very alike yet, at the same time, very different. Eva was much more easygoing than Barbara, but their fierce personalities could not be rivaled.

Dr. Silverstein finished his examination of Victor, noting multiple times at how astonishing his case was. It was rare for a person to come away with few to no issues after the gunshot wound Victor sustained. He happened to be lucky that the bullet exited his body through the other side. It managed to miss his major internal organs by only a hair. His recovery time would be long, but it was clear he was definitely going to live without any major health issues.

"You're a lucky man," Dr. Silverstein said as he held his chart.

Victor nodded, without a response.

"You're going to come away from this almost unscathed. You don't seem to be happy. Is there a reason?"

Victor nodded.

"Yes," he said shortly. Victor didn't want to be questioned by the doctor. He was anxious to see his mother and Eva.

"I just need to see your chest for a moment. I want to make sure your scars are healing."

Victor could barely move, having never been so delighted to feel pain before. Feeling pain from his surgery meant he was alive. Dr. Silverstein helped him untie the gown he was wearing. Victor looked down to see a large, half-moon-shaped scar near the center of his chest.

Dr. Silverstein could see that the healing was going exceptionally well. He raised his eyebrows at these findings, for this was next to impossible for him to even consider. He thought about the term, "medical miracle." Dr. Silverstein hadn't seen one in his career and this would be the first.

"I'll let you be now," Dr. Silverstein said. He left the room and waved at Eva and Barbara, letting them know they could see Victor.

They both stormed into the room, almost pushing and shoving each other out of the way. Barbara triumphantly was the first to sit in the seat next to Victor's bed. Eva backed off, wanting Barbara to share this special moment with her son.

"My baby," Barbara cried as she hugged him.

Victor cried, thinking about what his mother had gone through these past couple of days. She had so much stress in her life, and the last thing he had ever wanted to do was burden her. For a quick moment, Victor thought about telling his mother about what he'd seen while he was in a coma. She'd love to know that he was with her family.

"Ma," Victor said cautiously, "I have to tell you something."

"What is it, sweetheart?"

Victor paused. He thought about what he was going to do. Was it a vision he saw in his coma? Was he really so close to death that he happened to be in some sort of a purgatory? The questions raced through his mind. How could he ever explain this to her? He had to decide in a split second if he should tell his mother. He battled whether or not it was reality or a vision.

Maybe it was a very powerful dream? He thought about how real it felt.

"I love you, Ma," Victor said with a smile.

Barbara kissed him on the forehead. Standing behind her was Eva, quiet and timid now that he was awake. Since he'd woken up, Eva wondered if he had the same dream as her. Eva wondered if their souls had actually found a way to meet outside of this world. She wondered if he remembered the words they had exchanged.

"Would you mind if I have a few minutes alone with Eva?" Victor asked.

Barbara begrudgingly complied. She thought Victor would want to spend this time with his mother, but she did understand that he hadn't seen Eva in a decade. She left the room without a complaint, though Victor and Eva both knew she was thinking them. Eva kept her distance from Victor out of nervousness. Victor noticed, smiling at her, showing his white teeth.

"What are you doing over there?" Victor said cutely. "Come here."

Eva couldn't look at Victor without smiling back. She slowly walked over to him, like she wanted to tease him, making him more anxious every step she took. Victor gathered his strength, forcing himself to sit upright. He felt the pain flaring throughout his body, especially his chest, but he didn't care. Victor wanted to look his best for Eva. Eva sat on the side of his bed. She placed her hands on his thigh, gently stroking it.

"Victor," she said quietly, "I don't know where to start. I had the weirdest—"

Victor interrupted her, finishing her sentence. He could see she was hesitant.

"Dream?" he answered.

Eva smiled thinking back on it.

"Yes, a wonderful dream. You were there and we...well... we made love...for the first time. It was just as I always imagined it. Then we spent time with our families. My Nana and your grandparents, Camille and Vito. We were at your Uncle Paul's house! There was so much food. Sausage and peppers, apple pie. It was amazing. It felt so real...."

She gently pulled down his gown, curious to see how his scar had healed.

"It wasn't a dream," Victor said happily. "It was real. What we experienced was real. I remember it all too. I remember your Nana and Grandpa Fred. They were playing cards at the table. I remember dancing with you until the wonderful night ended. Then, *of course*, I remember us making love. I remember how captivated I was by you, how I stared at your body, dying to touch you and come closer. It was like the spell a siren would cast."

"How could it be real?" Eva asked. "You were here in the hospital. I was at home in the bathtub. How could we have experienced the same thing? It's impossible."

"Do you love me?" Victor asked.

Eva nodded.

"Of course, I do," she said confidently.

"Did you pray?" he asked.

Eva nodded.

"When you love someone the way that we love each other, it means something. Our souls found each other, no matter the obstacle, even in a matter of life and death. We refused to be separated any longer. Because of our faith and our love, we found a way to be together."

"I thought so too," Eva said. "I was afraid to admit it, or even say it out loud. I was afraid I would have to explain everything to you all over again. I was nervous the circumstances wouldn't be the same. I especially wanted our *night* to be real. That would have been heartbreaking if it had been a dream."

Victor rubbed her back with his hand. He tried to grip her shoulder tightly, showing comfort for her even while he was still sick. Victor felt his emotions coming to the surface. He thought about losing Eva once again. She never said she was going to leave her husband. Now that he was awake, what if she didn't want to? What if she changed her mind? Victor couldn't handle losing her twice.

Eva saw the internal struggle Victor was facing, wiping away the one tear that rolled down his cheek.

"Why are you crying?" Eva asked responding with tears of her own.

"I don't want to lose you again," Victor said. "I heard everything you said to me. I heard you reading me *Lady Chatterley's Lover*. I heard your fight with Cindy. And I even heard you read me your letter. I heard and saw the gifts you gave me."

Victor could see the look of relief on Eva's face. She really wanted him to see her in that moment. Eva wanted him to know how much he had impacted her life, and that letter had been the perfect way.

He continued, "My body died, but my soul was still alive. I can't explain it. I saw this bright flashing yellow light. Then I could hear everything around me. After you stopped reading the letter, a loud booming voice told me I was going to be okay. Then I woke up."

Eva kissed him, not once, not twice, but three times. She held his face between her hands, touching his lips. Her lips felt soft and silky compared to his. The touch of her body to his made his pain slightly go away. Their hearts were fluttering with the freshness of a love sealed with a first kiss. It was all real, just like Victor had said.

Eva response was automatic. As she promised, she was going to dedicate her life to Victor. She wanted to spend the rest of her life with him. She needed to follow her heart, even if the road ahead was going to be difficult. Eva never felt more satisfaction than when these next words passed her mouth.

"I'm yours now," Eva said. "We can have a life together."

These few words told Victor everything he needed to know. Eva had made her decision, and he felt proud that such a strong, beautiful, and intelligent woman was choosing to spend the rest of her days with him. He repeated the words over again in his mind.

"She chose me."

CHAPTER 21

Victor looked out of the window of his new home in the Upper West Side of Manhattan. He now lived in one of Manhattan's historic brownstones. A brutal snowstorm raged outside on Christmas Eve. The streets were covered in fields of white, glistening snow. Victor always enjoyed snowy days. He loved the idea of sleeping next to a wood-burning fire. The steam from the cup of hot tea he was holding reached his nose. He breathed in the steam, taking in the wonderful smell of the green tea. Victor shook his legs and clenched his hands, still in total amazement of his speedy recovery. It had been nine months since he'd woken up from his coma, and so much had changed since then.

A little puppy ran up on the side of Victor's leg, scratching him to get his attention. The puppy's name was Minnie, a Shih Tzu that Victor had adopted when he had moved into his new home. Minnie pulled the cuff of his pants over to a large red couch, situated in front of a beautiful fireplace. Sitting down on the couch with her legs crossed was Eva, reading Victor's latest manuscript. She smiled as Minnie jumped onto her lap, interrupting her train of thought. Eva placed both her legs on Victor's lap, swinging her feet in the direction of his eyesight.

"Look what I'm wearing," she giggled.

Victor instantly noticed the purple thermal socks he'd gotten her many years ago. He held her feet with his hands.

"I'd warm your feet with my hands if I had to," he said softly.

The past nine months had been far from easy, especially with Victor's recovery, but it was still nothing short of a dream. Victor and Eva had finally gotten their chance at life, both working equally hard to build their relationship. They both understood the work it took to help a relationship flourish and grow. Naturally, it came easier for the two of them, because they were drawn to each other.

While Eva often had her head in the clouds, Victor always had something on his mind. When he worried, she calmed him down. When she didn't worry enough, Victor got her thinking. They would laugh for hours on end, finding humor in anything. Fights brewed with the sound of roaring thunder, only for the storm clouds to quickly disperse. A deep longing lay beneath the anger. Their minds were forever in tune, and they always found delicious satisfaction in getting lost in each other.

Eva whipped her legs underneath her and over to the other side of the couch. She leaned on Victor's body, looking into his eyes. Today, her eyes were blue and clear, sparkling with the shine of a woman in love.

"Did you ever think we'd have all of this? Each other, a house, and, of course, a little baby."

Eva slowly stroked her hand over Minnie's soft fur.

"You mean Minnie?" he laughed.

"Hey!" Eva yelled. "She's our little baby."

Minnie jumped between the two of them, bouncing with excitement when she heard the sound of her name. Victor looked at Eva and Minnie. Two of his favorite girls in the whole world were sitting here with him.

"I asked God for this every night," Victor said. "I prayed that somehow, someway, I would have a life with you one day. I always complained about God stiffing me, but I can't anymore. God gave me my life back.... More importantly, he gave me you."

Eva could feel the pounding of his strong heart beating against her ear. She was happy to know that Victor was healthy and that he'd always be here to never leave her alone. Victor was continuously nervous when telling her these intimate feelings. The butterflies in his stomach never went away. Even until this very moment, Victor was nervous about what he was going to do next. He had prepared a special Christmas gift for Eva, and he couldn't wait until tomorrow morning to give it to her.

"I have something for you," Victor said happily.

Victor walked over to the fireplace that had Christmas stockings hanging above it. Each stocking had the first letter of each of their names stitched onto it. There was a *V*, *E*, and *M* hanging exactly in that order. He placed his hand into the stocking that had a large *E*. Inside, was an unmarked envelope. The envelope looked like it had been written just that very day, without a crease on it. He handed it to her.

"Merry Christmas," he said softly.

Eva looked up at him in shock. Without Victor saying another word, she knew what was in the envelope he handed her.

"Eleven years ago," Victor said with a smile, "I wrote a letter on the day that you asked me to never see you again. I kept it under my mattress, where no one could ever find it. I fought with myself for every day of those eleven years on whether or not to send you this letter. I prayed for the strength to send it, but I never could. I was afraid of disrupting your life. Now, I'm ready to give it to you."

Eva felt many emotions traveling through her, but the most prominent was curiosity. She grabbed the letter from him, carefully opening the envelope. Inside were three pieces of loose-leaf paper, handwritten with blue ink. Eva unfolded them, straightening out the letters.

She read the letter aloud for the both of them to hear, "To my dearest Eva."

ABOUT THE AUTHOR

Photo by Sofia Monge

Anthony Sciarratta was born in Maspeth, New York, to Italian-American parents. Being very nostalgic, Anthony takes great pride in labeling himself an old soul. His love for classic films, music, and literature shows through his work. Anthony started his career as a young writer through Amazon self-publishing, which lead to the republication of his first novel, *Finding Forever*. His success story as such a young writer is inspirational to all aspiring writers and self-published authors.

LOVE YOUR SCAR

LOVE YOUR SCAR

HOW TO HEAL BEAUTIFULLY USING NUTRITION, MASSAGE, HOMEOPATHY,
YOGA AND MANY MORE NATURAL THERAPIES

Andie Holman

LightMind Healing
Boulder, Colorado

The author is not a medical doctor, and the content of this book is for information
purposes and in no manner replaces the relationship with your primary physician or
medical team. You should inform your medical doctor of any supplements, exercises,
and/or remedies you choose to use. The reader assumes all responsibility for following any of the suggestions within.

Cover by Carolyn Baltas
Cover photo by Andrew Goldman
Illustrations by Ali Crossman

ISBN 9780998426433
ISBN: 0998426431

ACKNOWLEDGEMENTS

FIRST, THANK YOU Carolyn Baltas, my roommate from University, for designing my logo and cover. You get me even after all these years.

Thank you to Andrew Goldman for taking my photo, with the stunning backdrop of the mountains, and to Amy Freeth-Rice for tidying up my windblown hairs.

Thank you to Jody Berman and Laurel Kallenbach who edited my book. I appreciate your professionalism and enthusiasm.

Deepest thanks to the Oncology department Consultants, nurses and support staff at London Bridge Hospital. You gave me the freedom to help our patients in whatever way I could. Thank you for your confidence in me.

Blessings to my friends who read this book in all its various stages and then convinced me it was time to stop fiddling and publish.

For my dogs – it's time to make good on the long walks I promised.

Saving the best to last – thank you to my love for your faith in me and belief in my work.

*This book is dedicated to all the courageous people
who came to me for help with their scars.*

*I send my never-ending gratitude to my patients at London Bridge
Hospital for helping me develop a treatment for scars. I am honored to
have been a part of your recovery, and this book carries our collective
knowledge into the world to help others find freedom from pain.*

"No mud, no lotus."

—THICH NHAT HANH

CONTENTS

INTRODUCTION

THE ORIGINAL VERSION of this book was titled *Love Your Scar: Breast Cancer,* and it was written to help my patients recover from mastectomies. For twelve years I led the Complementary Therapies Team for the Oncology (cancer) Department at London Bridge Hospital in England; in addition I treated patients with scars at my private clinics. I used a combination of my training in different natural therapies to help people regain their full range of movement and be free from the pain of tight scars. We also worked on the mental and emotional component in order to reach a place of peace and acceptance around scarring.

The book was popular and soon people outside of the hospital asked if my techniques would work for them too. I treated people with burns, multiple scar patterns, scars from repeated surgeries, gunshots and internal adhesions that required some trial and error until I found ways to release them. Most of all I taught my patients how to do scar release on themselves, so that they had the tools to heal and did not have to rely on me. I wrote this revised version of natural scar care for *everyone*, regardless of where on the body a scar is located, how it got there or how old the scar is. I kept the title because your scar needs your love and attention to heal beautifully and remain supple for life.

My first "scar release session" happened quite by accident and changed the course of my career. Faye was in a wheelchair when I met her; she was unable to walk due to restricted breathing. She had recently undergone numerous tests and was fearful that the breast cancer had returned and spread to her lungs, but all tests came back clear. She told me the doctors were puzzled.

At the nurse's suggestion, Faye booked a relaxing massage with me to pass the time until her oncology consultant could see her. After helping her onto the table, I noticed she was panting and unable to take a full breath into her belly. I asked if I could take a closer look at her mastectomy scars. Even though I had been taught to avoid working on the breast area, I felt her scars might be the root of her breathing problems.

As suspected, the scar tissue and surrounding area had tightened and restricted to the point of clamping down her entire rib cage, which prevented Faye from being able to inflate her lungs. I told her my own scar story, which you will read shortly, and explained that I could free her restricted tissues, but it was probably going to hurt some. She trusted me, and together we launched into something amazing. After two simple half-hour massages, using techniques you will learn later, Faye was out of her wheelchair and walking again. I thought my heart was going to escape from my chest with joy and more than a little touch of terror at what had just happened. No one I knew worked with scars like this.

Faye's doctor was astounded, and from then on he regularly referred patients to me and my team for scar management. In the years that followed, I was asked to talk to the patients before surgery so they could prepare and hopefully avoid the pain and suffering caused by scars that didn't heal well. Each patient presented with a scar, yes, but each person had a different life and individual needs. We had to adapt the therapies to gain the highest compliance and therefore the best results for each patient.

I am going to give you a lot of information and suggestions. Take what you think can be useful and leave the rest to the next person. Most importantly, do not become overwhelmed with all that is in here. Pick and choose and play around. Your scar is going to be with you for the rest of your life so you have time to experiment and find what works for you. The information in this book comes from my professional career— twenty-eight years of clinical practice—as well as from personal experience with surgical scarring and a painful thirty year skin condition. I feel I must make a confession. I struggled with whether or not to share my story. After all, it is personal. However, the purpose of this book is to help you love your scar, and I want you to know you are not alone.

MY STORY

Since birth, I'd been using steroid creams to control a horrible, whole-body eczema. In my early teens, the creams stopped working, and the steroid pills the doctor prescribed made me violently ill. He gently told me he had nothing else to offer me medically and that I was on my own to heal myself. I started experimenting with aloe, salt baths, oatmeal baths, a cleaner diet, and anything else I could think of. I researched natural cures and tried them all, sparking a curiosity that continues to this day.

Along with the itchy oozing skin I was a late bloomer—flat-chested and very sporty. I loved high jump, tennis, running, swimming and ballet. Fast-forward one year and, seemingly overnight, hormones and genetics caused size D–cup breasts to develop. I was grappled into Granny bras with stiff, thick straps and an intricate network of wires and clasps to hold my breasts in place. I skipped the whole training-bra stage and went straight to full-on over-the-shoulder boulder holders. I had sweat stains and heat rashes in odd places (on top of the eczema), chronic neck and shoulder pain, and creepy and lecherous attention from older men. I wanted to hide forever.

After two years of misery and pain, a friend told me about breast-reduction surgery. My mom empathized with my physical pain and emotional distress, and just before my sixteenth birthday I went for the surgery, deliriously happy at the prospect of being free of my burden.

I did not heal well. I was a secret smoker and a vegetarian who lived on cheese sandwiches—plus I had an as yet undiscovered sensitivity to dairy and gluten. I was badly anemic, and the stitches didn't hold on my left breast. I had to go under anesthetic a second time for repair. Then my scar became infected which required daily bandage changes. It was a long and painful healing and once it was over I gave my scars no more thought or attention for the next five years.

Fast forward - I graduated from the University of Denver with a business degree emphasizing hospitality which at the time was our family's business. I had a brief stint at a prestigious establishment before deciding to follow my heart's path. For the next few years I managed a health food store using myself as the test subject for different detox protocols, supplements, juicing and other natural healing methods. My skin was in a pretty stable place at the time and I attended massage school at night. There I learned about skin, fascia, and the impact of scars on the body as a whole.

I was so excited to have someone work on my scars, as I was certain I had adhesions all over the place. But there was a major problem. Professional massage therapists are taught to never, ever touch the breast area of a woman. But what if that was where the work was needed?

For the next *fifteen* years I asked various massage therapists if they would check my scars for tightness or restriction, but not a single one would do so, even when I said I would sign a disclaimer. I explained that I too was a massage therapist and that I just wanted to make sure my scars weren't causing problems. I didn't want a boob rub, for crying out loud; I simply wanted my scars checked. However, it was too risky or too weird or too whatever and not a single person stepped up. I practiced on myself, experimenting with different techniques to free the fascia, and gained firsthand knowledge of how releasing a scar feels.

When I met Faye and realized the scars on her chest landed her in a wheelchair, I had the choice to help her or to be frightened by what might happen to me professionally if I massaged her scars. After wrestling with it for all of about three seconds, I gave her the option, knowing I had only worked on myself up to that point. We shared a quiet locking of the eyes and then she nodded yes. When she described the sensations, "The scar is burning; it is numb; that's electric," I knew what she meant.

My scar massages were not particularly relaxing – I needed constant feedback during the session so I could learn and develop my treatment. Also scars are tricky – it can feel as though someone is crushing their fingers down to bone when actually they are barely brushing the skin. Pain is relative and different for everyone. You will learn how to manage your scars or take this book to your massage therapist for help.

For the next ten years after Faye I worked with an astoundingly wide variety of scars and experimented with therapies and techniques. The result is this book. You hold the collective knowledge and experience of hundreds of people, including my own, in your hands. Now it's *your* turn to find freedom.

HOW THIS BOOK IS ORGANIZED

Love Your Scar is split into five sections. It might be tempting to skip right to the end where I tell you how to get to it. Please, read the book from the beginning. There is a reason for you to know it all. The science helps you identify what your body is doing, and the foundation helps you understand how you can best support it while it heals.

Part I covers the science of how your body makes a scar, what body systems are involved, and the possible complications of surgery. Part II explains the foundation for a healthy life—whether your scar is old or new. You will heal well and thrive by following a highly nutritious diet, learning to quiet your mind with meditation, using breath to de-stress, and practicing natural skin care, especially where scars are concerned.

In Part III, I explain additional support therapies for scars, including homeopathy, massage, lymphatic exercises, and healing oils, plus the benefits of skin brushing and salt soaks. There's also an important chapter on how to avoid infection.

Part IV offers a timeline and takes you from pre-op, your surgery day, and through the first two months after your surgery. It is a lot of information to take in initially. Don't stress. Each week builds on itself and by the time you get to the end of two months it is a really simple maintenance plan. Give yourself love and attention so that you heal well from the start and do not have the problems caused by adhesions.

Finally, Part V offers treatments for older scars that may be painful, tight, and restricted. The techniques are similar to those in Part IV, but you don't have to be concerned with the specific timing; you just have to put in the daily effort.

In the Appendices you'll find Resources and Shopping, Recipes, and a section on breast surgeries that was in the previous book.

"No mud, no lotus" sums up this work. The lotus grows out of the deep mud, pushing towards a light source it simply has to trust will be waiting for it. Once it breaks the surface only then can the beauty of the flower be revealed. You may be in a dark place right now, perhaps in pain and frustration, but you too will have your breakthrough. If you give your scar your loving attention, your blossoming is guaranteed.

PART I

THE SCIENCE OF A SCAR

"She wore her scars as her best attire.
A stunning dress made of hellfire."

—Daniel Saint

"I started chemotherapy in September 2009, having been diagnosed with secondary breast cancer. A month into chemo I began to have problems with my breathing. I couldn't walk more than twenty yards without becoming breathless, almost to the point of collapse. My breathing pattern was totally erratic.

I was sent for a heart and lung scan, but the scan came back normal. I then saw Andie who, after listening to my troubles, asked if she could work on my scars. She commenced deep-tissue massage, and I noticed an improvement after the first half-hour. After the second treatment the improvement in my breathing was dramatic and I could now inhale and exhale fully."

—Faye

WOUND HEALING AND TYPES OF SCARS

SCARS HEAL IN all shapes and sizes depending on the type of wound or surgery you have, your age, the site of the injury, your nutrition, overall lifestyle, individual genetics, and your personal healing capabilities. An associated infection with a wound can alter the final scar, as can repeated surgeries in the same area, as in the case of multiple C-sections. Trauma injuries, such as deep bruising, can trigger a scar response inside the body. These can potentially affect the proper functioning of the organs because scar tissue can pull them out of place.

THE FOUR STAGES OF WOUND HEALING

There are four stages to wound healing, and your body instantaneously goes into action to help you when you hurt yourself.

1. The first is the hemostasis stage, in which the body stops the initial bleeding. The damaged blood vessels constrict, little pieces of blood cells called platelet plugs form and clog the inside of the blood vessels, and finally the blood coagulates and thickens until the flow of blood has stopped.

2. Next is the inflammatory stage, which lasts for a few days. During this time, there can be redness, heat, and swelling around the wound as blood vessels constrict to control bleeding. Specialized white blood cells clean the wound of bacteria to prevent infection.

3. The proliferative stage lasts about three weeks, but it can take longer depending on the severity of the wound and whether or not there is an infection. In this stage a matrix of new skin cells and blood vessels form. Specialized cells called fibroblasts generate collagen to fill the wound, making a framework for the new tissues to build on and form your scar. Capillaries (tiny blood vessels) supply the new cells with nutrients and oxygen and support collagen production. The increased blood supply gives the scar its initial bright-pink color.

4. The remodeling stage can last up to two years—yes, two years to finalize a scar! Collagen continues to form, becoming more organized to increase the robustness of the resultant scar. During this stage the density of the blood vessels diminishes and the scar gradually loses color. The shape of the wound may change as the collagen restructures, and once this stage is complete, the area will have 70 to 80 percent of the strength of the original tissue. Quite amazing!

TYPES OF SCARS

Despite being formed of the same tissue and subject to the stages of healing outlined previously, scars come in several different types. Atrophic scars cause an indentation or depression in the skin, such as with acne and chicken-pox scars. Most surgical scars are hypertrophic scars which are elevated initially and subside over time, becoming flatter and paler. Keloid scars are non-malignant tumors formed by scar tissue that grows beyond the boundaries of the original incision or injury. Surgery is suggested to remove keloids but unfortunately they often grow back, so removing them can be a vicious cycle.

Stretch marks, technically called striae, are a form of scarring. These are caused by rapidly stretched skin such as we might notice during pregnancy, weight gain, or growth spurts in children. Sometimes stretch marks occur where the skin is put under tension during healing, such as near the joints.

Burns may also leave scars. A second-degree burn is deeper than a first-degree burn (sunburn) and extends into the dermis of the skin. Superficial second-degree burns are painful, pink, blistering and moist. They turn white with pressure and heal in about three weeks with little scarring. Deep second-degree burns are more likely to create a scar. A thick scab, or eschar, on the burn area indicates that healing is going to take longer. Third-degree burns are the most severe as full skin destruction leads to sensation loss. Skin grafting is almost always necessary and will probably result in a complicated scar pattern.

DANGERS TO YOUR SCAR

When you have an open wound, your body's natural barrier against infection is broken. If it is going to happen, an infection will typically occur in the first month after surgery. Having other medical conditions such as cancer, diabetes, or a weakened immune system increases the risk of an infection. Other factors that may contribute to infection include being elderly or overweight, undergoing a surgery that lasts longer than two hours, and emergency or abdominal surgery.

Post-operative infections are called surgical-site infections (SSIs), which are caused by microorganisms. If you've ever heard of someone having a staph infection, they are referring to the bacteria *Staphylococcus*. Other bacteria that cause SSIs include *Streptococcus* and *Pseudomonas*.

Infection of the incision causes redness, fever, pain and tenderness, warmth, swelling, and slow healing. If the infection spreads, pus may form from the dead blood cells and bacteria, reopening the wound site. In the case of an organ/space SSI—when the infection involves the organs or spaces other than the incision—pus may come out through a drain. When the tissue is disintegrating as a result of the infection, it's called an *abscess*. The degree of risk for an SSI is dependent on the type of wound you have.

Clean wounds are not inflamed or contaminated, and they do not involve operating on an internal organ. These wounds carry a very low risk of infection—about 2 percent. Clean-contaminated wounds have no evidence of infection at the time of surgery but involve operating on an internal organ. The risk of infection is less than 10 percent. Contaminated wounds are created when an outside object comes into contact with the wound, such as from a knife or bullet or when the contents of the gastrointestinal tract spill into the wound—such as with bowel resection or an appendectomy—which raises the risk of infection to 13 to 20 percent. Dirty wounds are infected at the time of the surgery and the risk of an SSI is about 40 percent.

An infection can really ruin your chances of a good-looking scar because it destroys the surrounding tissue and makes it harder for your body to knit the skin together. In the early stages of healing your primary focus is to prevent an infection, and Chapter 8 is dedicated to this. Once the initial danger of infection is over, the next obstacles to an inconspicuous, pain-free scar are adhesions and problems in the body's fascia.

CHAPTER 2

ADHESIONS AND FASCIA: WHEN STICKING TOGETHER IS A BAD THING

SOMETIMES THE BODY goes overboard in its attempt to secure the wound. This is a natural response to any injury, whether it's caused by infection, trauma, surgery, or radiation. Adhesions, which are fibrous bands of scar tissue, can extend beyond or behind the initial injury, sticking together parts of the body that would normally remain separate, which can lead to alterations in posture, movement, and function.

Imagine your scar is a boat in a harbor, floating around at the whim of choppy waves. You would want to secure your boat with ropes, ideally attached from different directions to give the best chance of keeping it steady. Your body does the same thing with a scar. It forms adhesions and secures them to other parts of the body to give stability to the scar. The problem is when the "ropes" get too tight. Adhesions develop slowly and pull on surrounding body tissues, restricting the ability of the muscles and bones to work properly. They can also irritate delicate nerves and blood vessels.

Fascia (pronounced FASH-ya) is an all-encompassing network of strong connective tissue that wraps around almost every part of the body. Only the tubes of the respiratory, lymphatic, and digestive systems are free of this intricate web of tissue. Any negative impact on the fascia will resonate throughout your whole body.

Do you remember the little song about how all the bones connect? "Toe bone connected to the foot bone, Foot bone connected to the heel bone, Heel bone connected to the ankle bone" and so on. Instead of being named "Dem Bones," it could have been called "Ode to Fascia" as fascia is what does the actual connecting.

To fully appreciate the interconnectedness of fascia and how a scar affects it, put on a tight-fitting shirt and stand in front of a mirror. Grab the fabric at the shoulder and note where the fabric bunches and creates cords on the shirt's front, back, and sides. Now grab in the middle of the shirt where a Cesarean section scar or appendectomy scar would be. Notice the creases and pulls of the fabric. Finally, hold your shirt on one side of the chest, perhaps where a breast scar would be, and see how the fabric pulls in the back as well.

You can imagine that a scar on the knee could pull the fascia of the thigh, forcing the hip to drop. This in turn could shorten the torso, perhaps rounding the shoulder on that side, which might pull on the neck muscles and result in headaches. You can rub your temples all you like, but your headaches will not stop until you release your knee scar. Crazy, right?

Fascia provides protection and support for nerves and blood vessels as they pass through body tissues. If the fascia around a nerve becomes adhered to something it should not, the nerve will be irritated and can cause tingling, burning, numbness, or weakness in the area.

Tendons and ligaments are made of fascia; fascia also surrounds and isolates individual muscles, letting them slide easily over each other. Restrictions in the fascia of the muscles and bones can affect posture and the ability to move freely.

Looser fascia, known as separating fascia, performs a different function. These fascia tissues sheathe all the organs and line the body cavities. Proper structural and functional relationships are maintained so that the organs can function properly. An example is the pericardium, which is a sack of fascia containing the heart. Another example is the fascia holding the pelvic organs in place. If these supportive tissues become weak or damaged, you can have something called a prolapse occur. You can see why we want to keep our different types of fascia healthy. Besides massage, what can you do? For starters, drink more water.

Being sufficiently hydrated is essential to fascia health because fascia is made mostly of water molecules so that it will be slippery enough to function properly. When stretching, fluid is pushed out of fascia much like squeezing a sponge. When the stretch is released, the area refills with fresh fluid from the surrounding tissue, drawing from the lymph and vascular systems nearby.

Human bodies are roughly 60 percent water, and we need to drink a fair amount every day, about 3 liters (100 ounces) for men and 2.2 liters (75 ounces) for women per day. Water transports nutrients, acts as a shock absorber for the brain and spine, lubricates joints, and is the major component of most body parts. The brain and heart are composed of 73 percent water and the lungs are 83 percent water. Even so-called solid bone is 30 percent water. When you're dehydrated, your health pretty much goes to hell in a hand basket, and nothing functions properly. This is especially true of your lymphatic system, which is intimately connected to your immune system, and ultimately to your scar.

CHAPTER 3

THE LYMPHATIC SYSTEM'S IMMUNE-BOOSTING, BLOOD-CLEANSING FUNCTION

IN ORDER TO create a great-looking, healthy scar, you need to ensure that cellular and metabolic waste gets taken away from the wound. The lymphatic system primarily handles this function. Being familiar with the lymphatic system helps you understand what is happening while you "build" your scar, and it also explains why I encourage you to do exercises to encourage lymph flow as soon as you wake up after surgery.

The cells of the body are bathed and surrounded by interstitial fluid, which is a water solvent containing amino acids, hormones, neurotransmitters, fatty acids, sugars, salts, and waste products from the cells. This fluid, called lymph, provides the platform for delivering materials to the cells and removing metabolic waste. This fluid also contains white blood cells to help combat infection.

The lymphatic system is made up of both deep and superficial vessels. The deep vessels generally follow the deep veins of the circulatory system, while the superficial vessels are in the superficial fascia. Lymph passes through vessels of increasing size and several lymph nodes (small, round, filter-like organs) before returning to the blood. Think of the lymph nodes as filtration plants where unwanted bacteria, viruses, and other wastes are attacked and destroyed by the immune cells stationed there. The cleansed fluid then returns into circulation.

12

One point of interest: lymph fluid travels in one direction only, with backflow being prevented by single-direction flap valves in the lymph vessels. This stops the waste from going the wrong way into the blood before it has been cleaned.

HOW DOES THE LYMPHATIC SYSTEM WORK?

One of the easiest ways to visualize the working of the lymph is to compare it to your local trash-collection service. It generally runs smoothly: the trucks come regularly and gather up the bags, tins, boxes, and other bits and take them away to be sorted and disposed of at a central processing plant. If the roads are well maintained and nothing gets in the way, it all happens swiftly and efficiently.

Imagine that the street is in disrepair and the trucks cannot move as quickly. Getting the rubbish off the street takes longer, and it begins to decompose in the sun. Likewise, when we are sedentary, the lymph does not get the activation it needs for good circulation, and waste builds up. Also, being dehydrated is akin to big potholes in the road, as the trucks cannot move freely.

Now suppose some of the trucks are permanently taken off the garbage route. This is what happens when lymph nodes are removed during surgery, as is often the case with breast cancer surgery. How many lymph nodes are removed depends on the surgery and will determine how much extra support you need to give your lymph system to ensure that all your body's waste products are still being collected.

With fewer lymph nodes, you now require a different strategy to remove the rubbish with fewer trucks. It is critical that you keep the roads clear and in good repair to facilitate the efficiency of the trucks you still have. Stimulating the areas of high lymph node concentration will help the body stay on top of waste removal.

Unlike the circulatory system, in which the heart pumps the blood, the lymphatic system has no such pump and relies instead on muscular contraction (i.e. movement and exercise) to move the fluid around the body. The vast network of lymph vessels flows against gravity as well, providing just that extra little challenge. Fortunately there are many ways to stimulate the lymphatic system, and I'll explain these methods later.

WHY IS THE LYMPHATIC SYSTEM SO IMPORTANT?

- **Healthy tissue drainage:** Every day about 21 liters (equal to 88 cups, 5.5 gallons, or 22 quarts) of plasma fluid carrying dissolved substances escape from the arterial end of the blood capillaries and into the tissues. Most of this fluid returns directly to the bloodstream, but 3 to 4 liters of fluid are drained away by the lymphatic vessels. The body's waste materials are removed by the lymph to prevent them from recirculating into the blood.
- **Nutrient absorption in the small intestine:** In the small intestine there are finger-like projections called villi, which increase the total intestinal surface area. Within each little villus there is a network of capillaries and lymphatic vessels. Amino acids and carbohydrates are absorbed into the capillaries, whereas fat and fat-soluble materials are absorbed into the lymphatic vessels. Fats are critical to optimal health throughout the body.
- **Maintenance of the immune system:** The lymphatic organs are responsible for the production and maturation of lymphocytes, the white blood cells primarily responsible for immunity. Lymphocytes fight infection and destroy abnormal or damaged

cells. Bone marrow is considered lymphatic tissue because lymphocytes are made in bone marrow.

- **Defense again antigens:** Lymph fluid plays a vital role in protecting the body from foreign materials known collectively as antigens. The immune system dispatches cells called phagocytes via the lymph system. These cells act like a Pac-Man, engulfing and trapping the antigens and releasing them when they come into contact with the white blood cells designed to destroy them.

COMPONENTS OF THE LYMPHATIC SYSTEM

Some of the different components that make up the lymphatic system are shown in Figure 1, Organs of the Lymphatic System. The fluid that runs through the system, lymph, travels through tubes called lymph vessels (e). You may be surprised to learn that the volume of lymphatic fluid in the body is about double that of blood. There are also roughly twice as many lymph vessels as there are blood vessels, so it is a significant body system.

There are three main areas of lymph node concentration where waste materials are removed from the lymph before the fluid returns into circulation. In the neck we have the cervical lymph nodes (a), in the armpits are the axillary lymph nodes (g) and in the groin are the inguinal lymph nodes (d). These are the areas we will stimulate through exercise in order to cleanse the lymph and keep immunity strong. Other organs involved in the lymphatic system include the thymus gland (b), the spleen (c), and diffuse lymphoid tissue such as the tonsils and adenoids. Finally we have lymphatic tissue, which is made in the bone marrow. As you can see, this system is very far reaching.

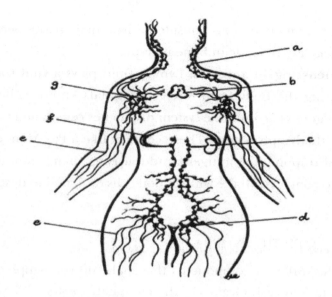

Figure 1: Organs of the Lymphatic System

a: cervical lymph nodes

b: thymus gland

c: spleen

d: inguinal lymph nodes

e: lymph vessels

f: diaphragm (shown for illustration: not part of the lymphatic system)

g: axillary lymph nodes

The lymphatic system is an intricate part of immunity. The spleen is the largest lymph organ and is highly active in the body's defense. The spleen is located above the stomach under the rib cage. Abnormal and old red blood cells are destroyed in the spleen, and the breakdown products are then sent to the liver. Along with the lymph nodes, the spleen creates lymphocytes, which are the body's defenders. Unlike the lymph nodes, the spleen is not entered by any lymphatic vessels, which protects it from diseases that the lymph fluid is carrying to the nodes for destruction.

The T-lymphocytes (the good guys who gobble up baddies) mature in the thymus. This gland is most active in childhood, and by puberty it starts to atrophy thanks to sex hormones. We stockpile T-lymphocytes as children, and the thymus degenerates to the point of being a blip of fat, which potentially contributes to susceptibility to infection and cancer when the person ages.

The tonsils and adenoids are considered the first line of defense for the respiratory and digestive systems. Waldeyer's tonsillar ring is an anatomical term collectively describing the arrangement of lymphoid tissue in the pharynx: the space that reaches from the back of the nasal cavity close to the bottom of the throat where food and air go into different tubes—either the esophagus or the trachea.

From the top to the bottom, the ring of lymph tissue has two adenoids (or pharyngeal tonsils) located at the back of the nasal cavity (nasopharynx) where the nose meets the throat, above the oral cavity. Next are two tubal tonsils near where the Eustachian tubes (from the ears) open into the nasopharynx, followed by what most of us call the tonsils, officially known as the palatine tonsils. These are located at the back of the mouth. Finally, there is more lymph tissue in the tongue and throat to complete Waldeyer's ring.

These lymph tissues defend against bacteria that enter the nose and mouth. They have specialized cells that capture antigens (things we don't want in our bodies). As they hold them, an immune response is activated, and the B-cells (made in the bone marrow) and T-cells (made in the thymus) come to destroy the antigens. As each antigen is demolished, the B-cells make a memory cell specific to it. If this particular antigen shows up again, the immune system, via the memory B-cell, can get on top of it much faster. This is why it is common to get sick when you travel to foreign countries, as you have no previous exposure to the different antigens, and your body has no memory of how to fight quickly.

ASYMMETRICAL LYMPH FLUID DRAINAGE

Because the body contains twice as much lymph as blood, it is critical to stay well hydrated in order to keep the immune system working efficiently, which will help you create a good, healthy scar. Your body will let you know if it is dehydrated through the following symptoms:

- bloating and water retention (counterintuitive but true)
- puffy fingers (you may notice rings become too tight)
- itchy skin, dry skin, flaky scalp
- swollen ankles or feet
- feeling stiff and sore when you wake
- cold hands and feet
- tiredness, fatigue, brain fog
- unexplained irritability
- headaches
- soreness and/or swelling of the breasts before menses

The lymph does not drain symmetrically in the body. I always found this a fascinating and rather puzzling fact. There are two principle lymph vessels, the thoracic and right lymph ducts, which pour into the heart via the brachiocephalic veins. The lymph returns to these ducts in a peculiar way. The head, neck, and right arm drain into the right lymph

18

duct, whereas the left arm, entire trunk of the body, and both legs drain into the thoracic lymph duct.

This is important to know because it may affect how you encourage lymph flow in the body through exercise. Remember we have three main areas of lymph node concentration: the deep and superficial lymphatic vessels flow through the cervical nodes in the jaw and neck, the axillary nodes in the armpits, and the inguinal nodes in the groin. So suppose you have swollen ankles. You will want to activate the groin and the left axillary nodes more often in order to drain the lymph from the legs. If you have headaches, you will want to pay particular attention to exercising the right arm to drain the lymph fluid from your head and neck.

Bear in mind that if any of your lymph organs have been previously removed (for example a tonsillectomy or adenoidectomy) you need to be more vigilant in taking care of yourself because you have lost some of your immune system's team members. Besides staying hydrated, there are other ways to help you stay or become healthy both during surgical recovery and well after. These include specific stretches to stimulate the lymph, skin brushing, deep breathing, bouncing on a trampoline, walking and yoga.

Part II covers the foundations of good health, which play an important role in scar healing, regardless of the age of your scar. When I ran my natural health practice in London, these fundamental areas of wellness were always top of my list to put in my patients' toolbox of self-care. Clients who embraced nutrition, dietary and herbal supplements, quiet time, breathing practices, and natural skin care all learned how to nurture themselves for the rest of their lives. I've always told patients that my aim was to get them better—and also to teach them how to do it for themselves. If a person kept coming back to me with the same complaint, clearly I was failing them!

Ideally you will start to integrate the therapies in Part II well before your surgery date. If you have picked up this book after the fact, no worries, just start taking care of your scar as quickly as you can.

THE FOUNDATIONS OF SCAR CARE

"There is a crack, a crack in everything.
That's how the light gets in."

—LEONARD COHEN

"I was first introduced to Adrianna [Andie] Holman about eighteen months after my mastectomy. I'd also had a lumpectomy just three weeks earlier. After the mastectomy I developed an infection that was treated by antibiotics, but it left the whole area around and below my scar tissue very tender. My surgeon recommended I try to massage the area, but I had obviously not found the right technique and was trying to avoid the very area I should have been massaging.

It was at this low point—when I found it uncomfortable to wear a bra for any length of time and still had a lot of numbness—that I met Adrianna. We discussed the problems I was encountering, and she advised scar massage to help the healing process and reduce tenderness. At first I had weekly massage sessions, and she showed me how to continue the massage at home.

I saw a slow but continued improvement. I think the massage took longer to have an effect because it had been so long after the operation before I started treatment. Eventually we settled on one session a month, sometimes every six weeks or so, and I continued to massage at home in between.

Now, nearly six years after the original operation, I am virtually pain free. I have almost no numbness or hard-tissue areas, and most of the scar tissue has dissipated. Without the help and encouragement of Adrianna I do not think I could have achieved so much."

—Eve

CHAPTER 4

HOW NUTRITION HELPS HEAL A SCAR

A NUTRIENT-RICH DIET is integral and essential to healing. I offer you the culmination of thirty years of personal experimentation and clinical experience as well as a Bachelor's degree in Nutritional Medicine. I have strong views as to what makes a nutrient rich diet, backed by science, and it is not going to appeal to those hooked on the Standard American Diet or SAD way of eating.

As with everything in this book, you get to decide just how far you want to go. I'll give you what I consider the best option, and you take it from there. Later in this chapter I will teach you how to tweak your diet to defend against infection and keep your healing scar supple and problem free.

It would be fabulous for your health if you chose to become a tree-hugging, unplugging, green-smoothie-chugging, meditating, levitating whole food guru for the rest of your life... but I will leave that up to you.

ANDIE'S BASIC NUTRITIONAL GUIDELINES

1. Choose foods as close to nature as possible, meaning unrefined, ideally organic.
2. Avoid highly processed foods, sugar, alcohol, and trans fats.

3. Eat foods rich in omega-3 fats and friendly bacteria.
4. Aim for ten servings of vegetables a day (forget five a day – it's not enough).
5. Eat everything else (meat, eggs, dairy, beans, grains) as suits your personal constitution.

Diets used to be much simpler and usually involved something that grew in the ground, ran on it, swam, or flew. In the past couple of generations there has been an explosion in food processing, and our taste buds have been manipulated by the food industry to crave fat, sugar, and salt. Commonly eaten foods are cocktails of chemicals created in laboratories rather than Mother Nature. Artificial colors, artificial flavors, preservatives, pesticides, GMOs, stabilizers, and goodness knows what else are now considered normal. It isn't called "junk" food by accident.

The World Health Organization sites a poor diet as the number-two cause of cancer and a major contributor to half of all cancers. It's also implicated in many other chronic health complications such as diabetes, obesity, heart disease, fatty liver disease, and Alzheimer's. So, let's start your healing diet by taking out the "trash" you may be consuming. Remember this is a diet aimed at giving your body the best possible chance of healing your scar beautifully. Dump the junk.

FOODS TO ELIMINATE FROM YOUR DIET

There are three categories of substances that should be omitted from your diet while you heal your scar and ideally for the rest of your long, brilliant life. These are refined sugar, trans fats, and excessive alcohol, and they pose myriad health hazards.

REFINED SUGAR

We were programmed to associate sugar with good times from a very young age. As children we were rewarded with desserts for eating our broccoli, and birthday celebrations included ice cream and cake. All holidays have a specific candy, whether it's candy corn, candy canes, or chocolate bunnies.

The problem is that refined sugar is a thief. It steals nutrients from our bodies, hijacks our hormones, and sets us on a course for obesity, inflammation, and chronic disease. More importantly for the purposes of scar healing, having high glucose levels or high blood sugar causes cell walls to become rigid and stiff. This slows the flow of blood and lymph to a wound and reduces the amount of oxygen and nutrients reaching the damaged area. For this reason, eating sugar impedes healing and threatens your chances of a healthy, flexible scar.

Having cured my eczema problems, I had a reputation as a skin guru in London. To give you an example of what excessive sugar does to your skin, I'll present a case study from my clinic. A gentleman in his sixties came to see me regarding his burning, weeping, painful eczema that covered a large portion of his body. We went through his diet and it turned out he loved a cup of tea—with eight teaspoons of sugar. I asked how many cups he might have in a day. He shrugged his shoulders and said, "Perhaps ten?" I struggled to keep my eyebrows in place.

I asked him to spoon eighty teaspoons of sugar onto a plate and leave it on his kitchen table until he next saw me. I did not tell him to cut back on sugar or stop drinking tea. I suggested that for every cup of tea he drank, he follow it with a cup of water, as he was currently not drinking any water at all. I asked him to add frozen veggies to his standard of canned soups and to eat one apple or pear a day. Because his eczema was so severe, he was given a homeopathic general-support remedy but nothing else. My focus was mostly on his diet as his sugar consumption was off the charts, and I hoped seeing the pile of sugar would motivate him to change.

Six weeks later at his follow up appointment, he proudly showed me that his eczema was completely gone – as if it had never existed. He was drinking four cups of tea a day, with no sugar, and was drinking two liters or more of water. He had added in the vegetables and fruit and had noticed he felt better, which led him to want to eat even more of them. The giant sugar mound had startled him into action, and a few simple changes were all it took for his body to heal the inflammation of the eczema. He was happy with his new diet, and was so delighted with his perfect skin that we never saw each other again. Case closed.

You will find sugar in almost all processed foods if you read the labels. Here's a short list of the names for refined sugar: brown rice syrup, corn sweetener, corn syrup or corn syrup solids, cane juice, dehydrated cane juice, dextrin, dextrose, fructose, fruit juice concentrate, glucose, high-fructose corn syrup (bad, bad, bad!!!), invert sugar, lactose, maltodextrin, malt syrup, maltose, mannitol, molasses, raw sugar, rice syrup, saccharose, sorbitol, sorghum, sucrose, treacle, turbinado sugar, and xylose. You can use honey and maple syrup in small amounts but bear in mind they can be enough to trigger cravings if you are susceptible to them.

The higher an ingredient is on the label, the more of that substance is contained in the food. One sneaky trick food processors use is to include three different types of sugar in a food and list them all separately so it doesn't look so bad. It may just be easier to avoid all processed food so you don't even have to think about whether it contains sugar. If that's too far of a stretch here at the start, just be vigilant at reading labels looking for hidden sugar.

For chocoholics who feel like a little part of them has just died, here is my peace offering: homemade chocolate. (You will find a delicious recipe in Appendix II at the end of the book.) When made with cacao powder, coconut oil, and real maple syrup, homemade chocolate is high in minerals and antioxidants, and it provides nutritious fat. In fact, it's practically a health food. Yes, it contains maple syrup, so technically it's not sugar free, but it is certainly healthier than most commercial chocolates. If it helps keep you on the greater plan, it's worth the small deviation.

TRANS-FATTY ACIDS OR PARTIALLY HYDROGENATED OILS

Next on our list of foods that foul up your health are trans-fatty acids (TFAs), also called trans fats or partially hydrogenated oils (PHOs). Liquid vegetable oils are processed into a solid form by adding hydrogen, thus the name partially "hydrogenated" vegetable oil. Processed foods have a longer shelf life when they contain PHOs, which makes them desirable to manufacturers. However, the scientific evidence concludes that PHOs are wildly dangerous and contribute to a wide range of diseases.

The cardiovascular system has been the main focus of research, which shows PHOs destroy good cholesterol while dramatically increasing bad cholesterol, leading to a much higher risk of heart attack. Research also indicates that PHOs increase risk of systemic inflammation, cell dysfunction, irregular heartbeat, insulin resistance, Alzheimer's, liver dysfunction, infertility, cancer, diabetes development, and stroke. In addition, hydrogenated oils cause the body to store fat around the abdomen, which is considered dangerous to health.

As of June 2015, the United States Food and Drug Administration (FDA) determined that PHOs are *not* "generally recognized as safe"

(GRAS) and placed them on the list of foods that are, well, not safe to eat. Based on a thorough review of the scientific evidence, the U.S. FDA has determined that removing partially hydrogenated oils from processed foods could prevent thousands of deaths and heart attacks in the United States each year—and they are only talking about the cardio-vascular danger of trans fats.

Given that these foods are now on the "bad" food list, the FDA has given food manufacturers three years to either reformulate their prod-ucts without PHOs or try to petition the use of them in foods. Until that time, the FDA recommends that consumers check a food's ingredient list to determine whether or not it contains PHOs.

Common foods that may contain partially hydrogenated oils, or trans fats, include:

- Baked goods such as cakes, cookies, pies, crackers, and donuts
- Vegetable shortening and stick margarine
- Coffee creamer
- Pot pies
- Waffles
- Pizzas
- Ready-to-use frosting
- Potato chips
- Microwave popcorn
- Ramen noodles and soup cups
- Fried foods (French fries, fried chicken, fried cheese sticks, fried anything)
- Refrigerated dough products such as cinnamon rolls and biscuits

Here's something critical to note: foods currently labeled with zero grams of trans fats may legally still contain small amounts (less than one-half gram per serving). These small amounts can add up and contribute to health problems. Suppose you usually start your day with coffee with creamer and a donut. For lunch you hit the drive-thru and order chicken nuggets and fries—and maybe a little apple pie for dessert. Someone in the office has a birthday and there are cupcakes with frosting. For dinner you have a frozen pizza, and later, while watching a movie, you eat some microwaved popcorn. See the problem? It is not the individual amount you have but the cumulative effect of trans fats on your health.

To summarize: processed foods, in particular partially hydrogenated oils, are going to cause damage to your health and healing capabilities, and therefore ought to be avoided.

ALCOHOL

Drinking alcohol—including beer and wine—impairs the early days of wound healing and increases the incidence of infection. In the short term, alcohol decreases your immune system's ability to fight, upsets re-epithelialization (scar cell formation), and decreases collagen production and wound closure. So for at least the first month of healing, skip the cocktail and stick to water to maximize your chances of building a great scar.

If stopping drinking for a month sounds like an impossible or intimidating goal, I would like to point you to an excellent book that will help you thrive without alcohol. It's called *The 30-Day Sobriety Solution* by Jack Canfield and Dave Andrews. After thirty days you decide how much alcohol to add back into your life.

So now you know how and why to cut out refined sugar, dangerous fats, and alcoholic beverages in order to dramatically aid healing. Next you will learn how to turbocharge your diet and help you speed-heal.

HEALTHY FOODS EVERYONE NEEDS AND SHOULD EAT MORE OF

Humans have certain nutritional needs in order to function optimally. Some of the nutrients I'm discussing become even more important during healing, and the following section guides you toward the foods that will help support your body as it heals. Focus on increasing these foods, especially in the early days of recovery, but also consider making them more of your day-to-day staples as you carry on through life. You may decide you feel so good you just want to keep eating this way. That's certainly what happened to me.

VEGETABLES + FRUITS = HEALING POWERHOUSES

The fastest way to improve the nutrient content of your diet is to eat more vegetables—probably a lot more vegetables. Aim for ten servings a day. Seems a lot if your idea of a vegetable serving is a slice of tomato on a burger (no, ketchup doesn't count). A serving is roughly what you can hold in your hand, so it really isn't that hard to achieve. A serving of leafy greens is two handfuls. If you embrace green smoothies you will knock out several of these servings in one swoop.

Veggies are loaded with nutrients that strengthen blood vessels and connective tissues and that boost the immune system, all of which is great for your scar. One of these super nutrients is vitamin C, which is a co-factor for collagen synthesis and a primary antioxidant. Antioxidants protect the cells by "loaning" an electron to chemicals called free radicals, which would otherwise steal electrons from a healthy cell, causing damage.

A recent study showed vitamin C is rapidly consumed by the body post-wounding. The researchers found that vitamin C supplementation suppressed inflammation quickly while exciting the expression of self-renewal genes. Supplementation also promoted the proliferation of fibroblasts, the specialized cells that make up a scar.[1]

Fruits high in vitamin C include all citrus, strawberries, black currants, kiwi, peaches, papayas, mangos, goji berries, guavas, and lychees. Vegetables high in vitamin C include spring greens, spinach, parsley, kale, broccoli, cauliflower, red cabbage, Brussels sprouts, bell peppers, and mange tout peas (snow or snap peas).

Quercetin is a well-researched antioxidant with anti-inflammatory and anti-cancer properties. A study released in early 2017 showed that quercetin reduced breast cancer cell viability in a time and dose dependent manner, meaning it increased cancer cell apoptosis (cell death) as well as inhibiting the cell cycle progression. The scientists conducting the study were looking for an effective and less toxic alternative to chemotherapy and radiotherapy.[2]

We are particularly interested in its anti-inflammatory action to support post-operative recovery, but I'm not about to knock its cancer killing properties. Quercetin is found in apples, red onions, green tea, broccoli, leafy greens, tomatoes, and berries.

Carotenoids, converted by the body into vitamin A, are essential for wound healing and proper immune function. A study in immunonutrition found that a deficiency in Vitamin A impairs wound healing. It has multiple positive effects on wounds, including collagen cross-linking, giving the wound strength, as well as increasing the monocytes and macrophages in the early inflammatory phase.[3]

Food sources high in carotenoids are usually red, orange, or yellow in color and include carrots, apricots, winter squash, mangos, plums, tomatoes, pumpkin, and sweet potatoes.

There can be some contention over the best way to eat your veggies: raw or cooked. Some veggies retain their nutrients better when raw, whereas others, like carrots and tomatoes, dramatically increase in nutrients when cooked as the heat releases antioxidants in the fiber. Steaming vegetables seems to be the best way to retain nutrients when cooking, followed by roasting. Boiling can destroy the delicate nutrients so that would be my last choice. The best way to prepare your veggies is the way you like them - so you will eat them!

TURMERIC, THE EXTRAORDINARY SPICE

The yellow pigment of the turmeric root, called curcumin, has powerful healing capabilities. Turmeric has been used in India's Ayurvedic medicine since about 1900 BC, and modern research confirms the spicy tuber's therapeutic uses for a wide variety of diseases and conditions. Specifically, curcumin exhibits antioxidant, anti-inflammatory, antibacterial, antiviral, antifungal, and anticancer properties.[4]

Turmeric has been extensively studied and is excellent for pain, inflammation, and for accelerating the various stages of healing. In particular, evidence shows it enhances granulation tissue formation (the creation of new connective tissue and microscopic blood vessels), collagen deposition (the laying down of collagen to stabilize the wound matrix), wound contraction (when the sides of the wound heal toward each other to close), and tissue remodeling (also called "maturation," the last stage of the healing process, which can take up to two years).[5]

Although there are turmeric-containing creams, I don't have experience in using turmeric topically, and I hesitate to recommend what I have not used with my patients. However, I *am* very comfortable suggesting you spice your cooking with turmeric; it's delicious.

Turmeric has been used medicinally for centuries in India, China, and Africa, and it's found in many countries' traditional dishes. You can add turmeric to curries, roasted veggies, smoothies, and rice. Or stir it into warm milk to make "golden milk," one of my favorite ways of taking the spice, especially at bedtime when it helps you sleep. (In Appendix II, you'll find recipes for Spicy Golden Milk and Turmeric Paste, which you can add into various dishes.)

ORGANIC FOODS

You can dramatically increase nutrient levels by choosing organic—called *bio* in some countries. Besides having fewer pesticides, organically grown foods have more nutrients than those grown conventionally with chemicals. A survey by the *Journal of Alternative and Complementary Medicine* compared the nutrient content of organic and conventional crops. Organic crops contained significantly more vitamin C, iron, magnesium, and phosphorus. There was a higher content of nutritionally significant minerals found in the organic crops because they contained far fewer heavy metals than conventional crops. Heavy metals are very toxic to your body. The conclusion? "There appear to be genuine differences in the nutrient content of organic and conventional crops."[6]

Typically the more fragile the fruit or vegetable, the more often it has been coated with pesticides. The following list of foods are the most heavily sprayed in conventional farming. They are known as the Dirty Dozen, and whenever possible, purchase them from an organic grower. (Please note that the list below is from 2016. The Environmental Working Group, an American nonprofit that specializes in research and advocacy about toxic chemicals in agriculture, updates this list annually to reflect changes in pesticide use, so please check www.ewg.org for a current list of the most toxic foods.)

Look for the organic options -

1. Strawberries
2. Apples
3. Nectarines
4. Peaches
5. Celery
6. Grapes
7. Cherries
8. Spinach
9. Tomatoes
10. Sweet bell pepper
11. Cherry tomatoes
12. Cucumbers

Special concern: Hot peppers, kale, collard greens

SUPERGREENS AND GREEN SMOOTHIES

As kale and collards are the last two on the 2016 must-buy-organic list, they make a nice segue into "supergreens." Green leafy veggies are rich in a group of B vitamins, called folates that maintain DNA stability. There is a widespread deficiency of folate in humans, and this deficiency has been implicated in the development of several cancers including cancer of the colon, ovary, breast, pancreas, cervix, brain, and lung. Supergreens are very protective— a powerhouse nutrient. Think of a superhero wearing a green kale cape.

Supergreens include broccoli, romaine lettuce, red- and green-leaf lettuce, spinach, endive, kale, chard, celery, bok choy, asparagus, arugula, carrot tops, beet tops, collard greens, escarole, frisée, mizuna, mustard greens, and radicchio. Some of these greens may have gone in your composting or trash can. Keep your beet and carrot tops and try them chopped up in a stir fry or blended in a smoothie.

I am inspired by Victoria Boutenko who wrote *Green for Life*. She conducted an interesting study on the myriad benefits of green smoothies. She asked study participants to drink a quart of green smoothie daily. According to the supervising doctor, after one month 66.7 percent of participants showed vast improvement with various health concerns. The testimonials and stories these participants contributed to the book are positively astonishing given the simplicity of the task. Boutenko's daily quart of green smoothie improved the health of two-thirds of her participants. One quart is not hard to consume, especially when you make it really tasty.

Before I offer some tips on making smoothies, I know there are readers who are thinking, "If one quart is good, then drinking only smoothies all day will make me heal even faster." If that's you: slow down, Sunshine! I don't suggest you go on a liquid fast or green smoothie–only diet. Smoothies are a supplement to a healing diet, *not* a replacement for other healthy foods.

Green smoothies look a little muddy if you use the very dark greens, but don't let that put you off. I like baby salad greens, spinach, and romaine lettuce for my smoothies as they are lighter and less bitter than the darker greens. If you want to go heavy on the kale, make a chocolate-banana-nut butter smoothie, which will balance out the bitterness.

Some folks love the really "green" flavor, and a friend of mine doesn't put any fruit in hers, instead preferring a big squeeze of lemon and a bit of fresh ginger. It's up to you and your taste buds. I keep peeled, broken bananas in the freezer along with bags of organic strawberries, blueberries, and pineapple. FYI: cherries will cause your smoothie to become very foamy.

I recommend you invest in a good blender. My old blenders made "chunkies" instead of smoothies, so I made the commitment and bought a Vitamix blender. It can chew up anything to create a silky drink and I use it daily for smoothies, blending ice cream recipes and making sauces, dips, soups, crushing ice into snow and more. Vitamix has been around for decades, and the machines are built to last.

Do your own thirty-day smoothie challenge and jot down any little health concern that's bothering you right now. Include even smaller issues such as bags under the eyes or lackluster skin. Put the list in a drawer, drink your smoothies, and look over your list again in a month. I think you'll be pleasantly surprised at the positive changes.

If you have blood sugar issues I would encourage you to make your smoothies more veg than fruit. You can also have your smoothie with a meal to slow down the release of sugar from the fruit. So if you're still wondering how on earth you are going to eat ten servings of vegetables in a day, start here - One quart of green smoothie per day, a salad of mixed greens, and a large portion of mixed veggies at dinner. I would put money down that this one change of eating more vegetables will dramatically improve the overall quality of your life, let alone your scar.

Okay, let's keep going with the therapeutic diet and investigate good fats.

ESSENTIAL FATTY ACIDS

Essential fatty acids, omega-3 fats, and omega-6 fats are literally essential to our good health. We must ingest them because our bodies cannot synthesize them. They are integral to keeping the cell membrane flexible, which we want for a healthy, functional scar. The essential fatty acids are the starting point for making hormones that regulate inflammation and blood clotting, which is important for wound healing. They maintain the suppleness of the arterial walls, protecting your cardiovascular system. And, they are highly concentrated in the brain and are necessary for memory and performance as well as for preventing mood swings and depression.

Our hunter-gatherer ancestors ate a ratio of omega-3 to omega-6 fats of about 1 to 1. This changed dramatically with the Industrial Revolution and mass-produced foods, which saw the boom of using refined vegetable oils in foods and the use of cereal grains to feed livestock instead of grazing. Nowadays, the standard diet supplies a ratio of 1 to 15, which is having dramatically negative consequences on our health due to the pro-inflammatory nature of omega-6 fats. Vegetable oils such as safflower, sunflower, corn, and soybean are cheap and widely used in packaged and processed foods, and they throw the delicate balance of essential fats way out of whack. Suffice to say, we need to dramatically increase the omega-3 fats and reduce the omega-6 fats to optimize health and, in particular, scar health.

There are three important omega-3 fatty acids:

- ALA, alpha-linolenic acid, found in a wide variety of foods, including flaxseed and walnuts
- EPA, eicosapentaenoic acid, found in fish
- DHA, docosahexaenoic acid, found in fish and seaweed.

Scientific studies indicate that supplementing with omega-3 fats, particularly EPA and DHA, dramatically assists wound healing by reducing inflammation and encouraging skin formation (epithelialization).[7]

Foods naturally high in EPA and DHA fats include oily fish like herrings, anchovies, mackerel, sardines, and salmon. The smaller fish are a healthier choice over salmon because they are lower on the food chain and less likely to contain high amounts of pollutants, including mercury, found in the oceans.

Vegans and vegetarians can obtain their omega-3 fats by eating seeds and nuts rich in omega-3 fats. However, these foods carry a high concentration of ALA as opposed to the wound-assisting EPA and DHA. Your body can convert some of the ALA into the other forms, but it is not as accessible as eating the fish oils directly.

The best vegan source of omega-3 fats is flaxseed. Grind the seeds freshly each time you consume them because you need to break down the seed coating to access the good fats. The oils can go rancid quickly, so buying them pre-ground is not beneficial. Be sure to store all seeds in the fridge to keep them fresh.

Other good sources of omega-3 fats are walnuts, especially English and Persian walnuts, followed by black walnuts. Personally, I also keep these in the fridge. Chia seeds are high in omega-3 fats as well in protein and fiber, which makes them an excellent addition to a vegetarian diet. Dark leafy greens also contain some omega-3 fats which is one more reason to jump on the green smoothie wagon.

The other way to increase your levels of beneficial omega-3 fats is to reduce your consumption of omega-6 fats such as safflower, grape seed, sunflower, hemp, corn, cottonseed, and soy oils. This tips the ratio in the healthier direction. It is easy to overeat cookies and cakes made with vegetable oils, but pretty darn hard to binge on sardines, unless you are a sea lion. Margarine, vegetable shortenings and any other artificially stabilized spreads are bad news as we discovered in the trans-fats section.

For the first month after surgery, I do suggest a supplement, as your wound is in the early stages of healing and we want to support it as much as possible. If you do not eat fish, there is a vegan omega-3 that comes from algae. Details are in the next chapter, Supplementing for Super Healing, as well as in Appendix I.

Once your scar has started to stabilize, which happens around four to six weeks, you can reduce the fish oil supplements (should you choose) and add more vegetarian sources of omega-3, such as freshly ground flaxseed, chia seed and walnuts. If you like eating fish, eat the little oily fish or wild-caught salmon three times a week. If you are a vegetarian, take the algae supplement or increase your intake of seaweed and algae in your foods. Everyone can reduce their omega-6 foods in order to help tip the balance in favor of the omega-3 fats, creating a more healing environment for your scar. Speaking of a healing environment, let's talk about friendly "bugs."

PROBIOTICS

We have more bacteria and microbes in and on our bodies than we have actual human cells. An average person has 30 trillion human cells and 39 trillion bacteria. Health and homeostasis requires working harmoniously with the bacteria we share space with. *Probiotics* means "for life," and these helpful bacteria come in many different strains such as *Lactobacillus acidophilus* and *Bifidobacterium*. They also help ward off harmful bacteria, create an acidic environment in the digestive tract (a good thing), and inhibit growth of other microorganisms such as yeast. Probiotic bacteria also help us heal: a study on burns found that supplementing the diet with probiotics reduces the time required to complete wound healing.[8]

Probiotics are generally recognized as having a positive effect in keeping harmful intestinal microorganisms in check, aiding digestion and nutrient absorption, and contributing to a strong immunity. They promote the return to harmony following a perturbing event (dysbiosis) such as antibiotic therapy, which is fairly standard practice in hospitals. We take care of our body's "good" bacteria by providing them with a supportive environment. *Prebiotics* are specialized plant fibers that nourish the good bacteria already in the colon. They encourage beneficial changes both in the composition and activity of the bacteria in the gastrointestinal tract. Probiotics introduce good bacteria into the gut, and prebiotics support the good bacteria that are already there.[9]

Imagine your body is a city where all your bacteria live. Balance and cooperation exists when there is an abundance of friendly bacteria. They love and take care of their beautiful city (you) and keep out negative elements that would upset their happy place. There are gorgeous, lush gardens and parks (prebiotics) for the bacteria to enjoy. All is harmonious until a natural disaster strikes the city (trauma, shock, antibiotics) and tragically many of the good citizens die. Mean, destructive bacteria start to infiltrate, setting up camps, creating mayhem and illness, and destroying the health of the city. A call for help is raised, and additional good guys flood the city (probiotic supplement) and edge out the destructive bacteria until they are contained and controlled. Harmony returns with friendlies back in charge of the city. You have a fair amount of control as to who gets to live in your body based on your food choices and supplementation.

Food sources rich in probiotics include fermented vegetables such as sauerkraut, sour pickles, kimchi, as well as kombucha, miso and tempeh, and kefir and yogurt. You will notice the last four foods are fermented versions of soy and milk. For people with intolerances or allergies to those foods, even the fermented form may be too much. However, you could try a water-based kefir starter and make your own concoction using coconut water instead of dairy milk.

I do believe that if you have a clean, organic, fresh diet, and you use certain foods therapeutically, you can attain many of your nutrients from your food. However, chances are pretty high that you are not going to eat sardines and sauerkraut every day. Given that these foods have nutrients you especially need when healing, I recommend supplementation for at least the first two months after surgery or injury, possibly much longer. I will give you some suggestions in Chapter 5 after we finish discussing the general food groups.

GENERAL FOOD GROUPS THAT MAY (OR MAY NOT) HELP *YOUR* HEALTH

Now you've read about my cornerstones of a healthy diet for *everyone:* loads of veggies (especially greens), omega-3 fats, and probiotics. Next we get into the more general categories of foods, and this is what splits people into different camps. I can assuredly say that in my search for an eczema cure I have tried every nutritional plan except for the cabbage soup diet: that just sounded disgusting. The Paleo Diet camp says no grains, no dairy, no soy, and no pulses (beans, lentils, peas). The Vegan Camp says no dairy, no meat, and no eggs. The Vegetarians say no meat, but dairy and eggs are an acceptable choice. The Raw Foodies don't eat anything cooked over 115 degrees F, and there are even Fruitarians and folks who claim to live on breath alone.

Where on Earth do you start? Well, you start with you.

The best diet to follow is the one that make you feel fabulous. This is going to take a bit of trial and error initially, particularly if you've been living on a SAD diet. Ideally, after we eat, we are refueled and ready to get back to our lives. If you do not feel full of vigor, consider keeping a record of what your food does to your body. Does a plate of pasta make you fall asleep? Are you still hungry after a large salad? Does meat sit heavily in your stomach? Does too much fat make you nauseous? Does dairy make you bloat? Any food can create problems for you if your body does not like it. You can keep a journal and slowly piece it together or you can jump in and do an elimination diet. This requires some pretty serious dedication but the rewards of knowing how to tweak your diet are priceless.

If you know you have a sensitivity to several foods I recommend the book *The Elimination Diet: Discover the Foods That Are Making You Sick and Tired—and Feel Better Fast* by Tom Malterre and Alissa Segersten. Rather than take you through an elimination protocol myself, I will let these two experts show you how. Another option is to work directly with a nutritional specialist who can guide you through the process. Yes you could spend money on a blood test but these are not consistently reliable. In my opinion the only way to know is to track your own reactions to certain foods. Once you know, you know, and then you can take steps to avoid foods that give you the mental and physical blahs.

GLUTEN-CONTAINING GRAINS

As a young child, I went to school in Bermuda, where our teachers often used the natural world to teach us science lessons. To learn how snails eat, we students made a paste of refined white flour and water, then put a dollop on a piece of glass. We gently pulled a snail off the schoolhouse wall and popped him on the glass, lifting it over our heads to watch the snail lick up the paste. The teacher told us to keep our bowls of wheat glue because after science came arts-and-crafts class. We returned our snails to their wall and used our glue to stick together paper projects. Clever teachers.

In my mid-teens, when conducting my first attempt at an elimination diet, I cut out all refined grains and found that my slow digestion, which had plagued my entire childhood, became normal. Could it be that the flour was acting like glue in my intestines? Indeed it can. Actually, it can cause far more damage than just constipation. The glue, called gluten, is a protein in wheat, rye, and barley that holds food together. The chronic autoimmune condition called celiac disease cannot be controlled by any means other than a completely gluten-free diet for life. There is no pill or potion. About 80 percent of Americans who have celiac disease are undiagnosed and suffer needlessly.

Celiac disease is one of the most common genetic conditions in the world, and if a family member is sensitive to gluten, there is a high chance you are as well. With celiac disease, the body starts an immune response to the gluten protein and attacks the small intestine and villi, which are tiny fingerlike projections that line the small intestine and are critical to nutrient absorption. If these are damaged, the body is unable to take in nutrients properly.

When undernourished, other things go wrong in the body including anemia, infertility, osteoporosis, intestinal cancers, bone or joint pain, arthritis, numbness, migraines, seizures, canker sores, dental defects, depression, short stature, and failure to thrive in children. According to the Celiac Disease Foundation, there are more than three hundred symptoms associated with celiac disease.

I used to get tiny blisters all over my hands, really deep in the palms and fingers, and they were maddeningly itchy to the point where I would scratch until I bled. This is Dermatitis herpetiformis, and it is a skin manifestation of celiac disease. Doctors simply told me I had eczema and gave me a steroid cream; there was no discussion about diet. I only pieced it together later in life after much suffering.

You might visit your doctor only to be told that the problem is in your head, or that the results of the tests are inconclusive. You might be told to eat prunes, use steroids or drink more water. The only way to stop celiac disease symptoms or any gluten sensitivity is to stop eating gluten. Continuing to eat gluten can lead to more chronic conditions such as multiple sclerosis (MS), Type 1 diabetes, and the horrors mentioned above. If you feel a little sick or tired or 'off' after eating wheat, rye, oats, or barley—or if you suffer from any of the above-mentioned conditions and you cannot figure out why—strictly eliminate all gluten for at least three weeks and see if you feel better. If you do, simply stay off of gluten for good!

Other people may scoff at your efforts, saying you are jumping on a trendy, gluten-free bandwagon. Ignore them. It is no one else's business what you put in your mouth. It is *your* body and *your* health. Remember most people have no idea they are sensitive to gluten. When folks try to coerce me to eat a slice of cake or dessert and do not respect my polite "No thank you," I briefly explain it will cause me physical discomfort. If the person is particularly persistent, "Come on, live a little, what's one piece, it's a special occasion, you deserve it, I made it especially for you", I may go into detail describing belly cramps, noxious gas and skin blisters. That pretty well stops it cold.

Two excellent books that discuss gluten's impact on health are *Wheat Belly* by William Davis, MD, and *Grain Brain* by David Perlmutter, MD. If you have a family member with Celiac disease I recommend you read these and see if you identify.

A note on gluten-free foods: they are still heavily processed and often high in sugar. Cake is cake regardless of the flour used, so please do not make gluten-free desserts, breads and snacks a staple of your diet. Reserve them for special events. In the Recipe section of the Appendix I will give you several different options for delicious desserts that are clean and safe for pretty much everyone.

MEAT

Meat is a highly concentrated source of protein, and a small amount goes a long way. Protein is a critical nutrient for efficient and effective wound healing. A deficiency of protein can impair capillary formation, reduce the cells that produce collagen, and negatively impact wound remodeling. Protein deficiency also affects the immune system, decreasing the body's ability to fight infection.[10]

Spiritually, emotionally and environmentally I want to be a vegan. I have tried quite desperately on several occasions to be a vegan, bringing my bread loving husband along with me for the experiment. If anyone can thrive on grains and veggies it's him. I put on my Nutritionist's hat and had us follow a stunningly healthy vegan diet with balanced plant protein, shakes and a wide variety of foods. Repeatedly I became lethargic, bloated, gained ten pounds (no lie – each time), had skin eruptions and wonky periods. One time I had blood work done before and after only to discover I became anemic after a short six weeks despite being vigilant about my iron intake. My husband is an endurance athlete and finds he suffers physically from the absence of meat. His energy plummets and he doesn't recover well after his long workouts. And so, we are not vegans.

Therefore, I am a conscious carnivore. I buy from local farmers and shop online, questioning the farmers and ranchers about their slaughter practices, looking for ones that have a high standard of compassion. I want to know that the animals have had access to fresh air, sunshine, plenty of grass and open space, and when the time comes for slaughter, it is done quickly with respect for the animal and the workers performing the kill.

With better quality meat you do not need to eat a steak the size of your face to get adequate protein – a portion size is roughly the same as your palm, so go by that measure. I will cook a "normal" sized steak and then eat half of it, saving the rest for a meal the next day. The website www.eatwild.com features a state-by-state directory of local farmers who sell directly to consumers.

As far as scars go there is a vital reason to eat organic meat and dairy. Approximately 80 percent of antibiotics sold in the U.S. are used in animal farming to promote animal growth and prevent infection. Even folks who eschew taking antibiotics for health reasons are getting a huge whack of them with every spoonful of commercial non-organic yoghurt.

The problem is that antibiotics used in food-producing animals kills their good bacteria, which allows antibiotic-resistant bacteria to thrive in the animal. We then consume the resistant bacteria when we eat the meat, and this can lead to infections. Thirty-five years ago scientists were already noticing that farmers and farm animals were showing signs of antibiotic resistance.[11]

Why does this matter? The antibiotics used in agriculture may be significantly contributing to the spread of antibiotic-resistant super-bugs that cause infections in patients in hospitals.

Scientists looked for a connection. They found that low levels of be-ta-lactam antibiotics, a drug class commonly used in both clinical and agricultural settings, accelerated the growth and spread of the (bad) bacteria *Staphylococcus aureus*. The effect was most noticeable among multidrug-resistant strains known as methicillin-resistant *Staphylococcus aureus,* or MRSA, which rapidly spread when exposed to low levels of antibiotics. The MRSA wasn't killed by the antibiotics—it actually thrived. *Staphylococcus aureus* and particularly MRSA continues to be a major cause of infections in medical settings such as health clinics and hospitals.[12] For this reason, choose organic animal products or ones that specifically state 'antibiotic free' from now on.

If you do not eat meat for ethical or spiritual reasons, make sure you eat adequate protein for healing after surgery or a wounding. Consider fish and seafood unless you have a sensitivity or if eating fish is against your beliefs. Non-meat sources of protein include pulses, beans, and nuts. Eating leafy-green vegetables, especially the dark greens, will contribute to your protein needs.

BEANS AND PULSES

Some people thrive on legumes, lentils, and peas, while others pollute the environment after eating them. Most often the reason for gas, which can be unpleasant and even painful, is that the beans were not soaked long enough before cooking. When using dried beans, soak them overnight in plenty of water. The next day, dump the soaking water, rinse the beans thoroughly, and add fresh water to the pot for cooking. Cook the beans until very tender.

If you buy canned beans, be sure to rinse them very well before adding to your soup or dip. If you still get gas after rinsing canned beans, try soaking the beans for an hour before adding to a recipe. If they *still* cause gas, you can try taking a digestive enzyme or resign yourself to the fact that your body finds them too difficult to digest and you may be better off avoiding them.

Soybeans are a touchy topic and there is research for both sides of the fence as to whether or not this is a healthy food. If you do eat soy, choose fermented foods like tempeh and miso, as these reduce the phytate content of the bean. Phytate binds minerals such as copper, iron, magnesium, calcium, and zinc in the gastrointestinal tract. You want zinc for wound healing and protein synthesis, so just take this as a caution if you consume a lot of soy. Keep in mind that eating refined soy foods such as tofu dogs and fake bacon can be hard on the body and redirect your precious energy from healing.

NUTS AND SEEDS

Tree nut allergies are one of the most common in children and adults. (Peanuts are often erroneously added to this group—they are actually legumes—but they are high on the list of allergenic foods, so I mention them here.) Allergic reactions to nuts range from mild (hives, itching) to severe anaphylaxis, when the throat swells and breathing is restricted. A severe reaction can result in death. If you eat nuts and find you have skin rashes, wheezing, digestive complaints, or itching in the mouth, nose, and sinuses, consider eliminating all nuts until symptoms clear, and then test them one type at a time for reaction.

You might have an easier time with seeds such as sunflower and pumpkin seeds. Tahini is creamed sesame seeds and can be used instead of nut butter. Sunflower-seed butter is pretty tasty too.

If you discover that you are sensitive to nuts or seeds—or for that matter to any other foods including grains, dairy, eggs, and nightshade veggies—you might want to dig deeper and consider an autoimmune diet. My favorite book on the subject is *The Paleo Approach: Reverse Autoimmune Disease and Heal Your Body* by Sarah Ballantyne, PhD.

If you are *not* allergic to nuts, here's the good news. Walnuts have the highest amount of antioxidants and are also rich in essential omega-3 oils. Almonds are high-fiber nuts that are rich in vitamin E, a powerful antioxidant. Cashews are high in zinc (good for healing), iron, and magnesium. A single Brazil nut contains enough selenium to meet the nutritional amount recommended daily. Selenium may inhibit the growth of certain cancers, particularly prostate and breast. It is better to eat your walnuts and flaxseed raw in order to gain the maximum benefits from their fats. High heat destroys the delicate omega-3 fats. In Appendix II, there is a recipe for low-roasting nuts that will keep the majority of these good fats intact.

STARCHY VEGETABLES

The Paleo Diet shuns grains but allows starchy carbs such as squashes, sweet potatoes, and white potatoes in reasonable portions depending on your level of activity. Vegetables with a higher starch content will break down in the body as sugar, so if you are sensitive to sugar, (it makes you sleepy, shaky, or cranky), experiment to find what portion size is okay for you. If you are very active or an endurance athlete, you are probably going to tolerate a larger serving of starchy vegetables. Some people find that eating starches after a workout helps them recover better. Others simply don't fare well with the extra sugar, regardless of lifestyle. Eating these with protein or fat will help slow down the release of sugar into the bloodstream.

MILK AND DAIRY PRODUCTS

The original version of this book was written for breast cancer patients, and I was greatly influenced by the writings of Jane Plant, PhD, author of *Your Life in Your Hands*. Plant is adamant about excluding all dairy products during cancer treatment—and beyond—based on her research and repeated incidences with breast cancer. While researching eczema, I came across many studies that concluded that dairy products cause inflammation—think arthritis, eczema, and acne. Therefore, dairy may not be a great food choice when you're healing. If you cannot bear a life without cheese (I have met many of you), make some concessions.

- Absolutely buy organic dairy to reduce your exposure to the antibiotics and hormone enhancers given to conventional dairy cows.
- Swap to goat and sheep dairy products as these have been found to be more easily digested than cow products. The protein and fat molecules in goat and sheep dairy are smaller and easier for the body to break down.
- Reduce the amount of cheese you eat by grating it on foods for flavor rather than eating large chunks of it.

I hope you have a better understanding of how the foods you eat directly impact the final outcome of your scar. My nutritional conclusion is easy. Skip the foods that steal your healing capabilities and boost up those that enhance it. Establish a solid nutritional plan now, even if your surgery is weeks away. Following these guidelines will give you the most nutrients possible from your diet while cutting out the "anti-nutrients," or health robbers, such as sugar, bad fats, and booze.

Ideally you would obtain all the nutrients you need from your diet. However, when healing, you may need some extra help, which you can obtain from supplements. In the next chapter, I want to introduce you to the ones that can help you feel like a superhero.

CHAPTER 5

SUPPLEMENTING FOR SUPER HEALING

THERE IS NO substitute for a clean diet, so please do not be fooled into thinking you can take your supplements with crappy food to compensate for it. These are called "supplements" because they add to your already excellent food choices. You may not eat curry every day, or drink golden milk every night, or eat kimchi and mackerel for breakfast. Yet in the early stages of healing, you need extra omega-3, probiotics, turmeric for its anti-inflammatory properties, and possibly a multivitamin to cover your bases.

I supplement on a regular basis for overall health, even though my diet is pretty supersonic. I figure the world is polluted, stress is rampant, and I'm getting older so my body could use the extra support. Plus, I have my own 'stuff' I am working on and prefer to use supplements rather than medication seeing as how I still have the option. If you are on medication and start to supplement, have your doctor monitor your reactions as your medication needs might change.

I have taken supplements since working at the health food store at the age of twenty-three when I first discovered their almost magical impact. I have tried many different brands and I offer you my current favorite ones along with tips for taking them. You don't have to buy the ones I do although I can personally attest to their effectiveness, at least on me. Just be sure to select high-quality ones that are not stuffed with fillers.

OMEGA-3 OPTIONS

Some folks are happy taking a slug of fish oil straight out of the bottle. I tried a chocolate-flavored fish oil once (yes, really) and, well, let's just say it didn't work out so well. The peppermint one tasted okay but I just couldn't get past the texture. Since I simply cannot "drink" fish oil, I take Ultimate Omega lemon-flavored soft gels from Nordic Naturals. These fish oils are high in the omega-3 fats EPA and DHA. Nordic Naturals' oils are very clean, surpassing the strictest international standards for freshness and purity. Additionally, each batch is tested to ensure there are no heavy metals present. On a more practical note, I never get fishy tasting burps from this lemony formulation, which is a good thing.

The vegan source of omega-3 DHA and EPA is derived from algae. Nordic Naturals Algae Omega is what I would choose.

PROBIOTICS

My probiotic suggestion is based on stability, quality, and convenience. Most probiotics require refrigeration. If you are stuck in the hospital for a few days or weeks you will need a high-potency, multiple-strain probiotic that is stable at room temperature. I recommend Jarro-Dophilus EPS from Jarrow Formulas.

As we discussed in the chapter about nutritious foods, the health of your bacteria plays a critical role in your healing. You will need double the regular dose of probiotics while taking antibiotics and I will explain in more detail in Chapter 8 where you learn how to avoid infection. Once you are back home or have access to a refrigerator, I recommend switching your probiotic over to MegaFlora, made by the MegaFood company.

TURMERIC

Curcumin, the active ingredient in turmeric, has anti-inflammatory properties. Both my husband and I use MegaFood Turmeric Strength for Whole Body because I don't always want a golden milk or curry. We know that inflammation is the common denominator in many chronic diseases so taking turmeric for life would be a smart move. If you are on blood thinners or other cardiovascular medications, please consult your doctor before taking turmeric supplements.

FOOD-BASED NUTRIENTS

It may seem as though I work for MegaFood, but I don't; I simply love their supplements. MegaFood products are made from whole foods, and the company has been going strong since 1973. I feel food-based supplements are more easily accepted, absorbed, and utilized by the body. Different co-factors and synergistic relationships in real food allow for nutrients to be optimally absorbed; supplements made from foods satisfy these complex relationships.

MegaFood works with local farmers to source the food, which goes through their Slo-Food process, in which they grind down the fresh fruits and veggies, concentrate the nutrients, gently dry the resulting mash, and form it into tablets. If you are curious to know more, check out their website www.megafood.com. This is my go-to company for most of my nutritional needs.

If you are not eating well or eating much, I recommend a multivitamin. MegaFood makes twelve varieties for women and twelve for men, so you have a large selection to choose from depending on your age and personal needs.

Now we have covered what to put into your body, we'll talk in the next chapter about what you put *on* it. The average woman is exposed to hundreds of different chemicals daily in personal care products including toothpaste, deodorant, perfume, makeup, facial cleansers and moisturizers, body lotion, hair-styling products, and more—depending on your routine. Rarely are these chemicals tested together for possible reactions in the body, nor are they regulated for their impact on health.

Now I don't want you to stop bathing or taking care of yourself but I do encourage you to think about making a switch to more natural skin care products. Gents, I'm talking to you too, although you typically put less "stuff" on your body than we ladies do. Everything that goes on you goes *in* you and can negatively impact your ability to heal quickly.

CHAPTER 6

NO MORE TOXIC SKIN CARE PRODUCTS

MANY SKIN CREAMS have preservatives and chemicals that have no business being on your skin, let alone a tender new scar. In London, I was known as an eczema specialist and helped hundreds of people find or make products that soothed rather than contributed to their skin problems. Most of them come from the health food store or from ingredients in your kitchen. You want to baby your scar and nourish it with oils and creams that boost healing. The specific oils to use in the early stages of healing are described later in Chapter 11. This section is more of a guide for getting rid of health-threatening skin care products that may be lurking in your house.

Outrageously, there are many ingredients that directly aggravate the skin in standard skin-care products, and this is known by the manufacturers. In the United States, there is no formal safety testing for cosmetics and personal care products, so companies can use whatever ingredients they want. Some common chemicals in commercial products are known carcinogens such as formaldehyde and coal tar. Others, such as phthalates, could disrupt the development of infant male reproductive organs. No health studies are required for personal care items—a sobering fact indeed.

INGREDIENTS TO AVOID

The Environmental Working Group (www.ewg.org) has designed a database in their Skin Deep section where you can check your favorite products for their chemical profile and potential hazard to health. You may be pretty shocked when you go through all the products you use and see the grades they receive. Add it all up and you'll see you are swimming in chemicals. I want to highlight just a couple of the most commonly used chemicals to give you a head start on healthy skin care.

Before we carry on, I would like to point out something that could cause some confusion. Later you will read that I love Dr. Hauschka products and have used them for almost two decades with never a reaction or problem. On the EWG website, Dr. Hauschka products receive a very poor score for the use of "Fragrance". Obviously I found this rather upsetting considering how beautiful the skin care line is and how carefully it has been formulated. So, I researched more.

According to the EWG website, "The word 'fragrance' or 'parfum' on the product label represents an undisclosed mixture of various scent chemicals and ingredients used as fragrance dispersants such as diethyl phthalate. Fragrance mixes have been associated with allergies, dermatitis, respiratory distress and potential effects on the reproductive system." A lot of unscrupulous companies list their chemical garbage as 'fragrance'. Unfortunately, there is no clarification for chemicals vs. essential oils.

On the Dr. Hauschka website, under Frequently Asked Questions, I found this: "Dr. Hauschka fragrances are carefully composed, proprietary blends of the purest, highest quality essential oils. European regulations require that we list our pure essential oil scents as "Parfum" while in the US the required declaration is "Fragrance". No synthetic fragrance or perfume ingredients are ever used to scent Dr. Hauschka products."

Hopefully that will clear up any misunderstandings. I used to send my eczema patients to my colleague Amanda Berlyn, a Dr. Hauschka

Esthetician, for targeted help with their skin. I promise that every single last person that took her advice and used the products saw benefits, myself included. You can visit the Dr. Hauschka website at www.dr.hauschka. com and read about their ingredients. They use biodynamic farming, which is even groovier than organic, use sustainable wild harvesting and partnerships around the world. With that cleared up, let's continue with what to avoid.

SODIUM LAURYL SULFATE

Sodium lauryl sulfate (SLS) and sodium laureth sulfate make soap bubbly. You use multiple soaps to wash your hands, body, face, hair, dishes, and household surfaces. Have a look on the label of all your different soaps to see if SLS is in the ingredients list. In laboratory tests, SLS caused allergies, dandruff, and skin irritations. In a study of sixty-seven patients, every single one of them showed a higher degree of skin-barrier disruption and inflammation in response to having sodium lauryl sulfate put on the skin.[13]

In fact, you can consistently damage the skin using SLS, making it a predictable tool for scientists when they need to test products on broken skin.[14] Yes, you read that correctly. Put another way, scientists depend on SLS to break the skin so that they can then test other products to see what happens.

In addition to soaps, this inexpensive chemical is found in toothpastes, mouthwashes, detergents, and anything else that is bubbly. SLS is strong enough to degrease your engine too! Imagine what it is doing to your skin. I was furious when I first connected the bubbles in my soap to my weeping eczema. I seriously question the people who formulate skin products with substances clinically proven to break open skin.

All my skin care products, shampoos, toothpastes and home cleaners are SLS free. I know as soon as I use it because my skin gets terribly dry and itchy. When my eczema was at its worst I used to carry a small bottle of castile soap in my bag for washing my hands in public restrooms. If you suffer from dry or broken skin, completely eliminating sodium lauryl sulfate from your daily life is essential.

MINERAL OIL

Mineral oil (also called liquid paraffin, paraffin jelly, and petroleum jelly) is inexpensive and widely used in skin care. Baby oil is simply mineral oil with added perfume. Mineral oil is a by-product from the distillation of petroleum to produce gasoline and other petroleum-based products from crude oil. Yes, pick up your jaw, I did say *crude oil.*

Although cosmetic-grade mineral oil is highly refined, which is why some people deem it safe for use on skin, there is still speculation about this. According to the Environmental Working Group, numerous studies show tumor formation in animals exposed to paraffin. CancerHelp UK warns that contact with petroleum products such as paraffin and mineral oil increases the risk of non-melanoma skin cancer. Knowing mineral oil is a refined version of the stuff I put in my car makes it very easy for me to just say no. Stop "cleaning" your skin with a ruthless degreaser and then applying crude oil afterward. It doesn't make sense and it certainly isn't healthy.

As an experiment, I read all the labels of all the lotions in a standard pharmacy in the United Kingdom. Every last one of them contained mineral oil. I then read the labels on all the shampoos and, sure enough, they all listed SLS. You may find that your very exclusive and expensive night cream has cheap ingredients and a fabulous marketing team.

When people came to me with terrible eczema, initially I would tell them to only put things on their skin that they would be happy eating. I wanted their skin to detox and have only 100 percent safe items put on it. Coconut oil is used by many cultures as a body lotion and hair treatment. Grapeseed oil is a very light oil, often used in massage therapy. Jojoba oil and rosehip-seed oil are gorgeous on the skin. Eventually my patients either found a natural skin care line they liked, such as Dr. Hauschka, or they learned to make their own.

MAKE HOMEMADE PERSONAL CARE PRODUCTS

Katie, known as The Wellness Mama (wellnessmama.com), has a beautiful website dedicated to natural products and healthy living. She provides loads of recipes for natural skin and hair products as well as tips for making your own household green cleaners.

Start by replacing the most noxious products in your cupboard and experiment with your own creations if you choose to. Otherwise there are plenty of natural and organic skin care lines available. And don't forget to purchase chemical-free makeup. Remember, you want to reduce the chemical burden on your body in general so that it can focus all of its attention on healing your wound.

Good nutrition and nontoxic skin care are imperative, but there are two more basics of good health: breath work and meditation, which we'll explore in the next chapter.

CHAPTER 7

WORKING WITH BREATH, MEDITATION, AND VISUALIZATION

So FAR, WE'VE been talking about healthy foods and household products, but now we turn to more internal methods of healing and maintaining wellness. Breathing exercises, meditation, and positive visualizations may seem intangible, yet they are powerful tools that let you take the reins of self-healing.

Our physical bodies are often at the mercy of our emotions. For instance, just thinking about your greatest fear can make your heart beat faster and your palms go sweaty. Your physical body responds to stress and fear in an instant, but practicing deep breathing and quiet mindfulness is like carrying your own parachute when you start to nosedive.

THE BENEFITS OF BREATHING

Deep breathing relaxes you and nourishes all the cells of the body by increasing oxygen to your brain and stimulating the parasympathetic nervous system, which helps calm you. Deep breathing can help cut through pain (think Lamaze during childbirth), encourage lymphatic flow and detoxification, and requires nothing more from you than a little focus and direction. Scientists can replicate experiments showing that psychological stress leads to clinically relevant delays in wound healing. Poor healing increases the risk of infection and complications, lengthens hospital stays, and slows your return to normal life.[15] As soon as you are free to breathe on your own after surgery you start making a beneficial impact on your healing with your next inhale.

In this section, I'll give you two breathing exercises. I encourage you to practice them both to see which one you like best. Perhaps one works better than another in a certain situation—you have to try it to find out. As a volunteer firefighter, I focus my breath when responding to a 911 call. I use it to calm myself as I drive to an accident and when I am on the scene. When volunteers are paged, they're given limited information, and often the situation can be much worse than initially reported. I need my wits about me, so I use my breath to keep me from going too far into my own stress response, which allows me to give better care to people in need. Stress reduces healing, so use your breath with intention.

In the yoga tradition, breath work is called *pranayama* and is the formal practice of controlling the breath. I mostly use the pranayama tools of alternate nostril breathing, *ujjayi* breath, and skull shining breath in my home practice. If breath work interests you, check out your local community for a class. Yoga studios are a good place to start and there may be natural health practitioners who also offer classes.

I give you two very basic "ways" of breathing: the Four Count Breath, which makes you very present in your body because you have to focus on counting, and the Pain-Relieving Breath, which helps you release pain, stress, and tension through controlled exhalations. These are the two I use in stressful situations to give me control over my physiology.

THE FOUR COUNT BREATH

This breath focuses the mind and reconnects you to the present moment.

1. Take a deep breath and shake out your shoulders. Focus on the count in order to still your mind.
2. Breathe in slowly for a count of four. Feel your face, neck, and shoulders relax as you inhale deeply into your belly.
3. Hold your breath for a count of four, allowing your body to soften and release. Drop your shoulders away from your ear.
4. Exhale slowly to a count of four, feeling your shoulders slide down your back as your legs, back, and feet relax. Pull in your tummy at the end of the exhale.
5. Finally, let your lungs stay empty for a count of four, further softening your body, letting any tension melt away.
6. Repeat.
7. Note: Each breath becomes deeper and fuller. Notice how you feel in each of the four phases. Consciously relax your body with each part of the breath work. The Four Count Breath helps you focus your mind to bring clarity and peace to a situation. The deep breaths increase oxygen levels and calm the nervous system. I use these counted breaths when I need to be present, powerful, and peaceful.

THE PAIN-RELIEVING BREATH

Researchers now know that controlled breathing used during childbirth is effective not because it distracts from the pain, but because it increases oxygenation, relaxation, mindfulness, and body awareness. It helps women be more alert, focused, and aware. [16]

This breath is ridiculously simple, and here are the steps:

1. Take a deep slow inhale right down into your belly.
2. Exhale for longer than you inhale.
3. Counting can help: inhale for a count of four, and exhale for a count of eight. Extend the exhale for as long as you can, maybe up to a count of sixteen!
4. If the pain is severe, purse your lips as you exhale. Focus intently on your breath rather than the pain. Continue until you feel your body relax and the pain begin to ease.

I coached my massage patients to use the pain-relieving breath when I would hit a sore spot on their scar. It is natural to tense up and hold your breath when in pain - but don't!

FINDING CALM THROUGH MEDITATION

Hand in hand with controlled breathing for relaxation and relief is meditation. As with pranayama breathing practice, there are plenty of guided meditations in the form of recordings, apps, and downloads that you can follow. If you are brand new to meditation and not sure where to start, I like the meditation app Headspace, as recorded by the extraordinary Andy Puddicombe, a meditation and mindfulness expert. Andy is a former Buddhist monk with a degree in Circus Arts – just the kind of quirky I adore. He is so easy to listen to and will teach you how to still your mind. Begin your free trial at the charming website, www.headspace.com. Also, Puddicombe has a wonderful TED talk about mindfulness that you may wish to watch.

The aim of meditation is to still the mind's chatter, turn off the running commentary, and give yourself a break. Meditation has shown to calm the nerves and reduce stress, which we now know is critical to healing well.

Start with five minutes at a time and aim for three short meditation sessions per day. Meditating early in the morning can center you and give you an opportunity to set intentions for the day. Taking five minutes after lunch can refresh your brain and refocus you for the rest of your afternoon. Meditating again last thing at night helps you drop the stressors of the day and encourages a restful sleep. Short and frequent meditation balances a life full of busy-ness. If yours is frantic, you need to find those moments more than anyone. Over time you might find you want to stay longer.

Here's how to prepare for either meditation or visualization (which you will learn at the end of this chapter):

- Silence your phone.
- Set an alarm if you need one.
- Put a "do not disturb" note on the door.
- Locate cats, dogs, children, parrots, and other potentially chatty creatures to safe places elsewhere.
- Find a comfortable chair, or sit on a cushion with your back against the wall.
- Take five slow, deep breaths, and on the exhalation audibly let out a big long "ahhh." Have a yawn and a little shake, then settle.
- Feel your body soften with each exhalation until you are very comfortable.
- Close your eyes and let them drift upward as though you are looking at the inside of your forehead.

How to "Do" Meditation

For your meditation, you can simply focus on breath, staying mindful of each inhale and exhale. If your thoughts wander, gently bring your focus back to the breath. You can do the Four Count Breath and concentrate on the counting, or try repeating a calming mantra in your head such as "Om," "I am healing," "I am free," "Love surrounds me," or "My scar is healing beautifully."

If a thought pops in your head such as "I have to make an appointment for the vet," or "Buy lettuce for dinner," or "Sign Johnny's permission slip," or ... or ... or... that's okay. Notice the thought and let it go, trusting that you will remember when you come out of your quiet time. Do your best to not attach to thoughts, to not obsess or worry about whether you are doing it right. Just relax and let your brain surrender to your mantra, your counting, or your breath.

Completing Your Meditation

At the end of your meditation or visualization, before you open your eyes, wiggle your fingers and toes, and take three deep breaths. Anchor in any details you want to remember from your journey. Think about any messages you received and how they can be incorporated into your daily waking life. Stretch gently and open your eyes. Journaling just after meditating helps you remember any gifts or insights you received.

MEDITATION AS MEDICATION: ANDIE'S VISUALIZATIONS

Meditation has a beneficial physiological effect on the body. I believe we can direct those healing qualities by using visualization and imagination. A couple of the following visualizations are ones I have given my fellow firefighters in our yoga classes and the others are more specific to healing. During a visualization, use all of your senses and fully imagine you are in the scene. Look around to see what is there. If you are on a beach, can you see birds, flowers, palm trees, coconuts, dolphins, or flying fish? Can you smell the tropical flowers? Feel the wind in your hair and the sand in your toes? Can you hear the waves crashing on the shore and taste the salty air? Use your creative imagination to make it seem real. The more time you have to give to your visualization, the more complex you can make the scene.

I have recorded these on my website www.andieholman.com to let you close your eyes and just be guided. Here's a quick overview of all six; the detailed visualization instructions follow.

- Column of Healing Light: Strengthens boundaries, is energizing
- The Tree: Is grounding and relaxing
- Angel Wings: Provides protection
- Waterfall of Light: Is cleansing, invigorating
- Ray of Starlight: Is peaceful and uplifting
- The Bench: Connects you to another person or being for insights

COLUMN OF HEALING LIGHT

This visualization can give you immediate peace and protection, connecting and grounding you deep into the Earth. Use it when you become agitated and want to regain some calm, or if you feel frightened and anxious and need to set some boundaries. With this visualization, you create an energetic boundary and will find it much easier to stand your ground, defend yourself, and speak up. Know that there is healing energy available to you always and forever. All you need to do is ask for it, and it will come instantaneously.

1. Take a deep breath and close your eyes. In your mind, ask for the Column of Healing Light to come to you now.

2. Imagine that high in the sky a switch flips on and a beam of brilliant, white light shoots down, encircling you like a spotlight. The light penetrates deep into the core of the Earth.

3. Within the column, your entire being—mind, body, and spirit—is bathed in safe, nurturing, cleansing light. The column anchors deep into the planet, keeping you grounded and solid. You are stronger, more confident, and happier with every breath.

4. If you need heavy-duty protection, make the outside of the column crackle with electricity to keep others from invading your space.

THE TREE

This is similar to the Column of Healing Light visualization, and it draws on nature for inspiration.

1. As you stand, envision your toes digging deep into the earth like tree roots. Feel them push down and down so deep, until you access the nourishment from Mother Earth. Keep pushing down until you feel the energy in the core that's nurturing, vibrant, strong, and sweet.

2. When you are rooted, picture your arms reaching up to the sky, your fingers becoming branches. Your fingertips are leaves, dancing in the breeze, stretching to the sun, reveling in the warmth, light, and generosity.

3. Bring the sun down your branches into the middle of your trunk to your heart center. Raise the nourishment from the earth up through your legs and torso and into your heart.

4. Feel the mixture of both energies and be grateful. Imagine beautiful, golden rays of light beaming from your heart center out into the world.

5. To end your visualization, bring your hands to your heart center, either in prayer position or one lying on top of the other. Breathe gently and come back to your body.

ANGEL WINGS

1. Take a deep breath, and on the exhale call in your Guardian Angel for protection, simply by asking or saying "Help."

2. The second you ask for help, your angel stands behind you and completely folds you in his or her wings, shielding you from harm and stress. Stay in the safety of the wings for as long as you wish.

What I love about the Column of Healing Light, The Tree, and Angel Wings visualizations is that much like the breathing exercises, you can use them with your eyes open. Flip the switch, and the column surrounds you. Ask for angelic protection and someone instantly has your back. Stressed out waiting in a long line? Become a tree.

Use these visualizations to calm yourself in pressured situations or to gain protection if you feel like your boundaries or buttons are being pushed. Feel your stress melt as soon as the light or the wings are around you.

The next three visualizations work best when you have at least fifteen minutes. In these, we go on a deeper journey, allowing you more time to explore your inner world and release your emotional and physical pain.

WATERFALL OF LIGHT

1. In your mind's eye visualize yourself in a beautiful natural setting. Turn around in a full circle, and take in the beauty of your surroundings using all of your senses. Over to the right lies a pathway lit by soft, golden light. Follow it.

2. In the distance you hear a waterfall; walk toward it. The waterfall starts high above, crashes into a large pool below, and empties into a river that stretches far into the horizon. There is a smaller pool off to the side that has a ledge under a slower stream of water. You go to investigate and find that the water is the perfect speed and temperature. Stand on the ledge and feel the water flow over your body.

3. Slowly, from the top of your head down to your toes, scan your body. Ask it to show you where you are tense, in pain, or holding emotions. Give the tension or pain a shape and a color. Keep scanning and see if you can find all your trapped emotions. You might have a red ball of anger, a blue cloud of sadness, or a grey mist of fear in you. Once you can see the shapes and colors and can identify the emotions or tensions, call in the light.

4. See a shimmering light-beam come down from the sky and merge with the water. As you stand under the waterfall, the light pours into your body through the crown of your head. See it filling all your cells with pure, white, healing light that surrounds the shapes and colors of your pain.

5. Like a watercolor in the rain, let the white light saturate the shapes—breaking them up and diluting the colors. As the colors start to run, visualize the pain also melting out of your

body. The colors and emotions are carried far away by the river, never to harm you or another being. Stay under the light, letting the colors bleed and the shapes melt until they are gone.

6. Now imagine you hold the light in your hand; it is the consistency of fluffy cotton. Stuff the light into all the spaces where there used to be pain. Pack the cottony light tightly as if the spaces were wounds, and imagine your body fully healing from the trauma and pain.

7. Take a few deep breaths and scan your body to see if there is anything else that needs to be released. When you are finished, thank the waterfall and the light. Walk back along your path until you reach the place where you started. Take a few deep breaths, wiggle your fingers and toes, and open your eyes.

RAY OF STARLIGHT, OR 70 BILLION-TRILLION STARS

Astronomers estimate that there are 70 billion-trillion stars in the Milky Way Galaxy alone. In this meditation, we use the softer yet still powerful light of all these stars.

1. Imagine you are in the wilderness looking up at a beautiful, starry sky. Take your time, point out some constellations or planets you recognize in your mind's eye, and let your body relax.

2. As your gaze drifts across the Milky Way, you see stars begin to shoot and dive together, rapidly forming a ray of light, brighter and more solid with each joining star. The column starts to stretch toward you, closer with every breath, until it fully envelops you.

3. Picture the light directly accessing your immune system. Visualize the light assisting the healer cells, cleansing the lymph nodes, and enhancing repair and restoration throughout your body. See the starlight glow around your scar, shimmering like glitter, working with the collagen fibers to create a healthy, smooth structure.

4. Ask the starlight to go anywhere in your body where healing is needed. See those areas light up with stardust glitter.

5. When you feel completely sparkly, thank the light, wiggle your toes, take a deep breath, and open your eyes. Keep the image of your sparkling, healing scar in your mind. Any time you feel disheartened, picture the glitter—and trust that you have Divine assistance helping you heal.

THE BENCH

Sometimes we want to talk things through with a certain someone. This visualization makes that happen, even if they have passed on or live far away.

1. Imagine a beautiful setting in nature. Ahead of you is a large bench; you go over to it and sit. Then you close your eyes and imagine the person you want to speak to.

2. When you open your eyes again, that person is sitting next to you on the bench and is eager for conversation. Stay and talk as long as you wish. Know that your words, whether they're full of love or pain or anger, will be accepted by the person you're talking with.

3. Thank the person for coming to see you, and after you say your goodbyes or so-longs, walk away from the bench and return to where you started.

Visualizations let you harness the power of your mind to help you heal your body. With all your faith and trust, see your body creating a healthy, tidy scar. See yourself playing your favorite sport or participating in a beloved hobby, all with a scar that moves freely with you and that has no negative impact on your joy whatsoever. Your body often follows the directions you give yourself; make them positive and uplifting.

If you get stuck in a loop of fear in your brain—mulling over what could go wrong or worrying about how it is all going to turn out—shout "Stop!" either out loud or in your head and imagine a large stop sign. Replace the negative thoughts with something positive such as your protective angel wings or stardust-glittering scar. You must use the power of your mind and direct it to healing, safety, beauty, and light.

Sometimes though, even with the best nutrition, mindset, friends, and support, things can go wrong. As they say, s*it happens, so the next chapter will help you know what to do if it does hit the fan and you get a scar's worst enemy: an infection. I recently (and stupidly) got in the middle of a fight between our cat and our new dog. They were both fine - I was the one who got wounded. However, I used all the techniques in the next chapter and came away with some nasty bruising but no infection, much to the surprise of everyone who saw me scratched and bitten, including the vet who has a long professional history of such injuries.

CHAPTER 8

AVOIDING INFECTION IN THE
HOSPITAL AND BEYOND

IN THE FIRST chapter we talked about dangers to your scar. Recall that surgical site infections, or SSIs, are unfortunately common after surgery. I don't tell you this to scare you but rather to get you prepared. An infection can cause healthy skin around your scar to deteriorate, making it much harder for you to heal well and make a neat and tidy scar. I want you to be ready with all of these items before going in for surgery so that if you sense even the slightest hint of trouble, you'll be ready to do everything you can to support your body while it fights the infection.

Signs of infection include:

- general feelings of malaise
- fever
- pus
- swelling
- red streaks radiating from the wound
- heat at the incision site
- pain (continual or increased)

Superbugs, bacteria that are resistant to antibiotics, are a major threat to patients in hospital. In March of 2016, Tom Frieden, MD, MPH, the director for the Centers for Disease Control and Prevention (CDC), said far too many patients were getting infected with drug-resistant bacteria in healthcare facilities. Ironically, we go to the hospital to get better, but this is where patients are most likely to become infected. A shocking one in four people in the hospital develops an antibiotic-resistant bacterial infection, according to the CDC—and staying in the hospital for more than twenty-five days increases the risk. [17]

This book helps you take charge of your own health, both while you're in the hospital and at home. Using natural methods for avoiding infections can work as a perfect complement to conventional medical treatments. When you're in the hospital, you may need to ask permission to use the treatments I'm about to tell you about. It helps if you can consult your doctor *before* your surgery or hospitalization about the potential benefits of these adjunct treatments. He or she is more likely to say "no" after surgery when there's less time to consider.

BANDAGES AND TOPICAL TREATMENTS

Prior to your surgery, talk to your doctor about adding natural antibacterial agents to your wound dressing to help healing and prevent infection.

Manuka Honey

One remedy you can try is placing Manuka honey in your bandages. Manuka honey, which comes from the *Leptospermum scoparium* bush (also called New Zealand Manuka), eliminates some bacteria and prevents certain other bacteria from creating a biofilm and spreading. A study in a 2014 peer-reviewed journal showed that methicillin-resistant *Staphylococcus aureus* (MRSA) is destroyed by Manuka honey. Even better, the bacteria did not become resistant to the honey, so the honey stayed effective as long as it was applied to the wound. Manuka honey has two principle antibacterial components, methylglyoxal and hydrogen peroxide. In clinical research, when the methylglyoxal was isolated and used on bacteria it was not effective in eradicating it. There is a special synergism in the Manuka honey that makes it effective. [18]

The interest in honey as a healing agent is spreading amongst scientists. There are promising clinical trials for the use of honey in wounds and there are companies developing impregnated bandages as well as topical honey ointments and gels for use after surgery. Honey has been used medicinally for eons—and now that we have antibiotic-resistant bacteria, we may need to revisit this ancient wonder.

COLLOIDAL SILVER

Another antibacterial that can keep infections from occurring is colloidal silver, which researchers are showing significantly reduces the formation and spread of *Staphylococcus aureus* bacteria. [19] To help reduce the chance of infection, buy colloidal silver spray and lightly spray your wound three times a day, or as often as your bandages are being changed.

There does seem to be precedent for the use of colloidal silver. Recently, medical-supply companies have developed waterproof wound dressings that contain silver as an antimicrobial.

ORAL SUPPLEMENTS TO HELP YOU PREVENT INFECTION

EXTRA PROBIOTICS

Probiotics are critical in the early days after surgery because they shorten the amount of time needed to heal, as discussed in Chapter 4. If you have an infection, you need friendly bacteria even more than when your immune system is not being challenged.

Your doctor will most likely prescribe antibiotics, which kill all bacteria, good and bad. Even though antibiotics are going to kill the friendly, supplemental bacteria that you take, you still want to have them in your body in between the doses of antibiotics. This may seem like a waste of probiotics, but look at it another way. Suppose you take your antibiotic at 9 a.m. and 9 p.m., and the doses wipe out all bacteria in your body. Your general health is already under par and fighting an infection, and sometimes the antibiotic doesn't kill all of the dangerous bugs. Because your friendly bacteria have also been destroyed, you're wide open for the opportunistic baddies to get even stronger. But let's say that two hours after your antibiotic, you flood your system with the good guys. You now have friendly bacteria taking care of your body for the next ten hours, until you take your next antibiotic. Yes, they will then be destroyed, but you stand a greater chance of healing faster when you have friendly bacteria in your body.

So I recommend that two hours after you take the antibiotic as prescribed by your doctor, take a high-potency probiotic, meaning it has multiple strains and lots of them. For example, the Jarrow EPS formula I previously mentioned contains eight beneficial, clinically documented strains—at 25 billion viable bacteria cells per capsule.

Make sure to finish the course of your antibiotics—all of it—and keep taking the strong probiotic twice a day for the next month to ensure repopulation of the friendlies.

GARLIC: THE NATURAL ANTI-BACTERIAL

Garlic has been celebrated as a healing agent for centuries. Current research into garlic's beneficial impact on immunity found that it stimulates certain cell types in the immune system such as macrophages, lymphocytes, natural killer cells, dendritic cells, and eosinophils. Garlic has anti-inflammatory properties and stimulates the beneficial bacteria in the colon, which further assists immunity. [20]

Scientists have found that raw garlic juice is effective against many common pathogenic (disease-causing) bacteria, even against strains that have become resistant to antibiotics. Garlic also prevents the bad bacteria from producing toxins that can damage health. [21]

The beneficial properties of garlic come from the thiosulfinates. When crushing or cutting a clove of garlic, an odorless amino acid called alliin is metabolized by the enzyme allinase. This yields allicin and other thiosulfinates, which give garlic its characteristic smell and its superpowers. When the thiosulfinates are removed from the garlic in processing, the antimicrobial activity of garlic is completely obliterated. In other words, to get the maximum benefits, you have to take garlic fresh and raw.

Yes, garlic is stinky, and you can smell it coming out of your skin in the beginning. To reduce the smell, consume plenty of chlorophyll, which is found in green vegetables, or chew a sprig of parsley after your meal to freshen your breath. Your body adapts quickly and the smell of garlic on your skin will soon pass.

Use garlic in your cooking for flavor, but if you want to take it medicinally, remember it is best served raw. You want to cut, chop, or crush the garlic clove and leave it to the side for about twenty minutes before eating. This allows the enzymes to work and produce the allicin and thiosulfinates.

One way to get your raw garlic is to take it like a pill. Slice one clove of garlic into small pieces, wait twenty minutes and swallow with water as you would a vitamin. This will be the easiest way to consume garlic while you are in hospital recovering. Have it with a meal or snack so it doesn't upset your stomach.

To incorporate raw garlic into a meal, make a dressing for salad or steamed vegetables. You will find an easy recipe in Appendix II.

HOMEOPATHIC REMEDIES FOR INFECTION

Chapter 9 provides a detailed explanation of how homeopathy works and how it focuses its healing on the immune system. For this particular chapter, I emphasize two primary remedies for general infection: Hepar sulphuris calcareum (Hepar sulph) and Pyrogenium (Pyrogen). These remedies are not specific to scars per se but rather how an infection "feels" in your body. The site of the infection may be your scar but you will feel its effects throughout your body first, and you will usually sense indications of a threatening infection well before it shows up in your scar.

1. Hepar sulph: Typically, a person who needs this remedy will feel chilly and irritable, wants to be wrapped in a warm blanket, and may have a sensation as if they had a splinter in their throat. They hate to get cold or feel a cold draft. They may also be sweaty with a chill.

2. Pyrogen (Pyrogenium): This remedy can be used when the infection has taken a stronger hold and the person has a fever, red streaks, and feels sore or achy and is restless. The person's body may smell putrid and offensive. Emotionally, they will be more weepy and self-pitying or showing signs of delirium.

Take both remedies in a 30C potency, two pills of each under the tongue every hour. I like to take both because I do not want to wait around to see if one or the other is more indicated or will work better. You cannot hurt yourself by taking both, and it may save valuable time getting the infection under control. Take them for as long as you have the symptoms described above and stop when you feel "normal" again. Homeopathy is very subtle, and my patients usually said something like "I know I still have the problem but I feel better in myself—lighter, stronger and happier." Your overall vitality and energy will feel better with the appropriate remedies. Continue taking the remedies until the physical signs of infection are gone.

WRAP-UP OF THE BASIC SCAR-HEALING STRATEGIES

Whew! Now we are halfway through the book—and we have only covered the basics. If you make healthy dietary choices 80 to 90 percent of the time; take high-potency, targeted supplements; stop using toxic chemicals on your skin; and harness your breath and your mind for stress reduction and visualized healing, you will do very well after your surgery.

If you carry on with these basic changes when life gets back to normal, you will find yourself looking and feeling more energized and vibrant each and every day. That I can promise you.

Moving forward, I'll cover different therapies and healing modalities that you may or may not use depending on how you feel, how well you are healing, or how well you have healed. I offer detailed explanations of each therapy and explain the healing benefits and how to use it. In Part IV, I'll give you a timetable of how to put it all together in a healing method based on whether your scar is new or old.

PART III

ADDITIONAL THERAPIES FOR SCAR HEALING

"A scar is not always a flaw.
Sometimes a scar may be redemption
inscribed in the flesh,
a memorial to something endured, to something lost."

—*Dean Koontz*

"I was diagnosed with breast cancer in April 2009. As is always the case with this diagnosis, the doctors move fast, and patients are required to make some really big decisions. Given the size of my cancer, I elected to have a mastectomy together with reconstructive surgery using my own tissue.

The SGAP flap operation had a 98 percent success rate and seemed like a really good option. But there's a danger in statistics: I happened to be in the other 2 percent and had a really fraught time, including four days in intensive care, four operations, and six blood transfusions. To think it was the chemotherapy I was most worried about! So I was left with no reconstructed breast and massive scarring to my breast area, a huge scar on my buttock where the donor tissue had been taken, and a graft site on my thigh to repair the skin that was taken. It was going to take a lot of work to heal from the operation and get back full mobility in my arm, shoulder, and buttock. Being a sport and fitness person this was really important to me.

Fortunately I met Adrianna, and she has taken "holistic" to a whole new level. She has given me homeopathic advice, massage, deep-scar massage, and has been a great listener. I feel very fortunate to have met her, and I question where I would be in my rehabilitation without her skill. It is a highly personal thing showing your surgical scars and allowing someone to touch them. Adrianna's skill in scar healing and the benefits I gained from her understanding of this area were phenomenal."

—Sue

CHAPTER 9

HOMEOPATHY: ENERGY HEALING WITHOUT SIDE EFFECTS

FROM 1997 TO 2000 I studied homeopathy full time in London, England. Homeopathy is well recognized and widely used in India, Europe, and in the UK where the Royal Family are avid supporters. After my training I gained my registered status with the Society of Homeopaths, accredited by the Professional Standards Authority. After moving to the United States, I registered with the North American Society of Homeopaths to continue my professional status.

My patients at London Bridge Hospital used homeopathic remedies for surgical support and to help with the side effects of chemotherapy and radiation. The oncology consultants and medical board of London Bridge Hospital approved the use of homeopathic remedies to complement the medical care they were providing. In twelve years of using remedies alongside orthodox cancer medication, no patients or doctors ever reported a negative reaction, and most reported a positive effect.

In the following pages I will explain how homeopathy works and will suggest remedies that I have found to help the body heal and form smooth scars. I like the term complementary medicine, meaning alongside. Use the remedies, and stay in close contact with your primary physician.

Keep your doctor informed of your self-care regimen so that she or he can adjust your prescription medications if necessary.

There's the one definite caveat, and I will say it a few times to make sure you get it: **Do not take Arnica *before* surgery and do not take it at all if you are on blood-thinning medication.** You do not want to thin your blood before surgery nor do you want to enhance your current blood-thinning prescription.

HOW HOMEOPATHY WORKS

Homeopathy differs from herbalism in that through the method of preparing the homeopathic remedies, only the energetic imprint of the original raw material is left in the final remedy. Herbalism uses raw plant material as the medicine, whereas homeopathic remedies are prepared in a certain way (discovered by German physician Samuel Hahnemann in the late 1700s) so as to release the energy of the plant while avoiding possible complications from otherwise toxic ingredients. (This is important because a number of homeopathic remedies are made from poisonous ingredients such as arsenic, snake venom, and plutonium.) The energy of the remedy then "speaks" to the body's immune system and energy system, encouraging healthy changes.

All day every day your body is trying to maintain balance. If you get too hot, you sweat. If you get too cold, you shiver. Your mind and body work in tandem, each influencing each other instantaneously, oftentimes well after an event occurred, or even far in advance. Sometimes the physical manifestation of a mental complaint is immediately apparent, and sometimes it takes a bit longer to show up.

Let's suppose a man has chronic stress headaches and neither aspirin nor painkillers is helping. He goes to see a registered homeopath. As part of the consultation she asks him to tell her about his work environment. The man instantly describes a heated argument with a colleague over a project. "As always, the boss decides to go with the other guy's suggestions instead of mine," sneers the man. "That gosh-darned, hot-air balloon Stanley always gets prize."

The homeopath notes that the man's voice has become louder. He has loosened his tie and his eyes are getting a little manic as the stress hormones come flooding back through his body, as though the argument is happening at that very moment. She puts a little star in her notes next to how he describes his co-worker Stanley and how he reverted to a childish voice. She notices that he is taking shallow breaths, his forehead is getting sweaty, and his face is flushed. The arteries in his temples and neck are showing, and the energy in the room has shifted considerably. He snaps out of his reverie, almost embarrassed to have shown her his inner mind.

All this man has to do is think about work and his body goes into a full fight-or-flight response, creating a stressed body and a continual loop of fiery energy that has to go somewhere. In his case, it goes to his head and creates headaches. This stress energy could just as easily become a stomach ulcer, heart attack, depression, or eczema. Where and how it will show up depends on lifestyle, genetics, food choices, environment, and self-care practices.

The homeopath understands that the problem is not really the headaches. It is how the man handles stress in his life. With a little more prodding, she tries to narrow it down into smaller components. She asks if there was any other time in his life that he experienced headaches like these. He says, "Yes, as a teenager." She asks what was happening in his life at that time. He explains that his father wanted him to play football, but he was not very good so the coach kept him on the bench.

While sitting on the sidelines, he knew his father would yell at him when he got home, telling him to try harder and that he was a disappointment and that a monkey could play ball better than him. He would work himself into such a frenzy he would get a crippling headache, which provided distraction from his father's tirade. It also offered protection as he would soon be able to escape and go lie down. The man's body goes back to this familiar pattern whenever he feels inferior, unworthy, small, insecure, and just not good enough—as is happening in the present when Stanley's ideas are chosen over his.

We know that balance or homeostasis is the bull's-eye for the body, which will always try to get there. We use homeopathic remedies to harness and direct that inherent intelligence. Here is where I think homeopathy gets really fun. Using the energy of the remedies, we can essentially pull a fast one on a body and mind that is stuck in a dis-ease pattern, encouraging the built-in homeostasis. We use the remedies to create a similar, yet slightly stronger version of the patient's complaint, allowing the body to wipe it out as it pushes back to center. As a result of purposely directing the inherent healer inside you, the illness or discomfort is extinguished as the body strives for balance, overcompensating for the remedy.

To treat our man with the headaches, we narrow his symptoms down to grief, shame, disappointment, and/or rejection (having established there is no physical cause for his pain). Then we give a remedy that addresses those emotions. I would ask this man to do additional supportive therapies such as writing and burning letters to his father, focused meditations to release pent-up emotion, and physical movement such as yoga and deep breathing. If the homeopathic remedy is right and it has worked well, I would expect a follow-up appointment with the homeopath to go like this: A month later the man returns and reports that not only are the headaches gone but he is going to visit his father next month, is getting along better with his boss, and now sees that Stanley the blowhard from the office actually has some great ideas. He has a lot more energy to do fun things with his family, and work just doesn't stress him out nearly as much as it used to.

As much as we cannot physically hold an x-ray or radio wave, science cannot yet explain why homeopathy works, and yet it does, often quite dramatically. It will not behave predictably like prescription drugs, because we are not aiming to suppress and mask the disease; we actually want to get rid of that energetic pattern. If a homeopath suppresses a symptom, we generally consider it a failure and search for a better remedy. Trying to compare headache pills to releasing deep grief is like comparing apples to orangutans. We are working from completely different perspectives.

One thing you will notice is that homeopathic remedies have a number and letter after the name. This is the potency. There are volumes of books covering the science and technique of how to make remedies into their various strengths and potencies. I will give a very rough example of how this might work. I grow calendula flowers in my garden. I crush and preserve them in alcohol to make a healing tincture, and this is herbalism. If I alter the tincture to the first level in homeopathy, it becomes an X potency (to the tenth) and is still very close to the original tincture I made. While this is fine for calendula flowers, it would not be so great when using snake venom. So I take it to the next level of potency, diluting and energizing the tincture to a C potency (to the hundredth). This can carry on up and up, continuing to energize the energy of the calendula, releasing deep healing vibrations to assist in healing the human mind and body.

Have you ever been to a concert where the bass is emphasized and you feel it hit your body with every chord, making your heart go ka-thump and your stomach flip? These are the lower potencies that have a very physical impact on your body. The more refined and higher notes of an opera singer might impact your emotional body, causing your heart to swell in your chest and tears to spring to your eyes. Remedies work in a similar way. The higher the potency, the more a remedy will impact your emotional energetic field, releasing anything that is stuck there, and then filter it down through your physical body. The higher potencies usually carry a letter of M, CM, MM, and beyond to LM.

For the purposes of this book, we will not go over a 30C, keeping the strength of the remedies at a general therapeutic potency. Please do not be tempted to buy your remedies in higher potencies as you can cause what is known as a "healing reaction" (I will describe mine in a minute), and it can cause great discomfort. I want the remedies to support you, help you heal, and be nothing but an asset in your toolbox. If you want to go deeper into this remarkable healing modality, find a professional homeopath.

I offer a different method of prescribing homeopathy than the classical way, which is one remedy at a time. I want you to use two or more of the most-indicated remedies at the time you need them, and then stop taking them when you no longer have the symptoms. My methodology is more of a practical nature, and you will need to pay attention to how you feel so that you can select the best remedy. The remedies suggested in this book are more pertinent to surgery, wound healing, and scar and emotional support, and they are by no means exhaustive. Some of them cast a wide beam of light for the immune system, whereas others are more targeted.

HOW TO TAKE HOMEOPATHIC REMEDIES
Should you study more about homeopathy you may find dire warnings to avoid coffee, mint, toothpaste, and other strong flavors while taking

remedies because these might interfere with their action. A quick side story for you. Throughout my three-year fulltime course to become a homeopath, I and the other students had to undergo treatment ourselves. Early in my training, and thus my treatment, I was given a bang-on remedy but in a very high potency that my body was not ready to handle. Sadly, this coincided with my homeopath leaving the country for two weeks, and my eczema erupted in full force, causing my face to resemble a boiled tomato that had lost its skin.

I thought, *No problem; I will antidote it.* I ran down to the shop below my apartment and bought supplies. Remember, I have had eczema from birth so I know what an outbreak feels like in all its stages. I drank two pots of very strong coffee and my face continued to swell. I ate two packets of extra-extra strong mints, and the eczema started weeping. I proceeded to drink wine: no better. I chain-smoked cigarettes: no better. I drank beer, then more beer and it only got worse. I tried all the substances that were supposed to make homeopathic remedies fail but all that happened was I got wired and wasted.

The next morning, I figured my skin couldn't get much worse, and I courageously took the same remedy in an even higher potency, accessing more of the emotional and energetic levels as this matched my history. I figured my face wouldn't slide off my skull, but I wasn't entirely sure. Slowly and surely my skin started to settle down taking about four days to fully clear again.

I tell you this story because I tried to antidote a homeopathic remedy with coffee, mint, booze, and cigarettes. They had no effect at all, or at least not in my case. Today I drink coffee and use mint toothpaste and my remedies all still work.

Here's the disclaimer: if you are easily affected by strong substances, you may find that indulging in said substances will overpower your delicate constitution, rendering the remedies less effective. If you know you are sensitive, your health will dramatically improve anyway by cutting out giant coffees, shots of tequila, and packs of cigarettes or huge spliffs. Use your judgment, and if you are not certain, book an appointment with a registered homeopath for guidance.

So, let's get back to how to take the remedies. They only work if you take them! I can't tell you how many times patients came back and sheepishly admitted, "Nothing changed, but actually I keep forgetting to take the remedies." The traditional way to take remedies is to put one or two pills under your tongue and let them melt, handling them as little as possible. You take them with a "clean" mouth, meaning you have put no food, drink, or toothpaste into it for twenty minutes before or after taking the remedy. Even for me, a great lover of homeopathy, this is challenging to remember. I want to make it easy for you because juggling remedies, supplements, and medication means you're likely to forget something.

Taking Homeopathic remedies the Easy Way

First, put three pills of each homeopathic remedy you are taking in a bottle of water and sip throughout the day. Replenish the pills each time you refill your bottle. Be sure to use the potency and frequency of dose I describe unless otherwise instructed by a professional. I will help you determine the best remedy to take for the symptoms you are experiencing.

You may wonder how long you need to take the homeopathic pills. This is where your powers of observation come in to play. Emotional remedies are used often, even every ten minutes, until you feel calm and back to your normal self. These are "in the heat of the moment" remedies to help you through the ups and downs pertaining to your situation.

Other remedies such as Calendula 30C will be taken daily until your scar is healed over, and sometimes even longer. The remedies for infection should be sipped continually throughout the day until your infection is gone. I will walk you through it when we get to the week-by-week guide in Part IV. And please know: you do not need to take these homeopathic remedies for life.

SUGGESTED REMEDIES FOR SCARS

None of these remedies is prescribed for you as an individual. If you want to be precise in your prescription, you need to see a qualified homeopath for a full consultation. These remedies are suggested in a general sense as having healing action in the context of scars and wounding. Also, the remedies are listed in alphabetical order, not in order of importance.

- **Aconite** (AH-con-ite) is made from the monkshood flower. It is used for fear, anticipation, and panic attacks. This remedy helps when terror grips, causing palpitations and anxiety. The fear can be so great that a person thinks horror or death is imminent.
- **Arnica** (ARE-ni-ka) is leopard's bane, from the daisy family, and is recommended for trauma, shock (emotional and physical), soreness, stiffness, and bruising. When someone is badly hurt or in pain they may fear having anyone approach them or touch them. Arnica helps with oversensitivity of a person's body and mental stress, allowing them to relax and accept help. **Caution:** Do *not* use Arnica before surgery as it has blood-thinning

properties. People who are on blood-thinning medication should avoid Arnica altogether. Also, do not apply Arnica gel, cream, or oil on broken skin.

- **Calendula** (ca-LEN-juh-luh is made from marigolds and has a long-standing reputation as an overall healing superstar. It is used for wounds, cuts, lacerations, abrasions, burns, or any broken skin surface. It promotes the formation of favorable scar tissue while warding off infection.

- **Fluoricum acidum,** commonly called **Fluoric acid**, (FLOOR-ic acid) is made by distilling a fine powder of calcium fluoride with sulfuric acid. This remedy is indicated for old scars that become red and itchy, or when the scar is surrounded by small pimples. If there is edema accompanying the above symptoms, this is a great remedy.

- **Graphites** (GRAPH-i-tees) is made from graphite, the black lead of English pencils. This remedy is good for an older scar that is thick and hard or has a burning or tearing pain. The skin around the scar might be broken and sticky (like eczema or seborrhea) or be ulcerated. Graphites helps with the absorption of scar tissue.

- **Hepar sulphuris calcareum** or **Hepar sulph** (HEP-arr sulff) is one of my favorite remedies. It is used at the first sign of infection, and your body will give you warning signs well before any pus appears. Generally, people who need this remedy are exquisitely sensitive to everything: one wrong word, a slight draft, a wee chill, and boy do they get irritable. The tiniest thing can set them off in a temper. Another indication is a sore throat and inability to get warm. This is the body asking for Hepar sulph, as there is an infection under way.

- **Ignatia** (igg-NAY-sha) is made from the St. Ignatius bean. This remedy is helpful for emotional shocks, bad news, loss, and feelings of vulnerability or sadness. The person may be putting on a brave face, swallowing tears that feel like a lump in the throat, and yet they are unable to hold it together, getting wildly upset over seemingly trivial things. Ignatia helps diffuse intense emotional outbursts and is useful for loss or distress of any kind— physical, mental, or emotional.

- **Nux vomica** is made from poison nut and is the number one remedy for toxicity. For our purposes, I would suggest this remedy for general sluggishness after strong medication, such as constipation after pain killers. The patient will be angry, impatient, and very sensitive to everything (light, touch, smell, noise, sounds). Think of someone who is thoroughly pissed off about being in the hospital and everything that goes with it. Also, for someone who is a workaholic and frequently indulges with coffee or booze, this remedy helps them detox from a hectic life, stimulants, and alcohol, as they will be undoubtedly uncomfortable without them. For scar healing, this remedy is only used short term because it can antidote other remedies.

- **Phosphorus** helps bring you back into your body if you feel spaced out or sick after anesthetic. You will likely only need a few doses to ground you.

- **Pyrogenium** or **Pyrogen** (PIE-row-gen) is excellent for a more advanced infection or when there is oozing pus. Please remember that if you suspect an infection, call your doctor right away. An infection eats away healthy cells and can greatly reduce your chances of a tidy scar. You will probably need antibiotics, and I suggest you use this remedy alongside them, as well as the extra nutritional support I'll give you in Part IV. A person who needs Pyrogen may feel confused, restless, aching, and sore and may have a fever. The scar site may have red streaks or oozing pus, and the person may smell pretty offensive and septic in general.

- **Silica** (SILL-ica) is for scars that are painful to touch, become thickened into keloids, are nodular (lumpy or bumpy), or heal slowly. The emotional state of the patient may be shy, overly sensitive, or withdrawn. Old scars may become painful suddenly, or be sore after you have been massaging and freeing the fascia.
- **Thiosinaminum** (THY-o-SIN-a-MY-num) is made from mustard seed oil and has a dissolving action on scar tissue. This remedy is used more on older scars that are restricting full range of motion. It is also indicated when there is tightness around the scar or keloid formation. I do not suggest it too early in healing as we do not want to impede the initial stages of scar formation.

USING THE REMEDIES THERAPEUTICALLY

Using remedies therapeutically means prescribing on the more general themes of a remedy rather than individualizing the prescription. They are used as a support to help you through your healing and are discontinued when they are no longer needed.

Remedies for emotional states: Ignatia, Aconite, Nux vomica
Wound healing remedies: Calendula
Post-op helpers: Arnica, Phosphorus
Infection remedies: Hepar sulph, Pyrogen

Healing helpers for old or painful scars: Fluoric acid, Graphites, Silica, Thiosinaminum

At the back of the book is a Resources section with the contact details for Nelsons, a London-based homeopathic pharmacy where you can order your remedies. Nelsons has been selling the remedies since 1860, when the pharmacy was started by a student of Hahnemann, homeopathy's founder. They ship worldwide, have very fair prices, and an extensive remedy bank. Some of the more common remedies I've listed are available in larger health food stores; some you will need to special order from Nelsons. I was lucky enough to be a founding practitioner at their clinic and I would fill in at the pharmacy from time to time. I loved being a part of such a legacy.

Next we move on to exercise and the immune-boosting benefits it has to offer, particularly when you use different movements for flushing the lymph and stretching the fascia around a scar.

CHAPTER 10

EXERCISE FOR A HEALTHY RECOVERY

I DON'T EXPECT you to jump out of bed the day after your surgery and go for a run. In fact, I would really rather you didn't. When you exercise too much too soon, your scar is going to get a bit nervous and develop extra adhesions to stabilize itself. Instead, go nice and slow, honoring the deep work your immune system is engaged in. On the same theme, an old scar might not adapt to intense stretching right off the bat and could feel quite painful. You may need to ease into the movements that will ultimately aid your recovery.

Exercise is important for the physical health of your scar, your lymphatic system, and to body in general—plus it's critical to a healthy state of mind. Even if you feel like the dog's old dinner after surgery or during hospitalization, gently move your body every couple of hours, or at the absolute minimum do five minutes of deep breathing sessions every hour.

We start with the most basic of exercises, having a friend help you move your lymph with arm sways and leg pumps, and progress to more challenging movements. Again, as with the homeopathic remedies, this will all come together in a program for you to follow, which is presented in Part IV. We avoid stretching a new scar in the early stages of healing. However, if you are working on an *old* scar, choose the stretches that activate the area around your scar the most in order to start pulling apart the adhesions.

EXERCISE TO INCREASE LYMPHATIC FLOW

Muscular contraction moves the lymph, so in the early days of recovery you need to enlist a friend, nurse, or massage therapist to help you with the exercises at least twice a day. The end result of your scar greatly depends on early-stage healing, and we want to move the lymph to help the immune system capture and destroy any bad bacteria in the body—as well as increase circulation and nutrient exchange.

Move and activate the non-injured limbs at first. Let the stronger parts of the body do the bulk of the work in the beginning. A high concentration of lymph nodes are located in the armpits and groin, and these are the areas we aim to stimulate. Avoid pulling or stretching the wound area or incision.

Do not perform the lymph exercises if you have an active infection, fever, bleeding, extreme lymphedema, or swelling. Instead, call your doctor. If you are experiencing cording in your arm after having lymph nodes removed, a professional lymph specialist or massage therapist may be needed for a short time. Cording is the term used for axillary web syndrome (AWS), which may develop after a lymph node dissection, removal of lymph nodes in the underarm, or from scar tissue after surgery to the chest. You can often see the "cords," which are thick, ropelike structures running under the skin down the arm. They are painful and tight, and they may restrict your ability to raise your arm to the shoulder or above your head. Cording can happen days, weeks, or months after surgery. It is unknown why some people get cording, but stretching and massage are imperative for treating it and keeping the connective tissues supple and flexible.

There are four, possibly five, ways to have a friend help you in the hospital, and you may want to try out some exercises together before you are in recovery at home. If you can do all the movements that follow while you're in the hospital, terrific! If not, just do what you can, and add in the other movements when possible. You will find videos on my website www. andieholman.com showing you how to do these exercises with your friend.

FRIEND-ASSISTED EXERCISES IN THE HOSPITAL: UPPER BODY

Head Lymph Flush

1. While you are lying down, a friend sits behind you and cradles the base of your head in both hands. If there is no room at the head of the bed, she sits next to it and places one hand under the base of the skull and the other on the forehead.
2. As you inhale, your friend squeezes lightly at the base of your skull. Hold your breath while she holds the gentle pressure for a count of three. Release your breath as she releases the gentle squeeze.
3. Your friend moves her hand about an inch lower, and you repeat the breath as she squeezes. Every time you inhale, she holds the pressure while you hold your breath, and then as you exhale, she releases the hold. Work slowly down your neck.
4. Repeat three to five times.

Chest Lymph Flush

1. Your friend uses the flat of her fingers to gently press (feather-light) on your chest, starting in the middle on the breastbone, moving out toward the armpit.
2. Inhale as she presses, and exhale as she releases.
3. Your friend moves her fingers along your chest in one-inch increments while you take deep breaths in time with her pressing.
4. Repeat both sides twice.

Arm Sway

1. Your friend holds your upper arm while you bend your elbow and go floppy, letting your forearm rest on his.
2. As you exhale, your friend moves your arm as far back as is comfortable. Pause at the top of the stretch and inhale.
3. Exhale as your friend brings your arm back to neutral or to 90 degrees. Inhale.
4. Exhale as he moves your arm overhead again with the hopes of stretching a tiny bit further with each breath.
5. Inhale slowly while he holds the stretch. Exhale back to start.
6. Repeat ten times and do the other side.

FRIEND-ASSISTED EXERCISES IN THE HOSPITAL: LOWER BODY

Leg Pumps

1. Lying flat, have your friend sit close to you on the bed next to your hip or upper thigh. Bend the leg closest to her and rest your ankle on her shoulder. She can put her hands around your thigh for support or hold one hand at the ankle and use the forearm of the other arm to push into the back of your lower thigh.
2. Take a deep breath in. As you exhale, your friend leans in, bending your leg slowly toward your chest. Hold for a slow count of three while you inhale. She sits up again slowly as you exhale.
3. Take a slow breath in, and as you exhale she leans in again. Repeat five times for each leg.

FRIEND-ASSISTED EXERCISE AT HOME

Once you are recovering at home, continue with the previous exercises and add the next two if you can. If you have had abdominal surgery, just do Legs Up the Wall. Do not start the bending movements until your scar is secure enough and you have been given the "all clear" for exercise from your doctor.

LEGS UP THE WALL

Rest your legs and feet up the wall and breathe deeply into the abdomen. This helps the lymph tremendously, as gravity drains the lymph into the groin while the deep breathing activates the lymph in your torso. Double bonus! Stay here for as long as is comfortable. If you are moving into Frog's Legs, put on socks so your feet slide easily up and down the wall.

FROG'S LEGS

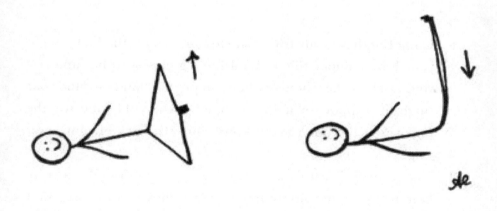

1. Keep your feet up the wall. Engage your core or stomach muscles by sinking your belly button to your spine, then tighten the muscles and hold them strong. This helps to protect your lower

back, while also giving you a sense of grounding and purpose; the very core of you is solid. Keep your core engaged and breathe into your rib cage, expanding your ribs out to the sides. Take a couple of breaths like this to get used to the feeling. Exhale when moving the legs, whether up or down. Pause at the top or bottom and inhale.

2. Stage One is to have your friend nearby to assist your balance if necessary. He can simply be near you to help when you want to get out of the pose, or he can assist you with bending your legs.

3. Bend one leg at a time. Your arms are wide by your sides with your hands facing palms-down for stability. Your friend can either help move the leg or can apply gentle pressure across your hips to hold you secure. Be sensible about your scar.

4. Stage Two is to slowly bend both knees outward, keeping the soles of the feet together to make diamond-shaped frog's legs. Slowly slide up and down the wall from fully bent to fully straight.

NEXT UP: LOVE YOUR LYMPH!

I designed Love Your Lymph Moves which is a gentle flow of twelve consecutive exercises to flush your lymphatic fluid in order to boost your immune system and keep your fascia flexible. As you are ready, progress from the friend-assisted lymph exercises to some or all of the Love Your Lymph Moves. I have suggested repetitions, but it is up to you to determine how far to go. Little and often is better than overdoing it one day and feeling terrible, then skipping all exercise for the next week.

I suggest you start these lymph exercises three to four weeks after surgery, but if you like, start them *before* surgery to prepare. If you recover swiftly and feel you can start this sequence sooner than Week 3—or if you can do at least some of them—that would be wonderful.

As before, be careful of where your scar is and modify or skip poses that cause too much pull or pressure on it. If you feel any pain, stop immediately. If the pain persists, contact your doctor or physical therapist for advice.

Ideally you will do all or part of the Love Your Lymph exercises daily, working up to twice a day. Feel free to break it up as well, maybe doing six in the morning and six in the evening. Just keep that lymph moving.

The exercises are described here and repeated again in Chapter 15, during Weeks 3 and 4 after surgery, which is when you are hopefully ready to try them all. At the risk of sounding like a broken record, remember there is no one path to healing, and you are on your own personal journey. Deep breathing and friend-assisted exercise will go a very long way to helping you recover. The Love Your Lymph Moves are simply the next in the progression of techniques to heal your scar. Start when you can!

Props: I like to have lots of props for these movements, as they are in essence "yin"-style yoga—plus it is reassuring for the body to have support available. Keep four cushions or pillows handy, or you could buy yoga bolsters and blocks. (See the Resources section in Appendix I for ideas).

THE 12 LOVE YOUR LYMPH MOVES

Before you start, do the Legs Up the Wall or the Frog's Legs first. Harness gravity to flush your legs and then progress to the moves. You can do the lying down exercises on the floor or the bed. Just be aware of stability and use props if you need them.

Start by lying on the floor or your bed. Bend your knees and place your feet flat on the floor, knees pointing upward. Take ten deep, slow breaths; use the counting to calm yourself and access the parasympathetic nervous system. Visualize healing light for your entire body. Ask for your lymph to be nourished and refreshed as you mindfully do the twelve exercises.

I. ROCK THE BOAT

This is a very small movement that helps warm up the smaller stabilizing muscles of the pelvis, hips, and lower abdominals.

a.   Exhale and slowly curl your pelvis up, squeezing your pelvic floor muscles and letting your belly button drop further toward the floor.

b.   Hold for the count of three and slowly inhale into your ribs.

c.   Exhale, release the hold, and let your pelvis stretch and rock forward toward the floor.

d.   Repeat ten times.

2. Twister

Twister massages the internal organs and can help peristalsis if you are constipated. If you had abdominal or back surgery, skip this one unless you have the okay from your doctor to do gentle twists.

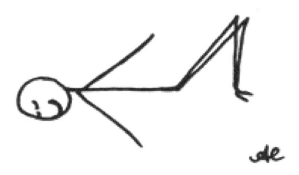

a. Lie on your back with your feet flat on the floor. Place one or two pillows on either side you, just below your hip where your thighs will land in the twist.

b. Keeping your knees pointing up, extend your arms comfortably to the sides, and steady yourself with your hands palms-down.

c. Take a deep breath and scootch your hips over to the right about four inches. As you exhale, gently allow both bent legs to fall to the left, resting on the pillow (or two or three).

d. Relax your stomach muscles and breathe deep into your belly. Feel the stretch in your rib cage, lower back, arms, and neck. Stay for seven deep breaths, continuing to relax deeper into the pose on each exhalation.

e. To come back to center, exhale fully, pull your belly button toward your spine, and slowly turn your knees back to center.

f. Take a full breath and repeat on the other side, doing two for each side.

3. Backstroke

Backstroke helps stretch the chest, arms, and shoulders while activating the lymph nodes in the neck, arms, and chest. Be very careful if you've had chest, breast, back, arm, or shoulder surgery. If this is too much, continue with your friend-assisted Arm Sway exercise.

a. Close your eyes and imagine a beautiful ocean scene. Picture yourself having a leisurely paddle through the crystal-clear waves.

b. Bend your knees bent upward and place your feet flat on the floor, arms straight by your sides.

c. Lock your core by sinking your belly button to your spine and holding it there. Breathe up into the ribs.

d. Bring one arm slowly over your head and extend it as far back as you are able. Then reverse the movement, bringing your arm back to your side whilelifting the other arm up and backward as if swimming the backstroke.

e. Complete twenty strokes in total.

f. Relax your stomach muscles and breathe into the belly.

Roll onto your side and push yourself up onto your hands and knees.

4. CAT-COW STRETCH

The Cat-Cow Stretch benefits the whole spine by stretching the front of the body from the chin to the pelvis, and the entire back from the top of the head to the tailbone. Use the breath consciously with this exercise. Be mindful if you have a scar on your torso, and take care not to overstretch.

a. The first picture is Cow. Inhale and drop your belly toward the floor, then stretch your chest forward and lift your chin.

b. As you exhale, arch your back like the second picture, which is Cat. Pull up on your core as you push every little bit of breath out of your body.

c. Inhale to Cow, exhale to Cat.

d. Repeat five times.

5. Child's Pose

In yoga this is a posture of surrender and serenity. In this pose your belly and face are soft. This stretch is so good for the arms, back, and shoulders, and it will be of particular benefit for tight cording, painful connective tissue in the arms.

a. Take your knees a little wider than hip distance apart and lean your bum back to rest on your heels, keeping your fingers stretched away from you. If this is uncomfortable, place a pillow or two on top your calves and move your hips back.

b. Rest your forehead on the floor, a pillow, or a yoga block. Make sure your neck is relaxed. Close your eyes and let your face go mushy.

c. Envision your Column of Healing Light nourishing you and re-moving anything that is not in line with your Highest Good.

d. Take ten long, slow breaths, and exhale fully with a sigh, letting all the tension leave your body.

Move into a comfortable sitting position. If you sit on a small cushion you may find your knees and hips relax more because your pelvis is slightly raised. When sitting cross-legged, you can prop up your knees with a pillow on either side or with your knees straighter (but still a little bent). Keep your back against a wall if sitting up straight is difficult.

6. SEAWEED

This flowing movement helps open the sides of the body from the armpit to the hip. Have a yoga block or pillow to either side of you if reaching the floor is too much of a stretch.

a. On an inhale, reach your right hand out to the side and place it on the floor about a foot away from your right hip.
b. Exhale and lean over to the right, raising your left arm overhead until you feel a stretch from your hip to your fingertips.
c. Inhale for a count of four.
d. Exhale and slowly change sides.
e. Try to keep both butt cheeks on the floor. Gracefully float your arms through the air as if they were sprays of seaweed rolling gently on the waves.
f. Repeat for a total of ten times, five on each side.

7. Seated Twist

The Seated Twist is similar to the lying Twister, but it has a different action on the hips and groin because of the seated position. This move mobilizes the internal organs gently, improving digestion and elimination while freeing possible rib adhesions. As with Twister, go very gently if you have had abdominal or back surgery.

a. Sit on a little cushion in a cross-legged position, and inhale.

b. On the exhale, twist your whole torso gently to the left placing your left hand on the floor or a block directly behind your spine.

c. Place your right hand on your left knee to help hold the position.

d. Gently turn your head to look over your left shoulder.

e. Take two deep breaths and return to center. Have a relaxing breath.

f. Then take a deep breath, and on the exhale twist to the right, with your right hand behind the spine and left hand on the right knee, looking over the right shoulder.

g. Take two refreshing breaths and return to center.

h. Repeat twice more either side.

8. Neck Rolls

Stretching the neck activates the lymph nodes, which drain the lymph in the head, and releases tension in the shoulders and any restrictions in the chest and front neck muscles.

a. Roll your shoulders back so you feel your shoulder blades flatten against your back. Engage your core to straighten your spine, and actually sit on your hands, palms-up, so you are grabbing your bum, keeping your shoulders away from your ears. You can also sit against the wall if this helps your posture.

b. Allow your head to drop gently forward and let it rock a little bit side to side. Gently roll your head to the right so that your ear is over your shoulder. Take a couple of breaths.

c. Slowly roll the head forward and to the center, then roll to the left. Keep going side to side, nice and slow.

d. Undoubtedly there will be some spots that feel tighter than others. When you find your neck feels "stuck" at some point, pause there and breathe. The weight of your head gently stretches your neck. Often you will feel a release in the jaw and ear.

e. Try not to let your shoulders creep up. Keep them down and rolled back so the neck receives the full benefit of the stretch.

9. SCRATCH YOUR BACK

This exercise opens up the chest and shoulders.

a. Holding a belt or dishcloth in your left hand, raise your left arm over your head, bend at the elbow, and reach your hand down (still holding the belt) as though to scratch between your shoulder blades.

b. Twist your right arm up behind the back into a chicken wing, or as if you were scratching the middle of your back. Grab the dangling belt with your right hand.

c. On an exhale, gently pull the top arm down to its maximum stretch, keeping the spine long and straight. Inhale deeply, and on the exhale gently pull the bottom arm up. Creep your hands toward each other on the belt to see how close you can get to touching your fingers. When you are as far along on the belt as you can be, take two deep breaths.

e. To release, drop the belt completely, and slide your bottom hand down toward your bum before untwisting it. Shake your arms, do a couple of shoulder shrugs, and repeat on the other side.

Stand up and shake out your legs. There are just three more exercises to go.

10. Opera Singer

This simple exercise helps mobility between the ribs and deep into the armpits, improving lymphatic flow through the torso. Moving the arms in opposite directions from each other gives a diagonal stretch to the chest and ribs.

a. To lock your core when standing, exhale, pull up on your pubic muscles, and feel the connection to your lower abs. Keep them engaged but not clamped down tight.

b. Take a deep inhale, and as you exhale stretch one arm up high, looking at your hand as though you were on stage singing your heart out. Move the other arm down and away in the opposite direction.

c. Inhale deeply, stretching all the muscles between the ribs, as though you were about to hit the high note of the aria.

d. Exhale and change sides, repeating five times on each side.

II. DOOR-FRAME STRETCH

This exercise stretches the chest. After breast or heart surgery there can be a tendency to naturally and instinctively roll in the shoulders to protect the scar, but this can lead to restrictions. Using the doorway as a stabilizer gives you confidence to stretch.

a. Place your hands or forearms on the door frame at chest height. Inhale deeply, puffing out your chest.

b. As you exhale, take a very small step forward, feeling the pull in your chest and shoulder muscles.

c. Inhale deeply and slowly.

d. If this amount of stretch is okay, exhale and take another very small step forward.

e. Keep going until you reach your comfortable limit. Then stay here and just breathe, filling your lungs deeply until you feel the stretch on your entire chest area.

12. Spider up the Wall

This is our final exercise, and it helps flush the lymph nodes in the armpits and chest area.

a. Face the wall and place your hand as high up as you are able.

b. Crawl the spider (your fingers) up the wall and allow all the small muscles in the arm, chest, and shoulder to gently open and release.

c. When you reach your limit, inhale for a count of four and very gently press your hand into the wall, activating your arm muscles.

d. As you exhale, release the tension on your arm and try to creep your fingers up again.

e. Go as high as you comfortably can, doing the little presses in between. This helps your body release tight muscles.

f. Repeat on the other side.

BOUNCING ON A MINI-TRAMPOLINE

Our next progressive exercise is for when your scar is secure—not necessarily fully healed, as that can take a couple of years, but enough that when you gently bounce it does not hurt or pull with any discomfort.

The best part of bouncing on a mini-trampoline—also called "rebounding"—is the activation of your lymph. The lymph system works against gravity, and every time you bounce you go from two to four times normal gravitation to zero gravity, over and over, as you land on the trampoline and rebound. Bouncing is incredibly efficient exercise when healing (and beyond). It excites the immune system by moving the lymphocytes and antibodies faster, making them more efficient, thereby decreasing the potential for infection. Additionally, bouncing is fun! It releases endorphins, the feel-good chemicals in our bodies, making us happier and more likely to continue the activity.

A study conducted by NASA concluded that trampoline bouncing is better and safer than running for exercise. Whereas both workouts provided similar benefits through increased heart rate and oxygen uptake, bouncing on a trampoline distributes the impact from exercise throughout the whole body, whereas running causes the knees, ankles, and feet to bear the brunt. A rebounder is said to take up 85 percent of the shock the body would experience otherwise on hard ground. [22]

There are varying qualities of mini-trampolines available on the market. I had one with squeaky springs for a while before upgrading to my Bellicon, a rebounder made in Germany. I love my Bellicon and have a link to the company on my website. These have bungee cords instead of springs, creating a smooth and silent bounce. Other bungee rebounders are sold on Amazon, but I haven't used them. The higher end rebounders will have options for either a T-bar accessory or support bars that connect to the legs of the trampoline. These would be an excellent idea if you are unsteady, weak, or off balance after surgery.

When you first start, simply do a little bounce, keeping your feet in contact with the rebounder, enjoying the rhythm in your body. Even bouncing slightly will help your lymph move around your body. If there is any pain or pulling in the wound area, stop immediately and wait another week until the scar is more secure before trying again.

Aim for little and often in the beginning, maybe two to five minutes three times a day. Gradually increase your time spent on the trampoline being mindful of your scar and how it feels. As you get stronger, start adding arm movements such as jumping-jack arms, or just move them over your head for more flushing. Also you can bounce a little harder to let your feet come off of the rebounder for a more vigorous workout.

You can also sit on a large fitness ball and gently bounce. It will not have the same full-body effect as a trampoline, but it will certainly get the lymph moving.

In the next chapter, we'll focus on what types of oils to use on your scar—and also the most beneficial way to touch and massage the scar and surrounding area.

CHAPTER 11

MASSAGE AND HEALING OILS FOR A SMOOTH SCAR

Usually after about two weeks, the doctor will remove your stitches, and the scab will fall off your scar. With your doctor's approval, you can now apply healing oils. My top three are calendula (*Calendula officinalis*), German chamomile (*Matricaria recutita*) and lavender (*Lavandula angustifolia*). Numerous studies indicate that these essential oils have tremendous healing powers even greater than standard orthodox medical treatments. As mentioned in Chapter 6, in which I discussed skin care, we want to use the purest products on the skin—especially on your new scar. Ideally you should purchase organic oils and use an organic base, or carrier oil.

Trolamine, a topical pain killer used in medical centers, was compared to calendula cream to investigate which one worked better for pain. Over two years, 254 patients were given either tromaline or calendula to use after each radiation treatment. Women who used calendula suffered significantly lower rates of acute dermatitis (skin rashes) as well as significantly less pain after radiation. [23] We use calendula in its homeopathic form for wound care, and research shows that the raw topical form is also powerful.

German chamomile was compared to corticosteroids for the treatment of ulcers. Those treated with chamomile had significantly faster wound healing; in fact, they healed a full nine days before the corticosteroid groups. The researchers rather obviously concluded that German chamomile dramatically promotes wound healing. [24]

Another study shows that German chamomile extract taken in drinking water significantly accelerated healing. On day fifteen of the study, the chamomile group showed a greater reduction of the wound area, faster epithelialization (wound coverage with epithelial, or skin, cells), and stronger wound construction compared to the control group. [25] Time to put on the kettle and make a cup of chamomile tea!

Our third healing oil is lavender. Applying lavender topically to recurring ulcers resulted in a significant reduction in inflammation level and ulcer size, a much faster healing time, and pain relief from the first dose. [26] We know that stress reduces the body's ability to heal, so using aromatherapy to calm the patient before surgery will also assist better healing. Besides its healing properties, scientists found that the anxiety levels of people who inhaled the scent of lavender oil before going into surgery were significantly reduced. [27]

MIX YOUR OWN HERBAL MASSAGE OIL

The are oodles of essential oil distributers. Find a good one meaning one that is ideally organic and ethical meaning they take care of the planet when sourcing their materials. I use primarily Mountain Rose Herbs and Rebecca's Apothecary (a local store in Boulder that ships across the US). Both Rebecca's and Mountain Rose Herbs have an organic calendula in an organic olive oil base. However, if you want a different carrier oil, such as rosehip-seed oil, you can buy that as well as your straight Calendula oil from Rebecca's. As I have more input from friends and companies around the globe, I will have an international resource page on my website.

When you are using these oils on a newly healed wound, it is recommended to use a 1 percent dilution because keeping the essential oils relatively low initially allows you to see how you react to them. If at any time your scar is aggravated by the oils, discontinue use and contact a qualified aromatherapist or herbalist for guidance. If all is well and you wish to increase the oils, the National Association for Holistic Aromatherapy gives suggestions for dilution.

To make your own massage oil, choose your base oil and add the following oils: Calendula herbal oil, German chamomile essential oil and Lavender essential oil.

Start with a one-ounce bottle of carrier oil. To make a 1 percent dilution, add two drops each of chamomile, lavender and calendula oil. Shake well and apply to your wrist or upper arm as a patch test. Wait twenty-four hours to test for a negative reaction. These are rare, but they are certainly possible, so please be patient and do the patch test first. You can gradually add more essential oils as you heal. Personally I keep mine low because I have sensitive skin.

I love using rosehip-seed oil as my carrier oil as it is packed with essential fatty acids and vitamin C, both of which help accelerate healing. Use rosehip-seed oil if you know you are sensitive to essential oils or if you do not wish to purchase the different oils. Buy an organic version of rosehip-seed oil, ideally one that's stored in a dark-glass bottle to preserve the oil's integrity.

MASSAGE THERAPY: HEALING AT YOUR FINGERTIPS

Massaging your scar helps you become familiar with how it feels so that you can respond immediately if you feel tight tissues forming on or around your scar. The idea of regular scar massage is much like regularly checking your breasts for lumps—you know your body best and can take action if something changes. Massage therapy also releases the fascia and adhesions of scars in a fairly short time if performed consistently; it was my main tool for liberating tight and painful tissues.

When starting, we use very small movements and light pressure. This is to allow the body to open up willingly rather than forcing a response. If you've ever had a massage that was too deep and found yourself resisting and tensing away from the therapist, you know that pressing too hard or trying to muscle through it defeats the end goal. You want the body to soften and relax, so be gentle and patient.

HOW TO MASSAGE YOUR SCAR

Before you start massage, take a few minutes to slow your breath and do a healing visualization. Focus on your scar forming beautifully, without any adhesions, knots, or complications.

TINY CIRCLES MASSAGE

Put a couple of drops of your healing-oil blend on your fingertips. Apply very soft pressure on your scar and surrounding area, tracing small circles. Note the feelings and sensations. There may be hardness, numbness, tingling, or burning to varying degrees. You may find that the ends of the scars or the point where a drain was placed are particularly sensitive.

If you find the initial contact painful, ease off slightly with your pressure but keep your fingers on the painful spot. Breathe deeply, slowly, and fully down into your belly. After two or three breaths the pain should subside.

Continue with the small, circular motions and work to your own limits, simply becoming familiar with the sensations around your scar. You are looking for numb areas, tender spots, burning, pulling, cording (sensation of tight, painful ropes extending from the armpit down the arm), or any other type of restriction that causes your fingertips to stop moving easily over the skin and scar. This massage also warms the area before you do any deeper work, so please be polite and check in with your scar before applying any extra pressure. Do the Tiny Circles Massage twice a day for ten minutes.

As you continue to work with your scar, you will find it changes as a result of the massage, good nutrition, healing oils, and exercises you do. As you become more active, the entire area will be different due to the stretching and exercise, so stay curious and be willing to work with whatever comes up day by day.

BASIC SCAR MASSAGE

If you have found adhesions with your Tiny Circles Massage, now you should gently pull them apart without stretching your scar too much. Adhesions will feel like little cords running off from your scar into the body—or the area may simply feel stuck and unable to move.

Start with your healing oils, and make circles to warm up the scar and surrounding area. Then, with a light touch, hold the skin around your scar with one hand to keep it from moving. Using your thumb or fingertips in a zigzag pattern, stroke gently across the scar where the adhesion is. Follow the adhesion as far as you can feel it. You may find it anchors into something else such as a bone—work it all the way to the end point.

If you hit an area that is painful, drop back to tiny circles, or just hold your fingers on the sensitive spot and use your breath to clear the pain.

Do your massage at least twice a day, for ten minutes each time. Ideally follow up with the Love Your Lymph Moves or another form of exercise such as walking or rebounding to help your body move the waste you have released from the massage.

DEEP SCAR RELEASE

Working with restricted scars requires grit, determination, and a willingness to work through pain. Massaging may set off shooting pain that can be severe to the point of taking your breath away. This is neuralgia, or nerve pain. The larger the scar, the more nerves have been cut. Remember fascia wraps around the nerves too, so they may be impinged or restricted and shouting out their distress. There can also be a sensation of deep burning that is particularly uncomfortable.

In time, some areas along the scar will feel pretty close to normal, while others may stay numb or sensitive for longer, most often when you have had a drain. Scars formed by repeated surgeries in the same area may take more time to change. Trust that with consistent attention they will continue to improve.

For deep scar release, use less oil in order to have more friction. You need your fingers to stick to an adhesion in order to break it apart. Warm up the area around your scar with little circles before moving on to the basic massage. Starting on one side, work across your scar with a zigzag stroke to warm up the deeper layers. After a minute or so of zigzags, hold the area around your scar taut with your other hand and start at one side, moving across the entire scar slowly.

If you find an area that feels "stuck," or if the skin won't move, drop your finger down into the scar, as though trying to poke inside the body. Gently move your finger in a deep, tiny circle to further isolate where the adhesion is and which direction it is moving. If you have one of those electric-shock pains or deep burns, stay right where you are and breathe. You can lighten up a little on the pressure, but stay with it and use your breath to move through it. Make your exhale longer than your inhale and purse your lips when breathing out.

When you have recovered, focus on that particular area and try again to move the adhesion. You may again get the shooting or burning pain. Stop and breathe through it. You have found one of your key scar trigger points; once this releases, other fascia around it can start to release as well. Work this area for as long as you can and then move on. You may want to take a break, have a stretch, and do some deep breathing before carrying on.

With old scars that hurt, the natural reflex is to pull away. Adhesions are usually painful, so give them loving attention in short bursts so that you are able to break them apart. Gritting your teeth for half an hour while trying not to cry is cruel—please don't do it to yourself. If a ten-minute massage is too much, do five minutes four times a day. If that is too much, do two minutes eight times a day. Just do it. Trust that the adhesions will release, trust that your fascia will unfurl, and trust that your nerves will settle. It will happen so long as you put in loving effort, one minute at a time.

The next part of your self-care is soothing and stress relieving. You deserve it after the exercise and scar massage!

CHAPTER 12

SKIN BRUSHING AND SOAKING IN DEAD SEA SALTS

As YOU KNOW, the lymph has its own system just beneath the skin that runs alongside the circulatory system. Brushing your skin against gravity moves the lymph into the larger nodes, which encourages cleansing. With consistent brushing, ingrown hairs are released, old skin is sloughed off, and cellulite can dramatically diminish. The result is smooth, velvety skin and a fired up lymphatic system.

Below are eight steps for brushing your skin:

Avoid fresh scars and sensitive or sore skin. Brush around the area but never right over the new scar or broken skin.

1. Use a *dry*, natural-bristle brush with a long handle, and brush your *dry* skin. It is best to do skin brushing just before your shower or bath.

2. Always move the brush toward the heart. You want to push the lymph fluid toward the lymph nodes. Make the strokes long and sweeping. Use a gentle pressure at first, becoming more firm as you get used to it.

3. Start at your feet, and with long strokes brush up the shin and calf to the knee. Take a little time over the tough kneecaps, and then brush from the knee to the top of the thigh, including the

front, back, and sides. Spend some extra time brushing up areas of cellulite to encourage circulation. Do the other leg from the foot to the groin.

4. Next, start at your sacrum and brush over your butt cheek to the front, sweeping round to the groin in front. Do the whole glute muscle and repeat on the other side.

5. Brush from the hips up the lower back, up the sides of the body and the front of the torso, always stroking toward the heart.

6. Move to your upper body. Brush down the back of your neck, and brush the upper back in a V shape toward the heart. This is where you are most likely to need a handle on your brush.

7. For arms, start with one arm in the air and brush from that hand up to the elbow. Then brush from the elbow to the armpit. Take some extra time on the back of your arm if you have little bumps or loose skin. When you get to the armpit, be gentle because the skin is delicate. Brush gently across the entire chest from the shoulder to the breastbone. Repeat on the other side.

8. Finish with a little extra sweeping of the breastbone from the bottom to the top.

To maximize the benefits of skin brushing, do it just before you hop into a gorgeous, warm, salt-soak bath. The dry brushing will have sloughed off old dead skin, opening your pores for the healing of the salts.

DEAD SEA SALT SOAKS

Mineral salts used for bathing are rich in magnesium, the fourth most abundant mineral in the body with 60 percent in the skeleton and the remaining 40 percent in the body's cells. It is essential for more than three hundred chemical reactions in the body, including energy metabolism and cell replication. Magnesium helps the heart function better and protects the blood vessels. It is also extremely beneficial when healing. [28]

The Dead Sea is actually a salt lake bordered by Jordan to the east and Israel and the West Bank to the west. It is about ten times saltier than ocean water and has a high concentration of magnesium, potassium, calcium chloride, and bromides. The name "Dead Sea" refers to the fact that no creature can live in such high salinity. These salts play a key role in accelerating skin-barrier repair.

Scientists studied the anti-inflammatory properties of Dead Sea salts using thirty people with atopic dermatitis (broken skin—usually eczema rashes) as their test group. Steroids, often used to suppress dermatitis, were discontinued for three weeks before and during the experiment. Every day for six weeks, subjects soaked each arm in different containers of water, some of which contained 5 percent Dead Sea salts. The study was randomized and double-blinded, meaning neither the scientists nor the subjects knew which container held the salts and which was simply water. The data collected tested different aspects of the skin, namely barrier function, hydration, roughness, and inflammation.

First, the scientists tested trans-epidermal water loss (or TEWL) measurements as a marker of barrier function in the skin. TEWL is defined as the measurement of the quantity of water that passes from the inside of the body through the skin (epidermal layer) to the environment outside, such as when we sweat. When large amounts of the skin are compromised, as with eczema or burns, the barrier is broken and water-loss increases. The scientists found that in just three weeks of soaking, the Dead Sea salt arm showed significant improvement in the barrier function of the skin.

The results kept getting better. Skin soaked in plain water lost hydration, whereas the salt-soaked arm increased in hydration. Skin roughness was measured, and again the salt group showed improvement at three weeks and continued to improve for the full six weeks whereas there were no changes for the plain-water group. Finally the researchers tested skin redness, or inflammation. The entire group who had been soaking in Dead Sea salt had significant decreases in skin redness after six weeks of treatment. The study's conclusion showed that bathing in Dead Sea salts strengthens the skin barrier, increases hydration, smoothes the skin, and decreases inflammation. [29]

To bathe in Dead Sea salts, heat up your bathroom in advance so you do not get chilled while soaking. While the tub is filling, do a thorough skin brushing to open your pores and flake off dead skin. Have a large bottle of water handy to sip throughout your soak. You may get sweaty, so avoid face and hair masks during these treatments.

Twice a week, take a therapeutic soak using at least two and up to four cups of Dead Sea salts in the bath. Do this before bed as you will probably get sleepy from the high levels of magnesium. If you wish to have a third bath during a week, or even a daily soak, go right ahead. You can use less salt for those baths; one to two cups will do.

We now start putting it altogether. Part IV is for new scars and how to essentially build a self-care practice from scratch. I take you through pre-op, surgery day, and the first two months after your operation. Some of what you have already read will be repeated in this section so that you do not have to flip back and forth through the book to find the information.

Part V addresses older scars and shows you how to use the techniques to be free from your pain and regain your full range of motion.

The plan starts with week by week suggestions on how to start building a beautiful scar after you've had major surgery. If your scar is the result of a more minor wounding that only needed a couple of stitches, you will not need the depth this section offers. However, I would still recommend you read through it all.

At the end of this section, in Chapter 17, there is a maintenance plan. When you look at the final 'to do' list of scar self-care, it is totally manageable. Most importantly is to figure out what is going to work for you and that you will continue for a long time. Try to pick the things you love.

PART IV

A PLAN FOR HEALING A NEW SCAR

"Every day you either see a scar or courage.
Where you dwell will define your struggle."

—DODINSKY

"I met Andie through a network of friends and came to know of her ex-
perience and the book she was writing about healing scars. Having been
through a bilateral mastectomy and three reconstructive surgeries, I was
bound up in a web of scar tissue and lymphedema. I did physical therapy
and stretching, and I followed the doctors' orders, yet I was still very tight
and uncomfortable. I was excited to learn about Andie's book so that I
had techniques to loosen the scar tissue and address my discomfort.

Her book Love Your Scar *was helpful for the older scars, and it pre-*
pared me for the ones to come from a laparoscopic hysterectomy. This book
is a manual for preparing for surgery through nutrition, self-care, yoga,
and breathing techniques. I was so grateful to have this information and
the specific actions to improve mobility, range of motion, circulation, and
to promote healing and overall health.

This book empowered me to take care of myself because the doctors
and surgeons can only get you so far. Andie explains the physiology of
the healing process in practical and understandable terms. She provides
a step-by-step process to prepare and heal by coupling all of her expertise
in both traditional and alternative methods. Green drinks are drinks to
live by!

Thank you for this gift. We are our own healers."

—Dana

CHAPTER 13

HEALING A NEW SCAR AFTER SURGERY

READ THROUGH THE entirety of Part IV to get an idea of how your personal recovery might play out over several months after your surgery. You will need to order certain items, organize friends to help you, and anticipate potential difficulties such as constipation from pain meds, edema, slow healing, exhaustion, or anxiety. Being prepared before you go into surgery will help you relax afterward, which in turn speeds healing.

SHOPPING LIST

Here's a list of necessities that you should buy before your surgery. For information about ordering certain brands, see Appendix I: Resources and Shopping Tips, located at the end of the book.

HOMEOPATHIC REMEDIES:

- Calendula 30C: general healer
- Arnica 30C: for trauma and bruising (after surgery)
- Phosphorus 30C: for use after anesthetic
- Hepar sulphuris calcareum 30C: for infection
- Pyrogenium 30C: for infection

Remedies for emotional support:

- Ignatia 30C: grief, loss, crying, highly emotional
- Aconite 30C: fear, anxiety, panic attacks
- Nux vomica 30C: grumpy, irritable, constipated, toxic

Supplements: probiotics, omega-3 fats, turmeric, aloe vera juice, colloidal silver
Healing oils: Calendula, Lavender, German chamomile
Dead Sea salts
Body brush with a long handle
Vitamix blender
Bellicon rebounder (mini-trampoline)

PREPARING BEFORE YOUR SURGERY

I hope you've had a little time to start incorporating the foundation therapies (See Part II) into your daily life by improving the quality of your food, increasing your greens, learning to use breath as a stress buster, visualizing a healthy healed scar, and transitioning to natural skin care.

Before your surgery, be sure you are taking the supplements that boost wound healing, namely probiotics (as directed on the bottle), omega-3 oils, and turmeric for its anti-inflammatory properties.

Now we get to the nitty-gritty plan of how to build a beautiful scar.

Talk to your doctor about using Manuka honey in your bandages or surgical dressings. The benefits of Manuka honey were discussed in Chapter 8, which covered avoiding infection. Please reread that chapter and have all the items you might need at hand and ready to go.

At the first indication of infection you have to move fast and support your body as it goes into battle. I know I sound melodramatic about infections, but I have seen so many scars "gone bad" as a result of an infection. I want to minimize your chances of winding up with a difficult or painful scar for life. Be prepared!

Your Circle of Support

Reach out to your friends, family, sports team, book club, work mates, church, or community and create a Circle of Support. Chances are that people you know will want to help you and will appreciate knowing exactly what you need from them. Many times people want to get involved but they don't want to seem pushy, so ask them for help.

Take a piece of paper and brainstorm all the daily chores and tasks you're responsible for: laundry, dishwashing, cooking, cleaning, shopping, driving the kids to school or after-school activities, picking up dry cleaning, taking out garbage, raking or mowing the lawn, shoveling the driveway, walking the dogs, cleaning the cat's litter box, mucking the horses, exercising the birds of prey, milking the goats, or feeding the llamas. The list depends on your lifestyle.

Where and when will you need help? How long is your estimated recovery time? Can you divide your to-do list among several people? Do you need to teach people how to do things in advance? If you do not have the strength to be the main coordinator, enlist a partner or friend to be your main point of contact.

HOMEOPATHY AND YOUR EMOTIONS

Preparing for surgery is a big deal, and it can bring up a lot of emotions. For help, you might turn to homeopathy's three "emotional support" remedies:

- Aconite 30C is good for fear and anxiety.
- Ignatia 30C is good for grief, loss, and feeling as though your emotions are overwhelming.
- Nux vomica 30C helps with irritability and toxicity. This remedy may be helpful pre-op if you have to give up a lifestyle full of booze, smokes, drugs, etc. because it helps your body detox.

Put three pills of the remedy in a bottle of water, and sip it throughout the day. If you are using Nux vomica, take it by itself because it is a notorious antidote to many other homeopathic remedies.

If you feel totally overwhelmed by emotion, put a pill under your tongue and let it melt to get immediate effect. Take an additional dose every five to ten minutes until you feel calm again.

WHAT TO DO ON SURGERY DAY

The morning of your surgery can make anyone jittery, so your most important task for today is to do a calming meditation and visualize your Column of Light protecting you. Follow these suggestions for some peace of mind before your procedure:

- Use your emotional-support homeopathic remedies. Usually you are not allowed to eat or drink for four hours before your surgery. However, homeopathic remedies were acceptable to the consultants at London Bridge Hospital, but be sure to ask your doctor just in case. Put one pill of your chosen support remedy under your tongue as needed.

- Imagine the operating room full of healing light, just for you. Let that light pour onto your surgeons, doctors, anesthesiologist, nurses, and all attendants participating in your procedure and recovery.Tell your circle of friends what time your surgery is so they can focus their healing intention on you as well.
- Sniff lavender oil to keep you calm and reduce anxiety.
- The heavens are cheering for a successful procedure and swift recovery! Let that feeling embrace you as you go into surgery.

HOMEOPATHIC REMEDIES TO TAKE AFTER WAKING FROM SURGERY

When you wake up after surgery you might feel disoriented or irritable. This is when you use the more specific remedies for those situations as well as starting the main healers: calendula and arnica. Homeopathy is very unlikely to negatively interact with any medical drugs but talk to your doctor to make sure he or she is on board with your plan.

- Phosphorus 30C helps bring you back into your body if you feel spaced out or sick after the anesthetic. Take one pill every half hour until you feel normal and grounded again.
- Calendula 30C is our primary healing remedy. Dissolve two pills in water to sip throughout the day. Refresh the pills each time you refill your water bottle or glass.
- Now you get to take Arnica. Arnica 30C is excellent for treating trauma, and it covers both physical and emotional shock. It helps with any lame, sore, and bruised feelings after surgery or injury.

You can put both Calendula and Arnica together in the same bottle of water.

- Nux vomica 30c is very good when you are feeling irritable, either from medications or because you are currently helpless, a state that is unsettling and unpleasant for independent, self-sufficient people. Nux vomica is a powerful remedy that has the potential to cancel out the others. Take it on its own, *not* in the bottle of water with Arnica and Calendula. Put one pill under your tongue on waking and wait half an hour before taking the other remedies.

CHAPTER 14

WEEKS 1 & 2 AFTER SURGERY

THE PREVENTIVE MEASURES for avoiding infection start now, when you begin taking probiotics, colloidal silver, and garlic. Preventing infection is your top priority in the first two weeks. Be vigilant with your cleanliness, and request that all your visitors wash their hands thoroughly and often, especially if they are touching you.

SUPPLEMENTS FOR THE FIRST WEEKS AFTER SURGERY

PROBIOTICS
In these first two weeks take the probiotics twice a day, and use your room temperature–stable version for convenience. You can continue taking these beneficial bacteria for the first month quite safely, unless your doctor has specifically said not to. If in doubt, ask.

While you're taking antibiotics, you need to adjust the timing of when you take your probiotics. Always take your antibiotic as prescribed by your doctor. Wait two hours after the antibiotics and then take the probiotics as suggested on the bottle or blister pack.

COLLOIDAL SILVER
This helps to fight bacteria. If allowed by your doctor, spray colloidal silver on your wound three times a day after washing with mild soap that

contains no sodium lauryl sulfate. This will depend on your incision and what is acceptable and possible given your injuries.

GARLIC

Increase your raw garlic intake, either swallowing slices of the raw herb, or adding it to salad dressing and sauces for your food.

HOMEOPATHY

If you do develop an infection, use Hepar sulphuris calcareum 30C and Pyrogenium 30C. Both of these remedies are excellent for suppuration (pus formation), and they help your body fight the infection. Put two pills of each remedy in your drinking water, along with the Calendula, Arnica, and any emotional support remedies you need. Sip this homeo-pathic-infused drink throughout the day.

EXERCISE

To recap, your lymph flows primarily upward and against gravity, yet the lymphatic system has no dedicated muscle to pump it through the body. Because lymph is part of the immune system and is necessary for healing, moving your body is crucial to your well-being. However, after your injury or surgery, your ability to move may be limited, so ask a friend to come to the hospital or your home and help you move your lymph. The friend-assisted exercises listed here are the same as from Chapter 10.

Have your friend read through the exercises before you start the movements or visit my website www.andieholman.com for video instruc-tions. Tell him or her to use feather-light pressure. Moving lymph does not feel like massage; it is more like Reiki or simply the laying on of hands. It may not feel like much is going on, but lots is actually happening. And this movement definitely should not hurt. If it does, stop and try again, using even less pressure or less range of motion.

Note: Do not move the limb with the new scar during the first two weeks after surgery. Focus instead on moving other parts of the body and allowing them to pick up the extra work and assist in healing.

FRIEND-ASSISTED EXERCISES IN THE HOSPITAL: UPPER BODY

Head Lymph Flush

1. While you are lying down, a friend sits behind you and cradles the base of your head in both hands. If there is no room at the head of the bed, she sits next to it and places one hand under the base of the skull and the other on the forehead.
2. As you inhale, your friend squeezes lightly at the base of your skull. Hold your breath while she holds the gentle pressure for a count of three. Release both the breath and the gentle squeeze.
3. Your friend moves her hand about an inch lower, and you repeat the breath as she squeezes. Every time you inhale, she holds the pressure while you hold your breath, and then as you exhale, she releases the hold. Work slowly down your neck.
4. Repeat three to five times.

Chest Lymph Flush

1. Your friend uses the flat of her fingers to gently press (feather light) on your chest, starting in the middle on the breastbone, moving out toward the armpit.
2. Inhale as she presses, and exhale as she releases.

3. Your friend moves her fingers along your chest in one-inch increments while you take deep breaths in time with her pressing.

4. Repeat both sides twice.

Arm Sway

1. Your friend holds your upper arm while you bend your elbow and go floppy, letting your forearm rest on his.

2. As you exhale, your friend moves your arm as far back as is comfortable. Pause at the top of the stretch and inhale.

3. Exhale as your friend brings your arm back to neutral or to 90 degrees. Inhale.

4. Exhale as he moves your arm overhead again with the hopes of stretching a tiny bit further with each breath.

5. Inhale slowly while he holds the stretch. Exhale back to start.

6. Repeat ten times and do the other side.

FRIEND-ASSISTED EXERCISES IN THE HOSPITAL: LOWER BODY

Leg Pumps

1. Lying flat, have your friend sit close to you on the bed next to your hip or upper thigh. Bend the leg closest to her and rest your ankle on her shoulder. She can put her hands around your thigh for support or hold one hand at the ankle and use the forearm of the other arm to push into the back of your lower thigh.

2. Take a deep breath in. As you exhale, your friend leans in, bending your leg slowly toward your chest. Hold for a slow

count of three while you inhale. She sits up again slowly as you exhale.

3. Take a slow breath in, and as you exhale she leans in again. Repeat five times for each leg.

FRIEND-ASSISTED EXERCISE AT HOME

Once you are recovering at home, continue with the previous exercises and add the next two if you can. If you have had abdominal surgery, just do Legs Up the Wall. Do not start the bending movements until your scar is secure enough and you have been given the "all clear" for exercise from your doctor.

Legs Up the Wall

Rest your legs and feet up the wall and breathe deeply into the abdomen. This helps the lymph tremendously, as gravity drains the lymph into the groin while the deep breathing activates the lymph in your torso. Double bonus! Stay here for as long as is comfortable. If you are moving into Frog's Legs, put on socks so your feet slide easily.

Frog's Legs

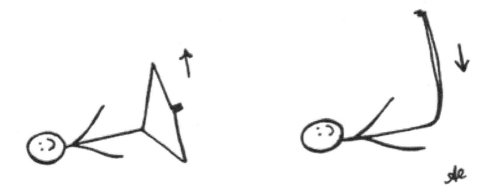

1. Keep your feet up the wall. Engage your core or stomach muscles by sinking your belly button to your spine, then tighten the muscles and hold them strong. This engages your core muscles and helps protect your lower back, while also giving you a sense of grounding and purpose. The very core of you is solid.

2. With your core engaged, breathe into your rib cage, expanding your ribs out to the sides. Take a couple of breaths like this to get used to the feeling.

3. Stage One is to have your friend nearby to assist your balance if necessary. He can simply be near you to help when you want to get out of the pose, or he can assist you with bending your legs.

4. Bend one leg at a time. Your arms are wide by your sides with your hands facing palms-down for stability. Your friend can either help move the leg or can apply gentle pressure across your hips to hold you secure. Be sensible about your scar.

5. Stage Two is to slowly bend both knees outward, keeping the soles of the feet together to make diamond-shaped frog's legs. Slowly slide up and down the wall from fully bent to fully straight.

6. Here's the breath: exhale while moving the legs, whether up or down. That means you inhale at the top and the bottom of the exercise and exhale as you move your legs.

BREATH AND MEDITATION

While you are convalescing, use the time to breathe and focus your mind on healing. Deep breathing helps you heal by increasing oxygenation in the blood. It also soothes your nervous system, reducing stress and inflammation. Meditation or visualization harnesses the power of your mind and directs your immune system to healing as quickly as possible. For a reminder of the specific instructions for breathing and guided meditations and visualizations, see Chapter 7.

THE IMPORTANCE OF SLEEP

Sleep a lot. Nap often. Rest and heal. The body regenerates when we sleep, so do not soldier through if you feel tired. Lack of sleep increases inflammation and thereby reduces immunity. The potential for infectious disease rises with sleep deprivation, and the body goes into a stress response. Poor sleep and consequent higher inflammation affects women more than men. Besides being detrimental to the health of your wound, sleep disturbance has shown to be a factor in cardiovascular disease, cancer risk, and depression. The excellent news is that taking a two-hour nap can be protective when nighttime sleep is disturbed; a very common occurrence both in hospital and when recuperating.

CONSTIPATION

If you are on painkillers, there is a very good chance you won't poop for a while because opioids tend to bring the bowels to a screeching halt. When constipation strikes, I recommend a natural laxative. Have a partner or friend prepare this simple prune-almond-aloe recipe and bring it to you in the hospital.

Place two handfuls of prunes and one handful of almonds in a container and fully cover with organic aloe vera juice overnight. (I prefer George's Aloe Vera Liquid as it is not bitter; see Appendix I.) Aloe acts as a gentle laxative for the digestive system and is an anti-inflammatory. Eat a few bites of the soaked prunes and almonds with each meal, and if necessary, have your friend make you a new batch every couple of days until your normal bowel movements are reestablished.

Deep breathing into the abdomen may relieve some of the pain or pressure of being blocked up. As you inflate your lungs, see if you can breathe all the way into your pelvis. This often gently stretches the abdomen and can help you relax and poop.

You can also try self-massage to stimulate the colon by massaging your abdomen with your hands or by rolling a tennis ball in circles in that area. Obviously, if your scar is on your abdomen, skip the colon massage and use the deep breathing and prune-almond-aloe combo.

How to Do a Colon Massage

1. Use the pads of the fingertips or a tennis ball.
2. Press or roll the tennis ball from the left hip toward the groin. Do this five times, from top to bottom.
3. Then press or roll from the belly button across to the left hip five times.
4. Again, press or roll from the left hip to the groin again, doing it from top to bottom five more times.
5. Now move from the right hip to the belly button five times.
6. Finish by rolling or stroking the entire colon from the right hip, across the belly button, to the left hip, and down toward the groin. Repeat five times.

The first two weeks after surgery can be physically painful as well as emotionally taxing. Take time to do the light exercises, take your supplements and remedies to stave off infection, and stay positive and calm with meditation. Use your visualizations and powerful imagination to help your body heal your wound and build a flexible, healthy scar. Finally, allow yourself rest—you should be feeling considerably better after the first two weeks.

CHAPTER 15

WEEKS 3 & 4 AFTER SURGERY

Assuming you were able to avoid infection, you should be ready to progress. By Week 3, the scabs on most people's scars have fallen off. Now, with your doctor's permission, you're ready to apply healing oils, get a bit more physical with the Love Your Lymph Moves, and add in skin brushing and magnesium rich salt baths. However if at this point you are still struggling with an open wound, please continue my protocol from the first two weeks after surgery until your incision or injury has healed over. Try not to stress or rush yourself. Your greatest gift to yourself is love and patience. You WILL heal.

HOMEOPATHIC REMEDIES FOR WEEKS 3 AND 4

Two weeks after surgery, you might not need any homeopathic remedies except the Calendula 30C. However, as your scar heals, you may start to note that it is painful. See if either Silica or Graphites fits the picture of your scar. If so, dissolve three pills in water with your Calendula, and use for as long as you have symptoms. If there is no change or improvement after two weeks, discontinue use and consult a professional. A homeopath will be able to prescribe remedies to fit you personally or a massage therapist or specially trained nurse can help with physical problems around your scar.

- Silica 30C is for scars that are painful to touch, become thickened into keloids (when scar tissue overgrows), are nodular (lumpy or bumpy), or are healing slowly. The emotional state of the patient who needs Silica may be shy, overly sensitive, or withdrawn after injury or surgery.
- Graphites 30C can help if the scar is hard or has a burning or tearing pain. The skin around the scar might be broken and sticky, or look like eczema, or be ulcerating.

HEALING OILS THAT NOURISH YOUR SKIN

After two weeks or so, the scab will dry up and fall off your scar. Do not pick it! I know it's itchy... don't pick. As long as you have your doctor's approval, you can now start to apply the blend of healing oils (a mixture of calendula, lavender, and German chamomile), or the pure rosehip-seed oil to your scar, as discussed in Chapter 11.

Wash your scar area with a mild soap—no sodium lauryl sulfate (SLS)! Then put a couple of drops of either the oil blend or rosehip-seed oil on your fingertips and gently apply to your scar and the surrounding area three times a day. It is too soon to begin massaging yet – simply let the healing oils soak in. I highly recommend the Ray of Starlight visualization here, focusing the light towards healing your scar.

EXERCISE FOR WEEKS 3 AND 4

The type of exercise you do now depends on how you are healing, how strong you were going into the surgery, and the type of surgery you had. If you are still feeling frail or are in pain, continue with the friend-assisted lymph movements that you've been practicing for the first two weeks. When you are feeling stronger, start introducing some or all of the Love Your Lymph Moves, beginning with the ones that do not involve the area around your scar. Use your best judgment and do only the ones that feel comfortable, not painful. The full twelve lymph moves are listed here so you don't have to jump around in the book to find them.

You will need a few props for the following exercises, so have either four cushions, pillows, yoga blocks, or bolsters handy.

Just a reminder – these moves are to activate your lymph which boosts immunity. Even if you have a wee little scar on your face or baby toe, still do the exercises. You are more than the bits and pieces of your injury. Your scar will heal better when your whole body is supported.

LOVE YOUR LYMPH MOVES

Begin with flushing the legs by using gravity and deep breathing. Put your Legs Up the Wall, and if you are able, bend your knees for Frog's Legs. If you're doing Frog's Legs, you are getting a triple blast of lymph action with breath, gravity and muscular contraction.

LEGS UP THE WALL

Rest your legs and feet up the wall and breathe deeply into the abdomen. Stay here for as long as is comfortable. If you are moving into Frog's Legs, put on socks so your feet slide easily up and down the wall.

FROG'S LEGS

1. Keep your feet up the wall. Engage your core or stomach muscles by sinking your belly button to your spine, then tighten the muscles and hold them strong. This helps to protect your lower back, while also giving you a sense of grounding and purpose; the very core of you is solid. Keep your core engaged and breathe into your rib cage, expanding your ribs out to the sides. Take a couple of breaths like this to get used to the feeling. Exhale when moving the legs, whether up or down. Pause at the top or bottom and inhale.

2. Stage One is to have your friend nearby to assist your balance if necessary. He can simply be near you to help when you want to get out of the pose, or he can assist you with bending your legs.

3. Bend one leg at a time. Your arms are wide by your sides with your hands facing palms-down for stability. Your friend can

either help move the leg or can apply gentle pressure across your hips to hold you secure. Be sensible about your scar.

4. Stage Two is to slowly bend both knees outward, keeping the soles of the feet together to make diamond-shaped frog's legs. Slowly slide up and down the wall from fully bent to fully straight.

Now move on to the Love Your Lymph Moves that work for you at this particular moment.

Start by lying on the floor or your bed. Bend your knees and place your feet flat on the floor, knees pointing upward. Take ten deep, slow breaths; use the counting to calm yourself and access the parasympathetic nervous system. Do some visualization to bring in healing light for your entire body. Ask for your lymph to be nourished and refreshed as you mindfully do the twelve exercises.

1. Rock the Boat

This is a very small movement that helps warm up the smaller stabilizing muscles of the pelvis, hips, and lower abdominals.

a. Exhale and slowly curl your pelvis up, squeezing your pelvic floor muscles and letting your belly button drop further toward the floor.

b. Hold for the count of three, and slowly inhale into your ribs.

c. Exhale, release the hold, and let your pelvis stretch and rock forward toward the floor.

d. Repeat ten times.

2. TWISTER

Twister massages the internal organs and can help peristalsis if you are constipated. If you had abdominal or back surgery, skip this one unless you have an okay from your doctor to do gentle twists.

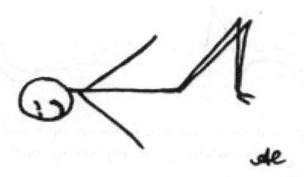

a. Lie on your back with your feet flat on the floor. Place one or two pillows on either side you, just below your hip where your thighs will land in the twist.

b. Keeping your knees pointing up, extend your arms comfortably to the sides, and steady yourself with your hands palms-down.

c. Take a deep breath and scootch your hips over to the right about four inches. As you exhale, gently allow both bent legs to fall to the left, resting on the pillow (or two or three).

d. Relax your stomach muscles and breathe deep into your belly. Feel the stretch in your rib cage, lower back, arms, and neck. Stay for seven deep breaths, continuing to relax deeper into the pose on each exhalation.

e. To come back to center, exhale fully, pull your belly button toward your spine, and slowly turn your knees back to center.

f. Take a full breath and repeat on the other side.

g. Do two twists to each side.

3. BACKSTROKE

Backstroke helps stretch the chest, arms, and shoulders while activating the lymph nodes in the neck, arms, and chest. Be very careful if you've had chest, breast, back, arm, or shoulder surgery. If this is too much, continue with your friend-assisted Arm Sway exercise.

a. Close your eyes and imagine a beautiful ocean scene. Picture yourself having a leisurely paddle through the crystal-clear waves.

b. Bend your knees bent upward and place your feet flat on the floor, arms straight by your sides.

c. Lock your core by sinking your belly button to your spine and holding it there. Breathe up into the ribs.

d. Bring one arm slowly over your head and extend it as far back as you are able. Then reverse the movement, bringing your arm back to your side, while lifting the other arm up and backward as if swimming the backstroke.

e. Complete twenty strokes in total.

f. Roll onto your side and push yourself up onto your hands and knees.

4. Cat-Cow Stretch

The Cat Cow Stretch benefits the whole spine by stretching the front of the body from the chin to the pelvis, and the entire back from the top of the head to the tailbone. Use the breath consciously with this exercise. Be mindful if you have a scar on your torso, and take care not to overstretch.

a. The first picture is Cow. Inhale and drop your belly toward the floor, then stretch your chest forward and lift your chin.

b. As you exhale, arch your back like the second picture, which is Cat. Pull up on your core as you push every little bit of breath out of your body.

c. Inhale to Cow, exhale to Cat.

d. Repeat five times.

5. CHILD'S POSE

In yoga, this is a posture of surrender and serenity. In this pose your belly and face are soft. This stretch is great for the arms, back, and shoulders, and it will be of particular benefit for cording, the sensation of a rope or tight cord running down the arm.

a. Take your knees a little wider than hip distance apart and lean your bum back to rest on your heels, keeping your fingers stretched away from you. If this is uncomfortable, place a pillow or two on top your calves and move your hips back.

b. Rest your forehead on the floor, a pillow, or a yoga block. Make sure your neck is relaxed. Close your eyes and let your face go mushy.

c. Envision your Column of Healing Light nourishing you and removing anything that is not in line with your Highest Good.

d. Take ten long, slow breaths, and exhale fully with a sigh, letting all the tension leave your body.

Move into a comfortable sitting position. If you sit on a small cushion you may find your knees and hips relax more because your pelvis is slightly raised. When sitting cross-legged, you can prop up your knees with a pillow on either side or with your knees straighter (but still a little bent). Keep your back against a wall if sitting up straight is difficult.

6. SEAWEED

This flowing movement helps open the sides of the body from the arm-pit to the hip. Have a yoga block or pillow to either side of you if reaching the floor is too much of a stretch.

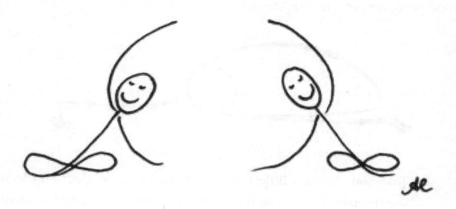

a. On an inhale, reach your right hand out to the side and place it on the floor about a foot away from your right hip.

b. Exhale and lean over to the right, raising your left arm overhead until you feel a stretch from your hip to your fingertips.

c. Inhale for a count of four.

d. Exhale and slowly change sides.

e. Try to keep both butt cheeks on the floor. Gracefully float your arms through the air as if they were sprays of seaweed rolling gently on the waves.

f. Repeat for a total of ten times, five on each side.

7. SEATED TWIST

The Seated Twist is similar to the lying Twister, but it has a different action on the hips and groin because of the seated position. This move mobilizes the internal organs gently, improving digestion and elimination while freeing possible rib adhesions. As with Twister, go very gently if you have had abdominal or back surgery.

a. Sit on a little cushion in a cross-legged position, and inhale.

b. On the exhale, twist your whole torso gently to the left placing your left hand on the floor or a block directly behind your spine.

c. Place your right hand on your left knee to help hold the position.

d. Gently turn your head to look over your left shoulder.

e. Take two deep breaths and return to center. Have a relaxing breath.

f. Then take a deep breath, and on the exhale twist to the right, with your right hand behind the spine and left hand on the right knee, looking over the right shoulder.

g. Take two refreshing breaths and return to center.

h. Repeat twice more either side.

8. Neck Rolls

Stretching the neck activates the lymph nodes, which drain the lymph in the head, and releases tension in the shoulders and any restrictions in the chest and front neck muscles.

a. Roll your shoulders back so you feel your shoulder blades flatten against your back. Engage your core to straighten your spine, and actually sit on your hands, palms-up, so you are grabbing your bum, keeping your shoulders away from your ears. You can also sit against the wall if this helps your posture.

b. Allow your head to drop gently forward and let it rock a little bit side to side. Gently roll your head to the right so that your ear is over your shoulder. Take a couple of breaths.

c. Slowly roll the head forward and to the center, then roll to the left. Keep going side to side, nice and slow.

d. Undoubtedly there will be some spots that feel tighter than others. When you find your neck feels "stuck" at some point, pause there and breathe. The weight of your head gently stretches your neck. Often you will feel a release in the jaw and ear.

e. Try not to let your shoulders creep up. Keep them down and rolled back so the neck receives the full benefit of the stretch.

9. SCRATCH YOUR BACK

This exercise opens up the chest and shoulders.

a. Holding a belt or dishcloth in your left hand, raise your left arm over your head, bend at the elbow, and reach your hand down (still holding the belt) as though to scratch between your shoulder blades.

b. Twist your right arm up behind the back into a chicken wing, or as if you were scratching the middle of your back. Grab the dangling belt with your right hand.

c. On an exhale, gently pull the top arm down to its maximum stretch, keeping the spine long and straight. Inhale deeply, and on the exhale gently pull the bottom arm up. Repeat the stretch for the upper arm and lower arm three times.

d. Now creep your hands toward each other on the belt to see how close you can get to touching your fingers. When you are as far along on the belt as you can be, take two deep breaths.

e. To release, drop the belt completely, and slide your bottom hand down toward your bum before untwisting it. Shake your arms, do a couple of shoulder shrugs, and repeat on the other side. In time it will get easier and you'll feel more balance between the two sides. Stand up and shake out your legs. There are just three more exercises to go.

10. Opera Singer

This simple exercise helps mobility between the ribs and deep into the armpits, improving lymphatic flow through the torso. Moving the arms in opposite directions from each other gives a diagonal stretch to the chest and ribs.

a. To lock your core when standing, exhale, pull up on your pubic muscles, and feel the connection to your lower abs. Keep them engaged but not clamped down tight.

b. Take a deep inhale, and as you exhale stretch one arm up high, looking at your hand as though you were on stage singing your heart out. Move the other arm down and away in the opposite direction.

c. Inhale deeply, stretching all the muscles between the ribs, as though you were about to hit the high note of the aria.

d. Exhale and change sides, repeating five times on each side.

11. DOOR-FRAME STRETCH

This exercise stretches the chest. After breast or heart surgery there can be a tendency to naturally and instinctively roll in the shoulders to protect the scar, but this can lead to restrictions. Using the doorway as a stabilizer gives you confidence to stretch.

a. Place your hands or forearms on the door frame at chest height. Inhale deeply, puffing out your chest.

b. As you exhale, take a very small step forward, feeling the pull in your chest and shoulder muscles.

c. Inhale deeply and slowly.

d. If this amount of stretch is okay, exhale and take another very small step forward.

e. Keep going until you reach your comfortable limit. Then stay here and just breathe, filling your lungs deeply until you feel the stretch on your entire chest area.

12. Spider up the Wall

This is our final exercise, and it helps flush the lymph nodes in the armpits and chest area.

a. Face the wall and place your hand as high up as you are able.

b. Crawl the spider (your fingers) up the wall and allow all the small muscles in the arm, chest, and shoulder to gently open and release.

c. When you reach your limit, inhale for a count of four and very gently press your hand into the wall, activating your arm muscles.

d. As you exhale, release the tension on your arm and try to creep your fingers up again.

e. Go as high as you comfortably can, doing the little presses in between. This helps your body release tight muscles.

f. Repeat on the other side.

You are done! I recommend that you do the Love Your Lymph Moves once a day. You can shoot for morning and evening once you get stronger. I demonstrate the exercises on my website www.andieholman.com if you want to follow along that way.

SKIN BRUSHING FOR A HEALTHY LYMPHATIC SYSTEM

This section on skin brushing also appears in Chapter 12. I included it here for convenience.

You may remember that the lymph has its own system just beneath the skin that runs alongside the circulatory system. Brushing your skin against gravity moves the lymph into the larger nodes, which encourages healing.

Here is the skin brushing flow:

Avoid fresh scars and sensitive or sore skin. Brush around the area but never right over the scar.

1. Use a *dry,* natural-bristle brush with a long handle, and brush your *dry* skin. It is best to do skin brushing just before your shower or bath.
2. Always move the brush toward the heart. You want to push the lymph fluid toward the lymph nodes. Make the strokes long and sweeping. Use a gentle pressure at first, becoming more firm as you get used to it.
3. Start at your feet, and with long strokes brush up the shin and calf to the knee. Take a little time over the tough kneecaps, and then brush from the knee to the top of the thigh, including the front, back, and sides. Spend some extra time brushing up areas of cellulite to encourage circulation. Do the other leg from the foot to the groin.

4. Next, start at your sacrum and brush over your butt cheek to the front, sweeping round to the groin in front. Do the whole butt muscle and repeat on the other side.

5. Brush from the hips up the lower back, up the sides of the body and the front of the torso, always stroking toward the heart.

6. Move to your upper body. Brush down the back of your neck, and brush the upper back in a V shape toward the heart. This is where you are most likely to need a handle on your brush.

7. For arms, start with one arm in the air and brush from that hand up to the elbow. Then brush from the elbow to the armpit. Take some extra time on the back of your arm if you have little bumps or loose skin. When you get to the armpit, be gentle because the skin is delicate. Brush gently across the entire chest from the shoulder to the breastbone. Repeat on the other side.

8. Finish with a little extra sweeping of the breastbone from the bottom to the top.

To maximize the benefits of skin brushing, do it just before you hop into a gorgeous, warm, salt-soak bath. The dry brushing will have sloughed off old dead skin, opening your pores for the healing of the salts.

SOAK IN SEA SALTS

Please double-check with your nurse or doctor to make sure you are cleared to take long baths before plunging into your salt soak.

Heat up your bathroom in advance so you do not get chilled while soaking. Have a large bottle of water handy to sip throughout your soak. You will get sweaty, so avoid face and hair masks during your bath.

Twice a week for the next month, take a highly therapeutic soak by using at least two and up to four cups of Dead Sea salts in the bath. We use this high amount of salt in order to fully maximize the healing effects of the magnesium in the mineral salts. Start with two cups and see how you feel. If you aren't sleeping well, or still feel stiff and sore, increase the salt gradually with each bath until you find your sweet spot.

If you wish to have a third bath during the week, use only one cup of salts. You can feel pretty sleepy or wiped out after the high-salt baths, and I don't want to put you in a healing crisis by using too much.

CHAPTER 16

WEEKS 5 & 6 AFTER SURGERY

HERE YOU ARE, one month after surgery. Hopefully you have managed to avoid infection, constipation, edema, cording, and any other complications. Your scar should be secure enough to start massage, but as always, check with your doctor first.

Continue any indicated homeopathic remedies for painful scars, but otherwise you can probably stop all other remedies such as Calendula and Arnica, unless you have not fully healed or you still have sore, bruised pain.

Carry on with the skin brushing and salt soaks; you can do those for the rest of your life if you like. Once you are back into the full swing of an active life, you will find the therapeutic salt soaks help your recovery. The skin brushing simply gives you velvety skin that is yummy and sexy to touch.

Continue the Love Your Lymph Moves, noting which particular exercises are still difficult given the location of your scar. These gentle movements are a wonderful measure of how far you've come as the weeks progress.

STARTING WITH TINY CIRCLES MASSAGE

Now when you apply your healing oils, you will also do light-pressure massage, as long as it has been approved by your doctor or nurse, especially if you have had complications with infection or swelling.

At six weeks roughly 50 percent of the collagen in your final scar is formed, so you want to be gentle with your touch and not disturb it too much. You will softly start to stretch adhesions that are forming so as to reduce the pulling on the fascia.

The full description of the Tiny Circles and Basic Scar massages can be found in Chapter 11 and what we have here is a recap. Please go back and reread that section if you have forgotten what to do.

Use the healing oils and start with the Tiny Circles Massage. All you do is make small circles on and around your scar, extending about two inches on either side. During this time, you are learning about your scar and figuring out where there may be painful spots, numb areas, or thickening.

Remember, if massaging hurts, back off with the pressure and just keep your fingertips touching the sore spot. Breathe through any pain, use your visualizations (especially the Ray of Starlight with its images of healing glitter) and try again later. Do not rush this. Your scar will guide you. Wherever you are in the process is perfect.

When you feel ready, move on to the Basic Scar massage. Warm the area around your scar with the tiny circles first. Then, anchor the skin around your scar with one hand, and with the fingertips of your other hand, move in a gentle zigzag motion across your scar, noting any sore areas, tightening, thickening, or numbness. The zigzag action breaks up scar tissue that is forming into adhesions. You do not have to go deep with your massage to gain benefits. Little and often is the golden ticket.

REBOUNDING AND BOUNCING

As with most of the therapies in this book we start slow and build up. Sometimes our enthusiasm runs away with us and we don't realize we've overdone it until we're sore. Oops.

So, a good place to start with rebounding is to do one minute of bouncing with your feet staying on the trampoline. If you are using a fitness ball, keep your feet on the floor and gently bounce up and down, breathing deeply. If you have a Bellicon mini-trampoline with support bars, hold on to those for stability. Otherwise please be very careful with your balance and keep your feet on the trampoline until you get the hang of bouncing.

Bounce three times a day, for a short time only, no more than three to five minutes. I know it doesn't seem like much, but you can add on time as you get stronger. For now, gentle lymph stimulation is our goal—not a hot, sweaty workout.

CHAPTER 17

WEEK 7 AND BEYOND: MAINTAINING A HEALTHY SCAR

You ARE NOW well on your way to taking care of your scar for life. Hopefully the foundation therapies are a normal part of your day and you no longer have to think about doing them. From here on we go to maintenance.

As much as I wish I could say "Congratulations, you've worked really hard and now you can forget about your scar forever," it doesn't work that way. You will need to stretch and massage your scar on a regular basis to keep it flexible.

MASSAGE

You may find that the Tiny Circles Massage is all you will ever need. However, sometimes the tissues tighten even though you've done all the right things and you need to go deeper. Next you would use the Basic Scar Massage techniques.

Start with your healing oils, and make circles to warm up the scar and surrounding area. Then, with a light touch, hold the skin around your scar with one hand to keep it from moving. Using your thumb or fingertips in a zigzag pattern, stroke gently across the scar where the adhesion is. Follow the adhesion as far as you can feel it. You may find it anchors into something else such as a bone—work it all the way to the end point.

If you hit an area that is painful, drop back to tiny circles, or just hold your fingers on the sensitive spot and use your breath to clear the pain.

Remember too that your scar probably won't feel homogenous - some bits will be bumpier or stiffer than others and may need even more aggressive massage. I know that in my patients, the area around the drains was always trickier to soften and we had to go into Deep Scar Release for those spots.

For deep scar release, use less oil in order to have more friction. You need your fingers to stick to an adhesion in order to break it apart. Warm up the area around your scar with little circles before moving on to the basic massage. Starting on one side, work across your scar with a zigzag stroke to warm up the deeper layers. After a minute or so of zigzags, hold the area around your scar taut with your other hand and start at one side, moving across the entire scar slowly.

If you find an area that feels "stuck," or if the skin won't move, drop your finger down into the scar, as though trying to poke inside the body. Gently move your finger in a deep, tiny circle to further isolate where the adhesion is and which direction it is moving. If you have one of those electric-shock pains or deep burns, stay right where you are and breathe. You can lighten up a little on the pressure, but stay with it and use your breath to move through it. Make your exhale longer than your inhale and purse your lips when breathing out.

When you have recovered, focus on that particular area and try again to move the adhesion. You may again get the shooting or burning pain. Stop and breathe through it. You have found one of your key scar trigger points; once this releases, other fascia around it can start to release as well. Work this area for as long as you can and then move on. You may want to take a break, have a stretch, and do some deep breathing before carrying on.

MAINTENANCE PLAN

DAILY:

- Skin brush before your shower, and follow with scar massage using healing oil, going to whatever depth you need as an individual.
- Do your lymph stretches, rebounding, or other exercise.
- Take homeopathic remedies as needed.

TWO TO THREE TIMES A WEEK:

- Have a long soak in a tub of Dead Sea salts

That's it! If you run into any troubles down the road, such as an infection or pain, go back to the earlier weeks and apply those suggestions.

HOMEOPATHY FOR ADHESIONS OR KELOIDS

There is a chance that even with the most careful of attention your scar can form adhesions or a keloid. We use homeopathic Thiosinaminum to help. This remedy has a dissolving action on scar tissue. Should you notice restrictions to your range of motion, a tightness around your scar, or keloid formation, take Thiosinaminum 30c once a day until your scar softens significantly and you no longer feel the restriction in your movement.

At that point gradually reduce the remedy, settling on once or twice a week for maintenance during the next couple of months—possibly years—until your scar keeps its flexibility and smoothness. Additionally, dedicate more time to your massage and stretching if you have adhesions, or seek out the help of a massage specialist.

EXERCISE: THE LONG-RANGE PLAN

You can keep doing the Love Your Lymph Moves (described in Chapters 10 and 15) for the rest of your life if you find them beneficial. You might decide you want more of a challenge and go on to explore yoga for your deep stretching. All I ask is that you listen to your body and do not push its capacity until you are ready.

It can take two years to "finalize" a scar. If you ignore that fact, you run the risk of tearing the scar-tissue matrix, which would set you back significantly. Be respectful of your scar.

So long as everything is going well, keep massaging, keep stretching, keep moving, keep bouncing, keep living, keep loving, and keep healing.

Should your scar start hardening and pulling on the fascia or restricting your range of motion, read through the next section about caring for older scars. You may need to apply some of the techniques to keep a full range of motion and ability.

PART V

WORKING WITH OLD SCARS

"Never be ashamed of a scar.
It simply means you were stronger than
whatever tried to hurt you."

—*Anonymous*

"In the last two-and-a-half years, I've had three hip surgeries—all done at the same incision site—to remove benign, recurrent tumors from the joint. After the first surgery, my scar faded to a smooth, white line. After the second surgery, however, it became puckered. In the following months I neglected it, partly because it was a visible symbol of a recurrent disease (PVNS) that has hijacked my life. When the pain and tumors returned a third time, requiring yet another surgery, I went into denial. I focused on my rehab and ignored my increasingly ugly scar.

A month after the third surgery, Andie Holman hired me as copyeditor for this book, and the first chapter she sent was about infections. I started editing the list of infection symptoms and suddenly realized I was experiencing a number of them! I called my doctor, who started me on antibiotics; luckily I had Andie's advice for taking probiotics to minimize the side effects.

Andie's encouragement about how even my three-times-opened scar could be healed changed my perspective. I started with the visualizations; the Ray of Starlight practice was truly uplifting. I also wrote a letter to my scar in which I apologized to it for projecting all my anger and frustration over my disease upon it.

After Andie massaged my scar and pointed out spots—some of them two inches away from the incision site—where I could lavish my hip with loving self-massage daily. Thanks to her, I now have hope that if I do dry brushing, soak in bath salts, and gently work on the disturbed tissue, my scar will improve in appearance and feel—and I will no longer harbor negative emotions about it."

—Laurel

CHAPTER 18

RELEASING OLD SCARS

BECAUSE YOU ARE not sitting in front of me giving me your personal history, I cannot see or feel your scar or evaluate your range of motion. Therefore, you will have to take note of where you are today so that you can see whether or not my suggestions are working. I am confident you will experience release in your scar—I just do not know your starting point and cannot give you a time frame for results.

A general rule of thumb is to do a month of work for every year you have had a complaint. So if your scar is ten years old, expect your full liberation to take about a year of dedicated work. I can promise that if you work diligently and daily to improve your health and the mobility of your scar, you will be free, quite often sooner than you imagine.

Remember my patient Faye? After one hour of treatment she was out of her wheelchair, and with each scar-release session she had less restriction and more energy. This fed her desire to keep going in order to reclaim her life and expand it beyond what she thought possible.

As is the case with new scars, your nutritional status is important because your body is always regenerating. Supplementation is also useful for you as you are actively stimulating tissue and encouraging change. Do the work and trust that change is just around the corner. All of the suggestions used for the new scars, such as massaging with healing oils, skin brushing, rebounding, and taking salt baths apply to you as well. These measures are therapeutic for everyone and not just for immediately after surgery.

EVALUATING YOUR SCAR WITH PHOTOS

The problem with old scars is that they slowly contract and shrink our movements, curling us in and restricting our posture. They are so insidious it feels as though we suddenly wake up and can't fully stretch, when actually scars tighten the fascia day by day, eventually preventing a full range of movement. You also might find a seemingly unrelated part of your body is in pain, and yet it comes from compensations around your scar. This happened to me and you can read about it in my next book about avoiding hip surgery.

After all the work I did with my patients, I ruefully regret not taking before and after photographs. As you do the massage and exercises your scar tissue *will* release and seeing the photographic evidence will motivate you to keep going.

Evaluating your range of motion gives you an idea of how much your scars impact your life and provides a record of how wonderfully you're doing as you release your scars. For the photos wear tight-fitting clothes, a bathing suit or your birthday suit. You want to measure how much freedom versus restriction you have in your scar. Take your body through the movements I suggest below, and have a friend snap a picture when you are at the limit of your range. Chances are the side with the scar will be more restricted in its motion.

Pay particular attention to the joint closest to the scar and take it through its range of motion. For example, if you had knee surgery, photograph how straight you can extend your leg as well as how much you can bend it. Take a photo of your "good" leg so you can compare.

I would like you to take photos of all the following movements, even if your scar is far away from that particular joint. Sometimes fascial restrictions travel far away from the original injury, and it's good to know how your entire body is affected by your scar.

Arm Motion:

- Standing tall, raise both arms out to the side, going as far as you can and eventually reaching overhead.
- Raise your arms in front of you, trying to lift your hands over your head.
- Lift your arms behind you. (They probably won't go very high).
- Take your right arm through a backstroke movement, and if you feel any restriction or hitch, take a picture at this point. Repeat with the left arm.

Torso:

- Place your left hand on your left hip. Raise your right arm out to the side, then lift it over your head, and bend your torso to the left. Repeat on the other side.

Legs:

- Rotate your foot in a circle, testing to see if there are any restrictions in the fascia of your foot and ankle.
- Bend and straighten your knee.
- Holding onto the back of a chair, bend your leg up at the hip as though pulling your thigh up to your chest, then slowly move your leg behind you. Torso scars may inhibit this movement too.
- Lie on the floor, and with your knee bent gently move your hip in a circle, noting any pulling or tightness.

General Posture:

- Stand as you normally would—no posing or trying to stand up straight. You want to see if your shoulders roll in, if you put more weight on one leg than the other, and whether there any other imbalances. Take a picture to the front, back, and both sides.

Save all the photos in a special file, and take new ones every two weeks. Soon you will see the changes in the pictures – great job!

HOMEOPATHY FOR OLDER SCARS

Thiosinaminum is the main remedy to use for older scars because it helps dissolve the rigid tissue. Use the remedy in a 30C potency. Take the remedy in water throughout the day; and at bedtime dissolve one pill under your tongue. Use Thiosinaminum as long as it takes for the scar to soften, and be sure to exercise and do the self-massage.

As mentioned in Chapter 15, we can use Silica, Fluoric acid and Graphites as well if there is pain with the tightness.

Silica is for painful scars that are thickened or nodular. These scars can hurt even when you are at rest. Take it in a 30C potency in your drinking water with the Thiosinaminum.

Fluoric acid is indicated for old scars that become red and itchy, or when the scar is surrounded by small pimples or fluid buildup as you begin releasing the scar. Use in a 30C potency as needed until the symptoms subside.

Graphites is for scars that are hard and have a burning or tearing pain associated with them. This burning sensation is very common when massaging old scars, and you can put one pill (30C potency) under your tongue as you start your massage. It may help lessen the pain. If you have the burning when not massaging, put Graphites in your water with Thiosinaminum.

Arnica is particularly useful the day after you have done deep massage on your scar when the area feels tender. Dissolve a 30C potency pill in your water.

STRETCHING YOUR SCAR

You may find that the Love Your Lymph Moves give you more than enough stretching for your scar. If there is a particular stretch that feels difficult, do it more often, or do more repetitions of it, always aiming to stretch a little further.

Just to reiterate, it's okay and necessary to stretch your scar, letting it pull more than usual, but you should not be brutal or mean to yourself. Instead of the mindset of pushing through the pain, relax and melt instead. Find your edge, take a deep breath, and consciously relax and let go. Really… let go. Let go of doing it right. Let go of being further along by now. Let go of the 'should be, want to be, ought to be'. You will get there when you relax.

MASSAGING THROUGH THE PAIN

Your massage therapy will depend on the level of your scar's sensitivity. I have worked on people with old scars that are exquisitely painful, and even the slightest touch made them jump. The chapter on massage therapy, Chapter 11, gives you the three different levels of intensity for massage: Tiny Circles, Basic Scar, and Deep Scar Release.

You may find your needs change often. Suppose today you feel like you're having a breakthrough and you go deeply into your scar, tearing up old fascia and releasing the tissue. Well, the area may be sore tomorrow, possibly feeling bruised and tender. So tomorrow, all you may want to do is Tiny Circles Massage and a long mineral-salt soak. Honor your process and be gentle when your body needs it.

However … this is not an invitation to be wimpy with your scar. You are going to be uncomfortable at times. Every single person who came to see me had to go through pain in the scar-release massage. There was no other way or else I would have found it. Be brave and be willing.

When you come across a painful part of your scar—and you will—breathe deeply and tell yourself you can do it. Face the pain, acknowledge it, cry through it, breathe through it, but do not run. Melt into it emotionally, mentally and physically. The pain is coming to the surface so that you can see it and then free it.

You are much stronger than you know. When I hit a sore spot on my patients, I lightened up the pressure and had them take deep-belly breaths, making the exhale longer than the inhale, while pursing the lips and pushing out the breath forcefully. As they were ready I would slowly increase the pressure again. You can do it; I know you can.

"DEAR SCAR": RELEASING TRAPPED EMOTIONS

Most of my patients were carrying heavy emotional burdens, some decades old, which were entangled with their scars. The fear, anger, betrayal, hatred, resentment, grief, horror, terror, and other intense emotions came up when we worked on their scars. My advice was the same regardless of the feelings: let it all out. Scream, cry, swear, and breathe through it. Keep your fingers on the scar in the place where the emotional pain has been triggered, and let it all out.

It can be frightening to relive these emotions or to acknowledge they exist within us, especially if we have been raised to keep a stiff upper lip, to soldier on, or to suck it up. Big boys need to cry, and good girls need to show fury. Your emotions are meant to flow; it is okay to feel sorry for yourself, to grieve, or to rage. The problem is when you get stuck in a feeling and stay in a state of self-pity or denial of how you feel.

Personally speaking I have a tendency to live in my head and rationally put emotions in little boxes deep in my brain filed under "DANGER DO NOT ENTER". Well, eventually those boxes will topple over and spill their contents into the present day, usually completely inappropriately. I've used the technique of writing and burning letters to unpack and collapse most of those boxes, allowing me to be mindful and far more compassionate with myself and those around me.

Emotions affect our physical self and can get trapped deep in the body's cells. The state of your mind has a direct impact on the state of your body. You can make your body go cold and stiff with fear by thinking about a poisonous snake or spider slithering across your belly. You can make yourself get hot and flushed from anger by focusing on injustice or a memory of when someone did you wrong.

Our common vocabulary describes the associations of the body and emotions: "rigid with fear," "seeing red," "eaten up with regret," "tied in knots by anxiety," and "swallowed by depression."

As a human, you have a wide range of emotions but, sadly, society teaches us to not express ourselves fully. Writing a letter and then burning it lets you get in touch with the parts of you that felt shameful or wrong and allows you to explore the depth of your emotions. Your letters will never be read by anyone, so you are encouraged to absolutely pour your heart out, use expletives, and write all the things you have wanted to say to others but filtered yourself.

Start by identifying who the letter needs to be addressed to. It can be a person or a situation. Or you might want to start with your scar.

For example, here is what Harry Potter might write:

Dear Scar,

I wish you didn't exist. You make me feel vulnerable, and I want to hide you. I feel like people are always looking at you and judging me because of you. I hate you. I hate that you show everyone what happened to me, that you live right there in the middle of my forehead like a damned brand. People always ask, "Hey, wow! What happened?" Like I want to talk about it. Like I want to relive what happened over and over, feeling the pain each time I tell the story. I hate you. I wish you were gone. You've ruined my face, and He Who Cannot Be Named will know me the second he sees you. My life is in danger thanks to you. Thanks a lot, you stupid scar.

Harry has to go through the loss of his parents, feel the grief, feel the fear of being discovered and killed, and feel the alienation of his peers—all because of his scar. However, in time, he realizes that he is much bigger than his scar, and he learns how to reframe his story instead of staying stuck. He grows.

WRITING YOUR LETTER

Give yourself at least half an hour for every letter you write. Turn off the phone and lock the door. You want complete privacy. You need a piece of paper, a pen, a comfortable place to sit, and something to write on. Personally, I like to keep writing over and over on the same piece of paper until nothing is left but thick, illegible scribble.

Imagine the Column of Light (from Chapter 7) around you before you start. Visualize that as you write and release your feelings, smoky cobwebs of old, stuck emotions are sucked into the column and taken high into the sky like a giant, spiritual vacuum cleaner.

Set an alarm for fifteen minutes. If you have time, go longer, but you will write for at least those fifteen.

Dear _____,

Do not stop, do not think, and do not worry about spelling or punctuation. Do not judge yourself for crying or wetting the paper with your dripping nose. Do not stop to pull yourself together or calm yourself down. Just write and do not stop until the fifteen minutes are up.

When the alarm sounds, sit back and be still. Breathe deeply into your belly and come back to the present moment. Simply breathe for the next two to five minutes, allowing your nervous system to settle down. See in your mind's eye the pain being lifted up and out of your energy field.

Finish with a visualization from Chapter 7 and go to the Waterfall of Light to clear any remaining emotion that is trapped. Then, call in your Column of Healing Light, Tree, or Angel Wings to ground yourself again.

BURNING THE LETTER

Now you *must* destroy the letter. This part of the process is critical so that you can fully release the emotion.

My first choice is fire. I watch the smoke rise and let all the pain contained in those words float away into the heavens. If it is not safe to burn paper, my next choice is to shred the letter. Again I imagine the shredder as rows of teeth tearing apart the pain so that it will never come to haunt me again. My final option is to tear the paper into itty-bitty pieces and then throw it in the trash like confetti, celebrating its destruction.

After destroying your letter, sit back and check in with how you feel. The next time you do your scar massage, notice if it feels less restricted or less painful. I am going to wager it does. If you want to thoroughly cleanse yourself energetically, go climb in the tub and soak in three cups of bath salts. Drink a lot of water while you're in the water, and let all the old memories and emotions swirl away down the drain at the end.

A final note on old scars: The most important part of treating old scars is consistency. Each and every day, do a little something for your scar tissue—perhaps a massage or some extra stretching. You have to fight against the natural tendency for scars to contract and pull in. Be vigilant in reclaiming your full range of motion and ability to pursue all the things you love.

Take the photos, record how your scar feels, and challenge yourself to push a little farther in life. Your scar does not define you. Do what Harry Potter did—and make magic!

It is time to wrap up the book – I could edit and fiddle and fuss over it for another two years but that would be useless to all of us. It serves you better to have it in your hands than have me trying to 'perfect' it and not share.

Obviously everything in life changes and grows, including me, my research and opinions. To stay current with my findings and with the feedback of people using the techniques in the book I encourage you to bookmark my website www.andieholman.com as all updates will go there first.

FINAL THOUGHTS

YOUR TASK FROM here on is to integrate your scar into your physical and emotional being. It is a part of you now and even if it fades to almost invisible, it will require your continued attention to keep it healthy and free from restrictions. Self-love and self-care are hopefully at the top of your 'to-do' list and you value dedicating time to yourself.

Depending on your age and state of health, your scar may have another two years to be fully formed, so continue to nourish it daily. Older scars will soften and release day by day. Soon you will be delighted with your full range of motion and freedom from pain.

Please share your progress with all of us. We learn best from each other and another person might have just the tip to help you out or you may be the curative balm for someone else.

I wish you love and great healing,

Andie

APPENDIX I: RESOURCES AND SHOPPING TIPS

ALL LINKS CAN be found on my website www.andieholman.com

HOMEOPATHIC REMEDIES

A large range of common homeopathic remedies can be found in health-food stores and natural pharmacies. I mostly see the Boiron range. However, I recommend some that are more specialized, and you will need to order them from a homeopathic pharmacy. I've put a little * after the ones you will need to source for yourself.

I buy these harder-to-find remedies from Nelsons Homeopathic Pharmacy in London, England (founded in 1860), which hosts an astounding bank of homeopathic remedies and ships worldwide. Here is the full list of suggested homeopathic remedies in this book, all in 30C potency:

- Aconite
- Arnica
- Calendula *
- Fluoricum acidum *
- Graphites
- Hepar sulphuris calcareum
- Ignatia

- Nux vomica
- Phosphorus
- Pyrogenium *
- Silica
- Thiosinaminum *

SUPPLEMENTS

I order my supplements from iHerb, which offers great discounts, has a large inventory, and ships all over the globe. The supplements I suggest below are brands I personally use—or those that my patients take and find helpful. There is a link on my website to give you an additional discount from iHerb.

- Ultimate Omega lemon-flavor soft gels from Nordic Naturals
- Nordic Naturals Algae Omega (vegan option for omega-3 fats)
- Jarro-Dophilus EPS from Jarrow Formulas (a probiotic that's stable at room temperature)
- MegaFlora probiotic by MegaFood (requires refrigeration)
- Turmeric Strength for Whole Body by MegaFood
- Sovereign Silver Bio-Active Silver Hydrosol fine-mist spray (for spritzing on your scar)
- George's Always Active Aloe Vera liquid (tastes like water with no bitterness) for constipation, sluggish bowels.
- Any product by MegaFood

HEALING OILS

I buy essential oils from the Mountain Rose Herbs company because what's not to love about an organic, fair trade, environmentally conscious business. I also love my local Rebecca's Apothecary. Rebecca's ships within the USA and Mountain Rose covers the USA and Canada.

- Calendula herbal oil
- Rosehip-seed oil
- German chamomile
- Lavender *(Lavandula angustifolia)*

DEAD SEA SALTS

I buy my salts from Salt Works through Amazon.

REBOUNDER/MINI-TRAMPOLINE

The Bellicon company in Germany makes the best rebounders I've ever tried and I have owned quite a few over the years. There is a link on my website to the Bellicon company - you won't be buying directly from me and it is important you understand that. You're buying straight from them.

MEDITATION AIDS

If you are just learning to meditate or have difficulty focusing your mind, try the meditation app from Headspace. I also love the app Insight Timer. Also have a look on my website for the visualizations in this book.

NATURAL SKIN CARE

To check on the safety of the ingredients in lotions, sunscreens, mois-turizers, cosmetics, and other skin-care products, visit the Skin Deep section of the Environmental Working Group website, which rates these products. (www.ewg.org)

For recipes for making your own nontoxic skin-care and other natural beauty products, check out Wellness Mama. I will also put my favorites on my website for you to try.

BLENDERS

Vitamix blender: There are plenty of other blenders on the market, however the Vitamix is the only one I've found that made true smoothies—no chunks, no green bits, no ice balls. I also use it to make soups, spreads, flours, nut butters, and more. I personally prefer to buy top quality products just once rather than have to buy lesser quality items that break and need frequent replacement.

RECOMMENDED BOOKS (MANY MORE ON MY WEBSITE)

- *The 30-Day Sobriety Solution* by Jack Canfield and Dave Andrews
- *Green for Life* by Victoria Boutenko
- *The Elimination Diet: Discover the Foods That Are Making You Sick and Tired—and Feel Better Fast* by Tom Malterre, MS, CN, and Alissa Segersten
- *Wheat Belly* by William Davis, MD
- *Grain Brain* by David Perlmutter, MD
- *Your Life in Your Hands* by Jane Plant, PhD

APPENDIX II: ANDIE'S FAVORITE RECIPES FOR HEALTHY EATING

MY BROTHER, THE chef, has a special food mantra I would like to share. Take a deep breath, rub your belly and hum: *Yum-yum-yum-yum-yummmmm.*

I have a huge range of cookbooks from complete vegan to full on Paleo. I love to cook but my recipes are pretty simple. My food focus is on the freshness and the nutrient content.

HOMEMADE CHOCOLATE HEARTS
Makes 26 1-inch-square pieces

I started making my own chocolate years ago after discovering "raw" chocolate while living in England. (I love you Booja Booja.) You can make this recipe sweeter—that's why the maple syrup is added incrementally. This is a basic chocolate candy recipe, so feel free to play around with ingredients. I use a silicon candy tray to mold the little hearts for my chocolates. An ice-cube tray works well too. Make your own peanut butter cups or dip strawberries in the chocolate before chilling.

If you want to use this recipe as a cake frosting, leave out step 4. After step 3, the consistency of the chocolate mixture will look and act like cake frosting, but remember it is raw so it will melt easily. Frost your

ANDIE HOLMAN

cake just before serving. You can also experiment with coco butter instead of oil. It has more texture or as chefs say, a different 'mouth feel'. I like both.

½ cup (100 g.) coconut oil at room temperature

½ cup (50 g.) cacao (cocoa) powder

¼ cup (30 ml.) maple syrup

1 teaspoon vanilla

½ teaspoon cinnamon

¼ teaspoon sea salt

1. Using a spatula, cream the coconut oil and cacao together.
2. Blend in half the maple syrup; then add vanilla, cinnamon, and salt.
3. Taste. Add more maple syrup until you reach the sweetness you like.
4. Mix in extra flavors/ingredients if desired. (See the list below for suggestions.) Fill your candy trays or ice-cube trays with the chocolate and place in the freezer until the candies have hardened.

Now, play with your food. Here are some suggestions for add-ins.

- Add cayenne powder (really) and use in savory dishes such as stews, tomato sauce, beans and chili.
- Mix in chunks of strawberries and bananas
- Stir in nuts of your choice. (I use ½ cup or 50 g.) or just stir in a large tablespoon of nut butter.
- Try different flavors such as lavender water, rose water, essential oils, orange peel, or anything your heart desires!

- For a homemade peanut butter cup, mix your peanut butter (or almond butter or seed butter) with a little bit of vanilla. Place paper liners in a muffin tin. Put a dollop of chocolate in first and squish it flat. Freeze for half an hour to harden. Then add a dollop of peanut butter mix. Freeze again. Put your final dollop of chocolate on top and squish that down. Freeze for the final time. Yay!

TURMERIC PASTE
Makes ½ cup of paste

Curcumin, the yellow pigment of the turmeric root, has antioxidant, anti-inflammatory, antibacterial, antiviral, antifungal, and anticancer properties. Be careful when working with turmeric; the bright yellow color will stain. First you make a paste out of turmeric, black pepper, and water. The black pepper robustly enhances the powerful properties of the turmeric, so don't skip it. The paste can be used to stir into the Spicy Golden Milk (recipe below) for a bedtime drink to help you sleep. The paste is also delicious stirred into rice, veggies, or other savory dishes.

¼ cup (30 g.) powdered turmeric
½ teaspoon ground black pepper
½ – ¾ cup (120.–180 ml.) water

1. Mix the turmeric, pepper, and water in a pan over medium heat, stirring frequently and adding a little more water if it gets too dry. I live in an arid climate so I need the higher measure of water.
2. Cook for seven minutes.
3. Let the paste cool; store in a glass container in the fridge. It will stay potent for about two weeks.

SPICY GOLDEN MILK
Makes 2 cups, or one large mug

I like this spiced, warm beverage best at night. Sipping it before bed helps me sleep.

2 cups milk (coconut, hemp, almond, rice, oat, cow, goat)
½ teaspoon of Turmeric Paste (recipe above)
¼ teaspoon powdered ginger, or a few grates of fresh ginger
¼ teaspoon cinnamon
¼ teaspoon cayenne pepper (omit if you don't like hot spices)
1 teaspoon coconut oil
1 tablespoon honey

1. Combine everything except the coconut oil and honey in a saucepan and heat on low temperature. Stir constantly until the milk simmers, showing tiny bubbles on the sides of the pan. Never boil as boiling will destroy the nutrients in the spices.
2. Turn off the heat and stir in the coconut oil and honey.

BASIC GREEN SMOOTHIE

Makes 5 cups, enough for two people or for you to have two servings.

Ideally, you should make a fresh smoothie daily—or at least every other day. Once veggies are crushed they start to lose their nutrients and vitality. This recipe is not sweet.

This recipe is also not an exact science; experiment to figure out what you like best.

2 cups (500 ml.) water
2 cups fresh, light-green leaves such as romaine lettuce (about two large handfuls)
1 cup of dark greens such as kale or spinach
½ peeled cucumber, sliced (about 1 cup)
1 green apple, peeled, seeded, and sliced (about 1 cup)
1 cup celery, roughly chopped (two stalks)
1/8–1/4 cup fresh lemon juice (half a lemon)

1. Blend the water and all greens together until creamy.
2. Add the cucumber, apple, celery, and lemon. Blend again to a smooth consistency. Depending on your greens, you may get a lot of foam on top of your smoothie which will settle.

SWEET ROASTED NUTS

Makes 2 cups

Roasting raw nuts at a relatively low temperature (no higher than 300°F, or 150°C) for a short time will not significantly reduce their nutrients.

2 cups (300 g.) raw nuts of your choice

3 tablespoons (40 g.) coconut oil or butter

1 tablespoon honey

2 teaspoons vanilla

¼ teaspoon sea salt or Himalayan salt

1 teaspoon cinnamon

1. Preheat oven to 300°F (150°C)
2. Melt the oil or butter, and stir in the other ingredients until fully blended.
3. Place nuts in a large bowl and pour the liquid over it. Stir until all nuts are covered.
4. Spread coated nuts onto a baking sheet—try to avoid nuts lumping together.
5. Roast for 10 minutes, then stir.
6. Roast for remaining 10 minutes, remove from oven, stir, and let cool before storing in an air-tight container.

SAVORY ROASTED NUTS
Makes 2 cups

The process is the same as the sweet nut recipe above—only the spices are different.

2 cups (300 g.) raw nuts of your choice
3 tablespoons of butter (or vegetable oil if you are dairy free)
1 teaspoon paprika (try smoked paprika sometime)
1 teaspoon cayenne pepper
1 teaspoon Italian blend seasoning
½ teaspoon salt
½ teaspoon garlic powder
½ teaspoon onion powder

1. Preheat oven to 300°F (150°C)
2. Melt the butter and stir in all the spices.
3. Place nuts in a large bowl and pour the liquid over it. Stir until all nuts are covered.
4. Spread coated nuts onto a baking sheet—try to avoid nuts lumping together.
5. Roast for 10 minutes, then stir.
6. Roast for remaining 10 minutes, remove from oven, stir, and let cool before storing in an air-tight container.

SIMPLE GARLIC DRESSING

Makes 1½ cups

Salads tossed with this dressing are excellent for warding off infection—and vampires.

1 cup (235 ml.) olive oil
¼ cup (60 ml.) balsamic vinegar (or white wine, apple cider, or coconut vinegar)
2 tablespoons fresh lemon juice (one whole lemon)
1 teaspoon of honey
1 tablespoon of Dijon mustard
1 clove garlic (two if you are feeling run down or infected)
¼ teaspoon of sea salt or Himalayan salt
¼ teaspoon of Italian spice blend

1. Crush or finely chop the garlic, and leave to the side for twenty minutes. This gives the enzymes time to produce allicin and thiosulfinates, aka "garlic superpowers."
2. Blend together all other ingredients, and stir in the garlic at the end. If you use a hand blender it will become creamy in texture. To keep the dressing more on the oily side, whisk with a fork.

APPENDIX III: TYPES OF BREAST SURGERY AND ASSOCIATED SCAR CARE

THIS CHAPTER IS from my book Love Your Scar: Breast Cancer, *and I have included it here to describe the more common surgeries for breast cancer and reconstruction.*

Where your breast cancer is located and what type of surgery you have will mostly determine the location and length of your breast scar. It will also have great bearing on the way your fascia is affected, which in turn can change your posture.

If you have reconstructive surgery using tissue from another part of the body—back, abdomen, or buttocks—you will have to invest more time and energy into your healing because you have more area to cover. With more intensive surgery it will take longer to restore flexibility and mobility. It is not impossible—just more involved.

LUMPECTOMY

After a lumpectomy, the scar is usually quite small, and sometimes there may be a small dent in the breast. The amount of tissue removed varies greatly from person to person. This is the least invasive surgery and therefore causes minimal impact on the tissues.

Approximately one in eight (12.5 percent) women will need a second operation to remove more tissue if on examination of the lump there is indication that precancerous cells are still in the breast. If further surgery is required there will be additional scar tissue in the area.

SEGMENTAL EXCISION (QUADRANTECTOMY)

This procedure is similar to a lumpectomy, but more tissue (a quadrant, or one-quarter of the breast) is removed from the surrounding area.

MASTECTOMY

- A simple mastectomy removes only breast tissue. The lymph nodes and muscles are unaffected.
- A simple mastectomy and sentinel node biopsy, or node sampling, removes the breast tissue and the lower lymph glands situated within the armpit.
- A modified radical mastectomy (also called a total mastectomy and axillary clearance) removes all the breast tissue and all of the lymph nodes in the armpit.
- A radical mastectomy removes all breast tissue, all lymph nodes in the armpit, and the muscles behind the breast tissue. This is done only if the cancer is found in the chest muscles under the breast.

Mastectomy scars usually run in a line across the chest from the breastbone to the armpit. When there are breathing difficulties, especially in double mastectomies, it is crucial to check the scars for adhesions. Full range of motion may also be compromised in the shoulders and neck, so look for adhesions anchoring up as well as down.

A NOTE ABOUT LYMPH

When lymph nodes are removed there is a greater chance of lymph-edema, or swelling in the arm, on the side of surgery. The more lymph nodes taken from the breast area, the more the other areas of lymph concentration in the body will need attention.

Varying degrees of lymph glands are removed in:

- the simple mastectomy and sentinel node biopsy
- a modified radical mastectomy
- a radical mastectomy

The importance of the lymphatic system is explained in Chapter 3. Please pay extra attention to this information if you have had lymph nodes removed. Do as mu-ch as you can to help the lymphatic system as it is integral to your healing.

RECONSTRUCTIVE SURGERY

Reconstruction after a mastectomy may take place at the same time as a mastectomy, or your surgeon may wish to wait—possibly up to a year—before performing reconstructive surgery. It is important to discuss this fully with your surgeon. Breast reconstruction may use an implant of some kind, in which case the scar will be localized to just the breast. Alternatively, there are "tissue-flap" reconstructions that involve other parts of the body.

Every woman is an individual, and scars pull the fascia in different ways depending on how you have healed as well as any previous postural habits. These descriptions are based on the most common patterns I have seen with my patients.

The following illustration shows the most common scar positioning for the various types of reconstructive surgery.

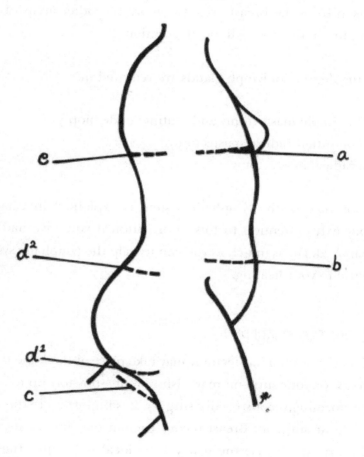

Common scar positions for reconstructive surgery. Details about the types of reconstruction follow.

    a.   Mastectomy scar

    b.   TRAM flap and DIEP flap reconstruction

    c.   Free TUG flap reconstruction

    d^1. IGAP (gluteal flap) reconstruction

    d^2. SGAP (gluteal flap) reconstruction

    e.   Latissimus dorsi (lat flap) reconstruction

TRAM FLAP RECONSTRUCTION (B)

This surgery uses the abdominal muscle, the transverse rectus abdominis (TRAM), and moves it into position to reconstruct the breast. The scar involves an oval shape around the breast and a long scar across the lower abdomen. Sometimes the belly button is reconstructed. If there are two scars on the front of the body, they are likely to pull toward each other. This may affect posture, making it feel difficult to stand up straight. Additionally, the lower back may feel tight. Work on the scars first to see if this releases the lower back.

If you have a TRAM flap surgery, my suggestion is that when you are ready you make sure to stretch the front of the body regularly. You can lie on your back over a Swiss ball or stretch over the back of a sturdy chair or sofa. The twisting exercises in the lymph-activating exercises will also be of great benefit. Please double check with your surgeon that this is suitable for you, especially if you have mesh inserted, and go slowly!

DIEP FLAP RECONSTRUCTION (B)

This surgery is almost identical to a TRAM surgery, but no abdominal muscle is taken. Instead, it entails microsurgery involving the blood vessels called deep inferior epigastric perforators (DIEP), as well as some skin and fat connected to them. This surgery takes much longer to perform than TRAM flap reconstruction. However, the scars will be the same as for a TRAM: an oval shape around the reconstructed breast and a scar along the abdomen above the pubic line. Do the same exercises as for a TRAM reconstruction.

FREE TUG FLAP RECONSTRUCTION (C)

This relatively new operation is suitable for slim women with small breasts. The procedure uses tissue from the upper inner thigh, namely the TUG (transverse upper gracilis) muscle.

The scar is at the top of the leg, and there can sometimes be a problem with fluid building up in the wound area on the leg. Be certain to ask your surgeon about the safety of doing leg exercises, particularly the Frog Legs, one of the lymph-activation exercises. It is important to know that with this surgery you will no longer be able to use the TUG muscle and this will affect your overall posture and functioning.

Adhesions on the scar around the gracilis muscle are more likely to create problems in the hip or pelvis. Once you are able, gently stretch the groin muscles and inner thighs in order to keep fluidity in the hip joint.

GLUTEAL FLAP RECONSTRUCTION (D)

This surgery uses skin and fat, and sometimes muscle, from the upper or lower buttock. It is usually performed when abdominal tissue is unavailable due to previous surgeries or when the woman is very slim.

The scars for a gluteal flap depend on the type. An IGAP (d¹) surgery, which uses the inferior gluteal artery perforator blood vessel, results in a scar hidden in the buttock crease, whereas an SGAP (d²) surgery, using the superior gluteal artery perforator, results in a scar that is higher up on the buttock or hip. In a gluteal flap reconstruction, the breast scar is oval. Watch for the potential of restrictions in the hip and lower back. I have also found the hamstrings can become very tight on the side with the scar. There may also be an over-reliance on the opposite leg, so both sides may be tight: one side from the surgery and the other from doing all the work. Check both.

LATISSIMUS DORSI (LAT FLAP OR MUSCLE PEDICLE FLAP) RECONSTRUCTION

This surgery uses muscle and skin from the upper back. An oval section of the latissimus dorsi muscle is used to create the new breast. The scar around the reconstructed breast is oval, and the scar on the back is usually horizontal along the bra line. There may be a pulling sensation around the side of the body between the two scars. Or, some women have a sensation of tightness inside the body between the front and the back. Neck and shoulder tightness can be a problem; so can the potential for overuse of the back muscles on the other side.

ENDNOTES

CHAPTER FOUR: HOW NUTRITION HELPS HEAL A SCAR

1. B. M. Mohammed, B. J. Fisher, D. Kraskauskas, S. Ward, J. S. Wayne, D. F. Brophy, A. A. Fowler, D. R. Yager, R. Natarajan, "Vitamin C promotes wound healing through novel pleiotropic mechanisms," *International Wound Journal* 13, no. 4 (August 20, 2015): 572–84, doi: 10.1111/iwj.12484.

2. Lich Thi Nguyen, Yeon-Hee Lee, Ashish Ranjan Sharma, Jong-Bong Park, Supriya Jagga, Garima Sharma, Sang-Soo Lee, Ju-Suk Nam, "Quercetin induces apoptosis and cell cycle arrest in triple-negative breast cancer cells through modulation of Foxo3a activity," *The Korean Journal of Physiology & Pharmacology* 21(2) (March 2017): 205-213, doi: 10.4196/kjpp.2017.21.2.205

3. Oliver Chow and Adrian Barbul, "Immunonutrition: Role in Wound Healing and Tissue Regeneration," *Advances in Wound Care* 3(1) (January 2014): 46-53, doi: 10.1089/wound.2012.0415

4. B. B. Aggarwal, C. Sundaram, N. Malani, H. Ichikawa, "Curcumin: the Indian solid gold," *Advances in Experimental Medicine and Biology* 595 (2007):1–75.

5. D. Akbik, M. Ghadiri, W. Chrzanowski, R. Rohanizadeh, "Curcumin as a wound-healing agent," *Life Sciences,* 116, no. 1 (Oct. 22, 2014): 1–7, doi: 10.1016/j.lfs.2014.08.016.

6. V. Worthington, "Nutritional quality of organic versus conventional fruits, vegetables, and grains," *Journal of Alternative and Complementary Medicine* 7, no. 2 (April 2001): 161–73.

7. J. C. McDaniel, K. Massey, A. Nicolaou. "Fish oil supplementation alters levels of lipid mediators of inflammation in microenvironment of acute human wounds," *Wound Repair and Regeneration* 19, no. 2 (March/April 2011): 189–200.

8. T. Mayes, M. M. Gottschlich, L. E. James, C. Allgeier, J. Weitz, R. J. Kagan, "Clinical safety and efficacy of probiotic administration following burn injury," *Journal of Burn Care and Research* (official publication of the American Burn Association) 36, no. 1 (2015), 92–99, doi: 10.1097/BCR.0000000000000139.

9. D. M. Linares, P. Ross, C. Stanton, "Beneficial Microbes: The pharmacy in the gut," *Bioengineered* Dec. 28, 2015: 1–28.

10. S. Guo and L. A. DiPietro, "Factors Affecting Wound Healing," *Journal of Dental Research* 89, no. 3 (March 2010): 219–29, doi: 10.1177/0022034509359125.

11. C. L. Ventola, "The Antibiotic Resistance Crisis," *Pharmacy and Therapeutics* 40, no. 4 (April 2015): 277–83.

12. Jeffrey B. Kaplan, Era Izano, Prerna Gopal, Michael Karwacki, Sangho Kim, Jeffrey Bose, Kenneth Bayles, and Alexander Horswill, "Low Levels of β-Lactam Antibiotics Induce Extracellular DNA

Release and Biofilm Formation in *Staphylococcus aureus*," *mBio* 3, no. 4 (July/August 2012): e00198–12. Published online July 31, 2012, doi: 10.1128/mBio.00198-12.

CHAPTER 6: NO MORE TOXIC SKIN CARE PRODUCTS

13. J. Bandier, B. C. Carlsen, M. A. Rasmussen, L. J. Petersen, J. D. Johansen, "Skin reaction and regeneration after single sodium lauryl sulfate exposure stratified by filaggrin genotype and atopic dermatitis phenotype," *British Journal of Dermatology* 172, no. 6 (2015): 1519-29.

14. A. Grängsjö, I. Pihl-Lundin, M. Lindberg, G. M. Roomans, "X-ray microanalysis of cultured keratinocytes: methodological aspects and effects of the irritant sodium lauryl sulphate on elemental composition," *Journal of Microscopy* 199 (Sept. 2000): 208–13, doi: 10.1046/j.1365-2818.2000.00724.

CHAPTER 7: WORKING WITH BREATH, MEDITATION, AND VISUALIZATION

15. J. P. Gouin, J. K. Kiecolt-Glaser, "The Impact of Psychological Stress on Wound Healing: Methods and Mechanisms" *Immunology and Allergy Clinics of North America* 31, no. 1 (Feb. 2011): 81–93, doi: 10.1016/j.iac.2010.09.010.

16. J. A. Lothian, "What Every Pregnant Woman Needs to Know," *Journal of Perinatal Education* 20, no. 2) (2011): 118–20, doi: 10.1891/1058-1243.20.2.118.

CHAPTER 8: AVOIDING INFECTION IN THE HOSPITAL AND BEYOND

17. "Superbugs threaten hospital patients," Centers for Disease Control and Prevention, retrieved on March 3, 2016 from http://www.cdc.gov/media/releases/2016/p0303-superbugs.html.

18. Jing Lu, Lynne Turnbull, Catherine M. Burke, Michael Liu, Dee A. Carter, Ralf C. Schlothauer, Cynthia B. Whitchurch, Elizabeth J. Harry, "Manuka-type honeys can eradicate biofilms produced by *Staphylococcus aureus* strains with different biofilm-forming abilities," *PeerJ* March 25, 2014, PubMed 24711974.

19. R. Goggin, C. Jardeleza, P. J. Wormald, S. Vreugde, "Colloidal silver: a novel treatment for *Staphylococcus aureus* biofilms?" *International Forum of Allergy and Rhinology* 4, no. 3 (March 2014): 171–5, doi: 10.1002/alr.21259.

20. R. Arreola, S. Quintero-Fabián, R. I. López-Roa, E. O. Flores-Gutiérrez, J. P. Reyes-Grajeda, L. Carrera-Quintanar, D. Ortuño-Sahagún, "Immunomodulation and Anti-Inflammatory Effects of Garlic Compounds" *Journal of Immunology Research,* April 19, 2015, doi: 10.1155/2015/401630.

21. G. P. Sivam, "Protection against *Helicobacter pylori* and other bacterial infections by garlic," *Journal of Nutrition* 131, no. 3s (March 2001): 1106S–8S.

CHAPTER 10: EXERCISE FOR A HEALTHY RECOVERY

22. A. Bhattacharya, E. P. McCutcheon, E. Shvartz, J.E. Greenleaf, "Body acceleration distribution and O^2 uptake in humans during running

and jumping," *Journal of Applied Physiology*: respiratory, environmental and exercise physiology 49, no. 5 (Nov. 1980): 881–87.

CHAPTER 11: MASSAGE AND HEALING OILS FOR A SMOOTH SCAR

23. P. Pommier, F. Gomez, M. P. Sunyach, A. D'Hombres, C. Carrie, X. Montbarbon, "Phase III randomized trial of *Calendula officinalis* compared with trolamine for the prevention of acute dermatitis during irradiation for breast cancer," *Journal of Clinical Oncology* (official journal of the American Society of Clinical Oncology) 22, no. 8 (April 15, 2004): 1447–453.

24. M. D. Martins, M. M. Marques, S. K. Bussadori, M. A. Martins, V. C. Pavesi, R. A. Mesquita-Ferrari, K. P. Fernandes, "Comparative analysis between *Chamomilla recutita* and corticosteroids on wound healing: an *in vitro* and *in vivo* study," *Phytotherapy Research* 23, no. 2 (Feb. 2009): 274–78, doi: 10.1002/ptr.2612.

25. B. S. Nayak, S. S. Raju, A. V. Rao, "Wound healing activity of *Matricaria recutita L.* extract," *Journal of Wound Care* 16, no. 7 (July 2007): 298–302.

26. D. T. Altaei, "Topical lavender oil for the treatment of recurrent aphthous ulceration," *American Journal of Dentistry* 25, no. 1 (Feb. 2012): 39–43.

27. S. Fayazi, M. Babashahi, M Rezaei, "The effect of inhalation aromatherapy on anxiety level of the patients in preoperative period," *Iranian Journal of Nursing and Midwifery Research* 16, no. 4 (Fall 2011): 278–83.

CHAPTER 12: SKIN BRUSHING AND SOAKING IN DEAD SEA SALTS

28. T. G. Polefka, R. J. Bianchini, S. Shapiro, "Interaction of mineral salts with the skin: a literature survey," *International Journal of Cosmetic Science* 34, no. 5 (Oct. 2012): 416–23, doi: 10.1111/j.1468-2494.2012.00731.

29. E. Proksch, H. P. Nissen, M. Bremgartner, and C. Urquhart, "Bathing in a magnesium-rich Dead Sea salt solution improves skin barrier function, enhances skin hydration, and reduces inflammation in atopic dry skin," *International Journal of Dermatology*, 44 (2005): 151–57, doi: 10.1111/j.1365-4632.2005.02079.

ABOUT THE AUTHOR

LIKE MANY NATURAL healers, Andie (Adrianna) Holman exhausted modern medicine searching for a cure for her horrendous eczema and multiple sensitivities. She started experimenting with her diet and natural therapies at age fifteen, and a burning curiosity was lit. Her body and soul became her science project which then led to the realization she could help others take control of their health and healing.

After completing a business degree (BSBA) from the University of Denver, she managed a health-food store and studied massage therapy at the Health Enrichment Center under the leadership of Sandy Fritz. Four years later, Andie decided to study homeopathy full time at the College of Homœopathy in London, England. After the three-year course she gained her registered status with the Society of Homeopaths UK and continued her homeopathic education studying toxicology, methodology, and understanding cancer. She also completed a foundation course in kinesiology and explored metaphysical energy healing training through Delphi University. She gained her Bachelor of Science degree in nutritional medicine from Thames Valley University in 2010.

Andie initiated a complementary therapy program for the oncology department of London Bridge Hospital in 2002 and worked alone for two years. As demand grew, she brought on more therapists and was lead practitioner for the Complementary Therapies team for ten years. The team provided massage, aromatherapy, Reiki, homeopathy, nutrition, and reflexology to cancer patients in various stages of treatment, including palliative care.

She worked in other clinics in London, being a founding member of two esteemed operations: Nelsons Homeopathic Pharmacy Clinic (the pharmacy itself being the oldest in Europe) and the integrated clinic, Third Space Medicine, where she was Head of Homeopathy. She gave workshops and was commissioned to write *Understanding Eczema* for Neal's Yard Remedies.

Andie lives in the mountains of Colorado with her husband and bevy of four-leggeds. Besides writing, she teaches yoga and is a volunteer firefighter for her mountain community.

To see more of her writing, videos and recordings, visit her website www.andieholman.com.